Renhala

Book 1 of the Renhala Series

Amy Joy Lutchen

CR

Renhala
(Book 1 of Renhala Series)
by
Amy Joy Lutchen

Dedication

❧

This book is dedicated to my husband, for his constant support of my numerous rendezvous with Earl Grey tea lattes, to my children for providing the spark that ignites, and to my mother, for simply being.

Other works by Amy Joy Lutchen

❧

Golden Dunes of Renhala (Book #2 of Renhala Series)

There is absolute silence.
Nothingness.
A change in consciousness.
A feeling of being watched.
The smell of mud, of earth.
The sensation of birth, of life, of love, of wholeness.
The sensation of pain, of desperation, of loss, of falling apart into a million pieces.

Chapter 1

Mad
☙

It's the incessant barking outside that brings me back to my senses. I stop fidgeting with the silver-braided ring in my hand and place it gently in my robe pocket. I gather my strength and rise from the couch to stand at the window, peeking through the slit in the curtains, not wanting to touch the fabric for any movement signals life inside.

The demons are out there sitting in their vans and talking between sips of hazelnut coffee, their subconscious gorging on the crimes spoken of by chattering scanners. All the while the eyes in the back of their heads screen this south side of Chicago's low-income home, hoping for a special photographic opportunity, perhaps the one that grabs and nails that promotion they've been cutting throats over.

I move from the window, trudging in my plaid baggy flannel pajamas and heavy, black terry cloth robe toward the kitchen and stop mid-way, staring at my house slippers buried in the brown shag-of-a-forest carpeting. The slippers sit there, all pink and perky, happy and smiley, with their sloppy floppy ears, staring at me with their stupid bunny eyes, their smirk attempting to defy the darkness of my depression.

My feet slip into the slippers and make their way to the kitchen, stopping at the mirror as I slide my hand inside my pocket, feeling the smoothness of the ring and slipping it onto my much smaller-sized finger.

My fingers then rise to touch where the stitches have dissolved on my lip and I brush away my long red hair from the incision on my throat. I clench my teeth and continue walking to the kitchen stove to prepare my daily cup of tea. As I grab the box of Tension Tamer, I find myself staring at a ridiculous princess sitting atop a dragon and wonder what marketing idiot came up with the idea. I plop the bag in my favorite teacup and notice a new sharp chip in the rim.

The cup is one my mom bought me, with a cute little cottage surrounded by lilac bushes and dragonflies etched into the china and a cool rune on the back.

The water steams as I pour it and I decide roulette on my lip shall be my excitement for the day. It beats opening and closing the front door repeatedly, forcing the camera-accessorized vermin outside to scatter, vying for the best position.

As I bring the cup to my lips and taste the tea, I decide it needs something—something strong, much stronger than just milk and honey. As I open a lower cabinet door, I reach in deep and pull out the hidden half-full flask from behind the blue Tupperware bowls and pour the remaining contents into my tea, hoping maybe this time will be different.

The ring keeps noisily clinging against the cup, so I take it off and place it on the counter.

I turn, returning to my indent in my mom's fugly couch and pick up Bear—my old and mangy stuffed teddy bear—and place him in my lap facing me. I then look around my mom's house, a house totally void of pictures, even of myself. I imagine my mom saying, "The best film is in here," as she points to her head.

Reaching over and pressing the flashing play button on my mother's digital answering machine I hear: "Kailey, it's Amber. I know you're probably just sitting there in the dark, sulking. You need to get out with me, or something. Please call. It's been three weeks now. I need to hear your voice. I need to know you're okay. Your mom says you are, but I want to hear it from you. I'll be home after nine if you want to call. I'm going out on a...date." Another pause. "I miss you. Bye." I bring the princess's drink of choice to my lips and gulp it as I stare at Bear, allowing images of

Amber, my best friend, to spill before my eyes, ending with an oddball one of Amber asking me if Bear has fleas.

I then feel the sudden movement of the hounds outside. My eyes tighten and I down my whole concoction, hoping for relief— anything. They are closer and I can feel their ridiculous eagerness, then I feel *her*. Three... two... one... The door swings open as she shouts profanities—something about cameras being shoved somewhere nameless.

"Damn reporters!" she screams as she slams the door with her foot, her hands busy with grocery bags most likely filled with my many requests. She freezes and looks at me. "Kailey, you need to change out of those clothes. And open the curtains! And let the dog in!"

She puts the bags down and throws open the curtains, letting the unforgiving rays of the sun pierce my eyes. As she bends over to pick up my empty tea cup, she sniffs it.

I look away, feeling no effects from the alcohol, wishing I would. "I'm an adult. Six years of experience at it, too," I murmur, ignoring her penetrating stare by looking down at my bunny slippers. I immediately sense her worry and add, "Mom, I'm sorry. I can't do this. I need something to take the edge off. Nothing is working!" I bite my lip, waiting for a reply.

"What do you mean, *nothing?* Kailey, what else are you doing?" I look up into her eyes which have begun filling with tears.

"It doesn't matter," I say, "because nothing works."

She says nothing as she picks a newspaper out of a grocery bag and tosses it to me. "Here's your daily newspaper, you junkie," she says. I see her hesitate at her poor choice of words. "Why do you even read those stupid personals?"

I pick the paper up and glance at the headline picture of some disfigured animal the nearby zoo attained, describing it as an unknown species found wandering Dan Ryan Woods. It apparently attacked three innocent joggers.

3

I begin shuffling the papers to find the personals. "Some SM has to be looking for a crazy, tattered and broken SWF," I whine.

My mom inhales deeply and I see her wince as she bends over to pick up the bags. It brings me to my feet quickly, and I say, "Mom, let me help you. You shouldn't push it. The doctors said-" Her piercing gaze tells me to sit back on my ass, immediately. I do.

She picks the bags up and heads into the kitchen. I hear: "I can do a simple act like bringing in groceries. Don't worry about me. But *you*, my dear, will be doing the cooking."

From where I'm sitting, with only a little maneuvering, I can see her standing near the counter, staring at the ring on the counter. The burrow between her eyebrows deepens, and then—in a flash—she moves about, stashing away the groceries with her unnatural speed that peeks out at stressful moments. It always baffles me.

"Don't let those idiots outside get to you," she advises, slamming the back door shut after letting our dog, Kioto, back inside.

Kioto, my huge 110-pound akita, walks swiftly with her wide-spread gait through the front room, staring at me as she walks by on her journey to the front window. As she peers at the strangers outside she growls a long and deep growl, one of pure disgust. She then barks one loud noise of warning to those who have gotten too close.

"It's not just them! Something is wrong with *me*," I sputter as I pet Kioto on her head. "I don't know what. Maybe psychological, maybe brain damage, something. These feelings... " I throw down the papers on the couch.

My mom walks to me slowly, then places her hands on both my shoulders. "Honey, anyone who has gone through something as traumatic as what you went through would undoubtedly have strange feelings. Feelings of mistrust, anger, perhaps a heightened sense of empathy, are all perfectly normal. Remember what your psychiatrist said." She then lets go of me and places the ring back in my hand as she walks toward the front window to scowl at the morons outside. She extends her middle finger through the window, humphs, and then turns to me and flashes me sign language for "I love you": thumb, pointer and pinky finger extended while the other two fingers are bent down. This is something we've shared since I climbed out of the womb, and it makes its appearance at special moments.

I return the gesture, but vent, "That quack of a psychiatrist? She never even really listened to me. She sat staring at that stupid picture of her boyfriend on her desk the whole time we were there. Oh, and occasionally glanced at the clock. I know you saw it, too. And when she *did* have questions for me, why were they all detailed questions about *it?*"

"*Him*," my mother corrects me.

"*It!*" I scream as I gaze into her eyes, pleading her to believe me as my scream turns to sobs. She grabs me and holds me tight as I sob into her shirt. I wipe the fabric where my nose begins dripping ooze.

"Don't worry about the shirt. Just let it out, Kailey. You are going to get better. Things will get easier for you. It's only been three weeks. It's just going to take some time and some work, by both of us. I am going to help you through this," she says as she squeezes harder, making my bruised rib scream in pain. "No matter what it takes, we are going to get through this," she whispers.

I flinch as her sudden anger actually crawls along her skin and onto me, constricting my throat like an anaconda on steroids, and I choke from *it*, as well as from my own tears.

5

Chapter 2

Damaged
❧

I pray for two months that, every time I wake up during the night to visions of my attacker and the sensation of being punched in the head, my pain would end, and the memories would stop. This was a mad thing which didn't even blink while cutting and punching. It seemed human, but the hatred in its eyes was more; something so dark couldn't be *only* human. And the arm: the grotesquely wet and slimy green arm that slipped from underneath my grip as I begged for mercy was far from human. The arm that groped and prodded private places. The arm that was *recorded on security video*—video footage from the rear of my apartment building that made its way to television channels, and played day, after day, along with other various recordings of other odd and extremely dangerous creatures that seem to be randomly appearing across the country.

For two whole months, my mom cooks me my favorite foods: fried, fattening things, and we rent movies and eat popcorn and chocolate covered raisins until we feel like puking. I enjoy bonding with my mom, but eventually feel the urge to be in my own place once again—somewhere I don't have to close the bathroom door when I pee, and somewhere I can hide without remorse. Also, the vultures that once camped outside have disappeared, to only have taken root in some others' misery, I'm sure.

One day, trudging through thirty-mile-per-hour winds in my childhood neighborhood and feeling exceptionally restless, a giant, blustery barrage of leaves hits me in my face, along with a page of the Chicago Tribune. I grab it off my face and quickly scan it before throwing it back to the wind. It's a list of nearby apartments for rent, all within my price range. I continue standing, allowing the wind to pound me, as I take the ring out of my pocket, twiddling it in my hands, unknowingly.

A bird caws, and I then make up my mind to make the move. The ring suddenly draws my attention, and as I stare at it, I think of the day it ended up in my possession. It was the second time that I could ever recall, that my mother actually spoke of my biological father.

Soon after my attack, my mom dragged me eighty miles to meet some old stoner acquaintance of hers from her "best-forgotten past." They spoke briefly as I waited on the front porch, and when my mom finally emerged, she simply said, "This was your father's, once. Keep it safe." I didn't reply, since I was angry from making the trip with her, since it clearly stirred up memories of "a stupid asshole that abandoned a mother and child" (exact words from the first time my mother mentioned my father). And why did I need any more drama in my life? But, I have to admit that once the ring was placed in my palm, the weight and coolness of the metal seemed to ground me, almost giving me a renewed sense of support.

I then lean forward and shuffle my feet home, gathering the courage to talk about apartments with my mother.

After much arguing, the only reason my mom agrees to let me search for a new apartment—since I can never go back to the old—is Kioto. Kioto can scare the stink off a skunk, and always gets people backing up on the sidewalk. It's odd thinking that the one day I needed her most, she was off at the veterinarian's office getting fixed while her mommy was being beaten to a blood pulp. I can honestly admit I'll still be afraid to be alone, even with her, but the thought of myself as an old maid living in my mom's house has me packing before I've even found an apartment.

After a week of viewing rental properties, in-between my mom's numerous doctor visits, I find a cozy third-floor, one-bedroom apartment in a six-flat with plenty of people around, not many windows, and plenty of locks on the front door.

My mother's uncle, Robert, and cousin, Ricky, who were there for my mother after my father left, help me move in, and make sure I have protection in my new place. It may be illegal, but who am I to argue? I feel silly, but they make sure there is something available in several rooms for self-defense. There's a Taser in the kitchen drawer, a few choice weapons (which feel mighty comfortable in my hands) on closet shelves and a five-pound decorative marble ball next to my couch, courtesy of my mom. Kioto is there, too, and she sniffs around the place, checking out all the dark spots, then returns to me, apparently agreeing with my choice. She nuzzles under my hand and licks me once before turning to walk to the front door, nestling into a ball.

After a lunch of Mexican food, permission to reside is granted by my relatives after much checking of locks and views from my windows, and my great-uncle and cousin leave, walking to their respective car and truck, leaving just my mom with me. I cannot say goodbye to her as she packs up her purse, preparing to leave, because I'm scared. Our eyes meet as she picks her head up, and she says one word: "Sleepover?" I nod, and she pulls out an overnight bag that I never noticed from a pile of my boxes. But as she does, she quickly bends over, reaching to her side near her back. I quickly grab her as she says, "I'm fine! I'm fine. Just a hard day for me."

"Your hard days seem to be increasing in number," I declare, as I help her unpack her pajamas and numerous heating pads. She brushes me off, telling me there's plenty other things to do besides look in her bag at her underwear.

"Believe me, they're nothing to look at," I joke. She whips me in the butt with a towel.

I rub where she snapped me and then attempt to move a box that I saw her carry in today and realize that it was most likely one of the heaviest boxes of the day. She moves into the bathroom to unpack her toiletries and I start crying to myself, softly.

Mom may be only fifty-five years old, but she has the body of a seventy-five-year old. She's been cursed with polycystic kidney disease, and has scars up the wazoo from various attempts at shunt sites for dialysis. She has a spine made up of some experimental foam never approved by the FDA, a clamp in her brain to keep an aneurysm from exploding in her head, *and* someone else's kidney in her body. Bad things do indeed happen to good people.

"Kailey," she says as she reappears next to me, pulling my chin up so that we meet eye to eye, "it will never happen again." She mistakes my pity for her, and as her arms embrace me, I cry heavier, feeling her compassion for me as an actual, *tangible* thing, like a warm, steamy towel enveloping me and I pull back, surprised by the solidness of it.

"Do you feel that?" I ask, my eyes wide.

"What? My stomach rumbling? Refried beans."

I start laughing, from insanity or the goofy look on my mom's face, I don't know. Then, to myself, I make a promise that if I ever become a mother, I want to be the mom she is to me.

Chapter 3

Enthralled
ଓ

Since the attack, I've really not had much human contact. I received tons of phone calls from loved ones while I stayed at my mom's house, and a great number of those being from Amber (who also sent me a cookie-gram and stuffed unicorns), but I didn't want anyone to see my battered face, so I refused anyone who asked. I didn't want that look of pity from anyone.

After four more psychiatric therapy sessions from a more caring psychiatrist, and a few prescribed self-defense classes, the doctor gives me the thumbs up to go back to work. And, funny thing is, I really feel I am ready. After much healing inside and out, and one tiny scar on my forehead and neck (which I did my best to cover up with makeup), I feel good about myself...until I step outside my apartment, alone, in my work clothes, and the visions come flooding back.

So much blood. I look down and see it, soaking into my new, crisp white, button-down shirt. The broken bottle used to cut my throat waves in front of me, threatening to slice up my delicate skin, daunting me to even try and move.

I close my eyes, attempting to wash the visions away, and let the sun of a new day shine on my face as I inhale deeply, gathering the courage to walk to the bus. I look down at my shirt, and once again, it's the cheerful yellow cardigan I put on this morning. I turn right back around into my apartment and call my mom.

"I'll be there in ten minutes," she states, no questions asked.

As we pull up to my ten-floor office building, downtown, I flash her our sign language, grab my bag, and head inside toward the set of elevators. As each door opens, I allow the other patrons to board, passing on their attempt to hold the door open for me. As I stand, watching them board, that familiar, creeping feeling from others' thoughts crawls over me, mocking me and my foolishness for not wanting to be in the elevator alone with them. I scan their faces as they shrug their shoulders and I watch them press the Close button.

Finally, an elevator arrives while I am the only one waiting, so I step inside, press the eight button and take my elevator up, breathing in deep breaths and telling myself how brave I am. I reassure myself that once I step off the elevator and into the office, my colleagues will be there to embrace me, and support me, and console me.

So why is it that when I enter the offices of Helping Hands, there are so many abrupt hellos and downturned faces? Where are the hugs and kisses?

Nancy, our receptionist, gives me the pity face I was so hoping to avoid, as she answers the endless phone lines, ending one conversation with, "Kailey Rooke, in accounting, is unavailable at the moment. I'll transfer you to her voicemail, *again*." Her annoyance is as obvious as a clown at a funeral. I grip my hands into fists, wanting to just turn around and run, but I continue to stand in place. I turn and stare at the soothing, sky blue walls, laden with the smiling faces of those that, we, here at Helping Hands, have helped. They encourage me to walk, to venture forth and topple the barriers before me.

I then hear a loud noise—someone dropping a box in our supply closet for the UPS man—and jump in place, suddenly anxious. I slip my hand in my pocket and caress the ring, begging it to give me the strength I need to last the whole workday.

I decide to head toward my mail, which is most likely the size of Mount Everest, and as I turn the corner, there I find Amber, bent over her in-box. She raises her straight blond-haired head and her beautiful green eyes widen just enough for me to notice. She grabs our office manager, Sienna, and immediately heads toward her office. I follow slowly behind them, and watch as Sienna breaks from Amber's grasp and ventures into a copy room, most likely to fix some paper jam left by some unknown individual who made no effort whatsoever to inform her of it. I hear Sienna huffing and puffing as she opens a copier door and numerous other hinged parts.

I stop in front of Amber's office, looking in from the doorway. "Hi Amber," I say. No response. "Amber." She stares straight at her computer as her eyes tear up, even as I walk into her office, toward her. "I'm sorry I haven't called."

At this point I have no idea how the tears are sticking to the wells of her eyes. As soon as I lay my hand on her shoulder, she relaxes, and the tears flow, heavily. After five minutes of sobs and no words, she finally blows her nose, waking anyone asleep within a five-mile radius. "How could someone do those things to you?" she says as she starts crying again.

Not knowing what to say, "Sometimes bad things happen to good people, I guess," slips from my mouth.

"Yes, they do," she whispers, more to herself, as she eventually sits up straight and sighs her "I've got it together now" sigh. "Kailey, please remember I'm here for you—I've always got your back. We're practically sisters." She looks at me, teary-eyed. "You and your mom have always been there for me, so I want to be here for you. Please don't block me out anymore, k?" Her eyes stare at me for a moment and I shake my head. "You sleeping at night? I don't mean to sound like a bitch, but you look exhausted."

"No, I am not sleeping. Every stupid sound I hear in my apartment has me up and running to the nearest weapon. And with every jump of mine, poor Kioto is right there beside me, watching and anticipating," I warble, sadly. Amber looks as though she may start crying again, so I decide to change the subject. "I just want this behind me, so let's not talk about it right now. How was your date?" I query, with a small amount of forced effort. The slight downturn of her plump lips gives me the hint it was probably not awesome.

She inhales deeply and says with a scowl, "Like usual. The asshole actually shoved his hand under the table and up my skirt. Twenty minutes flat." Her scowl then turns into a mischievous grin. "But I couldn't refuse his request to call me again this weekend." Her eyes widen as she catches my swallow and she immediately apologizes. "Oh, I said too much. That was so insensitive!" She then gets up and hugs me, practically knocking me over. "I love you, Kailey. Forgive my stupidness, especially after what you went through... It was so extreme... You mean so much to me," she whispers.

"Love you, too," I say as I finish the hug. "Amber, just please don't let yourself be taken advantage of. Don't settle. You're more than that. Look at you! You can have any guy you want, yet you continue to..."

Her sudden facial changes warn me that perhaps I stepped over some boundary—even best friend boundary. "Who are you to say?" she says, her voice suddenly becoming angry. "I'm truly sorry you experienced what you did, but you have no right telling me who and who not to see. Step back, Kailey."

"It's just—" I stop mid-sentence, knowing it's a losing battle. "You just worry me sometimes, that's all. Sorry." I wave goodbye as I leave her office. It was a typical Amber-Kailey boy-topic conversation, but I find myself brushing my clothes off from the strange creepy-crawly sensations gripping to me since our hug; surely my brain needs another scan at the hospital.

On the way to my office, I think about Amber and how she's usually the only reason I get out on the weekends and have any interaction with the opposite sex. We have fun together, but she's dangerously flirty and tends to pick the wrong guys. She *always* has, since I met her, at the spritely age of sixteen.

Amber's mother, once widowed, abandoned Amber at the early age of fifteen. They cohabited, but while her mother dated men half her own age, taking them on island vacations, Amber worked to support herself. That's when we met at Burrito Burgers and our deadbeat parent connection had us conjoined in a matter of days.

We would assemble burgers, side-by-side, gagging simultaneously every now and then on the stench of overly mature avocadoes and bean spread. Our overweight gigantasaur of a boss would just laugh at us as he shoved singles from the cash register into his forty-four-waist Lee Dungarees, and goosed Amber—his only reason for repeat customers—behind my back. And never once did Amber report him.

Anyway, my mom was the one who stepped in to fill Amber's maternal void. One unforgettable evening, after running out to a late-night Delta Chi frat party while I attended a nearby community college, and gorging on some questionable barbeque chicken, Amber introduced me to vodka and cranberry juice. After both of us became ill, I finally convinced her it was time to leave, so she had a "friend" of hers—granted she just met him that night—take us home, to my house. As we both sat in the front seat of this gentleman's car, smack dab in front of our destination, with Amber directly to his right, he decided it wasn't time to say goodbye, yet. His hands moved quickly under her shirt and as he groped and attempted to simultaneously touch me, I vomited. She told me to leave the car as she tried to play the offensive against his advances, but he was much larger, and stronger. As I knelt on the ground, vomiting barbeque sauce and vodka, I saw my mother run out the front door of our house to his car. As the boy continued with his conquest, ripping Amber's bra, my mother had opened his car door, had Amber seated in the grass next to me, and the boy in a headlock within five seconds. To this day, my mom says we were too intoxicated to really know what happened. But I remember, clearly, for at that moment I was not feeling a bit drunk.

I snap back to my senses after justifying my comment to Amber, and decide to stop in the office kitchen for a cup of hot black tea. Tea seems to cure everything for me, from stress to lethargy. My colleagues even say it's unnatural how excited I get over a cup, but what can I say? It's my drug, if you will. It's a bit of homey warmth that seems to tame the nerves no matter what is going on around me, especially these days, when even a fifth of vodka leaves me cold and unaffected.

As my Lipton bag brews, I reach for my honey bear in the highest cabinet, all the way in the back, and see that it's now completely empty; leave it up to office colleagues to sniff it out and use it all. I add a shake of powdered creamer and decide to search the mountainous stack of newspapers on the kitchen table for the personals. Reading the lines of hidden angst and desperation are a guilty pleasure of mine. I'm not the only one, right?

One in particular catches my eyes immediately. I do a double-take and reread it.

ROOKES and pawns. Chess is played by the gods K-Lee. Search for double happiness over the rainbow.

"Guess they don't proof the personals." Evan, my boss, appears next to me. "Why are you reading these, anyway? Don't you have a budget to go over?" He's joking, but I don't react. "You ok? We've missed you." He hugs me and I immediately tighten up a bit from his closeness, but eventually relax and hug him back. There are no creepy-crawlies, but instead a comfortable feeling of safety.

"I'll be ok. Thanks." He smiles at me and leaves the kitchen.

I return to the ad, without knowing what to do or even how to feel about it. *Is this for me?* My mind whirls enough to give me vertigo. *Is this for some weirdo, or some lovers' rendezvous? Am I totally overreacting?*

I tear out the ad, imagining who will be the one to cry, as the papers are public property and now they won't be able to read "Who's Screwing Who in Hollywood Now" or "So and So Gets a Boob Job" on the flip side.

I stumble to my office. It takes me all day to just get through my lousy junk mail and voicemail messages. I then find myself staring at the framed copy of Helping Hands' mission statement centered on my office wall.

The company is small, but dedicated to helping those that help—but not, like, on an extreme scale. Helping Hands is more like, we hire a personal chef for a woman who spends her weekends working at a soup shelter—simple things, but things that count. People hire us to coordinate special events for special people. Our clients range from sports stars to city governments, but unfortunately, we're not getting a steady flow of new money. My boss informs me that people seem to be less willing to reward others for their generosity than they were just over the two years or so. If we don't get new clients soon, I may no longer have a job. And if *I* leave, Amber most likely would be out the door with me.

Without major surgery, we, as conjoined twins, will most likely never part. When I knew they were hiring at Helping Hands, I made Amber come with me for support. She sat, reading quietly in the front lobby while I interviewed, but once the pervert HR manager got a look at her, she was hired on the spot—I had to wait a week for the welcoming call—for "public affairs," he said. Let's just say he didn't last long with Amber on the payroll. After one of his many advances were witnessed publicly, my boss had him fired.

Four o'clock finally rolls around, and I'm out the door, my coat whipping in the wind behind me.

When I get home, after hugging and repeatedly kissing Kioto, I reread the ad for the quadrillionth time and decide it's gonna be the death of me, so I have to get rid of it. So I light my ginger vanilla candle and, voila! Bye-bye, ambiguity.

From there, I slump onto the couch and turn on the television, tuning in to local channel 9, WGN. Wow, the news, go figure. I really hate the news, because most newsfeed is a big brown bag of bullshit. Light the fire, because it's time to stomp it out.

My attack—"Bucktown Horror," as they called it—was on the local news every three hours, every channel, every day for about a week—my five minutes of fame. The media had such a way of twisting the facts that I was dying to see what they would come up with next, especially after seeing the report about me on my deathbed, asking to speak to the president of the United States. That was a good one, considering it stemmed from the scavengers rifling through my garbage, finding a ripped out personal ad, which just happened to have a picture of the president on the underside.

Throughout my life, my mom constantly turned the news off, asking me to instead play games with her. I'm quite the Canasta player, and can really give you a run at *Boggle*.

But like many a poor soul, despite my own animosity, I decide to watch anyway. So after ten minutes of warehouse fires, hit and runs, and what fruits and vegetables you shouldn't eat now, I find myself drawn to the picture of a supposed murder scene in Chinatown, specifically Twenty-Second Street. A store owner was found mauled to death, but no animal was found, only footprints. There were no witnesses.

As the reporter keeps talking, I don't hear a word, instead stare wide-mouthed at the sign above the door. It's the Chinese symbol for double happiness, which I recognize from the many trips I took as a child with my mother to Chinatown; the symbol seemed to pop up everywhere. But this sign is particularly familiar looking to me.

When the news segment ends, all I hear is "Raine Boman reporting." *Rainbow.* *"Double happiness over the rainbow."* I turn to read the personal ad once more and end up staring at its ashes.

ƆȢ

I spend my workweek catching up on e-mails and trying to figure out how messed up things have gotten while I was gone. It's only been about three months, but as Assistant Controller, I'll probably spend another month reconstructing the books. Things like the purchase of a box of office coffee shouldn't be depreciated over ten years, unless we're looking to have our employee emergency room visit experience rate skyrocket.

The week actually makes me yearn, a little bit, for a night out, in hopes that maybe if I was out until some wee hour of the morning with Amber, I'd sleep soundlessly for a night.

Finally, the weekend arrives, and I find I couldn't be happier. I call up my mom to see what she's getting herself into these days and it's basically nothing, as usual.

"Whatch'ya doing, Mom?" I ask.

"Just sitting, looking through the want ads."

I taunt quickly, "You're gonna get a real job?" I cannot even fathom my mother working a nine-to-five job. For as long as I've known, my mother has just done oddball jobs, like painting and weeding for friends, and friends of friends, leaving me with distant relatives for days at a time while on her ventures. Despite the fact she would return totally exhausted, never once did she not make up the lost time to me with movies, amusement parks, and moments like sitting in our garage, watching lightning storms.

"No, just said I was looking through the want ads. On my way to the garage sales section," she says with a hoarse voice.

"Oh." I pause. "You ok, Mom?"

"My throat is killing me today. Must just be a bit of reflux. I'll be fine. Always am, right?" She coughs, sounding extremely tired.

"I survived the week at work," I say.

"I knew you would, honey," she professes sweetly. "Maybe you can celebrate this weekend with Amber." She waits for my reply.

"Actually, I'm calling her next."

"Good!" She pauses on the phone for a brief few seconds. "Just please be careful. I trust you'll make the important decisions for the evening? Don't leave them up to Amber. I'm too tired to head out to save her ass this evening. You got your pepper spray?"

"If I can gather the nerve to make it out the door with her, yes, it will be in my purse."

"I love you with all my heart, Kailey. Be safe."

"Thanks mom." I hang up the phone, gently.

I dial up Amber, and when I hear her yawn right before she says, "Hello," I know damn well she checked her caller ID.

"Hi. What are you up to this evening?" I say, not sure if I want her to say she's busy washing her hair or if I want her to shout out, "Going out with you, of course!"

"Oh, I'm just waiting for the seven sexual deviants I contacted through Craig's List to come over," she prattles.

"Alright already, I get it. I'm sorry. Last apology," I blurt as I roll my eyes.

"Fine, I accept. So, what's up?"

I take in a deep breath and then say, "I want to go out with you tonight." I sit with my eyes closed, feeling my heart race.

"We'll do dinner first. I'll be there by six!" she shouts, excitedly.

"Ok."

She surely notes the lack of excitement in my voice, for her tone changes. "You sure? I can always just come over to watch movies," she says, genuinely.

I think about how I already got her all riled up, so I must continue with the plan, for Amber's sake of course. "Just get your ass over, all dressed up. See ya."

Six o'clock means she'll be here at seven, and that gives me plenty of time to get ready. I can hardly believe I'm the one who initiated a night out, but I'm riding the minute possibility that a few really strong, dirty martinis will crumble a few emotional walls of mine tonight. I'm willing to give it a try, but damn well know the probable outcome: me sitting, totally sober, while already-drunk Amber downs the countless drinks bought for her from overly-anxious meatheads.

I switch on the radio and get dressed while lightly shuffling to "Good Vibrations," by Marky Mark. As I check myself out in the bathroom mirror, I stare, unhappy with the somewhat low-cut shirt I chose—too revealing. While taking the shirt off, I bend over to plug the iron back in, and then the power suddenly goes out, engulfing me in total darkness.

I freeze for a brief two seconds. Then whirl about, using my hands as eyes in the darkness, searching for any weapons in my bathroom. Realizing that two previous nights ago I walked away with a pocket knife usually stored in the medicine cabinet, I grab my cuticle scissors in one hand and my hairspray in the other. Kioto had only been moaning in her sleep that night I moved the knife, but it sounded so alien. *Alien. Alien-like grunting.*

The guttural sound of grunting from my assaulter's throat echoes through my mind as I stand motionless, frozen from fear, remembering the noise as he tore off my cotton panties the day of the assault. *I lay there, on my stomach, on top of my newly made bed, staring at Bear—a feeling of despair so great and overpowering pulsing through me.* I also remember, too painfully, the blood-curdling scream that escaped my throat as I pleaded to anyone listening, a higher being even, to please save me. *Don't let this happen to me. This shouldn't be happening to me.* I wouldn't survive feeling that hopeless again.

After my eyes adjust, and as I wait for the sound of footsteps or breathing, I hear neither, so I peek around the door and see Kioto lying on the ground, head turned toward me—possibly perturbed by the roaring sounds emanating from my chest. I walk, shakily, with weapons still in hand, toward the window and I see the whole block is out. A quick check toward the sky reveals the approaching storm. I collapse on my couch and cry like a baby, doubting my ability to function like a normal human being ever again. Kioto walks toward me, and slowly licks my blackened tears from my face. "Thanks, baby," I whisper as I snuggle into her and regain my normal breathing.

I wipe my running mascara from my face and gather my composure. A glance at the clock tells me that Amber should be here soon. Sooner than I can fix my makeup, the power goes back on, giving me another heart attack when "Kung Fu Fighting" starts blaring throughout the apartment. What a wonderful start to the evening.

Amber arrives at 7:15 and lets herself in with the key I gave her last week, which was supposed to be for emergencies only. She is absolutely stunning. Her long, straight blond hair complements the lime-green baby-doll dress and her black stilettos. She's only five foot three, so the extra four and a half inches brings her closer to eye level, but not for long. I decide to wear my knee length, heeled, black boots with my new taupe silk tank top and black pants. I grab my father's ring off my dresser and slip it into my pocket.

She stares at me and then implores, "Girl, I need some of that leg length. If you die, can you donate your legs to me?" I laugh and tell her only if she shares some of the endowment on her chest. She's about a thirty-two E, compared to my thirty-four B.

"You sure you're ready to do this?" She emanates sincerity.

I shake my head no as the tears fill my eyes and I grab my purse.

Seeing my reaction, she steps softly toward me and hugs me tightly.

As she lets go, I say, "I can do this, really. I *want* to do this." I sniffle and grasp the ring in my pocket. I pull myself together and say, "I'm ready. Let's go." I smile at her.

"Let's go and find us some sugar daddies," she purrs mischievously. My eyebrows rise and she then says, "or some boring, but respectful male who loves his momma, and thinks of nothing but pleasing the female race?"

I laugh at her as we both say our goodbyes to Kioto, before walking out of my apartment. With a sudden change of tone as we walk downstairs, she asks, "How's your mom doing?" Amber is always asking about my mom and worries as much as I do.

"She's hanging in there. The doctors are repeatedly amazed at how she continues each day without dialysis—which she refuses. The kidney is not doing well."

Amber frowns and says, "I hope you tell her how much you love her. Every day." She looks to the sky and says, "I would," in a whisper. Her sorrow makes my own eyes tear up and I take a deep breath, holding it deep in my chest, and bringing myself back to my own emotions.

We decide that, with menacing clouds still lingering above, we don't want to go anywhere café-ish, where we could have sat outside if the weather was decent.

"How about that new hot spot over in Lakeview that serves all their food raw?" she suggests.

I imagine a plate full of vomit-looking butternut squash and steak tartare, and it makes me want to puke. "Sorry, I'm not into that whole raw scene," I snap. "I want something warm and comforting tonight—maybe with some grease to soak up the cosmos I've been daydreaming about."

We decide on a soul food restaurant that's been around for years. We both get excited as we jinx each other with a simultaneous

"Cornbread!" But after we hail a cab, we regret it immediately. The cabbie slowly scans us with his beady eyes as we climb in and smiles a smile I rather dislike, displaying his stained teeth. *The yellow, rotten teeth, brown-streaked from years of neglect, sneer as he comes close, sniffing my lightly perfumed neck.*

Amber, seeing my reaction, then leans in toward me and whispers with beautiful, professionally whitened, but clenched teeth, "If I smell like this cab at the bar, I am going to start smoking again."

She quit three years ago, thanks to my constant nagging, and her comment indeed pulls me back to reality. "I'll spill some kind of fruity drink all over you so you don't stink. Sound good?" I give her my best wholesome smile, attempting to wash away negative thoughts that may ruin my night out.

"You are such a true friend. Thanks," she says. "You'd probably light a match, too." She smiles quirkily at me, showing her full set of dazzling white teeth.

Our chatting turns my mind from the cabbie as we discuss how Helping Hands is doing so poorly. And how maybe, it's no coincidence considering the increase of strange and depressing news that scours televisions these days. We then both stare at each other, silently acknowledging that we've hit yet another topic we should currently steer clear of, so we then divert our focus to the cattiness of our female Helping Hands colleagues, and how we are just *so* above that as grown, mature women. Our laughs intertwine as we realize we are so full of shit. But my laugh soon dissipates as a glance out the window informs me we are in unknown territory.

I grab my purse and the pepper spray inside as I scan the area for street signs. Amber grabs my arm and gives me a glare I've grown accustomed to throughout the years—the one informing me I'm overreacting. She asks the cabbie where we are, and he replies, with the thickest Middle-Eastern accent I've ever heard, "Dragon Palace, just like you said."

"No, it was *Regina's Palate*, on Southport." Amber's voice rises quickly.

The driver's face contorts as the prospect of a decent tip flies out the window—and Amber hasn't even begun with him yet. "I think you need to pay me now," he says.

"No, you take us where we asked," demands Amber.

"Get out of my cab," he says, turning off his meter. I am about to scream at this point, so very afraid of being stranded. He turns to me and bends over the seat, then directly looking into my face, he yells, "*You* get out *now!*"

The sour breath, reeking like a rotting corpse might, has me gagging as his eyes look into mine, daring me to scream again.

The terror is so overwhelming I think I'm going to explode. Amber grabs my arm quickly and pulls me out of the cab. I fumble with my purse, and my makeup bag rips open and spills out everywhere. The cabbie burns rubber as he runs over my Chanel compact, breaking it into a thousand pieces. There are tears in my eyes, but for fear of ruining my mascara, they don't fall. I sit on the curb and look up at Amber. "I can't do this. Who am I fooling? I thought I could, but I can't." I look down at my hands that are shaking.

Amber pulls my chin up to look at her. "You can. Stop doubting, Kailey. If that was me instead of you, believe me, I'd be locked up somewhere in a straightjacket," she says. "Look—you've made it this far. I know where we are, and so should you. Your mom took us here after...you know..."

I look around and it dawns on me that this is the restaurant—hidden in one of Chinatown's many nooks—my mom took us to after Amber broke the nose of one of her mother's boyfriends, actually the worst on the extensive list. His request of a ménage à trois with Amber and her own mother was the final straw.

"Yeah! You're right. I remember they had the most *delicious* lavender jasmine tea." My blood pressure slowly drops to a livable level as I recall the delicate taste.

Amber smiles warmly at me. "Leave it up to you to remember their damn tea. Let's go grab some mai tais instead." She walks toward the front door, leaving me standing with Jell-O legs.

She's amazing—already back to her nonchalant self, enjoying life. With my hand in my pocket, I eventually—as she stands holding the door open—convince myself to follow her. Perhaps the simple thought that she might get us some free appetizers draws me in.

After a delicious meal of free potstickers, Kung Pao Dream, two Dragon mai tais, one pina colada, and a steaming hot tea, I head to the ladies room to touch up my makeup after mentioning to Amber how weak the drinks are. Her heavy eyelids disagree.

As I walk to the restroom, I'm amazed at how many different shades of red exist in the restaurant. It's not tacky, though, instead actually very comforting, in a strange sort of way. I admire the many decorations on the walls: fierce, four-toed dragons threaten kimono-clothed girls as they run on their stilted shoes, beautiful golden temples shining in the distance. I breathe in deeply as the smells coming from the kitchen make me want more food—go figure.

Once I reach a mirror, I raise my hand to apply some powder to my nose, but it never reaches its destination, for I notice a reflection in the mirror of a neon sign outside. It's a buzzing double happiness symbol—and I'm sure it's the same sign from the news. Every muscle in my body freezes, except for my heart, which decides it rather try beating its way out through my chest.

I scramble back to our table as quickly as possible, forgoing my attention to my shiny forehead.

"Amber, let's go walk around," I suggest. "See some sites."

"In these heels?"

"I've witnessed you dance in those shoes for *hours*. Come on."

After a bit more coercing, and a "whatever" from Amber, we walk outside to the end of the block, turn the corner, and her mood suddenly changes as she sees the thriving nightlife of Chinatown. The storefronts promise goodies if you're willing to dig through mountains of Chinese imports, and several cutesy candy shops advertise yummy milk candies wrapped in equally yummy bunny-laden wrappers. Decorative dragon spoon rests call to me as Amber buys a sushi set-up for two at Hong Kong Heaven.

As we step out of the shop, my eyes are drawn to the opposite side of the street. I stop right in front of Amber, who walks right into me, dropping her bag. "If you even broke this, I'll kill you," she warns in a very serious voice as she picks up her bag.

I tell her to shut up. Across the street is a young Asian man dressed in black, motioning for us to join him. I turn around to find my friend smiling, her eyes widened and filled with lust. Another glance across the street reveals that the man is indeed quite handsome. He's about my height, and thin, but he reeks of hidden muscle underneath his expensively tailored shirt. His silky black hair is short, accentuating his polished skin, and his smile rivals the streetlight in brightness.

Amber's smile fades, replaced by a look of determination. "Maybe he needs some arm candy for some cool party. Let's go." Before I can say no, she pulls on my arm, dragging me across the street. When Amber has a purpose, watch out, world.

I, on the other hand, no longer trust anything and the gears in my head churn in overdrive. Her arm drags me, against my will, behind her, through throngs of night owls littering the streets.

We make our introductions to the handsome gentleman, and he informs us that, yes, indeed, there is a party down the block, and we should join him. He points to the bar with the longest line of already drunk bar-hoppers and turns to look at Amber. I notice a brief emotion from him, but can only describe it as how one might think a dog feels waiting in its owner's car, eyes focused on the door they disappeared through.

I explain, "My friend's feet here are killing her, so maybe we shouldn't." Amber then jabs me with her elbow. But to our surprise, our new friend leads us straight to the front of the line, and we enter without even having to pay the cover. Amber pumps her arm, letting a "Yes!" escape her mouth as the girls in line shout at us with their plump, glossy lips, which only enlarges Amber's already large head.

Inside, after finding that I have highly underestimated the size of the bar—and the crowd inside is not seedy—I decide there's nothing scary going on. All the patrons are engrossed in the news feed playing above the bar, which keeps showing shots of a dead, but adorable and humongous, white rabbit. But as the screen pans to where its front left paw should be, we all see one large talon, like a hybrid gone terribly wrong. The men and women alike all shriek in disgust at the sight—Amber specifically grabbing onto Russell's arm. Apparently, this rabbit, alone, took down a wild pack of dogs before it was shot by an Idaho potato farmer.

Within minutes, Amber leans over to me, shouting, "Kailey, Russell and I are going to get a drink at the bar! Would you like anything?" Her eyebrows are slightly raised, giving me a clue she wants some privacy. Russell points to a reserved table with three empty seats where I can sit and wait like a good doggie. A sore toe obliges with no problem whatsoever, but before I reach the table, I see a short, elderly Asian man standing in a doorway, staring at me. I squint my eyes at him, trying to scare him.

He then smiles at me and motions for me to come over.

I shake my head, refusing the offer.

He then mouths the words "Come, it's ok." I reach in my purse, feel my pepper spray and suddenly have enough courage to actually follow this stranger. Plus, the kitchen aromas coming from his direction have won hands down in the arm wrestle with my better judgment.

Upon entering the doorway, he says, "Follow me, I've got something interesting to show you. It might make your day." He exudes confidence, as though no matter what he says, I'll listen. His words make my insides feel all excited and fuzzy like a child who has found a new neighborhood park. But I stand, allowing him to continue without me. He stops and says, with a bit of sternness, "Please, follow. Don't be afraid. You're a stubborn one, aren't you?" I follow, not feeling one bit scared or foolish in doing so.

He walks through another doorway, and this room is empty, except for a small table with a lamp and some kind of urn. Out of curiosity, I follow the man yet again, through yet another door. This room has only one door. It must be our destination.

It's perhaps the most beautiful room I have ever seen. The hardwood floors are mahogany, the walls alternating between a deep, rich, purple hue and a stunning gold, metallic sheen, and the ceiling is painted like the sky. There are striking purple and gold accents here and there, along with lovely vases of tuberoses—my favorite—and purple delphinium. And the smell—god, it smells of rain and grass on a spring morning. A large, curtainless window framed by white, distressed wood looms perfectly in the middle of a wall, beckoning me to look out. The man holds out his hand, giving me permission to observe. I don't know what I'm looking for as I walk to the window, but I find myself drawn to it.

My eyes widen as I see a cab pulled along the side of the road. It has started raining, and the driver stands, staring at his cab. As he turns slowly, I recognize his Middle-Eastern profile. My blood begins boiling as he bends over, his hands reaching toward the wheel, pulling out a black piece of plastic from the flat tire. I recognize it instantly: Chanel medium bisque. I feel happy, and know I shouldn't, but he *was* a jerk.

"Someone *has* to still be listening," the man with me whispers to himself, as he watches the cab driver.

"What?" I respond.

"Just talking to myself. Would you like a cup of tea, Kailey?" I jump at words I wasn't expecting, especially my name.

He speaks again: "I know you because you called, and of course because of who you are."

Suddenly, I feel I made a big mistake. The man has got to be insane. *Where's the door?* I turn to look for it, but—silly me—the door is gone.

Chapter 4

Tender
❧

I whirl around, thinking maybe *I'm* really the one who's insane, or else someone slipped me a roofie at the restaurant—or maybe the milk candy I secretly slipped in my mouth from Hong Kong Heaven was tainted with melamine, and karma is getting me back.

"Have some tea. It will calm your nerves," says the man while fiddling with a teapot and cups. "Don't fight it."

"It's probably drugged," I say, and at once I feel ashamed as he smiles his warm smile again. I hold out my hand, accepting the cup of tea he is suddenly holding before me, and I bow, something I do uncontrollably for some reason in the presence of elderly Asian people.

"You should sit while you drink your tea," says the man.

Behind me, a soft, comfy-looking armchair seems to hold out its arms for me, inviting me in. I hadn't noticed the chair there before, but now I sit. I drink. I savor the wondrous aroma and sweetness of the tea in my cup. It's like honey, roses, and crème brûlée all in one. At this point, I'd sit here for a week if he asked, if only I could drink more of this intoxicating elixir.

He drinks from a cup as well. Between sips, he says, "Did you get my message? You were bound to find it at some point."

The newspaper ad suddenly appears in my head:

ROOKES and pawns.

My eyes widen in surprise. "If you mean the scary ad in the personals, yes," I say "and if you even tell me you killed that store owner on the news, or had something to do with it, I'm going to get very scary in this room with no door." I mean it, too. After all,

I recently learned some highly effective protective moves in self-defense class and I did take those three Tae Kwon Do classes ten years ago.

His eyes never leave mine. "I don't like to lie, so indirectly I may be related to it," he hints. At this point, my face gets very warm—and yet I feel no need for fight or flight. "Kailey," he says, "there are big things in the works, and I have to explain so you understand your involvement."

"You must have me mistaken for someone else. I don't get involved in big things, and I've been out of commission for the past few months, anyway." I want him to get up and lead me outside, apologizing for the huge mistake he's made.

"Someone else named Kailey? You know, I do not."

Damn.

"I needed to get you here as soon as possible," he says. "You acted much slower than anticipated."

I laugh to myself, wondering why I dragged Amber out tonight and didn't stay home and veg on the couch like she suggested. Why do I attract all the crazies?

"What is your religion, Kailey?"

"I'm Catholic."

"Are you practicing?"

"Uh, if you count praying the 151 Sheridan will stay at the corner long enough so I can catch it, or that nobody picks up the medium-sized sweater I hid among the extra-smalls on the sale rack, then yes," I joke sarcastically.

He turns toward the window and speaks: "Do you believe in a higher power?"

My willingness to answer his questions suddenly starts diminishing. "I really think that maybe I need to go. Um, thank you for the tea." I stand up and place my tea cup on the small table.

"Kailey, sit please. We need to have this conversation without interruptions."

I sit right back down and as I do, my ring falls out of my pocket, unbeknownst to me. The man initially moves to pick it up, but then stops and simply informs me that I dropped it. As I pick it up, I look into his face and his brow softens while a warm sense of sympathy from him washes over me, like a heavy cloud above me just released its load.

"Thanks," I sigh, as I shove the ring into my purse, and figuring I should answer his question. "I believe that all religions are praying to the same higher power, so yes."

"Do you believe in spirits or ghosts, and that they wander the earth, connected to individuals, here?"

"Yeah, maybe a bit."

He gets up and walks to another piece of furniture I didn't notice: a beautiful, golden, three-drawer chest on a small, mahogany table. He pulls out some kind of pointed stone pendant on a half-foot-long chain. He puts the milky white and tan stone in my hands.

"What am I supposed to do with this?" I ask.

"Think of it as speaking to your spirit guides."

"What drugs are *you* on?"

He laughs, and again, I feel that creeping warmness, like a soft kitten in my insides.

"Humor me," he says.

"Fine. What do I do?" I fuss, feeling a bit silly and resistant.

"Hold the pendulum slightly above your palm, like this." He shows me what to do. "Now ask it, 'What is no?'"

I clench my teeth, asking myself why the hell I'm still playing along with this man and cannot come up with a logical answer. I figure it best to continue. I know through experience what irrational things strangers are capable of.

I do as he suggests and the pendulum starts swinging back and forth. I check to make sure he is not blowing on it.

"Now ask it, 'What is yes?'"

I do, and it starts swinging around in a circle. "Is there like a magnet or something inside of this? Are you playing magician with me?" I question, examining the pendulum closely.

He shakes his head no, and I feel he means it, for there doesn't exist the wavering feelings I usually sense from outright liars—like the simple dressed, ballet shoe-wearing pythons that often waited outside my mom's front doors after my assault, offering their help for nothing in exchange, except maybe just a quick, harmless interview.

"Ask a question, any question," he coaxes. "Try something simple." He is turned toward the window again and not at me, so he doesn't see my very furrowed brow.

"Are my shoes black?" I ask. I wait, and then, suddenly, the pendulum starts moving in a circular motion. But I must be shaking it. My concentration wills my heart to slow down and my head to clear. "Did I eat chicken tonight?" I think about that question and realize I really don't want the answer. "No, nevermind," I add rather quickly and shake the pendulum. The man laughs to himself. "Do I work at Helping Hands?" Again, the circular movement. "Will I win the lotto?" It swings back and forth. "I had to try."

"Ask it something more meaningful now," the man suggests eagerly.

I think for a bit, and suddenly, "Is Amber okay right now?" The moment I say it, I can't believe I'd forgotten about her this whole time—I'm always concerned about Amber. I wait for the pendulum to do the whole circle thing, but to my surprise it doesn't move. And then, slowly, it starts swinging back and forth. I widen my eyes, and fear surfaces.

"Kailey," the man says quickly, "You must be more specific— in fact, *very* specific. Think about your question and what you really asked."

He's right. That question could mean anything. What is "okay," really? Any head-shrink would tell you there's no "okay" diagnosis. So the girl has some issue—don't we all? So I ask another question: "Is Amber safe at this particular moment?" Circular motion. Thank God.

The man moves to stand near me, and I let him. He locks his eyes with mine and delves deep, asking me to ask one more question.

I think for a short moment. "Am I safe?" The pendulum starts to move, and I cannot tell what it wants to do. Then, the motion begins—back and forth slowly, then more quickly, until it feels five pounds heavier. Suddenly, it feels like someone is pulling the chain from my hand. I let go, and it falls to the ground. My eyes move toward it as the old man quickly picks it up, then places it back in my hand.

His eyes meet mine, and I'm compelled to listen to him very carefully. "Some say it's spirit guides that make it move, while others say that pendulums like these are really only extensions of ourselves, and that we are in fact all-knowing creatures," he explains. "The pendulum just helps us focus on the truth and reveals it in a specific form. Omniscience is something I would love to believe in, but I don't know these days. You go home with this and return it to me in three days, before the full moon." He smiles again, but his expression emanates fatigue.

I feel like he looks. It's been a long day and I'm so ready to go home. I've decided Amber is definitely spending the night with me, whether she likes it or not. The strangeness of the evening, and my being frazzled beyond belief is enough of an excuse. The gentleman escorts me out the door, which is somehow there again.

After a few turns, we eventually reach the door to the bar, and I turn to the man. "Do you have a name?" I ask.

"My name is Gunthreon," he says, warmly, "and it's been a pleasure." He extends his hand and I shake it. A feeling of hurriedness and silent fear suddenly rushes over me and I pull my hand back, quickly, and rub it as he stares complacently at me, not making any movement or facial gesture to indicate my reaction.

"Come back in three days well-rested, because our next meeting may leave you exhausted, too." It feels like that soft kitten is now turning somersaults in my lower intestines. I wave goodbye and return to the bar.

I quickly scan the area and find Amber sitting at a table by herself. When she sees me, she doesn't even seem worried. "Here, Russell bought you a key lime martini, with extra graham crackers."

Yum. I love those.

"Did you miss me?" I twitter, waiting for some response from her, all the while giving her raised eyebrows.

"Geez, Kailey, I just wanted a few minutes of privacy with Russell," she spouts, arrogantly. She sips her whiskey on the rocks, frowning at me behind her glass.

I find I want a kudos for being brave enough to be out on my own, but I see that my actions have gone unnoticed. "Amber, can we go home? And please say you'll spend the night."

"Are you serious? We just got here! And I have so much more to talk to Russell about." Leave it to Amber to blindly connect to some strange male.

"Yes, sorry. That kung pao I ate isn't sitting so well."

"Ugh! Let me find Russell and tell him," whimpers Amber. "It would be rude if we just left." The daggers I suddenly feel bombarding me make me look down at my body. Nothing. I look up and watch Amber locate Russell and head toward him, swaying her hips in her best Marilyn Monroe fashion. He spots her and strides to meet her, like one of those old-fashioned couples in some black-and-white film. I'm ready for him to grab her and passionately kiss her as they meet, with the wind blowing her hair and her hands firmly squeezing his arms. They don't, but he does whisper something in her ear, then hands her a piece of paper. She waves a little goodbye to him, and he smiles at her, and then turns to me and waves a sincere goodbye. That was nice of him. I'm impressed. And Amber is glowing.

Her eyes scan the paper, and her glow intensifies. "Yum, I could gobble him up," she drawls. "He is just dreamy." *Did she really just say that?* She then realizes she's not alone, but rather has her best friend sitting next to her. "Shut up. Let's go, wimp."

"Yeah, I love you, too."

Finding a cab turns out to be difficult, but thanks to Amber's ability to run in stilettos, we grab one turning the corner and tail-hike it home. I get ready for bed, leaving Amber to herself on my couch.

As I crawl under my covers, with Kioto lying next to my bed, I hear Amber attempting to whisper on her cell phone. I sit up and turn my ear in her direction, and hear, "Russell, I most certainly accept your invitation." I bite my tongue and resist the urge to call her a slut across the apartment.

Time passes. I can't seem to fall asleep, so I decide to rummage through my purse for my new pendulum. I find it so intriguing that I end up playing with it for hours. Eventually, I move on to writing things on paper and holding the pendulum above and asking questions about various people at work, like: "Who stole the infamous frozen Lean Cuisine entree at work," or "Who is cheating on their spouse."

Delirious three hours later from lack of sleep, I gather the nerve to ask who is "around" me, since Gunthreon did suggest I might be chatting with my spirit guides. I've always felt there was one spirit in particular that might be following me around.

My mom had a psychic party one September many years ago in which she invited over a few select family members, and everyone took turns sitting with the psychic. I was quite the skeptic, but decided I'd give it a shot anyway. After she gave me lots of facts I already knew, the psychic suddenly told me that my aunt had entered the room. Since my Aunt Vivian lived in California at the time, I knew it wasn't her, and my father had no siblings. She could only have meant my mom's twin sister, Debra Kay, who had died in a car accident when they were only sixteen years old.

"She's telling me something, and I don't know what this means," the psychic said, "but she's telling you to dress up as a kidney for Halloween." This was quite the coincidence, as my mom was on the waiting list for a kidney transplant after being on dialysis for four years. I burst into tears, and I think the psychic felt bad, for she cleaned up her tarot cards immediately and lovingly placed her hand on my back. We both decided the reading was over and she suggested I go speak to my family. Sure enough, they all started laughing, telling me Aunt Debra Kay had always had quite a warped sense of humor, making my tears flow even harder.

So after asking my pendulum, I find out Debra Kay is in fact following me around. I ponder what kind of influence she may be having on my currently crazy life.

As I sit alone in my room, whether from lack of sleep or my belief it could happen, I feel a pair of arms lovingly embrace me, and I begin crying. Eventually, I cry myself to sleep, the pendulum in my hand.

Chapter 5

Disillusioned
ભ

It's 6 a.m. Monday, and the chiming of bells resonates throughout my head. I press the off button on my annoyingly cheerful alarm, but it continues to echo through my head anyway.

I get out of bed and start my routine: pee, throw on a coat and walk Kioto, eat a quick breakfast in bar form, dress in whatever I have clean, and then run like the wind to catch the bus. I take my shower before I go to bed each night, otherwise, I just don't get that wonderful, messy kind of beach look that actresses pay hundreds to acquire—and perhaps because I just don't have enough damn time in the morning.

But I *do* make sure that before I leave, I give Kioto a big hug and kiss her forehead as I breathe in her dogness—that dingy, earthy smell that can only belong to a canine. She leans into me, and I enjoy our brief moment, knowing that no other animal could ever take her place. She's the best. She warms my feet, kisses my wounds, and brings me her chew toys when I'm sad. What more can a mommy ask for?

Kioto sits at the door until I leave and watches me walk down the street from the front window—a dog's gesture for making sure their owners are safe. Hopefully, she'll soon find the pig ear treat I left by her food bowl, which should make her usually boring day a little brighter.

As I walk, I find myself watching a seedy group of gangbanger-looking teenagers—baggy pants, bandana-wrapped heads, heavy-chained necks—hanging out underneath the streetlight that I'm approaching. They're busy with a rap— something melodic about dubs and large genitals, as their German Shepard evil-eyes the beagle across the street. My grip on my purse tightens and I begin walking a bit faster than normal—actually racing to get past them, undamaged. I look down as they each see me approaching and carefully slip my hand in my purse, feeling for my pepper spray.

They stop their conversation and I hear, "Yo, Bitch, get back here!" *Bitch. Whore. Kailey. Tramp. They're the only words I understand in his mumbled speech as his punches connect to my face, bloodying his knuckles from the blow to my forehead and mixing my blood with his. He hates me. Hates me for something, but I have no idea why. He's never even met me before today, yet he knows my name. And I am not a whore.*

One of the gangbangers suddenly darts from his position to run in my direction. I pull the pepper spray out and hold it in front of me as he runs past, shaking his head at the me: a crazy lady. My hand falls slowly, and I hear, "Yo, did you see that? She almost peppered Joe!" and a mixture of laughter and snide remarks follows. I turn to see Joe yelling for his escaped dog, Bitch. Then, I notice that I passed by my bus stop by a half block and on the wrong side of the street.

As I walk back, I hear a cat call in my direction from a passing car—a new, ivory Mercedes SUV. The car stops ahead of me, and I instantly stop walking—my heart can't take any more. Deciding on becoming a moving target rather than a stationary one, I speed up, walking faster toward the bus stop and its regulars. If anyone jumps out of the car and grabs me they can be my witnesses.

The car door starts to open, and out steps a familiar leg: Amber's.

"Hey, want a ride? Or do you want to ride a stinky bus with the Chicago crazies?" she yells.

I look at her and the tears instantly start to flow from my eyes. I bring my hands to my face and she runs toward me. The sheer relief of seeing Amber, mixed with the adrenaline from the thought of bodily harm is too much and I can't control my emotions.

"Oh, Kailey! It's okay, hon." I grip onto her as Russell scrambles from behind the wheel to help. Amber responds softly, "She's fine Russell, thanks. We just need some privacy." He turns and heads back to the car as she pulls the tear-drenched hair away from my face. "Kailey, you need to get ahold of yourself. I'm calling your mom."

"No!" I suddenly snip.

Amber just stands with her hands on my arms. "Let us give you a ride to work."

As I crawl into the car and cast a glance at those still waiting for the bus, I grasp the fact that I'll most likely be an outcast, a deserted soul in that shelter, from now on—the crazy, emotional baggage girl, afraid of her own shadow.

Amber turns in her seat to face me. "See, isn't this better than sitting in a seat someone has probably peed on?" She has such a wonderful way with words.

The car is absolutely gorgeous, with its cream-colored leather and all-wood accents. It's immaculate and smells wonderful. The smell is so familiar—I can't pinpoint it, but it wakens visions of my mom and her incense burner.

Of course, Amber has run of the radio, because her favorite song is playing, the one about some country-western-dude whose heart ran out on him, and his best friend's semi-truck ran it over, or maybe his dog buried it—something like that.

"Dave Matthews would sound much better through these awesome speakers, I'm sure," I state. Russell gets it, because he laughs, and Amber punches him in the arm. "So why the special treatment?" I ask, gathering myself and brushing away my brief break from sanity, as well as the tears from my face.

"Just because you have an awesome best friend, that's all." Amber chuckles to herself as she applies lipstick, and I see her glare at me through her mirror. "Hey, did your mom tell you I went and saw her yesterday?"

She sees my questioning expression through her mirror. "You did?"

"Yep, and Russell, too. She just *loved* him. It was almost like they connected immediately." She smiles at Russell, then adds, "She was happy I found love." I roll my eyes behind them and I see her clench her teeth. "Give it up, Kailey. I'm not in the mood for your righteousness." She continues with her makeup and doesn't even look at my reflection.

I sit, broken-hearted. Russell then snaps, "Really, Amber?" He looks at me in his rearview mirror and says, "She's a bit crabby this morning. Please forgive her. They didn't have her favorite syrup this morning at Starbucks."

You already know her favorite syrup? I know her favorite syrup. I grow perturbed, so I go for the throat. "So am I to believe, Amber, you called Russell up early this morning to ask for the ride, or did he just happen to be somewhere very convenient? Hmm?"

They both blush. Great—I hit the nail on the head. I can easily return the attitude. For Russell's sake, I decide to change the subject.

"Thanks for driving me, Russell," I say, with a bit of sugar.

"Anytime!" he replies, cheerily.

We arrive at our destination, and I thank Russell, again. Amber gives him her own "thank you" and my, what a "thank you" it is. This time, it's my turn to blush. As we head toward the door, Russell steps out of his car, and then calls me back over.

"My grandfather really is a great man, and he deserves your utmost respect," he whispers. "Oh, and he also hates it when people don't keep their dinner dates." Then he gets in his car, winking at me as I stand, dumbfounded.

As we head toward the elevator, Amber asks, "What?" She missed the whole thing, but she can read me like a hawk.

41

I had shoved the promise made to Gunthreon way in the back of my mind all weekend, but now I realize I must go back today for dinner. But I gather myself and smile at Amber. "Russell and Amber sitting in a tree, K-I-S-S-I-N-G," I sing. I can't help laughing. She throws her keycard at me and laughs, too.

We get into the elevator. "Russell is like no other guy I've dated," Amber professes, her glassy eyes speaking volumes. "I've only known him a weekend and I feel more connected with him than I ever have with anyone—present company excluded."

"Just be careful, understand?" I think of Gunthreon and our odd meeting—and the fact that Russell is his *grandson* has me briefly thinking of mystery novel-type plots to frame the innocent. But when I concentrate on the thought of both Russell and Gunthreon, and focus on the feeling I get from them, any thoughts of evil plots dissipate. They feel good to me—whatever that counts for.

Amber says, "I will be careful. I always am, whether you think so or not."

"Don't break his heart…I want to borrow his Mercedes someday," I tease, and exiting the elevator, push her toward her office.

I stop in the kitchen, make my tea, and then pop a stale doughnut hole into my mouth. And then one more for good measure—two's good luck. Wait…that's three's a charm. One more won't hurt.

I head toward my own office, still chewing, and say a few hellos, and finally settle in. I'm already tired, feeling this is sure to be a long day, but I attack my e-mails with fervor anyway. *Let's see what forwarded messages from my friends were "quarantined" today by our IT staff.*

By the time I get to the very last two, I feel a wave of sleepiness come over me. I decide that, if I turn my computer just right, nobody walking by will see me with my eyes closed for a few minutes. It's office policy to leave our doors open, otherwise I'd slam it shut and sprawl out on the floor.

As my eyes shut, it suddenly hits me what the smell was in Russell's car—lilacs, a favorite of my mom's.

After a long while, I feel like someone is standing at my office door, so I open my eyes and peek around my computer. Nobody there. *Thank goodness*, I think. All I need is for Evan to catch me sleeping. I'm sure that would go over really well at my next review: "Yes sir, I concentrate much better with my eyes closed."

I turn to my screen to check those last two e-mails, and suddenly, my sight is blurry. I focus on the screen, and it seems to be getting worse, so I check my long-distance vision by looking out my door to the hallway.

Something is very wrong. The air is gray and thick, and my immediate thought is fire. I grab my purse and get up and walk to my door, yelling to a coworker whose office is next to mine, but I get no answer, and sniffing, smell nothing out of the ordinary.

"Hello?" I say questioningly to the haze before me. No response. "What the hell is going on?" I can't see where I'm walking, so I grab onto what I think should be filing cabinets outside my office, but feel tree bark instead. In feeling my way toward the reception area, my hand slides over something slimy— some kind of greenish-yellow ooze. It's sticky. I bring it closer my nose and gag. It reeks like rancid eggs and vomit.

Then, a faint, indistinguishable noise rises in the distance— something that sounds, and feels, big. I don't dare open my mouth. I only wait to see if I hear it again.

I do. This time it's a little clearer—closer. Still I wait, and don't move an inch. Again comes the sound, even closer. It's someone speaking very softly, in a kind of rhythmic tone.

I slowly start to back up toward my office, but the speed of its approach accelerates as I move backwards. So I crouch down, hoping this thing won't see me. I don't recognize the voice, and I'm scared that nobody else is around. Maybe they're dead. *Maybe I'm dead—he killed me.*

At this level, I can see that the fog is about a foot off the ground, so I get on my hands and knees to see if I can see anything. And I do see something—something that could possibly be very big feet, yards in front of me, but I have trouble wrapping my mind around the concept. When I squint, I see three feet—not two, but three brown, dirty, hairy feet, with toenails the size of bear claws.

Now I can hear it clearly.

"Kailey, Kailey, come and play with me. Kailey, Kailey, come and slay with me."

Bile rises to my throat as I start crawling, *crawling to my apartment door, my blood leaving its crimson trail behind me. I scratch at the door with my nails, and break one off as he drags me backwards, back through my own blood, making my attempt at grasping the hardwood floors impossible.*

The air is so thick I can hardly move through it, my lungs barely grasping enough oxygen. I realize I'm nearly to my office when I hear a thud. I stop and, with some effort, force enough courage to turn toward the feet. I see them again, along with the source of the thud—a bloody raccoon, which I assume from the angle of its neck is dead. It lies by the feet. Then, this thing—creature—somehow bends in a way that, though the feet remain where they stand, a face peeks under the fog directly at me, just enough for me to see huge eyes and nothing else.

Shit!

At this point, with all my might, I move as quickly as I can through the mist and back toward my office. I feel breath at my neck just as I slam my door shut. My panting is heavy, and I shake uncontrollably, as if I've run a marathon—or at least this is what I imagine it would feel like.

I run to my phone and sit in my chair. There is a soft knock at the door, and I hold my breath for what seems like minutes.

"Kailey, is everything okay?" It's Evan's voice. The door slowly opens, and I see his head peek in. "You slammed your door pretty hard there." I see another coworker standing behind him, attempting to peek in my office. No fog. "You know the open door policy here."

I think fast. "I just had to make a personal call—woman issues," I whisper. "Sorry."

"Uh, okay... Just checking," he squeaks in an embarrassed sort of way. "Hey, get some air freshener for your office. It smells like rotten eggs in here."

He leaves and I sit straight, looking forward, wondering if I should tell *anyone* what's happening to me. I choose to keep it to myself. Lunacy is not taken lightly with employers.

Chapter 6

Excited
○੪

After a swift walk past the gangbangers who are still lingering on the corner—and a snide remark about me being as white as they come, despite Joe's blonde hair and blue eyes—I get home from work and my Kioto waits open-eyed for me. She's a big comfort, especially after the nightmare I had at my desk today. *That's gotta be what happened. Note to self: No more food before work naps—especially stale office doughnuts.*

I hug her for a good five minutes, gathering from her stiff body that the hugs aren't going to do it. "I know, your bladder's going to explode, isn't it, girl?" I say. "Let's go for a walk—" Her ears perk at the word, "—before I leave again."

So we walk to South Lakeview Park and I let her empty her bladder. The guilt of leaving Kioto alone this evening gets the best of me, so I take a quick glance around, and then let her off the leash to chase squirrels, thinking that maybe the exercise will tire her out and she'll sleep soundly tonight while I'm gone. Stupid move on my part. I should know better. She's an akita—a prey-driven animal originally bred to hunt bear, and protective to a fault.

I never see the man and his dog, a beautiful Irish setter, enter through the gates. The moment Kioto makes eye contact with them, I scream at her as loud as my lungs will let me. I know the possible outcome all too well after a fight with a Rottweiler last summer. Kioto won, but I suffered for months after paying both dogs' vet bills. She does not get along with other dogs.

She takes off with the speed of a jet and runs toward the slim and graceful Irish setter. I run after her, yelling again for Kioto to stop.

The man steps in front of his dog and says some word to Kioto I barely hear. Instantly, to my surprise, Kioto stops and turns to me. I stop running and start walking briskly toward her before she changes her mind and attacks. I grab her collar and put her leash back on, apologizing up and down to this stranger while, reveling in the fact that my dog did not shred his like a piece of chicken jerky. Dog-fights are the worst ever. You don't know what to do because you fear for your own safety, but want to stop the snarling and squealing and the madness you can feel overtake them. It's so raw and feral.

"It's okay," says the stranger with a bit of an Irish brogue. At least I think it is. "Nothing happened. Except I think you may fall over from that rush of adrenaline. Do you need to sit?"

"No, I'll be okay. I just may throw up my lunch."

"I won't look."

"What did you say to my dog? How did you get her to stop?" Kioto is sitting now, just staring at the Irish setter, perhaps telepathically daring the dog to move.

"Oh, I took some strict guard-dog obedience classes long ago, before I got Cherry here. The word I used is the most stern-sounding German word I know, so I used it and it worked. Yeah, I know, Irish man speaking German—kind of funny. The instructor taught in German so that your typical stranger wouldn't be able to give commands to your dog."

"That was German? Didn't sound like it to me," I add. But I must have been too far away. "Your dog is so beautiful. I'm glad Kioto didn't get to her—him?" My head turns, trying to peek at where I may find the answer myself. I let the dog sniff my hand before petting it.

47

"Her. I have this thing for redheads, I guess." He says it without breaking his stare, embarrassing me slightly, and definitely satisfying his manhood, but it's non-threatening. It makes me feel...good.

I giggle girlishly. He's attractive—tall and muscular, with glowing blue eyes that make me hold my breath as I decide whether he's looking into my soul or just plain through me. My fingers want to reach out and sail through his sandy brown hair.

I collect myself, clearing my throat. Flirting is usually Amber's arena, not mine.

"You live around here?" My mind tries to replay what I've just said, hoping I spoke English and not girly boy-intoxicated gibberish.

"Just moved to the city from the south suburbs, but I've lived in the Chicago area since I was twelve," he answers. "I was born in Waterford, Ireland, though—land of four- leaf clovers, barley, and hops. Do you live close by?"

"You are stranger-danger. Can't tell you that!" I tease. "Unfortunately, I have to get going. I have a dinner date—not like a date-date, but like a friend date." Pretty sure that was English.

"Sure, don't mean to keep you," he says. "We will see you around?"

I stand motionless, and examine him in my special way. Intrigue. It's definitely intrigue I feel from him. "Probably," I say.

"What's your name?"

"Kailey, and yours?"

"Conner," he replies, "and it's nice to meet you—and Kioto." He extends his hand, and I shake it. His hand is much warmer than mine, and softer, if that's possible—definitely not a manual labor kind of guy. Feeling like a scaly alligator, I try to withdraw my hand—it's time for a change in lotions—but he holds on as a small static shock travels up my arm.

"Ow," I yelp as I pull my hand away.

"Oops, sorry. Did I do that, or was that you?" We both laugh as Kioto allows him to pet her head, without a shock.

"See you around, Conner." My turn to leave is slow, but with a twist of the head—my best attempt at a model's hair swish. *Amber's perfected it, so maybe I can?* I only end up with a mouthful of hair.

After a few feet, I turn back to see that Conner and Cherry are already gone.

"Let's go, my good girl," I say, genuinely smiling—maybe for the first time in months. Kioto leads the way home.

Chapter 7

Nonsensical
☙

Could I be any more nervous?

As dinner approaches, I keep asking myself all sorts of questions—questions like, did I wear the right clothes? Did I wear the right shoes? Is it all right that my hair is pulled back? When did I accidentally eat the hallucinogenic mushroom? What the hell am I doing?

The one thing that makes me decide to go is the pendulum. I have to give it back. I'm not a thief—never stole anything in my life, well, except that one bag of Big League Chew, but I chalked that off as a youth's rite of passage.

I call a cab, making sure it's a different company than the last I used. It arrives promptly, I take a deep breath, and direct the driver as I enter the vanilla-scented cab. We arrive in Chinatown, and I pay him, tipping him well, since we actually had some decent conversation on global warming. It was important that I take my mind off the trip or I might have opened the door while driving and just rolled out of the cab to avoid setting foot in Gunthreon's place.

When I get out, I see the sign above the bar, which I conveniently failed to notice the other day: "Spirit Cave". The neon sign of a champagne glass with tiny bubbles floating up to the roof flickers as I approach the door. But the ten steps to the door are absolute hell as I find myself fighting my better judgment. It's practically screaming at me to turn my bony ass around and go home, where I'm guaranteed safety with Kioto as my guard. My palm might now have a permanent indentation of my silver ring as I grip it with all my hand strength. The "Closed" sign seems the perfect excuse to run back after my cab, letting my better judgment be the winner of this round, but instead, I touch the handle of the door and turn. It opens. I force my feet forward.

"Hello?" My voice echoes through the deserted bar. I don't want to walk in any further, so I yell a bit louder, still hoping for an excuse to turn around and leave: *"Hello!"*

"Kailey, I'm back here. Come join me." Gunthreon's voice comes from the kitchen, along with some yummy smells. When I enter the kitchen, I swoon from the tantalizing aroma of sautéing mushrooms and onions and cream. I see a pot of noodles cooking and a quick glance in the oven reveals beautiful gargantuan lamb shanks. I think maybe I've died and entered heaven through a set of pub doors.

Gunthreon works on hand-rolled dinner rolls, speckled with oregano and garlic slices. He pats each one lovingly—like a baby's bottom—before placing it on the cookie sheet.

"And I thought you were Asian," I joke. "Turns out you're Italian?" I nervously smile at him. I keep my distance from him and the large chef's knife beside his cutting board.

"Can't help it—I like good food. I learned to cook from the best. Go ahead and put your purse down on a chair." Again, he exudes a strong and solid sort of confidence.

I walk to a chair and place my purse on it, slowly, not really wanting to leave my pepper spray beyond my reach. After I put it down, I sneak over to the small, hot saucepan on the stove—I could always use it as a weapon if things went awry.

As my nose sniffs the concoction in the pan, I can't help but dip my finger in the cream sauce and bring it to my tongue. I instantly want to cry. It has a touch of tangy lemon, sending my heart aflutter. On the counter is a filled wine glass. I start to speak, and Gunthreon, without looking up, tells me to drink.

I grab the glass without argument and slowly tilt it up, letting the wine barely touch my lips, and I slowly open my mouth, letting the deep, dark wine glide over my tongue and slide down my throat. It's warm, and it makes me tingle all over. I gulp the whole glass. It's not like any wine I've ever tasted, including the 1994 Cabernet Sauvignon—at forty-five-dollars a bottle—that I splurged on while I was a hermit in my mom's house.

"Hmm," mumbles Gunthreon, looking at my empty glass, "you downed that a little fast."

"No worries. Thanks for sharing it with me," I say, aware that he's worrying over nothing. "Can I help you with anything? I'm actually no stranger to the kitchen. My mom got sick when I was younger, and I did a lot of the cooking at home. She taught me many a trick." I expect him to ask about her, but he just nods while he slices a few strawberries and throws them in a bowl. Out of the blue, I suddenly feel a bit lightheaded and unsteady. "Whoa," I groan.

"Too fast," he jabbers under his breath. "How about you finish setting the table for me, please." He points toward the door I followed him through on that first unforgettable evening, then hands me two silverware settings.

When I walk through the door a bit unstable, I see the room that we entered on Friday, in which a lovely urn had sat atop a small table, but now the room is set up as a dining room. In the center is an extraordinarily long dinner table with several chairs set around it. The chairs are upholstered in a lovely fabric, which I determine I have to admire closely. The fabric feels like silk, and there are tiny little hand-embroidered hydrangea and buttercup flowers sewn randomly throughout it. The table's runner matches, and includes larger versions of the flowers.

On the wall are what seems like hundreds of lovely photos of different people of all shapes, sizes, and colors. Some are happy, and some just seem sad. But there is one thing they have in common: They all hold an urn—in fact, the same urn I saw when I first entered this room several nights ago, and the same urn now set upon the center of the table, embraced by plumes of hydrangeas. As I start to examine the pictures on the wall, I notice the urn seems to fit magically into each person's hands, perfectly.

My mind suddenly registers that the dining room table is already set with plates, but not for two—for three. The chair for the unknown guest is covered in plastic, and sitting on the top plate is a rather large piece of raw meat.

Turning around quickly—quicker than I should be moving right now—I practically run over Gunthreon and the bowl of au gratin potatoes he's carrying. He dodges me and shuffles the plate as if he just stepped out of a Jackie Chan flick.

"Kailey, please sit."

"No way!" I sit despite my spoken rejection. "What's on that plate? It's disgusting! And you never told me there would be another guest. Why am I really here? Surely not just to eat a good meal. Did you drug me?" It's the only possible reason why I'm feeling so shaky.

"Our other guest may or may not show up. That depends on you. You must trust me, please. All questions will be answered later." He then looks right in my eyes and I trust him, but not without thinking some choice words. "I did not drug you," he states.

"*My* damn lamb had better be cooked, because I don't feel like ending up in the hospital with salmonella," I prattle.

He proceeds to carry in each lusciously ladened dinner dish, one at a time. The dishes are an unmatched set, but each is lovely and distinct in its own way. My great aunt—Numa—we called her, had teacups and saucers that she gathered from around the world, and these remind me of her collection. As a child, I was mesmerized by their beauty. I always wanted to play tea party— Bear would have loved it—with them, but was forbidden. So now, I make sure to touch each one, satisfying the once-deprived child in me.

He serves me from each plate, almost knowing that I will not say no to *any* of it.

As he then fills his own plate, he very briefly glances toward our guest's. His frown scares me a bit, as well as the sense of nervousness I feel from him.

I decide it's time, so I reach in my purse and take out the pendulum. I move to put it in his hands, but he pulls them back. "Kailey, you are now the rightful owner. You cannot give it back to me," he says. "Please keep it and enjoy."

"For real?"

"For real."

"Thanks, Gunthreon," I say. "I was beginning to get attached to it."

"That's what I was hoping for. Did you learn anything?"

"I learned who my spirit guide was. Can you have more than one?"

Surprise flashes across his face. "Yes, you can," he says. "You learned fast, didn't you? Perfect." He smiles at me as he see my reaction—one of caution. As we stare at each other, I take a quick bite of the lamb, and it's the most tender my mouth has ever touched. The homemade gravy is to die for.

As I think about what I want to say next, he speaks before I can. "Enjoy your meal in peace first, and then we will talk about why you are here. Let's just talk some small talk. Tell me about your mother."

Finally—something I can go on and on about. I tell him all about my childhood and my mom and all the great things she's done in her life for others. I tell him about her debilitating kidney disease, how the doctors are amazed at how she's still alive and breathing, how she's the most important person in my life, and how I don't know what will happen to me if she passes away before me. I end my dialogue with how my mother has taught me about every living creature's connection to each other and how we should all treat each other with respect and love.

I never feel the tears flowing until Gunthreon hands me my clean napkin. I wipe my face, and I notice the napkin is so white it appears to be glowing. He takes it from me, then holds both my hands.

"Thank you, Kailey."

"For what?" I ask.

"For trusting me. It's very important that you do."

"I have plenty reason to not trust strangers." I wipe my eyes and blow my nose. "But you feel like a long lost friend... Does that make any sense?"

"Those before you have felt the same," he tells me with a gentle shyness. He pauses a bit, then asks, "Would you be willing to join a quest...for a friend? Simple question, and not a request."

"A quest?" I forget about my mom, intent on deciphering his words. *Why would anyone want me in a quest? And who even uses the word* quest *these days.*

"Let's just say you might be helping to save the world."

I stand up and walk towards the door. "No need to play with the vulnerable, Gunthreon. Thanks for the delicious dinner."

"You have not realized your power yet, have you?" he says quickly, just as I walk into the doorway. I stand with my back to him. "You have to let her go," he chatters matter-of-factly. "Just know that she will never be gone forever."

I turn back around, suddenly angry. "Let who go, where? And power?" I laugh, a bit maniacally. "I don't think so." I laugh again.

"You must concentrate and think about what I am going to tell you. I can guarantee it will be tough to grasp, but please listen, at least." He stares at me, longingly.

"Ugh! Fine! Try me. This is your last opportunity to get in my head."

I catch a brief lift of the corner of his mouth before he says, "Sit then." I sit, despite the lingering feeling I may have missed a joke of Gunthreon's. "During your unfortunate attack you let out a scream that was heard around the world," he hesitates, "and into other 'realms,' if I may call them that." My mouth opens to say something, but nothing comes out. "It was a cry for help to anyone who could hear." As my eyes fill with tears, he continues, knowing he has my full attention. "I am told you captured a certain entity's interest, and they, in turn, fully awakened something in you— something that hides in your brain—something that retreated when you were younger." He pauses enough for me to shake my head no. "In return for the help you were granted, you were given certain powers back, as well as a job to go with them: a quest. You have *such* potential, Kailey."

"Stop!" I yell. "If you expect me to believe any of this crap you are trying to feed me, you are indeed in need of mental help. Who put you up to this? Is this a cruel joke? Was it *him*—*it*? My heart thumps violently as I begin to shake; the synapses in my brain attempt to make logical connections, but get nowhere—I don't know what to do.

Gunthreon presses forward, ignoring my questions. "You are now what we call a karmelean—an energy manipulator of sorts, if you will. A deliverer of karma," prattles Gunthreon. "You help dish out what people truly deserve by *reading* them. You use people's energies."

"That is nonsense, Gunthreon," I grunt, shaking my head.

"Everyone emits sorts of vibrational energies, and you my friend, can read or *feel* these energies."

"This is insane," I say as I bite my fingernails, the anxiety wreaking havoc on my cuticles. I squirm in my seat, not finding comfort in *any* position. My body just wants to get up and run. And he's so sure of himself, only heightening my anxiety.

He continues, despite my complete discomfort in his words. "Every living creature's body exudes energy, it's been scientifically proven. This energy that's expelled stays close to our bodies, and karmeleans, like yourself, can feel or sense it. And depending on the individual being read, the energy can be good or bad, happy or sad, *good* and *sad*; the possible combinations of emotions are infinite, really. There are so many personality traits that are reflected in one's energy, too." He smiles at me, then amazes me by continuing to talk, without any concern of my thoughts, or so it seems. "The extent of your powers, though, we will learn as time progresses. And who, exactly, is still listening for *you*, particularly, is currently a mystery." He leans close to me and whispers, "The word 'coincidence' isn't in my vocabulary."

The extent of my powers.

It stands in front of me, staring, and I sense the evil intentions lingering behind the pitch black eyes. I'm a bloody mess: bruised, cut, and broken—body and mind. I close my eyes, feeling its presence, and concentrate on making it end. It has to end.

Gunthreon stands straight and walks to light one white candle sitting on a small shelf on the wall. "You need simple explanations right now. This will help. Relax while I continue."

My pulse slows as the candle burns, and a calm peace enters my body. I breathe in deeply, letting the soft scent of lavender relax my head, my joints, my muscles, my heart.

Gunthreon continues. "You see, karma is something like a bank. Everyone either puts good karma in or they take it out by failing to do the right thing. You are, let's say, the bank teller. Think of people you know who just happen to be very lucky, or unlucky, individuals. Now think of how they say you are five people away from knowing everyone. I'm sure everyone knows, in some way, a karmelean."

He stares at me as I say, "Gunthreon, how much wine did *you* drink?"

"The cabbie is one I witnessed personally through my window, and what about the...outcome of your attack?" he continues with raised eyebrows. "Relax and truly put some thought into it."

The bloody sludge. Everywhere. Its blood—gooey, black blood, trailing down my walls and sticking to my skin.

I try to wash the thoughts away, but suddenly feel, deep down inside, that I now need to listen to my self—my inner core reaching out to the girl broken by a monster—the girl with innocence lost, the girl with some possibly crazy shit going on in her life. With no shaking, and no fancy to run anymore, I say, "I thought karma just happens though, like the universe itself just does it."

"No, the universe doesn't just do it—the universe *and special people* do. There are those like you who influence and help karma along. It's actually an extra component in your aura. Your aura is equivalent to a beacon, which calls to the higher powers to dish it out. There are good and bad people everywhere, and you help right the world by feeding information from individuals to the Higher Ones.

"Now you must think about your mother," he holds up his hand as my body wants to suddenly stand and take movement. Towards who, or what, I don't know. "Yes, I know, a delicate topic. But we must. I know how important she is to you. You are holding her in this realm because you think she deserves to live—but, in reality, you are holding her here for yourself. Think, *really* think, of how your mom is possibly still here, with us. Her illnesses should have won, long ago. Let her go, Kailey. She has other duties to fulfill, and you do not need the bad karma yourself."

Memories of numerous visits to the hospital and endless doctor visits come flooding into my brain. "It can't be possible," I cry, still mesmerized by his knowledge of my life. "How the hell do you know my mother?"

He holds up his hand, slowly forming the sign language for "I love you." He says, "I've known your mother for some time now."

I bury my face in my hands and let the tears flow.

Gunthreon gets up and lays his hand on my shoulder, gently. "The right choices can be the hardest. Are you willing to hear the rest of the truth? Are you willing to accept anything I am to tell you and anything I may show you? You have committed in your heart, but I must hear it from your mouth, too." He stares at me, as if life and death teeter on what I say.

"Yes, Gunthreon." I feel things falling into place where I never before knew them to be missing.

"Kailey, close your eyes."

Chapter 8

Pure
❧

The strong scent of grass underneath my nose wakes me up. I pull myself up to a sitting position in a patch of bright green grass and try to see through the fog around me. I recognize this fog and close my eyes, trying to force myself to wake up, this time for real. When I open them again, I see that I'm still in the same place. "Gunthreon? I don't like this. Are you here?" I try not to be too loud.

I figure that the only thing I can do is try to relax. As I relax, the fog seems to lighten, and I can see further. It's dusk, and despite the nearness of night, I can see clearly within a minute or so.

Looking down at the ground next to me, I notice something peculiar. It looks like a locket and instinctively like a magpie I pick it up. An extremely long chain hangs from the locket, and I wipe the dust off of it, then fumble about trying to open it. Unsuccessful, I put it in my pocket, next to my ring.

A rocky dirt road lies up ahead, so I walk toward it. Along this road, I find old and once-beautiful buildings made of marble and slate, in ruins. I spot one unscathed building off the road, away from all the other buildings and I head in that direction, hoping I might find something or someone of interest, like Gunthreon. I can feel him here somewhere.

The building is smaller than the rest I've seen, and not as fancily built, but feels important, so I approach with caution. On each side of the modest wooden doors are finely-detailed, winged gargoyles, also fashioned from wood, with various metal inlay across their face and wings. They are identical twins, the only difference being their expressions. One has warm, pleasant eyes and a smile on its face, while the other looks as though it's snickering or just plain mean. I touch the one with the more pleasant face, and it suddenly winks at me.

I jump back, and I could swear it giggles softly. The other only stares straight ahead, so I choose to ignore it. As I push on the doors, I find they are surprisingly heavy, and I gather enough strength to nudge them open, giving myself just enough room to squeeze through.

They open to one big round room, and I see that the walls are lined with objects. They seem all to be weapons of sorts—extremely clean, usable weapons. Closest to me is a large, wooden hammer, and I touch it, caressing the wood. It feels old. I try and take it off the wall, but it doesn't budge. The next object that catches my eyes is a silver Chinese star with eight very sharp edges.

Each object seems to have its own personality and I'm wondering who they belong to. Next to the hammer, is a particularly long sword, inscribed with beautiful, intricately etched characters of an unknown language which seem to sing to me of a battle between the wind and sunshine. Again, it will not move from the wall. I try another, and another, and yet another, with no movement at all. Yet I feel I need one.

Frustrated, I sit, staring straight ahead of me. That's when my eyes lay upon the oddest weapon I've seen thus far. It invites me near, whispering to me, telling me not to be afraid, inviting me to touch. I stand and walk toward it, admiring its uniqueness.

The pole is made of a smoothly-sanded cherry wood, and on one end is a crescent-shaped blade, littered with runes. The opposite end has a flat, spade-like blade, which reflects my complexion flawlessly as I stare into the metal; both are sharp enough to slice hairs. I yearn to touch the wood, but then I sense that something is about to happen, so I hesitate.

As an unexpected warmth flows into the room, running over my feet first, I freeze. It slowly crawls up my body, touching my hands and forcing them to reach forward. As the heat envelopes my head, I suddenly yearn to possess this deadly treasure, so I touch it, and the pole comes off the wall with one pull. I embrace it, suddenly feeling I will never be disconnected from my new lover, because it is me and I am it. I swing, and it is light in my hands. The metal whistles as it slices air, singing its song of perfection—perfect balance.

Suddenly, I am torn from my find by a peculiar noise, accompanied by the faint smell of rotten eggs. I know the smell, and I run to the door, not wanting to be cornered in this room. That's when I see it standing in the road, and it's huge—at least eight feet tall and five feet wide, with dark brown skin and fur. I recognize the feet—all three of them, situated like a tripod, with the center leg slightly forward. Its full hideousness is far worse than its feet alone. The huge eyes that take up at least 50 percent of its head stare at me while its mouth, which seems to take up the other 50, quivers, drooling some dark liquid. I can't be sure, but it looks like it's hungry. It stares at me as though I'm a huge medium rare rib-eye steak. There are sprouts of fur here and there around its body, and its arms dangle below its waist. It wears a large loincloth and short pants, both shredded on the edges. There is also a band around its waist, somewhat resembling an extra, extra, extra large fanny pack. I stand, frozen with fear at the realization that I've been visited by yet another hideous creature. *It was not a dream.* The delicious meal I just ate starts creeping up my throat, but I swallow, keeping it at bay.

A noise escapes from behind the creature. Its ears quiver, and its head turns all the way around like an owl's, then swivels back toward me. I'm amazed by its flexibility. Its skin seems to be in constant movement, and it begins moving toward me quickly. *It's so fast. And so big.*

I grab the pole and stabilize myself, knowing I cannot outrun this abomination, and it's time to prove I can take care of myself.

Seconds before it reaches to grab me with its monkey-length arms, I duck and swing the pole out, but the creature jumps over me swiftly.

It lunges again quicker than expected, and I manage to somehow cut my leg with my own weapon. The flow of blood freezes me, vulnerability creeping up on me like a dark shadow. The creature makes the jump toward me. I fall directly down, sticking my pole spade straight up in its direction with my eyes closed. My movement is unexpected—by both of us—so the creature comes down slightly crooked as my blade nicks the inside of its leg.

Black ooze runs down its leg, dripping onto the dirt. *Black ooze.* Before I lose myself to the visions, I notice the tears in its eyes. This big, ugly creature—surely sent by Satan himself—is crying, and reeks of regret?

"Ow! You hurt Bu! How could you? Bu was only going to help you." Its voice is undeniably male and youthful as it wipes the dark ooze from its mouth on the back of his hand, then proceeds to lick some off.

"Oh, gross," I groan, totally disgusted. I hold the pole weapon out in front of me.

The tears are as big as his eyes as they roll down his cheeks, and I find myself feeling bad I hurt him, even if he was going to rip my throat out. I get closer to him, just out of arm's length, and say, "You were going to eat me! Is this a trick? You feign pain, I come close, and *then* you eat me?"

He then does something unexpected—giggles. It's then that I feel it—purity. Purity of heart and soul is spewing from him, like rays from a sun, warm and soft as cashmere.

"Wait," I say as I sniff the air. "You smell like chocolate."

"Want some?" he asks as he raises his hand, covered in goo to me.

"You did well for your first time. I see you found your weapon." I swing around with my weapon in hand and see it's Gunthreon who has snuck up behind me. The creature cries harder, turning toward Gunthreon for help. Gunthreon walks over and hugs him, talking to him in a soothing way, thanking him for his help in the "acclimation." "We have a nice treat for you. Come back with us," he whispers. "We'll take care of your cut." He then points to my leg. "Both of your cuts."

Chapter 9

Silly-willy
ɶ

Suddenly, we're back in the dining room, seated at the table as Gunthreon mends our injuries. My hands are sans weapon. I look around and see it nowhere, so I assume I dropped it. A feeling of despair comes and goes as I sit across from the giant creature, apparently named Bu. I stare in amazement at his size and despite his massiveness—and scariness—I feel comfortable sitting across from him, simply watching his delicate movements.

He eats his raw meat, smiling at Gunthreon all the while. He then gives me a hurtful glance, which actually makes me feel bad—but not so bad that I forget what just happened.

"So this was a test?!" I exclaim, suddenly back to my senses, and furious with both of them. "I could have been killed!"

"Yeah!" says Bu, smiling at me. Then he adds, "Yes, but no?" His eyes turn questioningly to Gunthreon.

My mind turns over what I experienced, and I try to determine whether I should interrogate them or run out the door and leave the country. "Where the hell were we?" I question. "It didn't feel like anywhere around here. Gunthreon, what did you put in that wine?" My eyes narrow as I glare at him. "Do you have more to tell me? What is he?" I point to Bu. "And can you tell me how *he* got to my work the other day?"

Gunthreon's facial expression shouts ignorance for a brief two seconds, and then he just stares at Bu with a furrowed brow.

"Bu," he growls in a fatherly tone.

Bu now stares at his empty plate like a scolded child. His feet shuffle and sweat beads on his body. With his head down, he says, "Bu couldn't help it. Bu wanted to meet Kailey." Then he looks up at Gunthreon and says, "Gunthreon showed me her office building once. Bu remembered where it was. Nobody else saw Bu!"

"You know, you scared the crap out—"

Gunthreon holds up his hand at me. "Bu, that was entirely wrong," he says. "You know you cannot make people visit you in Renhala, even if it's only in-between. You could have gotten Kailey hurt, or someone could have seen you. I should make you go home right now." Bu starts bawling like a grounded child. His tears somehow glow, lighting up the room with splendor. The twinkling lights are beautiful. They make me want to drink them up and dance around the room.

Reaching across the table, I touch Bu's face with one hand and reach into my pocket with the other, pulling out the necklace with the locket I found. An unexplainable need to give him the treasure I found has me handing it to him. He holds it gently, opening it with great dexterity. How he does so with his huge hands, I do not know.

"You found it! You found it!" he cries. He gets up rather quickly and hugs me, squeezing a little too hard.

"Bu, remember your manners," Gunthreon urges.

Bu lets go.

"Gunth, Kailey is cool!" He is dancing around his chair, making me smile, and making any tension left in my body dissipate.

"Kailey has blessed you because she knows how helpful you are when we need you. You are special and deserve a special present." Gunthreon mouths "Thank you" in my direction.

"Hey, I think it's my job now. Better get some practice, right?" I can't help but feel good watching Bu continue to dance as he attempts to do the running man.

"You need to know there are rules that go with your job," says Gunthreon, looking toward me. "There is still much to teach you, and learning will have to be fast, because the quest moves much too quickly, and things are starting to get bad. I will go get dessert, and then I will explain all about Renhala, the realm you have just visited. Bu, you want some, too? It's berry cobbler."

"Yes, yes, yes!" Bu is so worked up he can't sit.

"Realm?" I yell to Gunthreon as he leaves the room.

Then it's just me and Bu.

"Bu, if you only wanted to meet me, why the scary rhyming?" I say, "Kailey, Kailey, come and slay with me'? That doesn't sound very friendly to me. You really scared me today. Good thing I thought it was only a dream and didn't check myself into the loony bin."

"What's a loony bin? That's funny words."

"It's a place where they put crazy people," I say. "Somewhere maybe I need to go after tonight."

"Kailey not crazy! Kailey silly-willy! I was singing a greble song my momma used to sing to me. It's a...a...I don't know."

"A nursery rhyme?"

"Yes—a mursery rind." He is really cute, despite his ugliness.

"You're called a greble?"

He nods without looking up at me.

"I like you, Bu. Can we be friends?" I cannot believe I ask.

"Yes, oh yes! Bu don't have many friends." He examines his locket and appears happy and sad at the same time, tears and a smile gracing his face.

"Bu, what's in the locket?"

"This." He shows me a picture inside, which is a spitting image of himself, but with breasts, three of them at that. "Momma." He looks just plain sad as he puts the locket around his neck.

"That locket was yours? Wow." I whisper the latter to myself, amazed at the coincidence. *Coincidence is not in my vocabulary.*

"She's beautiful. You look just like her," I say. I lift his chin with my hand, and he smiles a smile at me that could melt the

North Pole. When Gunthreon comes back, my heart suddenly feels heavier.

"Better give me that cobbler first, because I have a feeling you'll need to sweeten me up before you start," I say. I brace myself, shove a *huge* scoop of cobbler in my mouth, and nod for him to begin.

"I want to start from the beginning. You need to know the whole truth about our existence, so listen, and when I am through, you may ask me questions," chatters Gunthreon. "Let's go and sit somewhere more comfortable. Follow me." He leads me and Bu to the purple and gold room in which Gunthreon and I first spoke, and there we find three armchairs. Bu frowns. Then, in the blink of an eye, there are one armchair and one loveseat. Gunthreon shakes his head at Bu, but he doesn't pay attention, instead pulls my hand toward the loveseat.

"Kailey wants to sit by me," he says, plopping his butt on the loveseat, still holding my hand. I have to sit, unless he lets go.

Gunthreon laughs, "Fine. Kailey can sit with you." I plead with my eyes to Gunthreon, and he only laughs harder. "You'll find some tea on the table over there. Fill a cup and sit."

I lift my body with lightning speed and proceed to speedily walk toward the teapot. I fill a cup and sniff the steam as it escapes my cup. It's the same tea as before! Excitement fills me, and I feel like a child who's been given one of those huge, swirled lollipops the size of my head.

Cup in hand, I sit next to Bu with folded legs, and he scoots over next to me, instilling a fear in me that the loveseat might tip up, dumping me atop him. But he is cautious, and I actually lean on him, quite aware I will probably smell like eggs henceforth. I lean against his fanny pack and something stabs me from inside.

"Bu, what's in this?" I query, touching the pack.

"My tools! Look!" He opens it up and shows me the many tools inside: screwdrivers, pliers, hammers, files—you name it. All are worn with age, and very sloppily—but most likely lovingly—have been scribbled on with the name "Bu."

"Cool collection, big guy." I smile at him as I give Gunthreon the thumbs up. I'm ready to be amazed, or scared shitless, whichever comes first.

Chapter 10

Bewildered
ᏫᏃ

"This is the story that's been passed down to me through thousands of years. You may take it as you like, Kailey." Gunthreon seems eager to begin. "Just remember, I am not a scientist, so take what you can from what limited information I give you." He clears his throat and takes a breath, inhaling deeply before he begins.

"The center of the world began with two atoms, and these atoms consisted of two opposing energies," he says. "After repeated contact with each other, these energies slowly produced other molecules, and the power of their opposition eventually created physical matter, and life was formed." I give him a dumbfounded look, which doesn't take much effort on my part. "Think of two pots clanging, and sound—a third matter—is formed, yes?" I give him the same dumbfounded look, but he continues.

"Despite the opposition of these initial energies, life was at first harmonious. Life matter continued to grow, until it formed creatures which ranged in size from bacteria to bigger even than Bu. As these life forms evolved, so did the two original atoms, and the complexity involved in their composition gave them great power. They oversaw all life that was created. Their creations roamed freely, developing many special traits, and many different abilities. Their world was called Renhala.

Those that walked Renhala named the two energies with which their life forces flowed. They were to be known as the Higher Ones: Neda the Kind and Velopa the Stern.

It is said that one day, a creature was born—a magnificent being of great beauty and strength. It walked upright, and was able to talk to all creatures and create wonderful works of art with its bare hands. It could sing and make joyful exhilarating noise, and rock you to sleep with gentle lullabies. It was smooth and voluptuous. It had long, silky, silver hair that flowed to its feet and reflected twofold any light which shone upon it. Sadly, this being lived without a name, because the Higher Ones fought back and forth, day after day, over who had the right to name the creature.

Neda the Kind insisted it had more to do with its birth, since the creature cradled all life in its hands and fed all creatures with the milk of its breasts. But Velopa the Stern felt it held the power to name the creature, because of the creature's ability to scorn and the aptitude with which it could persuade. The battle between Neda and Velopa became so horrible that the lands began to crumble and life began to die. Those creatures that remained began fighting each other and taking the side of either Neda or Velopa. You could no longer love both. You had to choose where your loyalty lay.

One day, Neda decided something had to happen to end the quarrelling. After much thought, Neda brought forth an idea to Velopa: This creature needed to be destroyed, or else all their other lovely creations would soon become extinct. Velopa felt it should be the one to finish the deed and agreed to give Neda one day to spend with the creature and decide how to destroy it. But Neda loved the creature so dearly, and the extra day only confirmed that Neda could not have the creature destroyed, so it came up with a plan.

When the new day began, Neda explained to Velopa, in its saddest tone, that the best death would be a quick jump off the edge of the deepest chasm. Velopa quickly agreed, eager to see how the creature would react to facing death. It found the beautiful creature and told it what it must do. Despite the fact that this creature held its own free will, it knowingly agreed to die to save all other life. The creature walked to the edge of the chasm and shed a single tear of glowing light before it walked off.

But unknown to Velopa, Neda had spidery creations weave a sticky web thousands of feet into the chasm, where the darkness swallowed all light, to catch the creature. It was there Neda decided that, to protect it from harm, the creature could not retain all its extraordinary abilities. So Neda immobilized certain areas of its brain and exiled it to a place where all life was limited in its abilities—a place where life was much simpler, and a place where vain Velopa would never lower itself to search. Neda also decided to name this creature in secret, whispering 'Wohmin' in its ear and deciding that, for its own sake, it was never to see this creature again. The realm it was banished to was this realm, here.

This creature roamed the new realm in solitude, until one day, it stumbled upon another creature similar to itself, which had grown from the Earth. They told each other their stories and loved each other wholeheartedly. Times were happy. They flourished, and life became what many know it as now.

Through whispers of the chasm, Velopa eventually found out what happened and decided to find this creature and keep it for itself. So Velopa descended to this level and found many creatures similar to its original, but not as powerful, and it seemed death came much easier here. It was evident the creatures were not using the powers stored deep within themselves. But still, the power involuntarily spewed from each of them through mighty surges, threatening Velopa. Velopa pondered their creation and thought Neda surely was behind it all. Overcome with anger, Velopa vowed to destroy all existence at this level, but to do it in a way that Neda would only realize the plan too late. This began what we refer to as 'The Surge.'

Slowly, this level of existence starting killing its environment. Wars of huge proportion began, and debilitating diseases, plagues and epidemics, were born.

One day, Neda decided to break its vow and visit the creature it so longed to see. But upon its arrival, Neda was appalled to see what had happened and knew that Velopa was behind the insidious actions. Neda restored some of the creatures' abilities, realizing this may be the only way to save them, but it took these creatures many a century to relearn all their gifts, and it was only a select few who wanted to use the gifts on this plane, because so many were afraid to challenge themselves. They had become too comfortable with their lives. So those who chose to use their reborn gifts saw that they could move between the two realms, and once again, those who traveled sided with either Neda or Velopa. This battle still thrives. Neda believes all creatures can once again live harmoniously, but Velopa has grown angry. Velopa, they say, is trying to build an empire of creatures to control all those it deems inferior.

To many here on Earth, Renhala is only the movement you see out of the corner of your eye—that unidentifiable smell that reminds you of childhood fairies and goblins, or the strange feeling of déjà vu. Then, there are those few of us who travel between realms and struggle either to protect what's left of a harmonious life or strengthen Velopa's army of cretins and misfits solely for the purpose of havoc. Velopa's forces are growing every day, and humanity as you know it, Kailey, is in grave danger—humanity in Renhala, as well as our realm here, known as Abscondia. Every day, more and more evil creatures show up outside Renhala, threatening our lives, here. We need your help."

Despite the look of desperation in Gunthreon's eyes, I don't know whether to believe this story and run to the hills for shelter, or instead laugh and proclaim my new friend a great comedian. Saliva starts puddling in my mouth as my brain churns through the information.

I glance over at Bu. He's snoring now with his mouth wide open.

"I need some sort of proof of my connection and that you're not some wacko trying to brainwash me."

He walks to the doorway and calls me to him. He grabs my hand and I walk with him into the dining room, toward the wall of pictures. His hand rises and points to one in particular, direct center. My eyes rise and stare in disbelief at the face that so resembles mine as I trace my finger over the innocent eyes. I realize at that moment that my life as I know it is going to change: No more caramel corn, stuffed teddy bears, and Fruit Loops.

Dead center on the wall, my mother sits, holding the urn with a delicate smile on her face. And now the real test of my strength begins.

"You have been given your powers back. You must use them to help create the harmony this land once knew," pleads Gunthreon. "You will find that many around you also have special abilities. Some know how to use them; others do not, yet. Evil creatures are lurking in the darkness, trying to establish a solemn world, of despair, in hopes that all beings will turn to Velopa. And as one who travels between planes, you must remember three things.

"One, drugs will not work for you, and alcohol will not get you drunk," he says. My heart skips a beat as I think back to all those hopeless moments I downed bottles of wine and rum, and popped countless pills. It was an attempt to silence my brain, and stop the pain. But, there was actually a solid reason why it did nothing for me—I wasn't a hopeless wreck.

Gunthreon continues with, "So sinus medicine, aspirin, pimple cream, whatever, will not help you and you will feel no effects from alcohol. But, you will not get sick as often—" He pauses and looks at the picture of my mom, "—and drugs and alcohol only muddy the senses, anyway. We don't need drunk idiots traveling between planes on whims.

"Two, as a traveler, when your body dies, your essence will travel to where you are, or are not, granted a true death by the Higher Ones. We also believe this is when you become a spirit guide, connected to a living individual, but we're not sure.

"Three, your weapon is always with you, as it is with most travelers. You may not see it now, but if you relax and let yourself believe it's there, you can faintly see it strapped to your back. Any questions?"

"You expect questions right now? I can barely even remember to keep breathing, let alone form questions! I don't know if I can believe this all."

"I'll wait," he chirps, standing in front of me, twiddling his thumbs.

"Fine! About my weapon, what is that thing?" I feel my back and start frisking myself, hoping to land on something. *Something solid, I can believe. And of course I don't feel it.*

"Ah, that was a perfect fit for you, I think. It is called a monk's spade," states Gunthreon. "Long ago, monks carried them on their missions through vast lands. They would use the spade as a shovel to bury the dead and the crescent served as a weapon against thieves. Monks would often travel between realms to observe, and write journals of their findings.

"You are going to need practice using your weapon and I will probably be the one to help you with training, as well as teach you about your powers. Now, to get to Renhala, we must practice as well—"

"I dropped it!" I wince, preparing for Gunthreon's anger.

"Dropped what?"

"My monk's spade."

"No, you didn't."

"Yes," I say, shaking my head and raising my eyebrows, "I did."

He points at my back and I feel warmth on my spine. I relax and slowly reach behind me, and sure enough, I faintly feel the shaft, but cannot grasp it.

"Don't worry, we'll work on that one," he proclaims.

I walk around in a circle like a dog chasing its tail. By the sixth round, I'm about to give up when I suddenly cut my finger on the blade. I instinctively shove my finger in my mouth and frown at Gunthreon. "If I'm to believe in karma," I say, "how come bad things happen to good people? Why was I attacked? What did I do so wrong that I deserved that? And what about my mom—her pain?"

Gunthreon ponders long and hard. Worn out from too much information, I sit in a dining room chair, waiting for whatever answer he may give me. "Bad things may happen to someone, but not always because *that* person committed some evil deed," he says. "It could simply be the butterfly effect. Then, that person's negative experience changes some other event, entirely elsewhere. Karma has her hands in *everything*. It's all about how you respond, and whether you build or deconstruct. Yes, bad things happen to good people, but it's these experiences that make a good person great! It's the ultimate test. Unfortunately, karma seems to grow quieter as the days progress. Less and less instances are seen in which positive outdoes negative. Do you understand?"

Uncertain how to reply, I try to take what Gunthreon says with a grain of salt. I shrug.

He puts his hand out towards me and I grab it once more. He leads me back into the room with Bu. I glance over at Bu, and he's not only still snoring, but also drooling.

We both walk to our previous seats and sit. Bu chuckles in his sleep.

Speaking to Gunthreon, I whisper, quietly, "You mentioned powers and abilities. What kinds of strange things am I going to be running into if I do join this 'quest' you speak of?" I shake at the visions my imagination conjures, like Bu-sized visions of my attacker and killer Venus flytraps. *I have a vivid imagination.*

"You might be quite surprised at the similarities between planes, like foods and animals. Those who travel bring certain items between planes, making them commonplace in *both* planes. Believe it or not, strawberries are native to Renhala," he says and I raise my eyebrows, "as well as flying squirrels—and cinnamon! And you do know at least one other traveler whose abilities you have witnessed," says Gunthreon. "My grandson, Russell."

Amber! "He better not hurt Amber!" I say, a bit loud. She's so fragile, despite the act she puts on.

"Russell is on our side—don't worry. Actually, he's used his power to create something wonderful I think, and you will probably agree. Russell is what you may call a sort of 'cupid'-type traveler. He can become the perfect companion for a willing soul, but can only make this transformation once in a lifetime," he says. "And Russell has made his choice."

My eyes grow wide.

"It's not exactly how I thought it would play out, but Russell has picked Amber. He will become exactly what Amber needs as a boyfriend, and someday husband. He really does love her already, but it is up to Amber to realize this and reciprocate the true love he will openly give."

"And if she doesn't return the love?" I say, knowing the probability.

Gunthreon thinks, then shrugs his shoulders. "I guess I don't know the answer to that. Hmm."

Gunthreon gets up slowly from his seat and covers Bu with a soft chenille blanket. "Kailey, before we conclude for the evening," he says, "let's get you to try one thing. Are you willing?"

"Sure... I guess..."

Gunthreon walks to the kitchen and I hear what sounds like him rifling through the garbage. My assumption is proven correct as he returns, holding a rancid cantaloupe halve in his hand. He brings it toward Bu's nose, which twitches. Bu's mouth also grimaces as it opens to gag.

"He hates cantaloupe," Gunthreon whispers.

"Gunthreon!" I try to whisper, not wanting Bu's peaceful sleep to be disrupted. Bu's ears twitch and he begins waking.

I instinctively reach to Bu with my own energy, closing my eyes as I do so. I think of beautiful thoughts and caress his energy, negating his repulsion, and coaxing him to fall back into peaceful slumber. My own energy vibrates a soothing lullaby as Bu smiles and starts snoring almost immediately.

Gunthreon smiles widely. I smile back, tears forming in my eyes from a newfound sense of pride.

"Everything happens for a reason, Kailey," he says as he approaches to hug me.

I immediately point to the cantaloupe and hold my nose.

"Oops, sorry," says Gunthreon.

"I should go. I have to check on my dog," I say, tired.

After I kiss Bu on the forehead, Gunthreon walks me out, and there is a limo and driver already waiting for me. "Ooh, is this one of my new perks? I could get used to this!" I say, climbing into the car, catching a glimpse of the burly, tanned man behind the wheel. Gunthreon laughs, waves to me, and walks back inside.

Chapter 11

Mysterious
ᆭ

I step out of the car, thank the driver who only smiles in return as he pulls away, and then stand in front of my building for a moment, just admiring the structure. It's plain, and really nothing special, but I love it. It's gotta be the inability to draw attention to itself. The apartment sits there before me, happy with its boring red brick and 1960 wrought-iron accents. I think of the possibility of any of the inhabitants knowing of Renhala. The thought makes me twirl around, scoping out the area, for my fear of monsters has increased fivefold since Gunthreon's chat about Velopa.

I eye the particularly interesting balcony across from my own. It's just odd. Several dried herbs hang from the gutters, and there are strange scribblings—most likely made by Sharpie permanent marker—around the balcony door. It's a door littered with scratches both on metal and glass, like some eager dog tried his damndest to get inside.

Suddenly, a quick movement of the curtains lets me know that perhaps I am intruding.

I gather myself and realize I should be feeding and walking Kioto, who now stares a hole through me from my own patio door, most likely cursing me for my time away tonight. And I came back so late.

My legs carry me speedily up the stairs, and my head spins from the rush of blood. Then, after minutes of searching, I finally find my keys at the bottom of my purse, connected to a few paperclips and hair thingies. Just as I bring the key up to the lock, the dizziness lifts slightly, and I turn to find myself staring at a beautiful little boy, around seven or eight years old—in my guesstimate—with the most gorgeous shaggy blond hair and the deepest brown eyes. The only thing that ruins his perfection is a small scar underneath his left eye. He wears black boxers and a tee-shirt with a skater performing an ollie on the front. He stands before me, motionless. I don't move, and he bites his lower lip slightly, tilts his head, squints his eyes, and stares at me, intensely. The "sureness" he emits makes me feel as though I've underestimated his age, perhaps.

The staring contest ends when his mother comes bounding up the stairs, her arms filled with groceries from the nearest 24/7 store. "Philip, what are you doing out here in your pajamas? Go back inside," she snaps. He turns and walks back, looking at me over his shoulder, throwing me an expression which makes him seem somewhat familiar.

"I'm so sorry if he bothered you, Miss," she says. "He should have never have come out here without me home. He usually keeps the door locked until I get back. Hi, I'm Karen, by the way. Nice to finally meet you." She holds out what she can of her hand.

"Please, let me help you carry those in, and I'm Kailey." I motion for one of the bags.

"Oh no, I can handle it, really." She moves toward her doorway and starts to enter. With a quick turn, she lets me know that I'm not going to be invited in right now. "It was a pleasure meeting you, and I'm sorry about Philip, my foster child. He's special-needs. I'll try and talk to him about giving you your privacy. Have a good evening." The door is closed, and locks are locked— all three of them.

I hear Kioto whimpering and scratching the door, so I insert my key into the lock and turn. As I open the door, she sniffs the air anxiously beyond me. Once her eyes meet mine, however, she scrutinizes and instantly scowls at me, rejecting my attempt at a kiss. She turns her head and walks toward the treat cabinet, sits down, and stares out the window. I laugh, and she growls a bitchy sort of growl. How can I help but give her a big sorry hug and two of her favorite treats?

I get ready for bed and tenaciously crawl under my cozy comforter, resisting a far happier Kioto's constant nudges to join her in play. She eventually gives up and humphs at me loudly before settling next to my bed. I drop my hand down to her, and she licks it gently.

As I drift into sleep, my mind keeps wandering to Philip and the judgmental stare he gave me, as though he was trying to decide which crime I was guilty of. It leaves me very unsettled, but still, I slip into a deep REM state, and the dreams begin.

രജ

Philip stands at the edge of a lake, muddy in his black boxers and skater shirt, continually transforming into several different people: People I've never seen, people who seem vaguely familiar, and a few people from my life, including childhood friends whose names I forgot. He emanates confusion.

Bu sits at an elegant table eating rotten cantaloupe with a rusty fork, and Amber and Russell play catch with a giant beach ball shaped like an embryo. Gunthreon plays chess with himself, and my mom stands in the middle of it all, crying. I try running to her, but hands are holding me back—hundreds of disfigured and non-human hands. They pinch and pull and hurt. I scream at the pain of being unable to reach my mom as I watch her melt into the ground. All that's left are her eyes and the top of her head, and that's when she homes in on me, her eyes widening with recognition. Her sorrow suddenly feels like an arrow to my heart.

I am suddenly released by the hands and thrown upright in bed as I gasp for air, sickened by the images burning in my brain. The sweat has dampened my pajamas, and when I get up to go into the bathroom, I feel the pain in my arms—a horrible soreness in my muscles. I pull up my pajama arms, and then I see the bruises—deep purple, finger-shaped bruises.

Kioto sits at the front door, sniffing underneath it and wagging her tail. I run to it and peek out the eyehole, only to see Philip's door close quickly and silently.

I call my mom immediately. The phone rings only once, and she answers, "Hello?" with no hint of sleepiness in her voice.

"Mom, are you okay?"

"Yes, honey, I'm fine," she says. "You must have had a bad dream. Go to bed." I don't. I stay on the line. These days I can't believe that any insanity I envision, or pain I feel is only a dream. It seems there's reality in every bit of oddness in my life.

"I'm scared, mom," I moan, holding back tears.

"You need me to come over?" she asks, hurriedly and worried.

I pause while reaching over to pick up the silver ring off my nightstand, and then say, "No. No. I will be fine," as I turn it over and over.

"I'll call you tomorrow before you go to work. *Go to bed,* Kailey," my mom says.

I hang up the phone, head to the freezer, grab a bag of frozen peas and try to nurse a few of the bad bruises. I fall asleep holding the bag to my arm.

Chapter 12

Deceiving
CB

"Mom, we have to talk. Are you going to be home tonight?"

As I chat on the phone, I'm also changing damp, stinky bedsheets reeking of freezer burn.

"I'll be home Friday. I gotta run to Frankie's in Aurora—needs some assistance with picking out new wall colors. Wanna come over then, and I'll do the cooking?" she says.

"Can I put in a request?" The drool starts puddling on my tongue from the thought. I can't help it that food excites me so much.

"You don't need to. Steak Diane and honey mustard-crusted potatoes it is."

"Yes! Thanks, Mom. You're awesome!" I can almost see the smile on her face. For a moment, I even forget the purpose of Friday night.

My next call before I head off to work is to Gunthreon who tells me that he actually had a really good night's sleep. There are wretching noises in the background on Gunthreon's end, as if someone is hacking up their lungs.

"It's Bu," Gunthreon states. "I'm thinking he may have eaten something really bad, and considering he eats raw meat and has a stomach of iron—"

"Gunthreon, my dream—this has to do with my dream last night!" I say. I tell him brief hints of the dream, and about the bruises on my arms.

"Was it only us in the dream?" queries Gunthreon. "Was there anyone else you knew besides us?" I hear emotion creeping into his normally indifferent voice.

"Philip was in it, too."

"Who is Philip?"

"One of my new neighbors. He seems to be quite a strange boy, but he's beautiful, Gunthreon. He's special needs I think, or at least that's what his foster mom Karen, says."

"What does Philip look like?"

"He's about eight, with blond hair and big, brown eyes."

"Is there anything different about this boy?" asks Gunthreon, who is seemingly trying to squeeze some important information from me. "Maybe an accent, or birthmarks, or anything like that?"

"No—wait—he has a scar on his face."

"Is it below his left eye?"

I don't know what to say, so I just sit there, stupefied. "Yes..."

"After all this time, he's right beneath our noses!" Gunthreon starts laughing. "Kailey, oh, Kailey, you have no idea what this means." He laughs even more.

I'm suddenly scared of Gunthreon's interest in this boy, which then turns to fear of the boy. "Should I be scared of him?"

"Oh, yes, be scared of him—be very scared." He laughs especially hard this time, making me want to hang up the phone, for fear of Gunthreon's hysterics traveling through the phone waves. "Kailey, you must go over there and talk with him. Don't let him know you know anything about him. Just pretend you're being neighborly."

"Why are you sending me out to talk with someone dangerous?" I stutter, praying that he doesn't laugh again.

"Just trust me. I'll talk with you later," says Gunthreon.

Then he hangs up. *He is going to drive me insane.*

My next call is to the office, because there is absolutely no possible way I will be able to work today. I would be a mess, and Amber would see right through me, expecting some logical answer to my odd behavior, which I cannot give *anyone* right now. I need to keep all this on the down-low, until I can fully grasp what the hell is going on.

Kioto tries to ignore me this morning, yet she keeps peeking at me out of the corner of her eye as I get dressed. She doesn't exactly know what to expect of me right now—whether I'm going or staying since I'm usually gone by now. I go to her and sit by her on my bedroom floor, nuzzling my head into her neck. She licks my face and smiles at me in her own dog way.

After a few minutes, I decide what I must do. I grab both my ring and pendulum and toss them into my pocket, then grab a cranberry-orange muffin—which I don't even like, and only accidentally bought on a recent grocery stockpiling expedition (I don't like venturing out much on my own)—and head toward the door. For a brief moment, I want to scream, because I don't know what course of action to take, but I decide that not rehearsing will be the best way to handle it.

"Just go and see what happens, right?" I say to myself. I step across the hallway, knowing it's Monday and that Philip is most likely at school, but knock on the door anyway.

Before I even finish the third knock, Philip opens the door. I hold out the muffin, and he stands motionless, inside the door. He puts his hand out, brushing my skin, and a small sigh escapes his mouth as he pauses before taking it, examining it, and sniffing it. I grab my hand where he touched it and mixed feelings of hostility, admiration and a sort of longing, meld to form a troubled sensation.

"Cranberry-orange—my favorite," he chuckles. "Trying to butter me up? Ha! No pun intended." I stare at him. "Butter, get it?" he asks as I continue to stare. He leaves the door open, turns around and starts walking away, not waiting for my reply. I assume he wants me to follow, so I move forward, but for some reason I cannot walk in. I bump against what seems to be an invisible wall. I shiver at the strange energy that seems to flow over my skin. I put my hand up, and against the barrier. It doesn't seem threatening, but more like a simple hindrance.

"Philip, if you want me to come in, I can't. But I think you know this, don't you?"

He turns around and walks back, then takes a post-it note off of the wall, just near the doorway and places it on a table near the door. "Try now," he says as we stare at each other.

"I swear we've never met," I say, "but you seem awfully familiar to me."

"I live next door, for God's sake. You have to have seen me at some time. Or maybe you've seen me on the cover of GQ magazine—wait, make that Parenting." He laughs.

I attempt to enter the apartment again, slowly, and sure enough, I can. In turning around once inside, I see Sharpie scribbles written across the door frame—a matching set to the ones outside on the balcony. Removing one of the symbols somehow breaks the chain that protected the doorway.

He turns around and heads toward the kitchen. When he's not looking, I grab the post-it note off the table, for fear of being trapped *inside* this apartment, somehow.

He grabs a mug and some milk, which seem harmless enough for me to stay. He then lights a flame on the stove and places a tea kettle on it.

The whole apartment is green—and not the walls and carpet, but rather plants and flowers, situated in every possible foot of the place. Lush and vibrant, they look as though they were just plucked from a rainforest.

Then I notice the itty-bitty little ball of mud in Philip's hair, near his neck.

"You have mud on your neck," I state matter-of-factly.

"What can I say? I have a green thumb and a muddy neck," he says, as he places a tea bag in a cup and then pours hot water over it. His actions resemble someone quite familiar with the kitchen—someone independent.

"Philip, I think if your mother came home right now and found me, a stranger, in your apartment, it would be very bad, and she may try to shoot me."

"Don't worry. She won't be home soon." Philip responds. "We don't own a gun. She'd only try to stab or strangle you."

"Great." I make sure to move as far from the kitchen and its knife set as possible.

Without even asking me, Philip adds a bit of milk and a dollop of honey to the tea cup—just how I like it—then hands it to me. As I take the cup, he places his hand on top of mine. I don't pull away, but instead, find myself curious of this boy's emotions. He pulls his hand away.

"How old are you, Philip?"

He looks in my eyes and hesitates. "Seven," he blurts.

He walks to the kitchen set and pulls out a seat. "Please sit," he says. "Before you ask me questions, I need to ask you one." Philip pulls out the chair next to me, and brings it close. "It's a simple question," he says. "How about I ask it, and you choose to answer or not. Deal?" He stares at me with what might seem to some like puppy-dog eyes, but I'm thinking "lion" is the better description.

"Agreed. Ask."

"Who is that creature that waits outside your door all night?"

The bile creeps up through my esophagus and I immediately jump up. "Outside *my* door at night?" My eyes are wide now, and he seems to realize that I honestly do not know what he's talking about. He grabs my arm lightly and pulls me back down into the seat. He then holds his hand over mine, in my lap, and looks at me with a soft face, one that holds years of experience—one that looks years older than seven.

"He's a stinky, big, brown, ugly thing with big eyes," he says as his hand tightens over mine, coercing me to stay seated. He stares into my eyes, looking as though he can read my thoughts. "He's always holding a necklace or something and he just sits there, like he's guarding your apartment." My shoulders release the tension built up as I realize who's been at my door.

"Oh. Philip, do you know Renhala?"

His eyebrows rise and he lets go of my hand as he sits up straight. He then gathers himself and speaks. "I feel you are an honest person, Kailey, and I'm really hoping that I am right," says Philip. "Let's be frank with each other, and I will share whatever information I have with you, as long as you reciprocate."

"Okay then," I say. "Special needs?"

"I am in whatever categories the doctors here want to lump me in." I see his throat force down a swallow before he continues. "I tried so hard to not be me, but we are who we are, Kailey. How do you explain the things I saw as a three year old, or how I understood the genetic makeup of an amaryllis at the age of six? Not genius, but 'special needs.' They just didn't like that I was smarter than them. I can guarantee you that a large percentage of us in this particular category also know of Renhala. There, I answered two questions for you. Please answer mine."

I agreed, so there's no backing out now. "I'm going to assume you're speaking of the young greble I recently befriended. His name is Bu, and is seemingly a gentle soul. Don't be frightened of him—he wouldn't hurt you."

He laughs. I furrow my brow.

Philip looks out the window at a morning dove sitting on his windowsill. The dove turns to him, and I feel an unspoken connection is made between them. The dove then turns away and closes its eyes. "I'm not scared of him," Philip finally says. "It's you who should watch out. He's more dangerous than you realize."

I feel the sudden need to defend Bu. "Funny, 'cause I've been warned you are the one to be careful around." I was raised not to beat around the bush, so I might as well run around the mulberry.

"And who told you that?" snaps Philip, his voice suddenly petulant.

"A small Asian man by the name of Gunthreon—" I am interrupted by his hand.

"I know Gunthreon, Kailey."

"Care to reveal how?"

"I bet he fed you lots of stories, didn't he? Special abilities, quests, legends?"

I clench my jaw as his face sprouts a sarcastic-looking smirk.

He seems on a roll as I feel anger growing in him. "And I'm sure he didn't even mention to you his power—maybe given you any clue of what *he* can do?" He's staring at me like I missed out on some joke, which at this point I'm sure I did. Come to think about it, Gunthreon never told me about any gifts of his, and I never bothered asking, either, even after he spoke of Russell.

"The power of persuasion—that's what he possesses," says Philip. "He can persuade anyone to do almost anything. Pretty powerful if you think about it, huh? If he gets in a fight, he can just persuade the aggressor to *not fight*. He can persuade a penguin it needs a pair of Nikes. It's the perfect gift, don't you see? He can persuade anyone to take up with *any* cause he may have. Do you see this now?"

Suddenly, I feel like I've been used. Maybe I never made any decisions on my own. Maybe that's why Gunthreon seemed so very trustworthy to me, breaking down my defenses so easily.

"Kailey, I don't want to be caught up in his or anyone else's stupid plans," squawks Philip. "I just want to live a normal, happy life." He looks down at his muffin.

As I contemplate what Philip has said, watching him stare at his muffin, I decide being angry at Gunthreon will get me nowhere, and I'm assuming it's the same story with Philip. There's definitely some sort of animosity between the two, and Philip is trying to sway me from believing Gunthreon. "Sorry, Philip, but your life doesn't seem very normal," I say. "Where do you go to school? Why aren't you there now? What games do you play at the park? Huh, Philip? You don't look too happy." I know I'm taking some long shots—I only met the kid yesterday—but I feel lucky right now.

And when I see his eyes are wet, I know I've hit a sore spot.

I sigh. "I'm sorry, Philip." I get up from my seat and hug him tightly, letting his body lean into mine. I stroke his hair as I talk to him. "Yeah, maybe Gunthreon is using me, but maybe I'm being selfish, too. I need something to be strong about—something to bring me out of my rut. And if it's gonna be a threat of monsters from an entirely different realm than the one I reside in that does it, sobeit." I kiss him on the top of the head and raise his face so I may see it. I take a step back.

Philip looks at me and just when I think he's going to feel sorry for me, or agree that Gunthreon may be on to a great plan, Philip sighs and says, "You are one foolish girl," as he drinks his last sip of milk.

I refuse to feed his jumbo-sized, too-big-for-a-seven-year-old, ego. "Thanks for the tea and enjoy your damn muffin!" I say as I storm to his front door.

Just as I reach his apartment door, tossing the post-it note back on the table, I hear, "Tell Gunthreon I'm willing to see him, as long as he doesn't try to cut my other eye out, my karmelean friend." When I exit, he locks the door, most likely reapplying his post-it note.

Why can't my life be simple? And why the hell does this feel like a break-up with a boyfriend and not an argument with a total stranger?

Chapter 13

Helpless
ᘒ

The whole rest of my day is spent lounging around and watching those horrible talk shows you just can't ignore, no matter how many educational cable channels you flip through. *Let's see,* Dr. Phil *or* The Fascinating Life of Dung Bugs? *Hmmm, easy choice.*

I start off laughing, telling myself how stupid these people are, but by the end I'm usually egging some baby's momma to punch the deadbeat father in his head. I don't even call Gunthreon, even though I know I really should.

Nighttime soon rolls around, and the moon is beautiful, just shining silently through my balcony door, lending me a brief moment of peacefulness. Watching one more TV show, I decide, won't destroy that many more brain cells than I've already lost today, so I sit on the couch sipping a relaxing cup of chamomile tea. I examine my favorite teacup in my lap as I sit, thinking it's just like me—damaged, but still able to perform its intended purpose. As I stare, my eyelids become heavy and when I slowly start dozing off, I feel I need to get up and go to bed before I spill the tea.

As I rise, Kioto turns toward my front door and I hear the beginning of a low growl from her throat. I stare at the door, recalling Philip's comment about Bu. I watch as the fog of Renhala forms before my eyes.

"Bu, you don't have to sit at my door," I say as I start for the door, quickly opening it. "If you want to come in-" but that's all that comes out before I realize that the horrible thing before me is not Bu. It's far uglier than Bu. It's a greble all right, but bigger and grosser, if that's possible.

I try to slam the door as the fog rolls in around me, but the greble catches it in its hand. Kioto snarls and growls, but I can tel she doesn't want to go near the creature. The marble ball my mom gave me lies on the table, catching my eye, so I scoop it up in my hand and throw it at its head, but it catches it mid-air and it crumbles in its grasp.

I grab Kioto by the collar, and as I start to drag her to my bedroom, the apartment suddenly disappears, and I find myself standing in a pool of slime the color of pus, surrounded by fog, without Kioto. I have no idea where I am. I pull myself out of the puddle, with much force, and stand still, listening.

Kioto barks frantically in the fog, and I yell to her, trying to coax her to me. Her barking abruptly stops, and then I feel soft fur rub against my leg. I feel better knowing she's safe, and I pet her head, only to find that the head I'm petting is some kind of giant raccoon with fangs.

Immediately, I scream and start running, but to where, I have no idea. I try relaxing in the hope that the fog will lift.

The greble laughs somewhere in the haze, and I try to pinpoint where the voice is coming from. "Kailey, Kailey, do you think you can run?" he says. "I see you. Mmm, your flesh is so soft and inviting. I'd really like to squeeze the life from it. I should have finished you when you visited last night."

I realize he must be talking about my dream. Once again, I didn't distinguish between a dream and reality by realizing the difference—the simple fact that I *felt*. *Felt their feelings*.

"You won't escape this time!" the monster grumbles in the fog.

I remember Gunthreon telling me my monk's spade should always be at my back, but as I grab for it, I don't feel it. I know it has to be there, but I can't bring myself to relax enough to really grasp it. The fear of what this creature can do to my fragile body is overwhelming, but I gather my courage and in a final attempt at defending myself, reach to the creature's own anger. *Maybe there's a chance. I can do this. Black sludge.*

Just as I grab the energy of the anger, I'm slammed by something so massive I am literally lifted off my feet. My head hits a huge rock, which resembles a headstone.

The blood is warm as it starts pouring down my forehead, dripping into my eye. As I sit, disoriented, the creature grabs at me, barely touching my shoulder. Then, he starts yelling, trying to swat away something at his feet.

It's Kioto. She's found her way to me. She bites the greble's legs and feet, dodging his blows.

Right before I faint, I see another figure running full force at the creature. This time, it's Bu, with his fists raised, charging the larger creature.

Blackness consumes me.

Chapter 14

Tense
ରଞ

The pain is excruciating. I sit up as slowly as I can and feel the top of my head, discovering it's still in one piece, and as my eyes peek open, I notice my own comforter is covering my legs, so I know I was not admitted to a hospital. Philip sits across from me in my desk chair, sleeping, while Bu, squeezed into the recliner beside him, also sleeps. Gunthreon stands next to me, staring at me intently.

"How are you feeling?" he asks very quietly. "I called in sick to your work for you, so don't worry."

The pain in my head leaves abruptly. I look to Gunthreon, confused. Smiling, he responds, "It was the last thing you felt, so the sensation just lingered. Your brain had to catch up with the rest of your body."

"What the hell happened? Where's Kioto?" I try to stand up quickly and almost fall on top of her. She jumps up and puts her tail between her legs, cowering from the surprise. "No, no, it's all right, baby, come here," I coo, patting her head and checking her over, feeling every bone in her body. She seems to be fine. But me on the other hand, I don't feel I'm ready to deal with another realm. "Gunthreon, I can't do this. I choked." I hesitate. "I should be dead now!"

"You have all your friends here to thank for your life, Kailey," says Gunthreon. "You've made wonderful, sacrificing friends, simply by being you. Don't give up that easily. That greble that attacked you is long gone. Bu and Kioto put up the fight of a lifetime. As for your head, 'Philip' fixed you."

I look at Gunthreon inquisitively.

"'Philip' has quite a coveted gift, you know," says Gunthreon, "something so special that wars have been started over it." He watches as my expression turns to one of worry. "That very being, sitting right there," he points to Philip, "somehow, magically, knows the genetic mapping of every living creature and how their life force flows. Everything from platelet regeneration to photosynthesis! With this, comes the gift of healing, along with a few other magic tricks. See why I was so excited you found him?" He smiles. "He is known as Ladimer, and as long as I've known him, he's never looked like *that*."

"I only kept my scar to remind myself." Philip's head rises, and his eyes are open, staring directly at Gunthreon.

Gunthreon puts his head down, looking like he's been run through the mill. "Ladimer, you have got to let go of your anger." He turns his face to Philip, with eyes suddenly full of power. "You know I can *make* you forget it, right?"

"Don't use those words on me, you fool." The anger between them rises, and I can feel the tension between them, as thick as maple syrup—but not so sweet. My lungs feel like they may collapse.

Philip turns to me and sternly says, "I can also take life away. He tends to forget that." He then turns to Gunthreon. "Oh, and so you know, I told Kailey of *your* special and unique gift. *I*, at least, thought that was of importance." Gunthreon ignores him.

"No way are you seven," I state. "How old are you really? Is this your true form? If I touch you, will you flicker?"

Philip turns to me and gives me the poutiest seven-year-old face he can muster. "This isn't Star Wars," he yaps. "Get real. Come on and use that brain I just shoved back in your head. I can *control* the force that gives life, along with these puny bodies of ours that hold our organs together. I can *manipulate body data*. I can be *anyone* I want to be."

"Does your foster mom know about all this?"

His laugh holds years of experience. "Karen? I've seen more foster homes than you can imagine, Kailey. I've probably been adopted forty times in the past century. I'm a nomad. I've deceived people my whole life. She doesn't know what I am, so best we leave it that way, for her sake." He sighs. "I thought I could lead a normal life, hiding away in her little family, but guess not, huh? Gunthreon here made sure of that. And he's trying to ruin your life, too."

I look at Gunthreon and it seems as though his glare at Philip might pierce right through his body. "I had nothing to do with finding you, 'Philip,'" spits Gunthreon. "Stop being so damn dramatic!"

The testosterone level in the room is smothering me—and the tiny seven-year-old seems to be the biggest contributor. "Can we stop this petty bickering please?" I say. "Gunthreon, why is Philip—Ladimer—whoever—so angry with you?" I turn to Philip with a finger to my lips, pointing to him with my other hand.

"Well, if Ladimer will let me explain," barks Gunthreon. "I can clue you in."

He waits until Philip gives him the floor with a hand gesture and Philip whispers, "Can't wait to hear *this*."

"Long ago," begins Gunthreon in his best fairytale fashion, "there was a disastrous battle, sparked by Velopa over a particular region of Renhala that it was claiming was its own. The fight involved hundreds of creatures and humans, and we two were in the middle of a particularly ugly fight—"

Philip interjects by adding, "—where I was falling at least twice the amount of enemies as my partner."

Gunthreon glares at him as Philip zippers his mouth shut. Gunthreon satisfied, continues, "My purse was cut in battle, and as I selfishly scrambled to collect all my fallen gold—I had a lot—I was speared through the gut by a meeple. Ladimer came to my rescue. He laid his hands on me, mending my insides.

"I fell unconscious, and in my unconsciousness," says Gunthreon, "my power came alive twofold. Disoriented as I awoke, the last thing I remembered was the meeple standing over me, shoving its talon into my belly so I persuaded the one bending over me to tear out his own eye. The pain I felt soon afterward was even worse than that talon, for I had hurt my best friend."

He turns to Philip. "I am truly sorry for what I did. You have to know this, Ladimer. I tried following your whereabouts for decades, hoping to tell you of my regrets, but since you can change your appearance, it has proved too difficult to find you."

"Oh," I say, not knowing what else *to* say. Gunthreon and Philip stare at each other, exchanging no words. I breathe in deeply, and with my mind open, feel the energy emanating from them both. I attempt to caress the hurt they both feel.

"Kailey!" I am suddenly interrupted by Bu and jump in my seat. I look to Gunthreon and Philip who are both staring at me with their mouths open, aware of what I was attempting. Gunthreon then smiles at me.

"I am sorry, Kailey. Bu was bad. Bu was late." Awake now, Bu comes to me quickly and wraps his giant arms around me. I feel I must remember to discuss with him the importance of hygiene, because man, he stinks. He's crying, lighting up the room—a daily occurrence, it seems.

"Don't feel bad, Bu. You can't protect me all the time. But Bu, you have to be honest with me. Have you been outside my door?" He nods his head. I then query, "Did you know this greble was going to attack me?"

His gaze turns to Kioto, and she licks his hand, coaxing him to tell me something. Philip nods sternly toward him, and the look of submission on Bu's face tells me he indeed knows something of importance.

"Bu heard talking at home," replies Bu. "Big grebles were talking to the ugly bunny. Bu heard your name. So Bu come and watch your door." He gets up and walks away from us, his anger and remorse fueling his temper. He turns to me and says, "Bu go get them. They hurt you!" And with this, he disappears.

"Damn!" yells Gunthreon, with enough power to slightly shake the room. Philip and I exchange glances, not expecting that out of Gunthreon's mouth. I'm not sure why the room shook. "They will kill him, or even worse, not kill him, but torture him. No, this is not going to happen. I need to go to him, *now!*"

I can see how special Bu is to Gunthreon. "Gunthreon, I want to help. Don't go alone, please. This is all because of me," I prattle.

Philip sighs. "Me, too," he adds. "I will help however you can use me. I will travel to Renhala if you will it. I'm bored here anyway." On his feet, he lifts his head from the bow he has given Gunthreon, his mannerisms not fitting his small frame. Adulthood peeks through the cracks, and I see someone other than Philip—instead, a man doing his best to eat his pride. This is the closest to an apology I think Gunthreon will get from him.

"You have no idea what you are getting yourself into," warns Gunthreon. "Kailey, you're so new, and Ladimer, you've been gone for so long. Bu's Gernwood is the worst it's ever been, its evil multiplying exponentially by the day."

"I'm scared shitless, and may faint at any particular moment," I pause, "but I am drawn to the idea of helping you, Gunthreon. I'm willing to jump in. If I don't, I may only barricade myself in my apartment. And, ain't it best that the insane keep the insane for company?" I pause as both of them stare at me. "I just need to know what Bu meant by 'the ugly bunny.' That kind of scares me."

"It's a meeple, Kailey—a cute little fuzzy meeple."

I recall the image flashing across Spirit Cave's television above the bar—the one of the taloned rabbit. Then I imagine images of Gunthreon getting speared through the gut in battle.

"You mean to tell me these deadly things are cute, little, fuzzy bunnies with talons?"

Gunthreon nods his head.

"They're here, in my realm!"

He nods again and says, "They've captured several, but it seems they all oddly disappear."

Philip stands before us. "If you want to save Bu, we have to leave now. No time for dawdling." He's frank, that's for sure. "The meeples have not kept their distance from me, Gunthreon. They know where I am. I've seen them at night, at my balcony door. They've begun travelling here in throngs. Something big's going down."

"The scratches?" I ask. "That's what those scratches are from?" *Creepy*. My pocket suddenly feels heavy, and I reach in, forgetting I had put my pendulum there. I pull it out.

Gunthreon sees it and questions, "Did you happen to have that in your pocket when the greble attacked you?"

"Yes."

"Great. We will use it to find Bu. Good job, Kailey."

"Cool." I guess I do cool things now, and don't even realize it.

Gunthreon grabs my hand and says, "Let's go."

Chapter 15

Repulsive
CR

The travel to Renhala is like sneezing, or even blinking an eye. One moment I'm standing in my room, and the next, I'm standing on a mulched path in the middle of a forest of black trees. It's less foggy than what I previously experienced, but the air feels sticky and mucky. There are puddles of the pus-filled goo scattered here and there. "Why has the fog lifted?" I ask.

Gunthreon turns to me. "With each travel, you get more acquainted, if you will, with Renhala," he says as he swats off a bug—half spider, half dragonfly—which has landed on his arm. "At the start, your mind has problems grasping the concept, hence the fog. You sort of teeter in-between until you get the hang of it. When you know where you want to be, you just arrive, with no fuzziness. Clear as crystal." Sure, that's what *he* says.

I pull out the pendulum and hold it before me. It just hangs, lifeless.

Kioto is beside me, right up against my leg, with every step I take. During our first attempt at leaving, we tried putting her in my front room and closed the bedroom door behind us, but somehow, she ended up with us in Renhala. *I don't even know how to travel yet, but my damn dog evidently does.*

Gunthreon said animals have the natural ability to travel and she must have really wanted to be at my side. Now I think I have a clue how the cats and dogs in news stories really journey thousands of miles to find their owners. Kioto's a stubborn one, I'll give her that, but I'd never trade her in a million years.

Gunthreon and Philip walk away from me, chit chatting amongst themselves, not knowing I'm purposefully giving them some privacy. I'm glad they're at least on talking terms, because the animosity could have suffocated me. And I couldn't imagine anything pulling me and Amber apart like that. I'd miss her too much, even if she is the biggest pain in the ass.

Growing more nervous with each growl from Kioto at some unseen creatures of the forest, I start fiddling around with my pendulum, kind of recklessly. "Come on, already," I mutter. "What are those two talking about?" I mutter to myself, and then see Gunthreon look over his shoulder toward me. I shoo him forward and mouth, "I'm okay," and continue following them at a brief distance, despite having my fear barometer ready to burst. I keep a hand in my pocket, caressing my braided silver ring, grounding myself.

A sudden howling noise from the forest makes me jump two feet straight up in the air, causing me to fumble my pendulum and drop it. It falls hard and cracks against a rock, breaking the pendulum in half, vertically. I cry to myself as I stand, staring at it. *Why am I doing this? Maybe I'm in purgatory. I must have died. I'm paying for my sins, surely.*

A small gnat-type bug then lands on my hand and bites me as I squish it. I bend over and pick up my broken pendulum. *Shit. Great, what am I going to do now?* Gunthreon may kill me, or Philip— Ladimer. After all, that's his thing, right? But I pull myself together. What I need is glue—something sticky.

A quick spin reveals one of the gross puddles of gook. I ponder whether it might be sticky enough to keep the halves together. Deciding to take the risk, I stick the smallest part of my finger in the goo. Kioto watches me closely, sniffing the goo and sticking her tail between her legs. The goo doesn't melt me or kill me, and it *is* sticky, so what the heck? I dip half the stone in the slop, only to find that I need to force my finger out before it and *my whole body* are pulled into the puddle.

I then attach the other side, just as Ladimer and Gunthreon walk back over to me.

"Kailey, take out your pendulum and ask it what direction we should head." Gunthreon doesn't seem so happy, and Philip is frowning. "And get away from that stuff. You don't want to fall into that."

I turn so that they can't really see the pendulum fully, then start asking out loud if Bu is located in each direction. Once I get the circle motion, I say, "It says that way." I point.

"Just what we thought, but we needed some confirmation," says Gunthreon. "Thank you." They continue on with their own conversation, which seems to have heated up a bit.

Phew. I shove the pendulum in my pocket and feel it fall apart as the sharp point cuts my fingertip.

Another howl has me and Kioto running to stand near Philip and Gunthreon. I scan the area for hidden grebles. "Gunthreon," I say, "that greble that attacked me told me he brought me to Renhala. Is that possible?" He nods. "How? Why?"

Gunthreon and Philip exchange a brief glance, and Gunthreon talks first. "Not sure exactly why, and actually how is also questionable. Travelers can take people with them back and forth, but the one 'bringing' had to have already been to where they're going, at least once in their life. Understand?" I nod, then freeze as I realize what Gunthreon is telling me—that the greble somehow knew where I lived. "Kailey," Gunthreon says, "you have to know what you are up against, and how unpredictably vicious these creatures can be, whatever their motives. While we're here, with my powers, I can block some things for you as we walk on to find Bu, but I cannot make it all entirely pleasant."

"So why is Bu not like them? You talk of these creatures like they're demon spawn. What if Bu's putting up a good front?" I say, petting Kioto's head as we continue to walk through the dark forest, trying to ignore the scurrying sounds of little feet on the forest floor. I see one of those raccoon things peek out from behind a tree stump as we walk by and Kioto growls.

Gunthreon shakes his head as his face softens. "He's not. Bu's an exception, as was his mother. You see, she was abandoned by her clan at birth because of her small size and was found by a weary traveler. This traveler took pity on the creature, despite knowing what it was and where it came from, so it took this creature with it on its many journeys. Bu's mother was raised outside the greble world and treated like the traveler's own child for many a year. She learned sympathy and kindness, and what it was to provide love and warmth to another creature.

"In time, as she grew bigger and bigger, the lands outside of the greble boundaries wanted nothing to do with her, so for her own safety, the traveler brought Bu's mother back to the greble lands. She also thought she could make a difference in the greble community—maybe instill some values. She did her best to fit in, sneaking kind acts here and there, and eventually became pregnant with Bu. As he grew, she instilled her own values in him, nurturing him and forming him into the lovely soul we know today. Before Bu's mother's untimely death by the hands of a jealous female, babe and mother traveled often to see the traveler, and the day before she died, she made the traveler promise one thing: to watch over the child when she was no longer around to do so.

"Bu was kept by his father's clan, but he snuck out every chance he could to meet the traveler, and they grew to love each other very much."

Philip then decides to add to the conversation. "Yeah, yeah. Guess who the traveler is, blah, blah. Well, hopefully we can do this quickly. My ideal plan is we find Bu, convince him how stupid he is, and bring him home. Done."

"He's only trying to protect something he cares about," says Gunthreon.

"I know how that plays out, all too well, don't I, Gunthreon? How stupid a mistake it can be."

"Come on!" My nerves can no longer take the bickering. "If you don't stop this, I will refuse doing anything you ask and just run and ask the nearest helpful greble if he's seen Bu. How would you like that?" The horror on their faces confirms I've made them realize they need to stop.

Gunthreon starts leading us west, I think. There are small noises and whispers on the wind, and it stinks like mildew. Occasionally, I see more of the raccoon creatures scurrying about, foraging—or so it seems. I almost feel like they're following us. Maybe they are, because they know we'll die and can eat our carcasses. Maybe my eyes taste good.

We pass several ruined buildings, all built very roughly, and I swear one owns a set of giant yellow eyes. The eyes watch us walk by, and I get a strong whiff of putrid egg.

Gunthreon spots the pair of eyes, too. "You must know that the grebles are very selfish creatures and will do whatever they can for themselves," he says. "Most likely, that one we passed will not let anyone know, but rather follow us to see if we have anything it wants."

We continue, but not for long. We abruptly stop, and I almost faint from the hideous scene hanging before me. There, looming ahead, is a giant, grizzly tree of redwood proportion with hundreds of silhouettes hanging from it like warped Christmas ornaments. Upon closer examination, some are human and some are not. The unfortunate commonality among them is they are all hanged by what appears to be their intestines.

"Oh God!" I cover my mouth quickly and Kioto walks around in circles, scoping the area, and perhaps feeling the residual evil of the acts performed. I find myself tempted to cover Philip's eyes, but he seems unfazed by the obscenity.

Instead, he stares at the display. "This is a sacrificial tree," he mutters. "The grebles will make sacrifices—rarely, but they do it—to one known as Devoten, one of Velopa's top men. He prefers the whole hanging, intestinal-noose thing. *He* is demon spawn, as you call it."

"Let's keep walking," Gunthreon suggests as he leads us. We continue walking in quiet, for fear of awakening anything hungry. I see Gunthreon and Philip exchange glances every now and then, most likely agreeing to cover something up from me, as Gunthreon whispers me suggestions, like "Don't be afraid." And "Kailey, imagine you're watching your favorite movie."

I know one thing—they both seem to have missed the woman lying behind a broken-down wagon with only stumps as appendages. Her face was also missing a nose.

Kioto keeps turning and checking behind us, growling as we continue on. She doesn't like those raccoons any more than I do. They only follow, though, apparently not wanting to do anything else. I even see one attack a small, gray, mouse-ish creature that lunges at my foot.

Gunthreon stops before a tall, creepy tower that seems to hold some authority. It makes my skin tingle and leaves me feeling strongly nauseated as we stand before it. I bend over, holding my stomach, feeling the retching about to be unleashed. Gunthreon sees my reaction and says, "Kailey, due to your *sensitivity*, you must do your best to repel the energy inside." I toss him a quick glance to tell him to eat his words, but then find myself feeling instantly better as I look to Kioto, who is staring into my face. She licks the tear which falls quickly from my eye and I stand up straight.

"This is it," Gunthreon says. "Don't be frightened of the ceetchans that have been following us. They're attracted to Ladimer, well at least his abilities."

Before we enter the tower, Gunthreon gives directions—he is to lead, I'll follow him with Kioto, and Ladimer will bring up the rear. We walk single-file, slowly and silently until we find Bu. We'll snatch him and bring him back to my realm, immediately.

I notice the ceetchans do not enter the building when we do, but rather wait outside the door. Once inside, the place seems empty, except for the occasional friendly scream.

We walk quietly, as agreed, but every single noise has me scurrying to be close to Philip. *Why him?*

On the walls are hideous, nasty things: shrunken heads, various animal feet, and one especially disturbing sketched picture framed in bones. At first glance, the picture looks to be a sweet little blond girl holding a dog of some sorts, standing on a pile of pillows. But when you look closer, she's standing on a pile of dead pigs and is choking one with her bare hands, with a smile plastered across her face. She's also wearing a pig nose over her face. Philip says, "Lenni Fontaine. Local legend."

"I'm not gonna run into her, am I?" I ask, frightened.

"Nah, been dead for at least ten years," he answers. "But you could have the pleasure of meeting her twin sister, Lorrie. She, however, is much more disturbing."

"More disturbing than that?!" I shout as Philip covers my mouth with his hand.

I shake the chill that has begun crawling through my skin and into my bones as we come to what seems the hundredth door. Gunthreon holds his ear to the door which is covered in what looks to be bloody handprints and paw prints of various creatures.

Suddenly, he runs from the door, dragging us with him to hide behind chain-mailled, greble-sized suits of armor.

Something opens the door partway, and we hear, "He is a child and malleable—you must remember this. He's not entirely worthless, but should be thoroughly punished for what he did. If he attempts something like that again, I will most definitely decide his fate, the pathetic greble. I wish Devoten would let us end this game now."

I peek out around the armor, expecting to see a hideous creature or human, but instead, see the cutest bunny. It's larger than bunnies on my plane of existence, but a bunny nonetheless—fluffy and white and floppy-eared. My inner child longs to run out and hug it, but as soon as it faces my direction, any hint of that thought escapes me. It has ugly, bloodshot eyes, and a huge, razor-sharp, blood-streaked talon where its right foot should be and its left ear is bloody, hanging in an unnatural position. It growls as it walks away, and I suddenly feel weak in the knees. Thoughts of my many weaknesses begin flooding into my head; horrible thoughts of my lack of defense as my freakish assaulter pummels me with his fists swim through my brain, making my self-esteem shrivel like a water-deprived, wilting flower. I feel as though I am a waste of matter, and that I should be fed to some stronger, greater god. I grab my head with both hands and, at the same time, Kioto whimpers a small, humble sort of noise, as though she feels exactly like I do.

Gunthreon crawls over next to me, energy leaking from him. "I didn't have time to react and shelter you from that. I'm sorry," he whispers. "The meeples are very strong creatures, so just don't let the thoughts linger. Think of what is good in your life."

"How do you stop thoughts like that?" I blubber. "I suddenly hate myself." I see my distorted reflection from a mirror on the wall and must fight myself to like what I see, but the faint sound of Bu whimpering pulls me out of my downward spiral.

Philip crawls over and wipes my eyes quickly, for the tears are brightening our dark corner of shelter, making the armor's shadows dance around the room. "Please know that I see before me a strong, beautiful, courageous woman," he remarks as he gently wipes the last of my tears, "who nobody could deny loving."

His lips meet my cheek and I redden in embarrassment as he turns and moves toward Gunthreon.

Gunthreon peeks around the armor and motions for us to start moving. We rise and enter the doorway slowly and cross the threshold of a large room of what I guess is torture equipment. I catch sight of a giant pinwheel, centered with an arrow, that resembles a carnival game. It looks as though it's supposed to be spun, the prizes indicated by multi-colored pie sections labeled with various body parts.

One greble with his back to us sharpens a hot fireplace poker in a fire pit, and another, smaller greble—Bu—hunches over on a bench made of what I think is some sort of reptile skin, facing away from us. The larger greble spins the wheel then turns to walk toward the bench. He turns back to look at the wheel as it lands on an ear, and he laughs, while grabbing a hold of Bu's neck, forcing his head back.

We each sneak closer, huddling behind various pieces of equipment. I make it within feet of the larger greble's back.

"I'm gonna make you pay for what you did," grumbles the greble, oblivious of the sudden infiltration around him. "Why risk your life for that scrawny piece of dirt? She's nothing." The poker starts to sizzle Bu's ear, and that's when his necklace and locket fall from his hand to the ground.

Something dangerous inside me stirs, and I do not care that this greble towers feet over me, and outweighs me by hundreds of pounds. I lunge at it and jump on its back. It's so massive that I cannot even grab onto it, and I end up just sliding back down over its rear.

Before I can get up and do any real damage, I see that Gunthreon has jumped out in front of the greble and is speaking to him, persuading him that what he's doing is not right—coaxing him to sit and think things over. The greble drops the poker and turns around, sitting compliantly on a chair. I don't trust it, so I eye the massive greble as I walk backward, until I bump into Bu.

I turn around to face him, and see what I couldn't before— that his mouth has been filled with dirty rags and sewn shut and his tear ducts have apparently been cauterized. The hurt in his eyes is so awful that I vow to continue on this quest, no matter where it brings me. Nobody should be subjected to this sort of mistreatment. *Torturous mistreatment. No woman,* or even greble.

Philip pulls a small, razor-sharp knife from his pocket and starts cutting the rope used to bind Bu's mouth.

"Bu tried. They are so quick," whimpers Bu. "Bu did bleed one, though!" I see the slashes and deep cuts all along Bu's body, and his rightmost leg is definitely broken. "He was mad at Bu, and said bad things about Kailey, so Bu pulled his ear almost off!" He looks to me for approval, but there is already a loss of innocence in him. I can feel the difference.

"Bu, you are so brave for sticking up for me," I say, "but you put yourself in grave danger. That makes me sad. I would be really happy if you gave up this fight and came back home with me now."

"But Kailey, *this* is my home."

I realize he's right, but I don't want him to stay here any longer. Philip begins healing Bu as we talk. I am amazed as I watch the cuts close and the leg reform to its original shape.

Gunthreon has the torturer painting a mural with oils and waxes. A lovely rendering of a bumblebee and daisy appear on the wall before us.

Then Gunthreon walks to Bu and holds his hand. "Bu, you can come stay with me until things quiet down here," says Gunthreon. "We can bake cupcakes and sing songs and watch *The Wizard of Oz* if you want. I know it's your favorite. But we must go now."

Bu perks up a bit, but sadly I fear this world is going to swallow him up as it did his mother.

"We have to leave this building," Philip comments quietly. "It has a protection spell on it. We cannot transport ourselves unless we're outside the walls."

Philip has Bu fully mended and able to walk, so Bu lifts me up and carries me to the door as quickly as we can all move, but not before kicking the newly inspired artist greble in the back, and grabbing his fanny pack on a nearby table. Not even noticing the jab, the greble continues with its masterpiece.

Just as Gunthreon reaches for the door handle, the door opens. "Oh, and keep him conscious enough for me to—" The meeple with the crooked ear stands in the door with its mouth still open, quickly scanning who stands before it. First, its eyes lock on Gunthreon, then Philip, then move to the beautiful mural, and finally turn back to the door. The meeple shoves something in its ears and runs full speed back out the door.

Both Gunthreon and Philip run in chase, along with Kioto. Bu runs with me in his arms. I am once again amazed at his grace and speed while running.

"He has closed his ears. I'm powerless. It's up to you," explains Gunthreon as Philip takes the lead. The meeple runs through a darkened doorway. We stop at the entrance and try to see in, but it's pitch black.

"Bu—you, Kailey, and Kioto stay here," advises Gunthreon. "If something happens, make some noise." With that, Gunthreon and Philip enter the darkened room.

I can't stand the silence. After a minute, I coax Bu into entering. Within seconds, I hear sounds of fighting, but I can't see anything. Bu falls and drops me, disappearing from sight, leaving me holding the rags he'd had in his mouth. Kioto barks frantically. Gunthreon makes some "oomph" noise, and Philip is silent.

"You idiots!" grunts the meeple. "How dare you enter our house and save that miserable good-for-nothing."

"Kailey, plug your ears!" It's Philip, warning me. I take the rags from Bu's mouth and rip them, shoving some small pieces in my ears. I'm now blind *and* deaf.

Crawling along the floor, I search with my hands for Bu. I find him and grab him as tightly as my hands allow. I hear loud clanging and fighting. Bu moves away from me and makes whimpering noises. Philip has fixed his tear ducts, so the tears start lighting the room in flashes, just in time for me to see Gunthreon crawling toward me.

I hear his voice over the ruckus and the rags in my ears: "Use its energy, Kailey! *Now!*" Both his hands appear bloody and broken.

His voice awakens my brain, and I reach from both within and beyond. I feel for the meeple's energy, but once I touch it, it's so repulsive I can't keep my grasp.

"Kailey, do something!" shouts Gunthreon. As the meeple approaches me, then disappears in the dark, I think of my weapon and reach behind me. I'm so stunned to feel the wood on my back that I freeze, and that's when the blow from behind knocks me into the wall. I drop the monk's spade, visible now, and it slides across the floor. The meeple stands over me, breathing in my face, its eyes full of hate—hate eager to shred me up like tissue paper. I feel its talon cutting my neck very slowly, and the familiar feeling of warm blood dripping my neck is all too personal. *It holds me down with its weight and grins as the broken bottle slices my neck, slowly spilling type AB down my neck and onto my crisp white shirt. I cry at the warmth, knowing these may be my last breaths.* This can't happen again, I won't allow it.

My anger explodes, and my hand dives into my pocket, grabbing my broken pendulum. I shove the sharp, pointy end right into the meeple's eye. It screams as it backs up slowly, and that's my break. I jump up as fast as my body will let me and grab my monk's spade off the floor. The weapon feels comforting in my hands, and for a brief moment, I am the stronger of us. I see defeat in the meeple's eyes, and in one long swoop, I slice its head off, showering the room with blood.

I take the rags from my ears as I stand, staring at the mess as Bu continues crying.

"You did it, Kailey. Are you okay?" Gunthreon asks as Philip stands over him, fixing his hands with a simple touch.

"This sucks. I think I'm going to throw up," I confess as I bend over, dry-heaving. "I'm never watching Bugs Bunny again, *ever.*" Fatigue overtakes me, and I sit beside Bu. Thanks to the remains of Bu's tears, I see that Kioto's collar is attached to a statue, and Bu says he didn't want to see Kioto get hurt.

"Gunth, I think my pendulum is lost forever," I say.

"Karma wills what she wills," he says as he comes and hugs me with his mended hands.

"Let's move it," says Philip.

No need to tell me twice. We all hike it to the entrance and barely make it out the door before a powerful clamor emerges from inside. I freeze. The ceetchans are still waiting for us outside, hovering near the doors, chattering to themselves nervously.

Gunthreon grabs my hand and drags me out of the shadow of the tower and into the sunlight, and as I turn around, I see throngs of grebles, filing out in army mode, with a tall man in a hooded cloak following behind. Instantly, the ceetchans start attacking the grebles' feet. Behind them, I see the robed man staring at me, at precisely the same time I feel a dark and menacing wave of energy approaching me. His eyes are questioning for a brief moment, and I turn to Gunthreon, whose eyes are already fixated on the figure.

"Devoten," he says.

Instantly, we're thrown into my apartment, and I run to the window. Gunthreon sees my distress. "They won't follow," he says, "so we're safe for now. They will not all enter this realm at once. At least, we hope."

I throw myself on my couch and scream into the pillows— one long, continuous, eardrum-blasting scream.

Chapter 16

Odd
○Ȝ

Morning comes all too quickly, and I wake up with the worst sore throat I have ever experienced. I reach for pain pills, but end up placing them back on the shelf, knowing that it won't help me.

Last night, as I freaked out over what had just happened, my friends agreed to a sleepover. This morning, I find them dispersed throughout my apartment on makeshift beds: couch cushion mattresses, pillows made of folded sheets, and Bu is lying on several bath towels—he didn't want to dirty my carpet. Philip even stayed, claiming Karen worked nights, and she wouldn't even know he was gone.

Everyone looks haggard and exhausted, so I decide to cook breakfast for everyone, considering I definitely have enough to feed an army—maybe even enough for a greble-sized appetite.

I call off work, and as I rummage through my pantry, both Gunthreon and Philip convince Bu that a shower will not melt him, and he takes a special liking to the yellow rubber duck I keep in the bath. His body stays hunched because of his size, but he does very well cleaning himself up. He even lets me spray him with some Coconut Dream body spray. It takes three towels to dry him, and he still stinks, but it's much more tolerable. The idea of hanging a tree-shaped car freshener around his neck is tempting.

I open my fridge, grabbing the bacon, and notice it feels a bit warmer than it should be and make a mental note to call my landlord. After a dozen eggs benedicts (Bu loved them), the pound of bacon, some chocolate-glazed donuts, three dog biscuits and some strong coffee—and tea—we all feel a bit human again—well, except of course for Bu, who rummages through my pantry, looking for something else to eat. (Another note to self: Check

Bu's pockets before he leaves. I see him eyeing my last three Oreos.)

"Thanks for staying last night," I say to the three of them. "I get chicken when I'm alone sometimes." I grab my throat and wince from the pain. Gunthreon and Philip exchange a glance, and then Philip lays his hands gently on my throat, and closes his eyes. The pain immediately disappears and I think back to the meeple and the decapitation, which *I* inflicted. "I did this to myself, didn't I?"

Philip nods. He stands and kisses me on my head and says, "*You* are a gentle soul, but unfortunately, karma is a boastful bitch."

"That sucks," I say, thinking that kind of language shouldn't be coming from his mouth.

"It was unavoidable. Don't be discouraged, Kailey," says Philip. "Truth be told, you will undoubtedly feel that your power is fickle, but karma has its own plan. Times like these are just...setbacks." He smiles sympathetically at me.

"Well, good thing I have you," I state, shyly.

With a deep sigh, Gunthreon adds, "I have a feeling that yesterday was not the worst of it."

"So gloom and doom, as always." Philip picks at the last piece of bacon. "I'm going home to sleep in my own bed, under my *Transformers* sheets," he adds with a sassy smile, "before my mom discovers I'm missing. I'll see you all later. Kailey, if you need me, just yelp." He leaves, and I hear his own door open and close.

"Are you sure you'll be fine today by yourself?" asks Gunthreon. "I can have my driver come and give you a ride to my place." I can see Gunthreon is really worried about me.

"Thanks, G, but I'll be okay, I think."

"Next lesson is meditation," he says. "You could ask your mother for pointers, too. She relies on it heavily, since she cannot take any pain medications. Come see me this weekend. Until next time."

He leaves with a bow. As I peek out the window, I see his driver ready and waiting. *Strange. He never made any calls.*

CR

"Let me guess. You're still 'sick.'" Amber can't hide the sarcasm.

"I need to see you sometime soon, just to talk and stuff," I say. "What are you doing tonight?"

"Well, since you asked, Russell and I are going out to eat tonight, and we were thinking of asking some people to go with us."

"Don't you ever cook dinner, Amber?" This is rhetorical on my part.

"Why should I, when so many other people are perfecting it? I just got a manicure anyway. I'd hate to chip one of these beauties washing dishes." I picture her staring at her French-manicured nails and roll my eyes for my own sake.

"You do the cooking," I say, "and what do you think Russell is for? The washing!"

"Oh, girlfriend, Russell is for plenty more than that." She giggles that naughty laugh of hers. "We were planning on Italian. Does that sound good to you, or were you planning on whipping up some eggplant parmesan and tiramisu for yourself tonight?"

A beautiful plate of spinach and ricotta ravioli bathing in a sage brown butter sauce appears before my eyes, and I feel myself salivating. "Okay, I'll take the plunge. Just know it may be the ugliest dive you've ever seen. Who else is going?"

"Oh, how about I surprise you? Let's just say it's a friend of Russell's from the recreation center. They run together, or something stupid like that." She's smiling. Fear of the unknown creeps upon me, but I gather courage. After cutting off a meeple's head, I can do a fix-up, a la Amber.

117

"What have I got to lose? Okay, hook me up. Guess I need some kind of action, right?" She has absolutely no idea the kind of "action" I've had lately.

"Wow," Amber stammers, evidently surprised by my reaction. "We'll come pick you up about six." The phone clicks without a goodbye, and I realize she didn't want me wiggling out of this one somehow.

With a couple of hours yet before the love couple arrives, I decide to take Kioto for a quick walk. She loves watching the squirrels romp around on the many maple trees at the park, so that's where we'll head. I show Kioto her leash and immediately, her tail starts wagging. "Walk?" She barks one loud "Hell yes" at me and we walk out my apartment door.

She stretches out her legs, her head scanning everywhere, looking for those sly squirrels. As we get closer, I see a recognizable figure standing amongst the kids at the playground. I decide to walk along a trail of nearby trees so I'm not noticed.

"You are so weird! Why don't you just play like everyone else?" squawks a small-framed girl with black ponytails and a Hello Kitty T-shirt, standing hands-on-hips, facing Philip.

"Maybe if you would actually think before you start running around like chickens with no plan of action, I could help formulate a wonderful strategy," proclaims Philip, aggravated. I hope he doesn't do something stupid.

"Weirdo!" The girl storms away toward her mother, and Philip turns to me. I wander on over to him.

He looks especially forlorn, and it's not pretty on him. "I don't think this whole seven-year-old thing is doing you any good," I say as I look to the girl and her mother. "Karen at home?"

His eyes agree with me before he even speaks. "I think I am finally bored of this seven-year-old life, especially when most are so absentminded and *cannot even focus*!" He says this last part loudly toward the little black-haired bully.

"Ladimer, you have so much to offer, but it's not for grade school." I smile at him.

"Thanks." He slowly slips his hand in mine, fitting perfectly, as we walk home together in silence.

Chapter 17

Surprised
CR

I pretty myself up, wearing dark form-fitting jeans and a cute short-sleeved cashmere sweater. I sit and wait like a nervous schoolgirl for Amber. Finally, around half past six—Russell seems to be a good influence over Amber's tardiness—my door buzzer screams, my heart beating faster than I thought possible. I let Amber up, and as she enters, I hold my breath and fear for my neck, for a sexy little goth vampire has crossed the threshold of my home. She's got on a tight little black number, accessorized with a long, black chain necklace disappearing into Neverland. Her velvet corset dress is practically painted onto her torso, and is tied with a deep red bow, begging to be untied as she bends over, welcoming Kioto first.

She loves dogs as much as I do, but not dog *hair*, hence the Amber-donated lint brush in the front closet. Amber and Kioto say their warm hellos as she bends over; her blond hair falling softly over her shoulders and her necklace spilling from her chest, revealing the silver-heart BFF charm I gave her when we were in high school. She quickly shoves it back into her corset, finally acknowledging me with a nod.

"Oh, thanks," I say. "Don't you want to rub noses with me or scratch behind *my* ears? No, wait, you might drain me with your fangs."

"Don't be jealous," teases Amber. "Maybe you can get some of that yourself later, after we all have dinner."

My deadly stare is ignored. "You better not embarrass me tonight," I warn her. "Who's the mystery man?"

"You'll see. He's cool, and very cute. Russell likes him, too. He's the perfect gentleman."

"Since you guys are in love with him, I guess we'll just arrange our wedding plans tonight, huh?" I say.

We both check the clock in sync and decide to go before the mystery guest decides to leave the restaurant before we show up.

Russell waits for us like a good chauffeur, and I give him a peck on the cheek. "My, my, Russell. You smell good," I purr. Amber hisses at me like a cat.

"I've heard you've been hanging out with my grandfather. Having fun?" Russell looks at me through his rearview mirror.

I don't know what to say at this point, because I don't know what Amber is privy to. She shows no interest as she fixes her makeup. I pause longer than I should, trying to come up with something smart. "Uhh, yes. He's a great cook, and I'm learning so much from him." I applaud myself for the fast thinking, but then I'm crushed as Amber gives me the "Yeah, whatever" face. She turns up the music, and I sink back in my seat, wrinkling my newly steamed sweater. As Russell sees my look of contemplation, he shakes his head for my eyes only.

We arrive at La Scarola and as we enter, I slip a peek at my armpits, making sure I don't have any wet marks, because it feels like I sweated at least a pint on the car ride. The maitre d' informs us that one guest has already been seated, and he proceeds to take us to our table. I glance back at the front door, thinking it's only a sprint away, and maybe nobody would even notice I'm gone, but my chance is lost as we arrive at our table. Our mystery guest sits facing us, and as I look up, I can't help but laugh.

"Nice to see you again, Conner," I say. "Small world, ain't it?"

"What? How do you know him?" Amber seems perturbed that I've pulled one over on her, by no action on my part.

"I know Cherry, too, don't I?" He nods.

He looks adorable this evening, and when he stands to push in my chair for me, he briefly touches my shoulder. I feel a static shock and jump.

"Sorry." He laughs, quietly, a hint of the Irish brogue peeking through.

Amber frowns. "What fun is a blind date when you're not blind?!" she says, angrily. I squeeze her hand. "You never even told me that you met someone—a male—by yourself." I let go of her hand both because I feel she is pushing her limits, but speaks the truth.

"Let's check out these menus," I suggest, "I'm starving."

After a quick rundown on who's ordering what, we nibble on fresh bread dipped in olive oil and parmesan. Dinner arrives after a brief wait, we enjoy the food slowly, and it's wonderful, both in the sense of taste *and tasteful* conversation, which ranges from breakfast cereals to world peace. I drink two glasses of wine, and convinced that it's not the taste I'm after, I don't order another. The wine does, however, affect my bladder, so Amber and I excuse ourselves and take a trip to the ladies' room.

"So, it seems like you two are really hitting it off, huh?" Amber makes kissy faces to herself in the mirror. "He's gorgeous, isn't he? And that accent," she says. "Kailey, really, how do you know Conner?" She says this with a hint of seriousness in her voice.

"I met him at the park," I reply. "We were both walking our dogs."

"Oh, okay. Whatever."

"I think I like him, but I'm not rushing anything." My lipstick needs a touch-up, so I reach blindly into my purse, searching for a tube.

"No need to wait for anything, Kailey. Learn to take what you want," Amber babbles as she examines herself for panty-lines.

A bit of frustration makes my mouth speak without thinking. "You tell that to your boyfriends?" I stand perfectly still, tube in hand, as I wait for the backslap.

But it never comes. Instead, Amber takes a deep breath and says, "You know I need to get myself some of that, especially these days." Amber eyes my hand. I've accidentally grabbed my travel pepper spray.

"Hey, you know me," I say. "I have about three of these at home, so please, take this one."

She grabs it, reads the label, and throws it in her purse. "Thanks, Kailey. I really appreciate that. Let's go back and give those boys their dessert." I smack her on the arm, and as we're leaving, I sneak a kissy face at myself in the mirror. I can't help it—she's a bad influence.

Before we reach the table she adds, "Don't ever judge my taste in men again. I've found the perfect one." Without waiting for a reply, she allows Russell to pull out her seat and scoot her in.

When the waiter comes back, I order what I knew well ahead of time would be my dessert: "Can I have the almond dark chocolate tartufo with the homemade candied lemon-peel biscotti?" I grin ear-to-ear as I talk.

"Um, sorry, miss, but that table over there just got the last tartufo dish," jabbers the waiter. "Would you like to try the blueberry cream cake with the orange sorbet instead, maybe?"

Saddened, I decide to peruse the dessert menu once again. But Conner then calls the waiter over, leans toward him, and whispers something in his ear. A quizzical look comes over the waiter's face, and suddenly, he disappears into the kitchen. Then he returns and exchanges glances with Conner before he explains to me that there is indeed one tartufo order left, and he'd be glad to serve it to me. I, of course, accept.

I then lean into Conner, basking in the good feelings flowing from him, and whisper, "What did you say to him?" I breathe in his cologne, and then blush as he notices.

"Oh, I used to work in a kitchen. The workers always save a bit of each dessert for themselves. I asked him nicely to let you have one."

"Well, thank you. I owe you." I wink a little wink at him, his grin widening.

When I finish, I feel so bloated, but it was all wonderful going down. "I vote we are done for the evening," I say, feeling the food coma about to hit. "I can't put another thing in my mouth."

Amber smirks at me and raises her eyebrows, which immediately causes me to scowl at her as she mouths, "I can."

Conner pats his own belly. "Yeah, me too." Both boys miss Amber's distasteful gesture.

Russell and Amber are playing footsie under the table, so I kick them. Amber pouts, and chirps, "Geez! Okay, yes. We are, too. Let's settle up and get you home."

Russell isn't quick enough as Conner leans in and swiftly grabs the black, padded envelope and sticks a gold card in it. Amber's eyes rise at the sight of gold. "I got this one," he states.

"No, here, let me add to it," I insist, "or at least give the tip." But he shoves my hand away.

"Let the man be a gentleman," Amber says. "Thank you, Conner, for your wonderful generosity." Amber smiles at him, her breasts taunting him.

Suddenly, I feel a slithering sensation from her that stirs my nerves a bit, catching me off guard and for I cannot believe what she's feeling: jealousy. I can't believe the position I'm in. Amber is jealous of *me*.

"Not a problem. Please let me perform yet another courtesy and drive Kailey home," Conner says. "You two need to get home quickly." He stands up as the waiter approaches to take the envelope.

Amber stands up and pulls me aside as Russell and Conner converse. "Kailey, I know how you are with men." I open my mouth to defend myself, and then decide not to, because she damn well knows me that well. "Timid and stuff," she whispers. "Especially after what happened to you. Maybe he's not for you. We will take you home. You don't have to be scared. I can spend the night if you like."

"But see, that's just it, I'm not. Not this time." It's true. I feel quite comfortable with Conner, and though I want to second-guess myself, I don't. "You brought me here to set me up, and look. You were successful. He can take me home."

Her righteous smile gives me the satisfaction that maybe she'll settle on what I'm feeding her. "Fine, if you say so," she says. She stares at me oddly, either holding in some remark glorifying her accomplishment at setting me up or fighting her inward struggle between stealing her best friend's new prospect and attacking Russell once they get in their SUV. But then, she turns back to Russell, tossing a sidelong glance at me before picking up her purse.

We all exchange our goodbyes and head to our cars. I know before we even walk to it that Conner's is the huge black Hummer looming before us. "Oooh, cool. I've never been in one of these babies," I say. "You must work for the gas alone."

"It's worth it when everyone on the highway gets out of your way." Conner smiles at his car like a husband should smile at his cherished wife.

We get in, and it's quite the smooth ride. The smell of his cologne lingers, along with the sweet aroma of vanilla. "Do you let your dog in this?"

"Yes, of course I do. She's well-behaved and pretty much lies down the whole time."

125

"You do have that certain power over dogs, don't you?" I say. "Maybe others, too?" He doesn't comment, which scores him points on my test.

He just smiles, and we drive home, listening to some awesome music. He's got some classical, and some *good* eighties, and some fifties and sixties, which I actually adore. The last song we hear is "Johnny Be Good." Sweet smells, good music, and a full belly create an absolutely enjoyable combination, making me smile at absolutely nothing.

Lightning suddenly flashes in the sky, startling both of us, making us laugh melodiously.

The car pulls over to my curb, and my happiness is suddenly replaced with fear of the unknown. I don't know whether to give him a kiss or a nice "Thanks." But before I have time to *really* get over-the-top anxious, though, he leans over, practically brushing his lips across my ear, and whispers softly.

The next few seconds flash by so fast, I don't know what hits me. I hear something that's not English as he then leans into me firmly with a kiss, catching me totally off guard. I know that he expressed his attraction to me, but I don't know how I know it. The feeling of vulnerability sneaks up quickly, and we are suddenly both standing in a slightly foggy Renhala.

Chapter 18

Defensive
ରୋ

"**W**hoa!" exclaims Conner.

I grab my monk's spade off my back, without even a second's hesitation, but as we stand face-to-face, I see that Conner has in his hand a short, quick kind of sword, runes engraved all over the blade.

The terrain around us screams Gernwood, as a few particularly nasty puddles bubble with goo.

"How did you do that so quickly, Kailey?" He sees me staring at the weapon. "I had to pull my weapon in defense," he states, slowly. "Please, put yours away."

"What the hell did you whisper to me?" I shout. "What are you—or who sent you, I should say?" I don't budge as I filter his words and the idea that I possibly just brought us to Renhala. "I didn't bring us here," I retort, snotty.

"Actually, yes. You did," he says. "I've traveled before, and know when I do it. And I am most certainly not going to voluntarily bring us here, of all places. You, are evidently new to this, so, Kailey, please put the weapon away," he says. "I'm putting *my* weapon away. I mean you no harm." Conner again speaks some language I cannot recognize, and I put my monk's spade on my back, slowly. Somehow I know he will not hurt me.

"What are you?" I stand my ground, but at the same time, struggle not to run to him on account of the scary noises approaching from behind me. They sound far from human.

Conner sees whatever is behind me and appears quite nervous. "I'm bringing us back home. Why you chose this area specifically, I do not know."

In a blink, we're standing outside his Hummer.

"You carried us into some dark territory, Kailey," Conner says. "Don't do that again."

"What do you expect when you're playing mind games with me?" I argue. "Did you not know I'm karmelean? If you mess with me, I will return the favor graciously. Whoever sent you should do their research first!"

He nods, but for what reason I do not know. "I apologize. And nobody *sent* me. Why would you think that?" he asks. "I like you, and I'm drawn to you. I only wanted you to know, and felt that you thought the same of me. I did take advantage with that kiss, and feel ashamed of what I did, so please forgive me." He smiles. "But it's nice to know we can both be open about Renhala."

My stance is one of kung fu, or in actuality more like tai chi, and not yet forgiving. "I accept your apology, on one condition," I announce. "Tell me what you are."

A sigh escapes his perfect lips, and he hunches his shoulders as rain starts to fall from the sky. "I am known as a soulspeaker. There exists an ancient form of communication used long before any languages evolved, and I possess the ability to speak it. I am able to speak to another's soul in a way that they know my true intent—the truth—in my mind, if you will. I can speak truth directly to your soul. There. Yeah, and the 'Irish' accent..." He then shakes his head no. "Wasn't born in Ireland."

"That makes perfect sense now. Yes, thank you." I try to seem all together and matter-of-fact, but really, I'm shaking in my boots. I quickly gather myself and my purse in hightail fashion. I hold my purse against my chest, as though he can hear my heart beating as frantically as it is. "Thank you for everything tonight," I say, "and if it's okay with you, I'm going to go in now and retire for the evening. Good day to you."

He looks like a heartbroken teenager standing before me, solemnness lingers like a weight in the air. The rain begins to fall heavily over us, but I can still feel both his emotion of regret, and embarrassment.

He speaks, but very sadly: "I totally understand. And again I'm sorry for my actions. That's all I can say." He then says it in soulspeak.

I move toward him, point at him to stand still, and say, "Stay." I cannot help but lean in and give him a quick peck on the cheek, despite his actions this evening. "This would have sufficed," I say. "Conner, I'll see you again soon. Bye." I turn and walk toward my building. He waits until I have unlocked the main door and stepped inside, then slowly drives away.

I run up the stairs to my apartment as fast as my legs will carry me and trip over Bu, who sits in the dark, asleep.

"Damn, Bu!" I almost regurgitate my fantastic dinner and dessert with all the adrenaline pumping through my veins.

"Bu sorry! Bu always messes up!" The tears start to form, but I immediately hug him and tell him I'm sorry, explaining I was just startled. I invite him in and let him sleep on the floor, since the couch is too small for him. He gets all my extra blankets *and* Kioto, who snuggles up next to him. I kiss them both goodnight above the nose and turn in for the evening. I figure maybe I'll actually sleep, knowing that they're both in the living room, guarding me.

I attempt it, but Conner, with all his dangerous cuteness, makes my consciousness scream, "Danger!" I wonder if maybe I've actually been in a coma since the assault. Maybe I'm dreaming this all up? But when I pinch my arm, I know damn well I'm not.

Gunthreon's comment about meditation pops into my head, so I do my best at what I think is meditation, and just relax and put my mind to rest. It must eventually work, because when I open my eyes, the early morning sun is peeking through my bedroom curtains, and I hear Bu playing with my television. I smell something that resembles food, but it doesn't smell very appetizing. My body tells me to get up, so I do.

"Bu made you breakfast, Kailey!" Bu says when I emerge from my room. "Bu cooked these for you. Just sit." I see the empty container of dog treats and a Cool Whip container on the counter. I pray that I do not have to eat this to make Bu happy. He lays out a plate in front of me, and I smile my best, holding back the gag begging to be freed. As he turns around, Kioto is at my arm, sniffing toward my dish. I quickly scoop a few biscuits up and shove them into her mouth. She walks away into the bedroom and I can hear her eating the mess.

Bu turns around right after I smear a bit of Cool Whip near my mouth.

"Yum, Bu. Thanks so much," I say. "I have to go take a shower now. You go ahead and eat the rest, because that filled me up." He accepts this and sits at the table and eats the remainder of the food.

The hot water runs over my body as I decide what to do today before I see my mom this evening. *Will my life ever go back to normal? Wait—was it ever normal to begin?* I lean against the wall and cry quietly, which turns into laughter, a rich laughter that drowns the self-pity and cleanses, renewing me and making one more day livable.

Chapter 19

Secret
☙

I decide I might as well chalk off a whole week of vacation time. I feel I have to do something for myself today, and just run from all the madness. I need to do something relaxing, and not just meditation—something splurge-worthy. A spa day! Only problem is that a whole day at the spa is not for doing alone. Amber is already at work, for sure. I know one other person I'd love to have join me.

"I have a plan, and you cannot say no to it today," I say to my mom over the phone. I'm lucky to have some gift certificates I've not had time to use, because my mom never lets me pay for anything, despite her low supply of cash. "How does a luxuriously relaxing day at Spa de Serenite sound?"

She doesn't even hesitate before she replies: "Let's meet there at noon. You'll want to call ahead of time and make sure they have two openings. Love you. Bye."

I'm left sitting with the phone to my ear and cannot believe she agreed so easily. Mom doesn't usually do spas. *Wow, this day might end up being good.* The phone rings while it's still in my hand, and I'm convinced it's her changing her mind already.

I push the talk button. "Don't tell me no now, because there's no excuse."

"My, my, Conner must be playing hard to get."

"Shut up, Amber," I retort.

"No need to be rude," responds Amber. "I was actually calling to tell you about last night."

"Yeah? Some new sexual position you want to enlighten me with?"

"Umm no, actually," she says. "After we left the restaurant and got to my place, me and Russell got out of the car and starting walking to the door when two guys tried mugging us. I used the pepper spray on both of them! Can you believe that? Little ol' me! Russell tied them both up with a neighbor's dog cable while I called nine-one-one. The cops came and took them away. I might be on TV, we'll see. See what happens when you fight back?" There's a long pause.

"Sorry, Kailey. I just meant that women aren't as weak as some men try to make them feel. I didn't exactly mean anything about what happened to you."

My knowledge of her past relationships keeps me from being offended. "Karma keeps me going," I tell her. "You know it all comes back in the end."

Under her breath, I hear, "Let's hope not."

I really don't understand her, but what else is new? "Talk to you later, Amber."

"*Adios.*"

The thought that maybe this karma thing I do is good keeps swimming in my head. She offered her protection, and I, in turn, provided it to her. If my abilities can do good things like this for Amber, I think I'll keep them.

I call the spa, and they have two spaces—thank goodness. Just as I hang up, my phone rings again. I don't recognize the number, so I just let it ring, and if they want, they can leave me a message. My thoughts return to my mom and how she must be so tired.

I call my voicemail, and the voice that I hear is so sorrowful, yet seductive—a dangerous combination. It's Conner. Amber must have given him my number, since it's unlisted. He again apologizes and I think about how long I'll let it go on. I *do* like him. I have to admit, I may have overreacted to an innocent gesture.

He leaves his number, and I write it down, thinking about when I should return the call. Maybe I will tomorrow. I'm spending today with my mom, and that's a good enough excuse not to call now.

After getting myself lazily dressed and dragging myself to Spa de Serenite by bus, I patiently await my mom's arrival. Finally, she pulls up, and I watch her from inside as she gets out of her car. It always takes her a long time to get out, and I wince as I see *her* wincing. It's sad seeing someone you love hurting, even if you don't understand their pain.

She finally makes it in, and her beautiful smile lights up the room. That's my mom. I stare at her and see she actually wore a short-sleeve shirt, revealing all her "Frankenstein" scars, as I call them, from dialysis and numerous surgeries. She is so strong, because there is no way I'd ever knowingly show those scars. After my attack, I hid mine the best I could.

"I'm ready for some pampering," she tells the girl at the counter. She then speaks quietly, and from her body language, I can tell she's trying to prepay with some cash. But I bested her this time. Ha!

She walks toward me with her pissed-off face, and I start laughing. "What's wrong, Mom?" I give her my "genuinely concerned" face. The punch in the arm she gives me in return is definitely going to leave a purple splotch. "Don't do that again," I say. "You may break your hand or something." I rub my arm when she's not paying attention.

We take our time changing into fluffy, white terry cloth robes, sipping on mango nectar, and eating apple slices with imported honey and manchego cheese. Ah, the life.

First, we get to do the sauna. You need to open up the pores to let all the good stuff in. We talk little. I only ask her my usual questions about how she's feeling and how her kidneys are doing. I know that, after her transplant four years ago, her body can reject

133

the new kidney at any time in her life, and we could end up back at square one. She gives me her usual, "I'm fine, stop worrying."

She also asks if Amber is doing all right, and I tell her, "That girl is messed up," which gets a snicker out of her.

Saunas are absolutely wonderful, until you get to the point where you start sweating so bad you feel you might faint. So I'm glad when the sauna is done, after which we are ushered to steel tables covered with towels. I sneak a peek at my mom, who looks horrified. Her eyes are glued to something directly above the tables, and the object hanging could indeed pass for an ancient torture device of some sort. But actually, it's a water dispenser, about the length of the average woman with hundreds of tiny holes. We are now to be scrubbed with a pumpkin exfoliant sugar scrub, then rinsed with the torture device.

Afterwards, we are given more fluids and another fancy-schmancy snack before our hot-stone massages. My mom and I sigh at the same time.

"Are you enjoying yourself, Mom?" I ask.

"I'm a little raw right now from that scrub, but I think I'll be okay," she says. "Was that sandpaper they used? Maybe four-hundred grit?" My rolling eyes seem to satisfy her. There's so much I need to say to her right now, but I know that I cannot start a crazy conversation like that in a spa. I'll wait until dinner.

They call us into two separate rooms, and I wave goodbye to her as she leaves for her pedicure. She flashes me our special sign as she disappears around the corner. The only light in my room is from the small candles placed strategically in two corners. The smell of lavender relaxes me, and I pick the mandarin orange oil for the massage.

My masseuse glides over my back with her magic fingers, and I cannot believe how heavenly it feels—so much, in fact, that I start to doze off. I fight it to the best of my abilities, but it's a losing battle.

CR

I wake to the sound of voices.

"I really hope you have some brilliant plan to stop them. They're becoming more than just nuisances." This voice is unfamiliar to me.

The closet I suddenly realize I am in is barely big enough for me to stand up in, and it stinks like compost. There are odd-looking metal and wooden objects strewn across the floor and I try to avoid stepping on them as I brace myself, trying to keep steady as to not move anything. I peek through the wooden doors, seeing only a seated individual's back to me, as I hold my towel up around me, asking myself how I ended up here. *Did that greble bring me? Did I travel here myself? No. I couldn't have.* I've never been here before.

"Oh, you wait and see. I have plenty up my sleeve, Tartarin. Don't you worry your pretty little self," states a male voice. I try to convince myself that maybe I am dreaming, but know from the evil feelings emanating from those speaking I am indeed, not. *Relax, Kailey—just breathe deeply and relax before you get yourself killed,* I think, *most likely by something painful.*

As I stand, balancing, the most horrible feeling of hatred and loathing hits me like a cannonball to the chest. I stagger a bit, and hold my breath as I nudge something that clinks near my feet. My head feels as though it might implode from the powerful vibrations that are firing off the individual seated outside the closet, repeatedly battering me. His energy is repulsive and I try wiping my skin, not wanting it to linger near my own. I try to shield myself, but it's as though *his* energy wants to devour *mine.*

"The armies are formed. Do you have your informant ready to strike?" The one named Tartarin is talking, but I can barely see him through the slit in the door. He sounds large.

"Don't worry about my informant. This will only work at the right moment, so do not rush things. If you do, you will regret it. We must cover much ground before," he says, then hesitates, "the releasing. Be patient, my friend. Everything must be in place."

"I will obey. After all, you are Devoten." I sense Tartarin leave.

This is where my bladder slightly gives in, and I can feel the wetness escaping. I feel no shame as I peek around the door behind Devoten's back. He is hunched over the table and seems downtrodden, his shoulders slumped. Slowly he turns toward the closet door, and I see a glimpse of his face and the blood-red tear streaming down it as his energy makes one final lunge at me.

☞

I am yanked back into my own reality by my mom shaking my shoulders. The masseuse is back in the corner of the room, staring at me like I've grown horns.

"Kailey! Kailey!"

"Stop already. You're gonna give me shaken baby syndrome or something," I say. I sit up on my own and realize my naked breasts are exposed to the world, so I cover myself up and discreetly wipe the pee off my leg.

My mom turns to the masseuse. "I'm sorry, hon. My daughter sometimes has fits. It's a medical condition." My mom is trying to reassure her that everything is fine. This must be bad.

"Whatever," stammers the masseuse, "but I know she disintegrated or something, because my hands just went right through her!" The poor girl looks like she may fall over the fence into hysterics. I grab my purse and pull out my smartphone and dial Gunthreon, but he doesn't answer. I then dial the numbers that I conveniently remember—must be the accountant in me—calling me this morning.

"I need your help. Do you know Spa de Serenite?" He agrees to rush over immediately.

My mom's energy churns in a way that I know she's inwardly questioning what the hell just happened, but she keeps all comments to herself. I tell her to console the girl as we wait for someone who can help. Conner arrives, and all the women fawn over him as he blushes, then spots me across the room in my robe. He smiles a crooked smile at me, forcing me to tighten my robe a bit. The manager allows me to escort him back to my massage room after a whisper in her ear assures her that he's no threat. Conner chats quietly with my masseuse, and she looks a bit calmer.

"I hope you enjoyed your massage," she comments as she eyes us questioningly before leaving the room.

"She'll be fine. I told her that ignoring what just happened would be in her best interest," Conner whispers. "Did you enjoy the massage?" His soulspeak accent is thick in his words, sexy. He stares at me *and* my robe, which seems to have loosened up a bit.

"Yeah, it was nice," I reply as my heart threatens to crawl up my throat. Suddenly, I remember my mom is standing here, too. My cheeks redden, and it doesn't take long for her to furrow her brow. My mom and Conner exchange glances, and I see a small bow from Conner toward my mom.

My mom bows slightly toward Conner. "Soulspeak. Wow, I haven't heard that in years," she says. And with that, she leaves the room, heading back toward her locker. "Kailey," I hear, "can you please meet me in the bathroom?"

"Yes, Mom. Be right there," I say, loud enough for her to hear me down the hall. I turn to Conner and sigh. "I really appreciate what you did for me and everything, but I have to leave," I say. "I have a lot to discuss with my mom right now."

"You do know you'll have to explain this to me, right? I'm at least owed that." His eyes are intense, and he seems too close to me, especially in my nakedness—underneath the robe and all.

"I'll call you tonight. Is that okay?" I don't make eye contact with him, instead pretending I am way too interested in my pedicure—anything to break the connection he's trying to make with those eyes of his.

"Okay. Go get dressed," he says. I leave quickly, grabbing my clothes and making sure my robe is fully wrapped around me.

I find my mom in a bathroom stall, throwing up her fancy-schmancy snacks. The sound weakens me, and I start crying.

"Kailey, don't cry. You know my nerves," she says. "I'll be fine. Just get me a wet paper towel." The wad of paper towels I give her is as big as my head, and she starts laughing. It makes me cry more. "Let's go back to your place where you can pack an overnight back," she says, "and then we'll go home and I'll make that dinner you've been wanting. Sound good?"

"Yes, Mom."

We eventually walk to my mom's car and I see the tail end of a black Hummer pull out of the parking lot.

My thoughts are haunted by the one red tear I witnessed, and I hope that my gut feeling is just bullshitting me right now. Otherwise, I fear we're in for some serious trouble.

Chapter 20

Quick
℘

I let my mom lead me to the kitchenette set and find myself just sitting, letting memories come flooding back of happy childhood days spent lounging and eating blueberry syrup-drenched pancakes shaped like Mickey Mouse decapitations. My mom always did her best to provide for me on her limited budget.

Suddenly, the doorbell rings, and in walks Amber.

"Hey girls!" She plops her purse on the ground and wanders into the kitchen. She kisses my mom on the cheek and says, "What can I help with?" She's wearing a low-cut halter top, some tight black jeans and four-inch espadrilles wedge shoes.

"What are you doing here?" escapes my mouth as I look at Amber, simply not aware we were having a guest. "And since when do you cook? And in an outfit like that?" I say, a bit sarcastically.

"And when did you turn into such a bitch?" she snarls back, walking to stand directly in front of me.

My mom suddenly walks between us. "Hold up girls! I invited Amber earlier this week, after you suggested dinner, Kailey. She's our guest, and I think she looks cute! Where did you get those awesome shoes, anyway?" my mom says, looking at Amber's platformed feet.

I sigh from the loss of opportunity, again, to speak to my mother about Renhala. Amber frowns, evidently mistaking my sigh for the disgust of her company, because she storms toward her purse and then the door. "I'm outta here," she yaps. "I'll go find someone who wants me there."

"Amber!" my mom yells as Amber slams the front door. Then my mom turns to me.

"What?" I say, as she walks toward the stove and continues cooking, without saying one word to me. I grab the newspaper on the table and read the personals.

A half hour goes by and I inhale as I smell the lemon Worcestershire sauce, then get a whiff of the godly Dijon potatoes baking in the oven. I shake my head, forcing myself back to reality—to the fact that I have to start *the* conversation with my mom.

But she gets there first: "Kailey, do you want to start, or shall I?"

"The food's done already?" I know it's not, but I'm trying to buy some kind of time to make up my mind what to do. *What the heck, just dive in, Kailey. That's the best policy.* "Okay, Mom. Can you come sit, or do you have to babysit the food?"

She jumps right in as she sits, placing a kitchen towel in her lap. "Well, I must tell you that Gunthreon is quite impressed with you and your abilities," she says. "He says you're a natural, but still need some practice, especially with traveling. I totally agree, especially after today's little episode." She raises her eyebrows at me, then continues. "Renhala can be so dangerous. You must have a purpose, and go in and get out fast. I do somewhat blame him, though." As she goes on and on, I sit, my jaw hanging down. "He's your teacher, and you've only been to Bu's Renhala. There are other places, you know, good places. Places you could mistake for heaven."

She seems dreamy, and I feel she's imagining some whimsical land of puffy clouds and cream-soda rivers. She smiles as she looks out the window toward a concrete wall.

"What the hell?!?" I exclaim suddenly. "Why did I have to find out the way I did? Why did you never tell me about any of this?"

She sighs deep. "I wanted you to have a normal life, Kailey," she says, looking at me. "The life I have lived has been so hard, and I tried to shelter you from the things I have had to do. Did you not live a happy life? Did you ever have to worry about your mother having her head chewed off by a spirithound?"

"Yes, I know you did your best. It's just so hard to take everything in—especially knowing the one person I trusted the most kept such important things from me." I hesitate. "So you know my 'powers,' right?"

"I know your powers. I've always known them." Her eyes tear up. "You've always been such a sensitive girl, but *now*, given your full access to them, it's absolutely wonderful," she says, taking my hands in hers. "Since you were born, I always had an inkling you were something extraordinary."

"Only an inkling, eh?" Her remark gets a faint smile from the corner of my mouth. "I'm your daughter. You're supposed to feel, without a doubt, that I am infinitely extraordinary. Now what makes *you* special?" I smile, squeezing her hands.

She sits motionless for a bit, looking as though she is gathering strength. Just when I'm going to ask her the question again, there is movement. It's almost as though a thin layer of film covers everything in her apartment, and she's no longer in her seat.

Suddenly, there are feathers and polyester stuffing and wood splinters everywhere as I look toward what I think is still her. One couch is torn to shreds, along with the pillows, as well as two of those portable "TV dinner" tables.

Then, she's more solid, sitting again in her chair, holding about three of my hairs from my head in her one hand and a long, elegant blade in the other. My mouth might as well collect flies.

"They call me Quicksilver. This is what I can do."

"You get that, and I get karma?" I wail. "That is so not fair! That is *soooo* cool!"

141

"Kailey, you have to understand something," my mom says, looking concerned. "Most of our powers must be kept secret—used only for helping those in need and making both our realms safe. You, on the other hand, can do something that people will believe without discovery threatening our lives. You can affect everyday life for far more than I can. All I can do is fight fast. You let all creatures know the golden rule is real. You change the world in a way that I cannot. See, your ability to feel others' energies doesn't make you crazy. It makes you a karmelean; it makes you *special*."

"Well, I don't like being special if it means putting myself in comprising positions, like Devoten's closet."

"*What?*"

"Yeah, that's where I ended up today, briefly. He spoke of 'the releasing.' Do you know what that is? It sounded very wrong to me."

"Did he see you?" I shake my head. Her strength seems drained after her little show, and her wrinkles are suddenly deep. "One thing I ask is that you keep your experience at the spa today to yourself for the time being. I need to roll it over in my head before anyone else knows, especially anything about a 'releasing,' whatever the hell that is. Please. It's very important you don't intrude on someone as dangerous as Devoten. Do you understand?"

I agree with a nod, even though I want to run and share with Gunthreon.

Changing the subject seems a necessity, so I say, "Guess Helping Hands could use my help, as a karmelean. You think?"

She looks confused, then says, "Yes! Maybe you're the answer. You have *no idea* what you are capable of. Believe in yourself, but believe equally in the need to play things smart and safe."

"Is it possible that I can just, maybe, inherit some of what you just did? I am, after all, your *extraordinary* daughter." I know I'm reaching.

She says, "I *have* witnessed a sort of passing of powers, but that always ends in tragedy, so let's not go there. And believe me, it takes a strong person to be me, I will openly admit this. Do you realize why?"

I shrug.

"All I've done in my life is fight. That's what I found I was best at, and so I do it. All those 'odd jobs' I do? It's not painting, or giving advice, but instead protecting and preventing. There's really bad stuff happening now, in both realms, and I have sworn to do what I can for Neda. But what does this oath give me?" She raises her arms to reveal her scars. "This is what karma gave me: health issues." My scowl only makes her shake her head. "I've learned to live with the lessons I've learned, but have chosen with my own free will to keep punishing myself. I am so very tired, running from the inevitable. But I cannot live any other way. To me, there's no escape. Just when I think there's a possibility for freedom, I am yanked back." I don't know what to say, so I sit, staring forward at her.

She stands, staring at her furniture and says, "I was actually planning on redecorating, anyway. I just got a head's start!"

I gaze at her and say, in a saddened tone, "Mom, I love you more than anything in this world." I look down at my hands. "Gunthreon has spoken to me, about your needed...freedom." The clock timer on the oven goes off loudly, drowning my sentence.

"Dinner is ready!" My mom gets up and moves to the kitchen with cheetah speed and starts piling the food on our plates. "Can you get our drinks and napkins, Kailey? The conversation can wait until after we eat."

My stomach rumbles, and I know I must eat despite my shaky insides. I dig my fork and knife into the steak Diane, realizing the meat is so tender that I don't even need the knife, but can barely gather the strength to bring it to my mouth. The potatoes are cooked perfectly, both sweet and spicy at the same time, with a wonderful caramelized, crunchy skin. The corn is perfect, slathered in salty garlic butter and dressed in fresh parsley my mom has sprinkled throughout. It's a meal made with love—an ingredient my mom always has plenty of on hand, and I can barely eat four mouthfuls.

As my mother finishes and rises to bring the dishes to the sink, I lay my fork on my plate and let one tear drop into my potatoes as I watch my mother wash a casserole dish. Deep in thought, she hums softly to herself, something I always thought was lame, until now. "Kailey, you need to eat," she says with her back to me. "I'll pack Amber up a doggie bag, and if your food's not gone by then...no dessert." She turns and smiles at me.

I agree to eat, and force down the food, followed by a whole helping of ooey-gooey monkey bread, which I sniffed out, hiding in the microwave. After all dishes are washed, we sit on the couch in front of the television and I lean on my mom as she scrolls through the channels. Within minutes, I'm out.

I sleep soundly until eight o'clock the next morning, and find myself covered with a blanket, still on the couch. I'd almost say my mom drugged me to avoid any further Renhala conversation, but I know that can't be possible. So I learn to accept that I was so comforted by home and a home-cooked meal from my momma that I was able to become that child again, and sleep with no thoughts of the monsters in my closet.

There's sausage in the fridge, and pancake mix in the cabinet, so I decide the least I can do is make my mom some breakfast.

She's usually up once the sausage browns, but not this time. I decide to let her sleep, because I'm sure her body can use it.

I sit and watch some bilingual Saturday-morning cartoons—when what I'm really craving is some politically incorrect *Tom and Jerry*—and decide that, after two hours, I have to wake her up.

As I approach her room, a scent drifts along my nose. I recognize it—the coppery scent of urine. Quickly, I open her door, and she's lying on the floor wrapped up in a drenched blanket like a taco. She mumbles something, and her eyes are open, but she doesn't see me. The inside of her mouth is black and blue, and her tongue is so swollen she barely has room even to open her mouth. She then passes out. There have been so many times I've had to take care of my mom when she got sick, but this is serious.

Chapter 21

Underestimated
☙

I call nine-one-one, fearing for the worst. Two paramedics arrive and inform me they're rushing her to Stroger Hospital, as she has no insurance. Unfortunately, Stroger Hospital is one of the scariest and craziest hospitals in the area; it's also the place I was born. Spend two minutes there, and you're likely to see five gunshot wounds, four domestic disputes, and a litter of injuries involving alcohol and crack. I ask if her normal specialists will see her there, and the EMTs just shrug their shoulders.

I agree to ride shotgun in the ambulance. I do not want my mom out of sight.

Upon arrival, our driver has to convince some bum to get up off the arrival dock, telling him he's not on stage at the Improv and that he should pull up his pants. What a beautiful start to what I'm sure will be a most wonderful stay.

They wheel my mom inside, where I cannot see her, and proceed to shoo me towards the outdated and depressing ER reception vestibule. Staff then gathers all her information from me. I make sure I only answer what is asked of me and don't give the nurses any lip, because they are some tough cookies.

An unknown doctor eventually finds me and informs me that, after examining my mom, he's going to run a gamut of tests to find out what happened. He also says she's awake now, but is still incoherent.

I find her in ER number six, babbling to herself. She stares at me as I approach, and yells something, angrily. My eyes tear as I feel the pain and sickness her body is exuding across the room.

As I lay my hands on her hand, my insides spasm and I become nauseous. My mom watches me carefully with hostile eyes as I close my own, and wish for simple relief for her—something to ease her pain. She doesn't deserve this.

I willingly touch her surrounding energy with my own, and begin to siphon it, carefully picking out the poison which has leeched into her energy from her body, and replacing it with my own clean energy. It takes a bit, for there is some resistance, but she once again feels renewed. I feel her body tremble slightly as I open my eyes, just before her tears fall from her eyes as she watches me. She shakes her head no once as her eyes begin to close, but before she goes totally under, I see a faint attempt to sign me our special signal. She's still in there.

By the look on her face and her wide-open mouth as she sleeps peacefully, I know she'll be in the ER for a while. The only thing I can do is pass the time by going for a walk.

I wonder what I may see today. Every day at Stroger Hospital is an adventure in itself. It's a resident psych major's dream come true. A few left turns take me to the nearest vending machine. *Junk, junk, one granola bar and junk.* I *should* eat the granola bar, but I go for the pork rinds, since there are several rows of them. Gotta keep the vending machine orderer happy, after all. It's my civic duty. Of course, I promise myself never to tell anyone I actually ate a bag of pork rinds from Stroger Hospital.

I turn the corner, shoving fried skin in my mouth, and notice a small man crouched near the waiting area, examining something under the nearest chair. His grin resembles a circus clown's exaggerated smile as he feeds some imaginary creature his last Flamin' Hot Cheeto. Several women are curled up in their chairs staring at nothing, while one delirious looking man actually spits in his hands, then proceeds to draw pictures of decapitated nurses on a hospital pamphlet.

The bathroom is not far from the waiting area, and I feel my bladder calling for help, so I enter, making sure I use my shirt sleeve as a barrier against the metal handle. The stalls seem empty as I peer for feet. I find one stall without several piles of toilet paper and unidentifiable liquid on the floor and take my seat after layering up the toilet seat with clean paper. Suddenly I hear whispering from the stall next to me.

"Quiet, quiet. They'll find me. Don't be scared, Sadie. They won't hurt you."

"Hello? Is everything all right in there?" I don't expect an answer, and don't really hope for one, either. I do my business as quickly as I can and wash my hands four times before I leave—and then use my hand sanitizer for safe measure. Just as the door closes, I hear, "They're only bunnies."

Visions of meeples flash into my head as I walk, and I shake to clear the heebie jeebies just as a particularly dirty man jumps in front of me, staring into my face. He whispers, "You have to let me use it, please!" His breath smells like fish and stale beer.

"I'm sorry. I don't know you." I turn and try to walk around him, but he's quick.

"You must! They know where I am and what I did to their daughter," he says. "Give me your blade, *now!*" His eyes do not stray from my back. I put my hand behind me and sure enough, feel the monk's spade, warm and affixed to me. It knows danger when it senses it. *Hey! He sees it.*

"No!" I shout, suddenly brave. "Get away now, or I will use this in a way where you'll never get to piss again." My glare frightens him, and he turns without another word and walks into the men's bathroom. I am officially insane on the Stroger scene as another crazy smiles and gives me the thumbs up, approving my actions.

Thoughts of Renhala dance before me as I twirl around, spotting the man with the Cheeto. Another glance down, and I see it now—a foggy form of a ceetchan cowering underneath, baring its teeth, evidently pregnant. The revelation of mistaking insanity for true sight smacks me upside my head. Somehow, these folks are in-between realms, and some poor creatures have also gotten stuck. I shoot the Cheeto man a look of craziness—I'm getting the hang of it—as I walk toward him, then look down under the chair, but the extremely scared ceetchan bares her fangs at me.

"It's okay, honey. I'm not going to hurt you," I coax. "Let me bring you home." She's kind of cute, with her big eyes; one is covered by a white patch of hair. I grab a handful of pig skins and coerce her out from underneath the chair. She wriggles out, and I feed her two of them. All the while, she watches me cautiously with her huge eyes, trying to fight her maternal instinct to feed the babies growing inside her. But once she seems comfortable with me, I grab her, close my eyes, and travel—just like that. I thought of Renhala, and needed to travel for the sake of this innocent creature, and I did it! I jump up and down in celebration before realizing where I landed, so I immediately put her down and attempt to travel out of Bu's land, back home.

But nothing happens.

I spin on my feet, taking in the scenery and start panicking as I hear footsteps and snarling approaching at a very quick speed from the forest. *The fear of no way out strangles me as the unknown approaches.* I freeze as the hideous half-man, half-dog creature emerges from the trees, grimy and famished, with its human, but sharp teeth bared at me. It stares as it examines its prey, calculatingly scoping me out and figuring the probability of me inflicting any damage when it attacks. It finishes its computations and suddenly lunges in the air toward me. Instead of letting myself become dinner, I stand my ground, gather courage, then grasp its savage, evil energy and pull with all my might, ripping the creature open as I tumble upon Stroger Hospital's floor, covered in black goo. *Black sludge.*

I stand, and as I assess my situation, several of those waiting to be admitted start applauding. A feeling of strength enters my being, and I allow myself one brief bow and then begin quickly walking to find my mother, smearing the goo as I hurry, trying to flick it off my body. I find my mom and her eyes are open.

"Mom, how are you feeling?"

She shrugs her shoulders. "Fine, I guess." Her face scrunches up as she sees the goop plastered across my clothes. Her eyes then widen, knowing what it is. She tries to sit up as a crisp white coat labeled M.D. enters and asks if I am Dena May's kin. After a nod from me, he then informs me that due to shift changes, he is my mother's new doctor for the next several hours.

"What did you find out?" I say.

"Well," he says as he eyes the sludge dripping off of me and onto the floor, "we tested your mother's blood and the results suggest total renal failure. But, strangely, we ran another set of tests and both of her kidneys are functioning, and functioning normal. We don't know how this is possible, but would like her to stay here for more tests."

My mom turns to me and there are now tears in her eyes. "No," she says.

"But Mom—"

"No!" she insists as she sits up straight. "I am discharging myself. Get me the papers."

"Ms. Rooke, I rather you stay," requests the doctor to my mom.

"I'm functioning normally, am I not? You cannot keep me here, legally." She gets up and starts dumping all her belongings out from the clear plastic bag they were stored in. "Get me the paperwork!" The doctor then leaves us.

"Mom!"

"Don't put me through the prodding and poking, Kailey, please. We both know it will get us nowhere," she says, slipping on her pants as she slips on goo. She says nothing, as though black sludge dripping from her daughter is a daily occurrence.

One prescription later—which we know is useless—and several agreements to watch her diet, she gets discharged. I promise my mom I'm going to disown her, or better yet drown her for not staying.

I dial Gunthreon's number on my cell, figuring I don't need to owe Conner any more favors. "Gunthreon, can we use your driver?"

"He'll be there in five minutes."

Three minutes is more like it. This time the driver actually gets out of the car to open the back door for my mom. He's huge, and I am amazed how he fits in the limo. His muscles ripple underneath his white, short-sleeved shirt as he offers his arm to her. "Hey, I never got that!" I squawk, furrowing my brow at him. I've never even seen the guy's legs.

"Fidello is an old friend of mine, aren't you?" my mom chuckles, giving him a great, big old bear hug. He just nods and smiles. He reminds me of a giant tree stump with two arms, which are also tree stumps, decorated with scrollwork tattoos. His dark skin shimmers in the sunlight as he picks my mom up off the ground in his hug. It is then I see his facial features clearly: broad nose, wide forehead, straight black hair, resembling one of Native American heritage. He then places her gently back on the ground.

Their friendliness bugs me in a jealous sort of way. "Well, take your old friend here home, because she's a pain in my ass," I say, crossing my arms. Fidello apparently thinks this is funny, and laughs a big, hearty, ear-splitting laugh. Then my mom chimes in, while I climb in and pout because there's some inside joke going on that I am not involved in. It happens a lot.

My mom is dropped off at her home, seemingly upbeat. She gets out of the car herself, brushing off Fidello, but before she leaves, she says to me, "If you see Gunthreon, tell him I said, 'Meadow's Edge.'" She waves farewell and runs faster than the wind to her front door, with still a bit of my energy clinging to her.

Chapter 22

Renewing
❧

When I get home, I see that Kioto has been well taken care of by a couple of friendly fellow travelers, namely Bu and Philip. It's nice to know they can make themselves comfortable in my residence while I'm away. I find Kioto's food and water bowl full, an empty microwave popcorn bag sitting on the counter, and *Willy Wonka & the Chocolate Factory* in my DVD player—oh, and a fern that has long been dead is now alive and thriving.

I take a long, hot shower to clean the black ooze that's caked on my skin and in my hair. Once I hit the couch, I'm out for the night.

❧

I decide to call Gunthreon first thing in the morning to ask if he'll at least come over for a chat. Within ten minutes, I see Gunthreon and Fidello pull up. Gunthreon waves to Philip's balcony.

Gunthreon makes it up the stairs slowly. "I still cannot believe you live across the hall from him," he says. "Talk about karma." He hugs me tightly. His hugs are getting better and better. "Talked to your mom. She's surprisingly in great spirits." I simply nod.

Gunthreon hands me a tin container as he enters my apartment. I open it and breathe the aromatics. "Tea!" I'm so excited, I rush him in and practically run to my kettle. Kioto greets him with a kiss on the hand and he firmly pats her on the back.

"Use it sparingly, please," he requests. "The Hymenaea protera tree is extinct from what I hear. Gone with the dinosaurs. Such a shame."

"No way! I'm drinking an extinct plant? That is so cool, as long as I don't suddenly have Greenpeace knocking on my door. Thank you, Gunthreon. It's fun having friends in high places."

"Oh, don't misjudge me. I have not always been the friend in high places. I've had my lows, too." I've never been one to judge people and their past, so I just nod, and he seems to understand that I won't ask. I expect he understands karma more than I do, and has most likely spent a lot of time making up for whatever he may have done in the past.

"This tea is just what I need," I state, "especially after the hospital. I always thought everyone there was crazy, but they just see the truth. They *really* see it. How come not everyone does?"

"It's because some people aren't as open as others. Lots of people lead sheltered lives and don't open their minds to what else might be out there."

The water in my kettle starts to boil slightly, and after I add the tea leaves, I drift into a comfort zone beyond belief. The scent is heaven. A glance at Kioto sprawled out on the floor with her ears relaxed and a dog smile on her face tells me she feels the effects, too.

"I can understand that. I guess maybe it's a blessing, though, in some ways, that not everyone knows what's going on. It could be chaotic," I assume. "That's what I wanted to ask you! Do those in Renhala all know of our realm? Or is it like here, where only some know?"

"It's like here," Gunthreon says. "Some know. And with most of those who do know, mothers protect their young, like in most species—well, except for that damn dodo bird. And a small minority travel often. I do believe, however, that some time everyone is going to need to know the truth. I feel a great disturbance in the air, plus Velopa's cretins are popping up *everywhere* in Abscondia. If the army isn't stopped, and it continues to grow in numbers, the general public will need their eyes opened. They'd have to be trained to fight." The look on Gunthreon's face is one of fear. "Let's pray it doesn't come to that," he says.

I pause before deciding to ask him another question, for fear I may betray my mom in some way. "Gunthreon, does 'the releasing' mean anything to you?"

Gunthreon's eyebrows scrunch and he responds, "No. Should it?"

"No, just wondering. I had a weird dream, that's all." He suddenly looks concerned. I then ask, "How 'bout 'Meadow's Edge'?" in hopes that Gunthreon's train of thought may switch tracks.

At the mention of this, I hear a faint noise from the hallway outside my door, and just as I do, Gunthreon jumps up faster than a kangaroo on amphetamines and opens my front door. Philip practically falls into my apartment.

He is thrown askew, but recovers quickly. "I was just coming over to borrow a cup of sugar," he proclaims.

"I'd say a cup of eavesdropping." I walk over and punch him in the arm. "Hey, want some tea?"

"And let that voodoo take over my mind? No way," says Philip. "I need to be on my toes with this one." A nod toward Gunthreon brings a smile to his mouth and evaporates any negative energy that may have been forming in the air.

"Well, in case you didn't *hear*, Ladimer, our karmelean friend here mentioned Meadow's Edge. Up for a trip?" Gunthreon has a sneaky, mischievous smile on his face—one which I haven't witnessed on him—and it makes me wonder what trouble this place might be. "It's actually quite a coincidence, isn't it? Having to speak with Hamm and all?"

"I thought 'coincidence' wasn't in your vocabulary?" I say to Gunthreon with a smirk.

Philip laughs loudly as Gunthreon puts his hands on his hips. "She got you on that one. And oh yeah, you know I'm up for the trip," says Philip, with a grin that makes me straight-out shiver.

Before I even have time to bring the teacup to my lips, we travel. I sincerely hope not to find my favorite cup in shards back at my apartment. So much for my Sunday, day of rest.

❧

The ground we arrive on is rocks, rocks and more rocks— just a great big land of rocks. I stumble as I take my first steps, wondering why on Earth my mom would send us here. Philip and Gunthreon are already walking ahead together, busily talking. A sniff of the air tells me nothing, but then again, do rocks really have a scent? The sky matches the rocks—gray. It's not even cold or warm. This place is just plain boring.

"Remember drunken Rihan and that sprite of a pixie he got caught with in the barn?" rambles Philip to Gunthreon. "Wow, the sparks that flew that night. The mead *and* the love songs got the best of him."

"Yes, and his horse! You can't forget how long it took him to get it white again. A pink horse. Ha!" As they laugh it up, I struggle to follow and not to trip and fall on my knees again. Kioto follows along with me, but looks confused as I continually stumble, and my struggle is futile, as I cut my knee on one jagged piece of unruly rock. Kioto licks the cut as I try wiping the blood off with my hand, but the blood continues to run, and there's nothing I can do about it. I decide to take a small piece of rock and keep it in my pocket to remind myself how mad I am at my mom.

Just as I'm about to groan in pain, a wave of scent practically knocks me over. *Lilacs.* I look ahead at Philip and Gunthreon, and am amazed at Gunthreon's sudden cheerfulness, when just earlier he was informing me that my plane of existence could be overtaken by blood-thirsty, maniacal animals—at least that's how it's forming in my mind.

I don't see anything yet, but there is definitely something alive here. We walk for another ten minutes across the rocklands, and I slowly realize this tricky terrain seems to repeat itself: large flat rock, smaller flat rock, taller pointy rock; large flat rock, smaller flat rock, taller pointy rock; and so on. I catch up to the two Chatty Cathys ahead of me.

"Hey, hey, remember me?" Hoping for some sympathy, I make sure to discreetly flash at them my hand, bloody from my knee.

"Forgive us Kailey, we kind of got caught up in the excitement." Gunthreon is still smiling.

"Excitement? Where? Do rock quarries get you all hot and bothered?" I prattle. "You guys are both weird. Think I can get some help with this cut?"

"No need," says Philip as they both turn and keep walking forward. "The land will recognize you."

I am ready to scream. Refusing to keep walking, I sit down square on my butt. Kioto sits down right alongside me. Gunthreon and Philip keep walking and don't even bother to look back—and then, suddenly, they disappear. This frightens me at first, but really, it's actually quite peaceful just sitting, having nothing to do but stare ahead of me at the patterned rocks, nothing and nobody to worry about. The lilac smell is still strong, and a slight wind seems to pick up as I lie on my back and stare straight up at the gray sky. Out of the corner of my eye, I see a quick, jagged movement high among the clouds and as I look up, Kioto growls deep in her chest. One small, but unusually long speck of black seems to be hovering miles above me. I try focusing and unfocusing, but I cannot make out its shape or size.

I decide to get up and do something other than waste time sitting, as whatever is circling could probably swoop down and eat me. As I get up, pushing my hands against the rocks below me, a tingling sensation comes over me. I walk toward where Gunthreon and Philip went, and the sound of falling water suddenly fills my ears. The land changes slightly as I walk. The rock patterns are different, and jutting rock walls sprout up like teeth out of the ground. But even so, everywhere I turn is still rock, making me dizzy.

Then, before I know it, just as the falling water becomes loudest, I walk right into a rock wall—right smack-dab into it. After I regain my composure, rub my nose, and realize the illusion of space before me, I feel the rock wall, looking for a change, maybe an opening. I find it and step through.

Appearing out of nowhere, I find a pool with a small cliff lingering above it, spilling crystal clear water into the pool. The sound and sight are breathtaking among the rocks—and still there is no vegetation in sight. The water looks refreshing, and I want to soak my whole body in it. The waterfall keeps emptying into the pool, but the water level does not move, despite its small size. It's only, maybe, equivalent to six hot-tubs of water.

As I stand before the pool, a feeling of familiarity overtakes my senses. Moving into a trance-like state of consciousness, I slowly begin to lose each piece of clothing, by my own hands. There are stairs of rocks leading into the pool, and, naked, I walk down each one carefully. As each body part meets the pool, the tingling in my body becomes orgasmic. Kioto paces back and forth quickly at the edge of the pool as I continue into it, wanting more and more, giving into the selfishness of satisfaction. I forget the disappearance of my friends as I totally submerge my body. Holding my breath, I am fully engulfed by the pleasure running over and into each and every pore. Soon, there is no need to hold my breath any longer, and a warmth so tender closes in on me, making me feel like I am being embraced—like this is where I am meant to be, forever.

I stand with my feet at the bottom of the pool and open my eyes underwater. Underneath my feet is a mosaic rock symbol, and it looks familiar, at once very endearing and thought-provoking.

Then I recognize it: the symbol from my teacup! This must be Meadow's Edge.

My cut is healed, and my skin has never looked so young, my breasts so firm, and my hair so sensuous as I walk out of the pool, deciding I can't really stay here forever. Kioto whimpers loudly and begins wagging her tail fiercely. I feel totally refreshed and ready to emerge into the world, ready to face whatever comes at me—at least until I see two pairs of eyes staring widely at me.

"Turn around!" I scramble for my clothes, and Philip seems not to hear my plea, but Gunthreon turns, being the gentleman he is. My clothes are assembled messily, but do their job of covering me up.

Philip hasn't moved, but eventually his mouth does. "I see you've tended to your cut."

"We're here, right? Meadow's Edge? Where did you guys go? And what kind of water is *that*? Because I need to bottle it up and make millions of women happy."

"Can't be bottled up. Feel your hair. The water cannot leave the pool."

I run my fingers through it, and it's totally dry and soft. It smells like lilacs, too. I breathe in deeply, and I see both Philip and Gunthreon step in to take a whiff themselves. "Step back, boys," I demand. "This is mine to enjoy right now."

"Well, stop your lollygagging and let's move." Gunthreon hoots. Hearing the word "lollygagging" from his mouth is funny enough, so Philip and I laugh as we venture forward. Gunthreon's most definitely smitten by Meadow's Edge.

"Why aren't you two eager to jump in?" I ask Philip, playing with my hair.

"This is a life pool for women only—no men are allowed."

"Cool."

Philip looks toward me and comments, "Only thing to know about Meadow's Edge is that there are many things here that are either masculine or feminine. Everything seems to be connected to either one sex or the other, creating a balance. When you come upon something that calls to both, hang on to your britches!"

The boys start up with laughter. Whatever.

I think of the sorts of people or creatures I may meet in Meadow's Edge and a question comes to my mind. I turn to Gunthreon. "Hey, do they speak English here, too? Is there any place in Renhala where I won't know the language? People from other countries travel too, don't they?"

"A universal language is spoken in Renhala, and it's the same for any written text," says Gunthreon. "Neda thought communication was of the utmost importance. No matter what language you speak in your realm, everyone understands each other here, and anything written here is easily read by any Abscondian. When a native Renhalan travels to Abscondia for the first time, there is a brief disconnect if they speak to a non-traveler, but a traveler would understand them. It's another reason for Renhalans to stay in Renhala."

"Like soulspeak?" I question.

Gunthreon stops and asks, "How do you know about soulspeak?"

"Oh, I met this guy. His name is Conner," I reply with a smile on my face. Philip suddenly looks at me and clenches his jaw a bit before turning around, not saying a word.

"What?" I say, as my smile disappears. Then I realize the emotion which Philip exhibited in his stare: jealousy. It heightens

159

my belief that Philip shouldn't be walking around in a seven-year-old's body.

Gunthreon disregards our interaction and says, "I know Conner, too. I met him through Russell. Nice gentleman. I wasn't aware you two met." He hesitates. "But anyway, soulspeak is an entirely different matter. He speaks from his soul to another soul, and it is truth spoken no matter where he stands. No lies exist in soulspeak. But language here can be anything, so be wary of words spoken, for words in Renhala hold ancient magic, and not always pleasant."

Chapter 23

Drunk
❧

The rocks finally end, and the world suddenly opens up to green, and green of every shade imaginable. Interspersed are shouts of cheery reds, sunny yellows, and popping pinks. Sunlight spills from overhead, and the grass reaches skyward as flowers spread their petals, welcoming the warmth of life. Happiness floats on the breeze, and the world here is good.

Soft white fuzzies float in the air and tickle my nose. In the distance are cottages made of moss and logs, sheltered by trees resembling weeping willows, swooping down low, lovingly caressing the cottages and gardens comprised of every flower imaginable. It's definitely heaven.

"Ah—beautiful, wondrous Meadow's Edge," sings Gunthreon, breaking the spell. "Let's see if we can find Lupa. She must be around somewhere, tending her rhubarb plants." In watching him go, it seems as though he's actually skipping to his destination.

Philip grabs my hand, and we follow far back behind him. "Kailey, it may seem perfect here, but, something bad is indeed going on in both our realms, and I need to stop ignoring it. This is why I'm here," he says, "not simply because your mom suggested we take a vacation. Keep your eyes and ears open, please. Take these trips seriously. We are here to speak to a few contacts."

"I pinky-swear." I intertwine my finger with his and he frowns, but seems satisfied enough.

Then he rubs his gurgling stomach. "Time to find some grub. I'm starving," he grunts. "How does homemade sweet cream biscuits and cinnamon rhubarb jelly sound to you?"

"Not bad. Not bad at all."

"Let's find that old fart."

"You callin' the kettle black?" I tease. He laughs whole-heartedly as we walk hand-in-hand.

We find Gunthreon lovingly embracing a short, stout woman, her gray hair up in a large bun. Her face is round, and the crow's feet around her eyes only seem to enhance the freshness she exudes. She is a beautiful woman, with a curvy figure, who has most likely only grown more beautiful with age and experience. She welcomes us with hellos and a smile as big as her face is wide. It is only when she hugs me that I feel the slightest bit of tension in her embrace, and in her energy. A strange resonance surrounds her. I don't know if Gunthreon and Philip notice, but I recognize her as a woman with a lot of weight on her shoulders.

She leads us to a kitchen I can see is truly used every day. The biscuits I was promised are laid out before us, and I cannot hold back the food lover in me. I gobble up three of them, wondering how many pounds heavier I'll be tomorrow.

Lupa, Gunthreon and Philip talk about the old days: gallivanting, travels, fights, and much more as they promise me that this evening will be the best night I've ever had.

After we're done, Lupa cleans up the table and sits with us. "Ladimer, I cannot get used to you in this body," she comments. "I keep wanting to ask if you have to use the outhouse."

"I had to make some adjustments since I was here last. I may make a few more before this trip is up." Philip smiles at me, and I smile back, all the while thinking of just one more biscuit. "After all, what seven year old drinks mead?"

Lupa refills his teacup. "I will be sure to tell Hamm we'll be stopping at The Wicked Whale tonight."

Philip says toward me, "Oh, you're gonna *love* The Wicked Whale. Hamm has a special ability of his own. You'll see." He smiles as I raise an eyebrow at him.

As Kioto hangs with Lupa in her cottage, the next hour is spent meeting all sorts of people throughout the town and eating whatever they have in their kitchens. I end up with five different varieties of flowers in my hair, too, and a beautiful silver-and-gold pendant around my neck that is always cool to the touch. The latter is a gift from a timidly strange metalsmith to whom I take a liking because of his ability to sneeze and forge at the same time.

The day seems to end too fast, but from the look of the town and its townspeople at sunset, nighttime seems really to liven up the place. Music is everywhere, and songs of love and lovemaking drift to my ears. I see musical instruments I've never seen, and soon discover that women and men each play their own sorts; women play instruments requiring handwork, while the men play those requiring mouthwork. Throughout the town, I see what is meant by the separateness of masculinity and femininity, but not in a chauvinistic sense. There's an air of refreshing chivalry. At one point I attempt to open a door for myself and a gentleman runs across the sidewalk, grabbing the door from me. Everyone's got their appropriate job here; women are cooks and bakers, dealing with delicate intricacies; men are laborers, dealing with all physically exertive tasks. Each couple seems to work together, perfectly.

While walking through one particularly narrow alley on our journey to The Wicked Whale, Lupa holds us all up and huddles us into a corner. "Before we head in, I must tell you something," she says quietly. She is nervous, and I sense the urgency in her voice, and the strange resonance around her vibrates faster than when I first noticed it. Whatever she is going to tell us really has an effect on her. "Something is going on in Meadow's Edge—something that makes me afraid of the shadows. I don't tell you this to frighten you, but to make you aware of the changes. A murder has occurred, here," Both Philip and Gunthreon inhale simultaneously. "And Greer is awake."

I notice Philip hold his breath for a moment, which he then lets go ever so slowly. Gunthreon looks up to the dark sky.

"Who's Greer?" I ask.

"Let's just say he's been asleep for a few years, and he breathes fire." Philip stares upwards.

Gunthreon walks to Lupa and puts his arm around her. "I was hoping it hadn't reached here, but I guess no place is safe now. Let's just find the serenity in the simple comfort of each other's company and enjoy the night."

Serenity. Spa de Serenite. I feel an overwhelming draw to give my recently discovered information about Devoten to Gunthreon, despite what my mother asked. Conversations with Gunthreon begin replaying in my mind as I try recalling him perhaps suggesting something of the like. "Gunthreon, I have to talk to you about something that happened to me recently," I say. He turns to me and nods, but the look on his face says that now is not the best time to talk.

We enter the merriment of The Wicked Whale with saddened faces. Fortunately, they don't last long, for the music, food, and mugs being delivered to numerous tables lighten our moods. There are many people in The Wicked Whale, but it never seems truly crowded, as if the place itself expands with each warm body that enters.

Hamm greets us at the door and hugs each one of us, tightly. He's a large man, with a big, bushy brown beard and a contagious laugh. Unfortunately, as soon as Gunthreon pulls him aside to talk privately, his laughter abruptly ends and a seriousness consumes his cheerful expression as he speaks to Gunthreon, who frowns, then pats Hamm on the back and points to me as they exchange a few words.

Gunthreon wanders back and leads us to a table. He whispers in Philip's ear and Philip exhibits the same frown as

Gunthreon's. Hamm then walks over and brings me my first cup of mead. As it's plopped down on the table, they each stare at me.

"What?" I ask.

"Take a few big gulps," urges Philip.

"Okay..." I then gulp half of the deliciously sweet ale mixture. Then it hits me, within seconds: the usual alcohol-induced giddiness I once felt, long ago after drinking. Apparently Hamm's gift is one for making alcohol that delivers results on Renhalan travelers. "Ooh. Wow!" I yelp as I hiccup. Philip smiles and walks away as I turn to the fellow patrons, smiling.

I am invited to dance by several males in the house, first by Gunthreon—as Lupa discreetly watches his hands—and then by others who anxiously await their turn with a smile on their face. They clap to the rhythm of the music and I feel many a hand exploring a few of my curves, but nothing violating. Roasted turkey legs, small starchy vegetables and garlic keep the tummy full, and I become so engrossed with the fun that I lose track of my friends. I want to live here forever and swallow up the laughter until I burst. Finally, a pleasurable night, with absolutely no hesitation on any actions of my own.

I find Gunthreon and Lupa engrossed in each other and inquire about Philip, for it seems he has disappeared, and he hasn't had his dance with me.

"You mean you haven't seen him?" replies Gunthreon. "You must find the prettiest girl—besides yourself and Lupa here—and you will find your man. Search for the commonality." With that, he turns back to Lupa and whispers something surely devilish in her ear, her cheeks blushing cherry red.

My eyes, meanwhile, scan each smiling, happy-with-life face, carefully. The mead has made my vision a bit on the fuzzy side, but I keep at my goal, finally landing on those seated and standing along the large main bar. It is then that I notice a particularly curvaceous, porcelain-skinned bombshell with long blond hair, holding the arm of a man who is close to her in beauty, but with one small scar below his eye. His hair is also blond, but cut short, and his eyes still an intense brown. He carries an air of authority despite his youthful appearance. He's tall and lean, and moves gracefully. In time, he turns to me, and his eyes meet mine. His smile loosens and after escaping the fair beauty's clutch, he makes his way toward me. He is gorgeous, and I blush like Lupa at his attention, for he takes my breath away.

"May I have my dance now?" He holds out his hand to me and I take it. His movements are calculating, but smooth, and I feel light as air as he spins me, then pulls me close. His eyes are glossy from mead, and he stares at me in a way that arouses feelings that I never knew existed. The music then changes to a slower, sexy beat and before I can lay my head on his shoulder, he is yanked away from me by a gorgeous and tantalizing brunette. Ladimer's eyes meet mine and apologize as another set of hands take his place. I follow the hands to the arms, and then to the chest, and then to the face. He's a rugged farmhand-looking fellow, mighty strong and very attractive. We dance to a song of hardships that luck and love overcome, and we sway in time to the flute and the crackle of the fireplace. Several more mugs of mead touch my lips, and I get to a point I've longed for with every vodka brought to my lips: drunk. My partner's hands explore more than the other men's, but as I glance at Ladimer dancing with yet another woman, I feel a sudden need for someone's attention, no matter what kind it may be. Conner suddenly enters my thoughts and I think of the possibility of dancing and drinking with him, here.

Things become foggy as the night grows. I barely remember being led out the back door to the alley; the foul stench of stale alcohol wafting on the breeze. As I continue my jig to the music, I trip over my own feet several times, allowing my new farmhand friend to pick me quickly. But when we reach a rather dark and foreboding barn, reeking of animal manure and riddled with pitchforks and nameless rusty tools, my drunkenness is soon overpowered by a sudden anxiety.

I freeze, and before I can say no, or perform the slightest sensible reaction, he whisks me in and covers my mouth with his suddenly rough hands. *Evil intentions.* The negative energy pouring from this man is enough to choke a horse, and I immediately regret my heavy intake of mead. *How could I have let myself ignore the warnings? How could I have been so stupid?* My monk's spade flares up, but he is so strong I cannot move. I hear the ripping of clothes and try to bite him as hard as I can, but he seems to enjoy the pain, for a smile appears on his face as I draw blood. I try kicking him in the groin, but he's got his weight against my legs. A hand crawls under my bra and I try to scream.

Just as I hear the fear-provoking clinking of an unfastened belt, he freezes mid-movement. His eyes open as wide as they possibly can, and his mouth twists in gruesome fashion. His weight drops heavily onto me, and I see that someone is standing behind him, a hand on his back. I do my best to wiggle out from beneath the man.

A musky voice rises above my whimpers. "You really shouldn't be doing that, you know. How does it feel to have each of your internal organs slowly pulled away from your insides?"

"Ladimer, stop, please," I yell. He appears wickedly beautiful in the dark, but I know I have to stop him. "If you kill him, I fear something equally bad may happen to you." He's motionless. "Do you hear me?" I yell.

He takes his hand away, and my attacker falls to the ground. Pain convulsions pulse through him as he breathes sporadically and mumbles some nasty words, evidently still alive.

Ladimer stands above him, lowering his own face to within inches of his prey's ear. "You're lucky I only got to your spleen, asshole." With the last word, his foot meets the guy's ass, forcing an "oomph" from the man's lungs.

I try standing before Ladimer, but practically take him to the ground with me. Despite the burst of adrenaline, the mead still has the better of me. I begin crying as I sit on the ground. I can barely speak without slurring, but I manage to get out, "How could I let this happen, again? What have I done to deserve this?" My tears run down my face as I stare at Ladimer, longing for a reason for my suffering.

He brushes my hair from my face as he says, "Don't blame yourself for what's happened to you, Kailey. Karma is definitely making a point to enlighten you on the seriousness of what's going on between realms. All I can tell you," he raises my face to meet my eyes, "is to dig deep and take her warnings for what they're meant. Prove yourself worthy of her attention." He kisses me gently on my lips.

"Please don't tell my mother. It'll break her heart. Just don't tell *anybody*." I'm embarrassed that I seem to be so vulnerable. "I attract crazies!" I start crying, burying my face in my hands.

Ladimer then kisses me gently on my forehead and whispers, "I'm not crazy." He then pulls me up from the ground, lifting me in his arms. "Come on. I know a place where you can rest peacefully," he says, "though it seems there is no place sacred anymore." All I hear is "sacred," and suddenly the world goes dim.

◌

Remnants of dreams melt away as I awaken, a single tear falling from my sleepy eyes. I open them slightly, and see Ladimer's back before me—my savior. His warmth is inviting, and I snuggle close to him, wanting to soak into the safety of his mere presence. The alcohol affects still lingering in my blood, I sit up slowly and begin kissing his ear. He turns his sleepy face and I kiss his lips, gently. The mere scent of him brings a warm, inviting, and familiar sensation to my senses.

He smiles, but suddenly his eyes open. He holds me back from him. "Kailey, we can't do this. I'm not who you think I am. I'm..." His breath smells like warm mead. "Believe me, I would *like* this, but it's not right. We have both drunk more than our fair share. Things shouldn't happen like this. And my history..." He seems thrown askew. My eyes search his face for something— something to explain his actions. Then my energy feeler emerges, also seeking an answer. A sense of strong refrain is my only clue.

"Then just hold me," I plead. I turn with my back to him and lie, teary-eyed, facing away from him. I speak no more on the matter, for fear of humiliating myself.

Our surroundings suddenly become clear through my eyes, and all thoughts of rejection dissipate. My eyes focus sharply, and that's when I scream.

Chapter 24

Egotistical
ℭℛ

If she disturbs my sleep again, I will eat her while you watch.
This comes not from around me, but rather inside my head. The
power of these words pours over me, yet as I read the energies
around me, my fear lessens. I do not feel threatened, but still stand
my guard as the egos I sense seemingly make the room feel smaller.

"Oh, come on, Greer. Imagine yourself in her position."
Ladimer still holds me tightly.

*I shall never be able to compare myself to a human, the
scrawny things that you are.*

The massive and magnificent creature is curled around us,
providing an encasement for peaceful privacy. We are surrounded
by a wall of green, opalescent scales that reflect the fire sconces,
warmly lighting the area around us. The dragon smells slightly
spicy, like cinnamon.

"You're gorgeous," I drawl, awestruck.

*Oh, please, don't try to flatter. That will get you
nowhere*, I hear, again inside my head.

"You're telepathic."

*Wow, Ladimer she's a bright one. Do you have any
other two-word sentences for me? I think maybe I'd rather
have you scream.* I hear the boredom in his voice.

Greer adjusts his position, and the ground moves with him. I
grab Ladimer's leg.

"Kailey, Greer here has done us a great favor letting us sleep
in his presence," states Ladimer.

Greer turns his head toward us, and I feel the fire stirring in
his insides. His eyes come close, and they are just as awe-inspiring
as his scales, but a bright blue. *Kailey, your friend here did me a*

170

favor once, and I owed him. Do not think, though, that I owe any other favors. We are even.

I turn to Ladimer, asking him with just my eyes what favor this dragon is speaking about. "Our great friend here once suffered a nasty cut from a gang of meeples," says Ladimer in a respectful tone. "I happened to be in the neighborhood and heard his suffering. I was afraid to get close, but seeing a creature as mighty as he suffer made me want to help, so I healed him."

We eventually found those pests and I had a nice, tasty snack that day. Nice texture and crunch if they're cooked just right.

"Dear Greer, forgive my being frank, but can I ask you why you're awake?" I ask, suddenly remembering Lupa's serious face as she spoke of Greer.

I appreciate that little one. Well, I, like many a dragon, am sworn to protect areas of Renhala. Meadow's Edge, was at least one of the most, if not the most, peaceful places in this realm. We never knew of strife, theft, or murder, and things here were pleasant. Many came here to relax and release their troubles. But recently, a great vibration reverberated through the air and through my mind. It awoke me, and I have not been able to shake the feeling of despair. Ladimer, I request you find Gunthreon for me, for I would like to discuss the situation with him. And as a personal suggestion, I say head east, to Socola. Whispers on the wind speak of Neda and mutiny, and Trudon's death shouldn't be taken lightly.

"Socola? Really?" says Ladimer, suddenly looking forlorn. "They do say 'we all meet our maker.' Your wish is my command. Thank you, Greer. I did not want Kailey to give up on Meadow's Edge. It's important that she feel home here."

This last statement holds something more than I feel I know. "What do you mean?" I feel Ladimer flinch.

You mean—she doesn't know? Greer laughs in my head, and it rumbles throughout my body. *Go ahead, Ladimer. What do you mean?* I taste the sarcasm.

Ladimer is uncomfortable, for he fidgets as he sits. "I mean that—well...Kailey, you were born here. Meadow's Edge is your birthplace." He stares at me, holding my hands.

I laugh and remonstrate, "No, I was born in Stroger Hospital, Abscondia."

Ladimer and Greer look at each other. Ladimer says, "No, you weren't."

"But my mom told me... " I stop mid-sentence, my childhood becoming a blur as the lies dissipate to make room for the truth. As I examine both Greer and Ladimer and reach for the feeling of truth in their energies, I know they are in fact telling no lies.

Your mother, what a card! Greer laughs to himself.

"Greer—you know my mom?"

Yes, of course I knew your parents. Why, your mother is one of my favorites. I valued fighting by her side in some distant battles. Ah, she is a beautiful creature. He leans in closer and examines me closely, as I hold my breath. *You actually resemble your father. No offense.*

I look at Ladimer as connections are made by my brain. *Gunthreon and Ladimer: friends. Gunthreon and my mom: friends. Ladimer and my mom?*

Ladimer twists uncomfortably as he stands. "We will go find Gunthreon for you, and I will ask him to meet you here. Thanks again for providing safety. We were both able to sleep soundly." He sneaks his hand in mine, already such a comfortable and familiar feeling.

Sleep? Is that what you humans call what you were doing? I feel the blood come to my face in embarrassment. Greer lays his head back down and opens a small passageway for us to exit. As I walk by, I cannot help but feel his scales with my hand as I walk by. I see his one eye open and wink at me as we leave.

Thank you, great Greer. I think this last thought with respect, and notice a small altar-type ledge at the entrance of the lair. It is laden with precious stones, chalices made of gold, and other priceless gifts apparently given to Meadow's Edge's great dragon. I reach in my pocket and pull out the gray rock I picked up yesterday and place it on the altar. *I think this is just as beautiful.*

After a touch on the forehead from Ladimer to relieve my sudden headache, he tries keeping ahead of me to get to Gunthreon first, but I keep up with him. After deciding that anger toward my mother is worthless, I decide that knowledge of my history might prove much more worthwhile. "Why am I the last to know everything?" I say. "You know my mom? What was my father like? What did he look like? When did I leave here?"

"We must find Gunthreon and send him to Greer. We can talk later. Stop asking me all those stupid questions. I don't know everything, you know." He's perturbed, so I just settle on daydreaming.

Lupa's cottage is ahead, and I see her and Gunthreon tending to her many fruits and vegetables. Kioto is barking at the many strange creatures roaming the nearby meadow, but once she spots me she bounds towards us at full speed. She stands on her hind legs after reaching us, looks me directly in the eye, then kisses my face. She jumps down and smells Ladimer, then licks his hand. He caresses her head as we walk to the cottage.

Lupa has an amazingly green thumb, and I only wish that my patio planter of cherry tomatoes would actually grow tomatoes, let alone plants nine feet tall. I pick a plump ripe bluish berry as we walk through her garden and know I don't even need to wash it since everything here is pesticide-free. (Lupa did, however, warn me about the topola bugs, which resemble flying chocolate sprinkles—cute, but one accidental swallow and you're in the bathroom for three days.)

"Remember when I said I had some of the best teachers?" says Gunthreon, as we arrive, seemingly in love with not just the woman of the house but also the pepper plant looming before him. "Lupa has taught me many a trick. If only I could get my plants back in our realm to grow like this. Just imagine what my tomato and onion tart might taste like! Just too damn bad she cannot seem to grow roses—her favorite. Must be the soil."

"Gunthreon, Greer requests your presence, immediately," Ladimer yammers, totally unaware of the culinary inventions that could be created from the produce around him.

"I will see him at once," replies Gunthreon. "Kailey, what did you think of our Greer?"

"Please go see him, sooner rather than later," says Ladimer, pleading with his eyes. "I'll take Kailey around for the day before we leave. Maybe you could do with some souvenirs?" he says toward me. He expects to divert my attention. For the time being, I allow it.

"He's sarcastic, but likable," I say to Gunthreon. I steal a glance toward Ladimer meant for Gunthreon. "Greer, that is."

Gunthreon looks like he agrees. "Make sure to pick up a replacement teacup."

"Crap!" I knew I broke that damn cup.

CR

So, first thing, I find a replacement cup, even though it just doesn't feel the same. Every shop in Meadow's Edge is teeming with items I feel I need to own, or at least buy for someone, don't know who, but someone would love them. I know that, by the time we get home, I'll owe Ladimer my whole life's savings. I was hoping that currency in Renhala would be something easily accessible, like geodes or sunflower seeds, but they use gold: coins, jewelry, nuggets, whatever weighs the required amount. I see Ladimer place a few gold chains on the counter. "Philip's mom won't miss them, right?"

I respond, "Maybe you shouldn't say that in front of karma."

He laughs, loudly. "Let's just say I have a hefty savings in the karma bank."

A snow globe with a beautifully detailed wooden base that I think my mom would love catches my eye. Inside is a miniature cottage and lilac bushes, with a mini Greer floating around. I pick it up and shake it, watching Greer fall over on his side. I continue shaking until I'm satisfied with him right-side up. I push a button on the back, and it actually emits the scent of lilacs.

For Bu, I get a stuffed dog whose collar tag is the rune of Meadow's Edge. When you squeeze *him*, he farts, and *it, too,* smells like lilacs. Amber is getting a pendant from my favorite metalsmith, so I tell Ladimer we shall see him last. Also, I should get something for Conner, since I never did actually call him back after Spa de Serenite. What to get a man I hardly know, but am very attracted to? I contemplate asking Ladimer, but feel that may not be the right step to take.

We scan the last store, and that's when I see it. *Perfect!* It's a small plaque made of slate, and engraved in simple block letters is "The truth shall set you free." We pay and head to my favorite metalsmith's forge.

As we approach the shop, we notice the doors are shut tight and the lights inside off. "Funny," mutters Ladimer. "Mortimer is always open." Ladimer tries the front door, then puts his ear to the door, but nothing. "Let's try the back entrance," he says, at the same time that shouts come from within. We step quietly. My monk's spade is warm, and I see Ladimer reaching inside his shirt, no doubt for his blade.

A man shouts from inside. "This has turned from a request to a demand, Mortimer! If you do not cooperate, we shall see how loud you scream when your precious metal penetrates your precious heart!"

A loud crash has us both on our toes, not daring to be seen before we can figure out who is causing the ruckus. The back door opens, and a rather large man comes limping out of Mortimer's shop in a hurry. As he runs around the corner, I catch a glimpse of the hands and know this man is the one from the barn.

"Let's check on Mortimer," I whisper, grabbing Ladimer's arm, restraining him from chase.

We enter the shop and find Mortimer sitting, startled by our entry. I walk to him and ask if he's hurt, but he's mainly stunned, petting his tabby cat, rather voraciously.

"Mortimer, what's that guy want from you?" asks Ladimer.

"He was just a customer who wasn't pleased with an order, that's all," responds Mortimer. "So what may I help you with?"

I can tell Ladimer is not happy with the response, but he chooses not to pursue the matter. "Kailey here would like a pendant for a friend of hers," he says as he watches the back door.

"Hmm, good friend, or just acquaintance?"

"Best friend, if you must know. Her name is Amber." I flash him my biggest smile.

"Beautiful! How about something representative of her name?" says Mortimer. "I have a pendant with a beautifully enrobed specimen of amber. It's not gaudy, and it sits wonderfully upon the womanly frame."

He wanders to the front of the store and comes back with a small, handmade wooden box. He opens it slowly and shows me a most beautiful piece of amber, with a few small specks of something within it. It's undoubtedly older than me.

I turn to Ladimer and tease, "Predate you?"

He smirks and says, "You'll never know." He pinches my cheek as he looks around the shop, clearly checking to make sure nobody else is hiding from us.

"I think it's perfect, Mortimer!" I say. I hug him and question how on earth he is able to lift a mallet with his small frame. "Ladimer, pay the man, please," I say with regality, as if I am the queen of England. I then walk around, admiring all the beauties in the shop.

Ladimer stands, holding out his coin purse. "Are you set yet, Kailey? I seem to have run out of currency, you know." Ladimer shows me that the purse is empty.

I make sure to hug Mortimer once more, and Ladimer offers his help if he has any more unruly customers. Mortimer shows him his weapons behind the counter and Ladimer seems to leave the matter at rest.

"Are you worried about the guy who ran?" I say, after we leave.

"Yes, but he, I fear, is only a speck in what's happening here. When we can, we must talk with Gunthreon."

"Why is it that everyone's gotta talk to Gunthreon? Gunthreon, Gunthreon, Gunthreon." Then I realize there's nobody better with whom I'd like to share my Devoten experience. "Okay, whatever."

"Mortimer is a very special person, Kailey."

"Yeah. He's cool, I like him."

"Yes, he's nice, but he has a unique power of his own." Ladimer points to my necklace. "He has an ability to produce a metal that is special in itself. Nobody knows how he does it. We call his metal 'lutheose.' This metal has certain...nasty effects for anyone with unhealthy convictions who touches it," he says, staring at my necklace. "First few seconds, the metal burns; beyond that, it leeches poison into the skin of those it's touching, and eventually, if kept in contact long enough, kills. Those who have turned to

Velopa, and believe in its need to rule realms through brutality and slavery should be very afraid of Mortimer's metal, but for some reason, I feel they may be seeking it out, instead." He turns toward Mortimer's shop for one last look. "But why?" he says to himself.

I touch my pendant upon my chest and feel its coolness. "Well, you know whose side *I'm* on." I raise the pendant toward Ladimer.

"It *is* stunning on you." I suddenly feel the need for Ladimer to touch it. His slow hand movement toward the pendant stops, as if I've just slapped him in the face. "Do you not trust me, Kailey?" His mouth is open slightly as he stands still, looking shocked. The suddenly overwhelming sadness that I feel radiating from him hurts badly. He feels betrayed.

"I was only joking. Cool down," I reply. Bad part is, I was actually not. Worse part is, he didn't touch it. But how could I not trust this man thoroughly? Why would I doubt someone who's come to my rescue? Simply because my mom taught me not to trust everyone, but I damn well want to be able to, especially someone as valuable as Ladimer. I shake off his sadness, not wanting my own emotions to mix with his. I need to think clearly.

Once again, Lupa's cottage is within our view. Gunthreon is apparently back and ready to leave. We say our goodbyes to Lupa, and I see the tears in Gunthreon's eyes as he kisses her, softly. "Stay safe, my dear love. My offer is always open, you know."

"Are you trying that persuasion of yours on me again?" Lupa kisses him on the cheek and smacks him on the butt to send him off. He grunts, and seems embarrassed that we witnessed it, which makes both me and Ladimer laugh to ourselves.

Leaving Meadow's Edge makes me sad, but as I look to the sky and see the long, snake-like silhouette so many miles above us, I relish the small amount of hope I have in my new friends, including a certain sarcastic, fire-breathing ally.

Chapter 25

Defeated

Ҩ

"Kailey, I admit you're a great worker, and one of the very best here, but you have not been very dependable lately. And you just can't *not* show up. We were worried about you." Over the phone, Evan sounds not angry, but disappointed, which is even worse.

"I'm so sorry," I murmur. "I've got some personal issues going on, and I don't like it, either. I don't know what to do, and you know this totally unlike me. How many paid personal days do I have left this year?"

"You have six left."

"Thanks for not firing me." I mean this sincerely.

"Just don't quit on me. I know you'll get through this," he says. "Call me if you need anything. Take care. Just please remember, business is down right now, and the board of trustees is looking to downsize." He hangs up.

"I don't know what to do. Will I ever be able to go back to work and lead a normal life?" I say this to Ladimer and Gunthreon, who are sitting at my kitchen table, sipping tea and eagerly exchanging news that each acquired in Meadow's Edge. With maps spread out and a safe place to speak openly, they seem to be coming up with plans for more traveling.

Gunthreon sits up a bit more straight. "Try to hold on to your job, because it's a grip on a normal life," he responds, "but if it really came down to it, you would be taken care of. Actually, I hate to admit it now, but I have helped out you and your mother before."

"Thanks, Gunthreon."

179

"It's the least I could do for your mother. She's come to many a person's rescue, my dear, present company included."

I want to tell him what happened to me the other day, during my massage, but I bite my tongue, remembering my mom's request.

"Ladimer, Kailey," says Gunthreon, "I've spoken with many people and creatures, and nobody seems to know where Neda and Velopa are. It's true that all their locations were generally kept secret, but I have always had a track on them, until now. He turns to me. "Energies this strong shouldn't be able to vanish like this. It's strange that they are both missing, but oddly reassuring to know that it's not just one that is gone. I think, in finding them, we will discover what is truly going on with both our realms. The only clue I heard was that Devoten's castle is now under lockdown."

I shudder at his name as it rolls off Gunthreon's lips. "That guy gives me the willies. Even just seeing him made me feel very strange," I comment. "What's his story?"

Gunthreon and Ladimer exchange a very brief glance, and Ladimer holds out his hand, giving Gunthreon the go-ahead. "Believe it or not," says Gunthreon, "Devoten is infatuation—that's his ability." My brain churns how dangerous that could be. "He can make you willing to give your own life just for a chance to stand next to him. Thank Neda he mostly chooses grebles, for they seem to be the weakest against him. Still, quite the deadly fan club." He hesitates. "In my experience, one knows they are under his control, bowing to his every need. It makes one feel small and unworthy. But it's draining for him. He must constantly keep control over his minions. Some have the natural ability to block his control, but he's very strong."

"Devoten was not always what he is today," begins Ladimer. "He was actually once a kind and gentle soul, capable of making anyone happy when the chips were down. Believe it or not, we shared the same circle of friends. We shared some good times together, but he came upon some much harder times after a bad deal with regards to a neighboring piece of land. He began talking nonsense and travelling with some strange individuals.

One day, he returned to town, and I remember his exact words: 'I've learned to hate in full strength, and the power is incredible. Fear tomorrow, Ladimer.' And with that, he was not seen again for a long time.

When he did show up again, I felt his new power and saw it in action. He had developed what the elders call sudo-abominor: a change in oneself in which hate takes over a portion of one's cognitive being, like a leech, sucking and draining all goodness until it's fed. It happens rarely, but when it does, the individual should be contained as soon as possible, for once sudo-abominor is fed, it can travel to a new host." Ladimer's energy briefly shudders, then resumes its complacency. "Unfortunately, Devoten was too wise to be caught. He appeared in town one day and began engaging with a local woman. The fire in his eyes was insanity itself. She deflected his passes at first, but he was so persistent, he made her fall madly in love with him. After weeks of her attention, he grew tired and annoyed with her, so he had her cut out her own tongue with Mortimer's golden knife.

Still, she followed him around silently for a month, doing all his nasty biddings. One day, I caught her alone in a horse stall, crying. I turned her face to mine and knew it had to end. I could fix her tongue, but not her infatuation, so I did what I had to do. I hate Devoten for what he has become, but I fear him. Infatuation is no simple emotion."

My doorbell rings. Ladimer reaches for one of my bags as I open the door for my mom. She seems excited to see us all. She gives Gunthreon a big kiss on his cheek and hugs Ladimer very tightly, confirming my belief they indeed know each other. I notice

Ladimer shake slightly as he releases my mom. But if they *are* acquaintances, or even friends, why has he not healed her?

Suddenly, Ladimer starts laughing, holding Amber's lutheose pendant and grinning ear to ear, evidently not burning his hand.

"Gunthreon, do you know what I'm holding in my hand?"

"Jewelry."

"It's that damn plant you get your tea from. I can feel it through the amber. I could probably get it to grow again."

"Why, I'll be," Gunthreon twitters.

As I run to see the pendant, the rush of excitement hits me so fast that I trip over my own two feet, but before I even hit the floor, my mom has me in her arms.

"Thanks, Mom." She helps me to my feet. "Since you can move like that, how come I remember a certain painful fall off the monkey bars at age ten that sent me to the emergency room?"

"You had to learn, honey," she says. "I couldn't *totally* shelter you."

I bite my tongue and just furrow my brow. "Well, I did get that pendant for Amber. I can't keep it for myself. Karma, remember? Maybe when she tires of it I can reclaim it. Well, giving it to her gives me a damn good reason to go to work." I hand my mom her snow globe and her eyes twinkle as she shakes it.

Ladimer stands up and announces that he's going home.

"Uh, don't you think your mom might freak out if you just wander in?" I ask.

He laughs heartily. "Yeah, well, I guess I'll go borrow your bathroom for a minute."

"Can I watch?"

My mom gasps. "Kailey, that's rude!"

"He's going to transform back into a seven year old." I'm intrigued.

But he doesn't let me follow him. Soon enough, "Philip" emerges from my bathroom in Ladimer's shirt which hangs below his knees and no pants. "Wouldn't she have noticed that you've been missing?" I say. "And what is she gonna think when you walk in like that!"

"Actually, she hired a sitter whom I have a certain relationship with: she gets paid for the time she stays in my apartment, having sex with her boyfriend, as I come and go as I please. But I need to figure something out fast. I need to be that knock out gorgeous guy with the ass you and your mother are always staring at."

"Don't talk like that in your current condition. It just weirds me out," I reply. My mom falls over laughing—a melodic sound to my ears—into the couch, but then grips her side from the pain, and I feel my love for her deep in my heart.

⚥

That night, as everyone has left, I decide that I will indeed go to work tomorrow after a good night's sleep. I heat myself up some tea and sit before the television in my nice, satiny pajamas. With nobody around except Kioto, it's peaceful, and I feel nice and comfy.

As Kioto curls up at the front door, I wonder if Bu is outside. Of course, I promise myself I will not doze off on the couch, but who really tries to fight that battle anyway?

The windows are open, and the air coming in is cool, promising fall is on its way. I can hear the last of the summertime crickets chirping their farewells.

Sleep wins.

⚥

I walk barefoot through a parking lot, the asphalt still warm from the day's sun. There's only one car in this lot, a familiar one—a black Mercedes SUV. Slowly, I walk toward it, drawn to its mysterious solemnity, for there is music coming from the car—a sad, haunting sound. Russell sits at the wheel, just staring forward. His eyes are blackened from lack of sleep, and there are dried-up tear stains on his cheeks. I knock on the window, but he's so lost in his own thoughts that he doesn't budge.

It is then that I look down into his hands and see something that my eyes don't clearly interpret. With a closer look, I see it's a soft, small, blue teddy bear covering its mouth with its own paws, like a "speak no evil" monkey, which, like all three of those monkeys, has always creeped me out. Closer examination reveals that something resembling blood is splattered all over the bear.

Russell turns slowly to me with unseeing eyes, and he mouths one word: "Why?" As I stare at him, I realize that he is not alone. Just barely peeking from the passenger seat, is another head, cloaked, and all I see is a very wide grin.

❧

As I jump from the dream, I find drool dripping down the lip of my mouth, and I wipe it off. "Whoa, Kioto. That was weird." Kioto ignores me, instead getting up and going to my bedroom, which is exactly what I should be doing. But I decide to stop in the bathroom first; I'd rather go now than wake myself up having to go half an hour before my alarm clock goes off. While rinsing my hands, I glance in the mirror.

My reflection stands with its hands over its eyes and a beating human heart in the sink. *How can I see myself if I'm covering my eyes?*

My heart skips a beat, and I suddenly stand up off my couch for the second time. "Damn! What keeps happening?"

Kioto is at the front door, asleep.

At this point, I'm frightened, unsure whether or not I'm still dreaming. But I reach over and turn on the light, and all seems normal. I keep thinking of the "speak no evil" monkey. Quickly, I run to my bedroom and slip under the covers. My breathing is heavy, and I remember the meditation techniques I've been working on.

The smell of lilacs is the last thing I remember.

Chapter 26

Shocking
ೞ

Ah, nothing like the familiar scent of toner and coffee brewing to soothe a worker bee. My desk is littered with mail and work to do—go figure. As I sit in my chair and sort through everything, I find I love the normalcy of it. It's sanity. It makes sense.

"Nice to see you again." Evan stands before me.

"Nice to be back."

"Is everything... You know, okay?" He looks genuinely concerned.

"Everything is just fine," I state. "Thanks again." With a nod, he's off to his own office, knowing I'll take care of everything I need to today.

"Well look what the cat dragged in." Amber of course. Her voice oozes contempt. She's as beautiful as ever silhouetted in the doorway, but is a bit on the trampy side today, with a low-cut blouse and too-short-for-work black skirt.

"You got a date or something?" I stare at her four-inch heels.

"Don't be jealous, hon. Just wanted to come over and check up on you, and give you this, too." She drops a candy apple-red envelope on my desk and blows me a kiss as she leaves. "Oh, and make sure your mom comes." This was not exactly the "hello" I expected after being gone a bit, but Amber is a fickle girl.

I pick up the envelope, noticing the smell of her perfume on it, and open it up with the tip of my pencil, rebel accountant that I am. But as I read the card inside, my mouth drops:

You are cordially invited for a small ceremony and reception to share in our happiness.

Russell Yu and Amber Hardy to be wed on Saturday, September 23rd of this year, 7 p.m.

Bring your appetite and dancing shoes!

I glance at my calendar. "A week and a half?!" I shout out loud, to nobody. *Why do I have to have such a strange best friend?* I can't decide whether to respond formally or go to her office and squeeze her to death. I decide to do the latter. I almost forget her gift from Meadow's Edge, but grab it quickly before I head off to her office down the hall.

As I approach I hear stifled weeping. When I peek in her office, her back is to me and she's wiping her eyes.

"Amber, are you okay?" I see her back stiffen up, and she turns around, smiling at me.

"Yes, I'm fine," she responds. "Just a little emotional this morning, for no reason, actually."

"Must be wedding jitters," I say. "Why on earth would you tell me like that, you weirdo? I mean, I'm happy for you, but it's kind of soon, don't you agree?" I am *so* not wanting to start an argument, but I had to get that off my chest first thing.

"Never satisfied, are you, Kailey? I'd think *you'd* be glad I've decided to get hitched and not continuing my whoring." *I can't win.*

She eyes my hand and the small box with the bow cradled inside it. "Presents already?" Instantly, I see the Amber I've grown to love before me: the bright-eyed child discovering all her material goods under the tree Christmas morning, yet void of any purity or innocence.

"Sure. Here, happy engagement." I hand it over to her. She rips the bow off in two seconds flat and opens the box. She stares at the necklace, and I grab it out of the box.

Her eyes well up again, and I can see she's trying to hold back the tears. She's quite emotional today.

"Let me do the honor." I unlock the clasp so I can put it on her.

"I love it. Where did you get it?" she asks.

"I took a little trip and found it for you. It's amber."

"Yes, I know that." I walk around behind her and grasp the necklace, holding it around her neck. As I move her hair away and attempt to clasp it, she yelps.

A nervous twitch runs through my body, and out of my mouth comes, "Did it burn you?"

"Why the hell would it burn me? You pulled one of the baby hairs on the back of my neck. Be careful!" Then she turns around in her chair for me to see, and the pendant is gorgeous on her chest. She produces a mirror from her desk drawer—quite large, but I expect nothing less. The smile on her face blows my nervous twitch to smithereens. She loves it, and I love that *she* loves it.

"You can go on trips more often, even if they're without me. Thank you, Kailey. It's beautiful."

"You're welcome. And, if I can clear my calendar, you can put me down as an attendee for September 23rd," I say.

"One or two?"

Oh, I didn't think of that. "Uh, can we do a tentative two? Who else did you invite?"

She smiles devilishly. "I specifically told Russell to not give Conner an invitation. Will it be one or two?"

Evil! "Ugh. I'll have to let you know later," I blurt. "What if I planned on inviting someone else, huh?"

She laughs all too loud. "Yeah, right. Well, spaces are filling fast, so tell me soon, like today."

The little giggle she tries to hide is so annoying that I stick my tongue out at her. "I'll let you know *later!*" I say, leaving with a pout on my face. As a female, she knows the pain of having to make the "Would you like to go to a wedding with me?" call. She did that on purpose, which is so selfish—so *Amber*.

I'll make the phone call this evening at home. I need to speak to Conner anyway to thank him, so it'll be like killing one bird with two stones: my death from two very embarrassing topics.

For the rest of the day, I spend some time chatting with coworkers and setting up a meeting with a famous baseball player to play golf with some man who donates his time to organizing Special Olympic events. The day goes by quickly.

On my way out the door, I stop in the bathroom to silence the sudden screams from my lower intestines. I knew the pepper steak I ate for lunch was going to give me trouble. I choose a stall and sit, trembling from the coldness of the toilet seat.

The sound of the bathroom door opening makes me stop before I do my duty. Funny how I can decapitate a meeple, but I can't even do my business in a work stall when someone else is in the room.

I wait for her to enter a stall, and wait, and wait, and wait. The hair on the back of my neck stands up, and slowly, I pull up my pants, listening closely for some kind of noise—anything. My monk's spade is warm on my back and I feel for its shaft. I try peeking through the gap in the stall door, but see only a faint shadow.

I gather my nerve. "Hello?" I say. "Could you possibly hand me some toilet paper? I'm desperate." I keep my hand on the blade, for the emotions reaching me from this individual are strangely ones of revenge. Whomever is here is definitely upset about something.

Delicate footsteps approach the stall next to me, and I hear the person unrolling paper in the handicap stall. Relief comes over me, and I reach my hand down. "Thanks."

I regret this all too soon. The hand reaching back under is not human, but greble. It grabs me and instantly pulls me under the divider. I struggle with all my might, but I might as well be a three year old. Before I know it, he has me pinned against the wall above

189

the toilet, my feet dangling, attempting to gain footing, somewhere. It's the same greble who attacked me in my apartment, and as he grins and drools, his stench makes me gag.

"Devoten may be too preoccupied with his ridiculous visions to come visit, but I am not," grumbles the greble. "Even blessed with sudo-abominor, he *still* has his weaknesses, but I am not weak like you humans. I'm the one known as Tartarin, and I am the one who is going to end your life, so pray to your gods, Kailey."

His hold on my neck tightens. *The slimy green arm weighs down on my neck, smearing its wetness on my skin, as its nose sniffs my skin.* I gather my will to fight and with all my might, I kick him right in the hard-to-miss groin. He doubles over in pain, and I slide down the wall, one foot falling in the toilet. I then slip between two of his legs. Tartarin, quick, grabs my foot, but I can now grab my monk's spade. It flares, and I stab at the back of his leg.

He bleeds dark ooze and breathes very heavily, but he does not scream. "I am going to eat your brain with ice cream when I get my hands on you next," he whispers. "Think that one over while you still have it."

As he suddenly disappears, I hear two women chattering, entering the bathroom. I stand up as fast as I can and regain my composure. I look to my monk's spade, regretting the blood still dripping down the blade, and place it back on my back as it fades from view.

"God, it reeks in here," spits Nancy, evidently on a break from the front desk.

I surely don't want them to think I'm responsible for the smell. I exit the stall. "Yeah, I know," I say. "They need to get one of those air freshener-dispenser thingies in here soon." I leave as soon as I rinse my hands as Nancy complains about the high cost of air freshener-dispenser thingies. I run to my office, ignoring the pleas from my bowels. My purse, sweater, and bag are soon on my shoulder, and then, I'm out the door. I fumble for my smartphone and call Gunthreon. He answers on the first ring.

"So why does this greble, Tartarin, have it out for me?" I query. "Why is everyone else afraid to travel here and just kill us all?"

"What happened?" he asks, worriedly. "Are you okay? Where are you?" It feels like he's going to jump through the phone and grab me to keep me safe. I tell him where I am and what happened. I ask again why they don't all travel here.

He pauses. "Advanced technology versus magic." That's all he says.

"Huh?" He's speaking again in that language called ambiguity.

"Renhala is a realm based on magical forces from within *oneself.* This is what they believe in and rely on. They are not as technologically advanced as we are. They think technology like ours, especially anything electrical, is a magic in itself—something bad, something generated from a fire demon of some sort that we let run our lives. They think that 'powers' like electricity, costs us our life energy. Those who live in Renhala *do* live *much* longer than those living here. Who knows?"

I ponder this. "But as our technology advances through the years, life expectancy goes up," I state.

"Only because we can make machines, that help our bodies live longer. Renhala has spies all over this realm, and they know that we depend on outside energy, rather than our own internal life power, to help us live our pathetically short lives. They watch us microwave our food, send e-mail to foreign countries, and even detonate hydrogen bombs. To most Renhalans, Abscondia is a place of nightmares, both to those who travel, and to even those who know nothing of the actual realm—those in which Abscondia is only an urban myth."

"It's hard for me to believe that none of the technology in this realm has been brought to Renhala."

"Renhala does have its own scientists, and sort of 'technology police' who feed information to the Renhalan public and prevent any imports," Gunthreon says. "I've got to say, though, their scientists have come up with some interesting theories regarding negative energy radiation within black holes—something Hawking would be proud of."

He pauses. "Those who choose to take the risk, like myself, come to live in Abscondia," says Gunthreon.

"You're native to Renhala?"

"Yes. I've established residency here to merely watch and protect those I can," he says. "And there are also those who take certain 'already produced' items back to Renhala. Your technology is taboo there, and most do not even want to experiment with it, but there are some risk-takers. I know that several governmental agencies around the world have something to do with items that end up in Renhala," he finally says. "They know Renhala exists. They're just good at hiding things. As a matter of fact, I could have sworn I saw Jimmy Hoffa meat cleaver-shopping in Meadow's Edge just recently."

I laugh, because part of me thinks the idea is silly, but another part of me thinks otherwise. Gunthreon ignores my laugh.

"But while most in Renhala fear your realm," he says, "some, do not care and are just set on one thing—like killing."

"So what you're saying is that I may be safer carrying around my battery-operated digital alarm clock rather than my monk's spade?" I snicker. "Bu doesn't seem to be fazed."

Gunthreon's voice changes at the mention of Bu, cheering up a bit. "Bu is fascinated with learning Abscondian technology and isn't concerned about any dangers," he says. "Bu is actually quite smart for a greble. Just last week, he fixed my stove when the pilot light broke. His ability to pick up on the workings of electronics is fascinating. I think it's his gift, and he's slowly developing it, since he spends little time in your realm."

"That's cool. Doesn't help with the greble who wants to eat my brain, though," I mention as I think back to work. Amber pops in my head. "Oh, hey, did you know Russell and Amber set a date?"

I hear the phone drop on the other end and really hope Gunthreon didn't faint.

Chapter 27

Concerned
ℭ

Kioto greets me at my door rather slowly, panting heavily but seemingly satisfied, and I realize it's her post-walk mode. Sure enough, her leash has been moved, and I see her water bowl has been refilled. I turn right back around and knock on Philip's door, because I really can't imagine an eight-foot greble walking my dog down the street to the park.

"Yes?" Philip answers the door in a Darth Vader shirt and torn jeans. I hear his babysitter talking on the phone in the kitchen. I try to peek in, but Philip closes the door behind him.

"My dog is quite worn out right now. Would you have any idea why?"

He pulls on a thick silver chain attached from his belt loop to his pocket and pulls out a black wallet embroidered with a white skull. He starts thumbing through his dollar bills. "How much are dog walking services these days? I think I need to start getting paid for it."

"Such a cool seven year old, aren't you?" I tease.

"The coolest," he replies, jerking his head quickly to move his hair from his eyes.

I think about the privacy of my apartment, but realize I don't have much to hide. Kioto gets to go outside during the day, and I don't have to worry about her poor bladder. "How's thirty bucks a week sound to you?"

"Wonder how long it will take you to pay me back for all those souvenirs you bought with my gold."

I totally forgot to pay him back. "Damn! Sorry. Let me check my purse," I say. I open my wallet and find it totally devoid of cash. A few receipts fall out, along with one of those scratch-off lottery tickets.

Philip reaches down, grabs it, and says, "This will have to do for now, I guess. Thirty bucks a week? Deal. That'll give me some extra cash when I move out. There's an apartment available in the next building." He shakes my hand, then holds it briefly before letting go and returning to his apartment. A sensation of longingness lingers as I touch the hand he held. I wonder how moving out will work with his foster mother.

As I put my wallet back, Amber's red envelope falls to the floor, still smelling of her sickeningly sweet perfume. I pick it up, pinning it to my refrigerator with one of my numerous Akita magnets. The damn envelope practically screams at me to make my phone call. So I do.

"Hello?" Conner sounds as if I've just woke him up.

"What would one do for a living if he's sleeping at this time?" I ask. Surprisingly, Conner's occupation has never come up. "Broker? Self-employed entrepreneur?"

"Phone-sex operator."

"What?!"

He cracks up on the other end. "Don't get your panties all in a bunch." He continues laughing, but eventually calms himself down. "Real estate, actually. Think about it. I've got to put my gift to good use somehow, right?"

Thank God for small miracles. "Sorry I haven't called you back," I say. "I know I promised I would, but lots of things have been going on and I couldn't find the time, and I'm actually calling you for another favor."

"My, my. You are really going to owe me one, aren't you?"

"Would you go to a wedding with me?" I ask. I practically hold my breath as I speak, wincing.

"That's not a favor. I'd love to." Praise the Lord again.

"Guess who?"

"Our two lovebirds?"

"How did you know?"

"Russell gave me an invitation, too," he says. "I must say he's been so quiet lately and hard to get in touch with, but anyway, you saved me a phone call."

How can I kill Amber quickly and painlessly, at least for me?

"Kailey, what are you doing right now?"

I'm sitting picking at my pedicure right now, but he doesn't need to know that. "Nothing. Why?"

He's silent. "I was just wondering if I could stop by. I got you something—something small. It just made me think of you, that's all."

I then realize I still have *his* gift from Meadow's Edge. "You can stop by if you'd like," I say. "I was just going to order takeout Chinese. Did you have dinner yet?"

"No, and Chinese sounds great." I decide to order a smorgasbord, and he can pick and choose, because I don't really know what he likes.

I'm starving, though, and can't wait until he gets here. My work clothes have to come off, and I decide on something comfortable, but something that shows my figure slightly—and, oh, a little strawberry lip gloss.

Eventually, the doorbell rings and I let him up. He's as handsome as ever, with his dark blue frayed jeans, white pullover V-neck sweater, stubbled chin, and slightly tousled hair. He gives me a warm peck on my cheek as he puts his hand on my shoulder and closes the door behind him. I shudder slightly. He smells divine, as usual.

"Here." He puts a small, black velvet box in my hands. I open it, and it's a sterling chain with a small silver and brass whistle attached. He helps me put the chain on, and I put it to my lips and blow. It's quite loud and shrill for its size. Kioto pulls her ears back and runs. "It's in case someone gets a little overzealous with you and you need to fend them off." His eyes soften and I instantly feel a pain from him, similar to a broken heart.

My own anxiety flares up. "What's wrong?" I say, concerned.

His eyes are tearful and he brings his hands to hold mine. "Amber told me what happened to you. I'm so sorry you had to go through that. No woman should ever feel that kind of pain."

"Thanks for both the gift and your concern. I hope I'll never need to use this, but I'll keep it close at hand," I say, as I turn the whistle over in my hand. I smile warmly at him. "Oh, oh, I got you something too!" I hand him his box, and he slowly opens it.

"'The truth shall set you free.'" A large grin appears on his face, and he leans in to hug me. It's one of those good, firm hugs one learns to appreciate.

There's a quick, single knock at the door and the door opens. I let go of Conner, quickly, but reluctantly.

"Oh, you little karmelean queen, I... " The look on Philip's face shows shock, embarrassment, and a hint of jealousy all at once. The fact it's from a seven year old is a bit disturbing. I can only imagine what is running through Conner's mind. Philip has now made me decide I *do* need my privacy.

"Conner, this is Philip, my neighbor friend," I say, a bit uncomfortably.

Conner's face contorts slightly, and I realize what Philip said as he walked in. "Nice to meet you, Philip," Conner says. "It's always nice meeting another traveler." He shakes Philip's hand, and Philip shakes back as firmly as a seven year old's muscles will allow. He holds on slightly longer than I would expect, and I hold my breath once again in anticipation of what he may do to Conner's insides, but he lets go and proceeds to turn around and leave.

"Hey, what did you come over for?" I ask.

"Just to hang," he sputters in his best seven-year-old impression.

In deciding I rather not have him slamming the door as he leaves, and the smallest bit of desire that I want him to stay, I request, "Don't leave yet, I've ordered a whole bunch of Chinese food and we won't be able to eat it all." I glance at Conner as I talk and he nods.

"Yes," says Conner. "Please stay, Philip, and I mean it." He speaks in his special way, and Philip does indeed come in and sit on the couch.

"Soulspeak, eh?" says Philip.

"Yep. Glad we can be ourselves here. What about you, 'Philip'?" I hear the question in his voice, as I know Philip does.

"You can call me Ladimer."

Conner adjusts his seating a bit and bites his lip, unknowingly. "Nice to be in the presence of such a celebrity," he says. "I've heard your tales, Ladimer, from my parents. How long have you and Kailey here known each other?"

"She knows who I am and what I am. It doesn't really matter how long we've known each other."

Conner smiles slightly.

The doorbell rings, and I shout, "Food!" I'm famished, and I need a break from the boys in the room. I run downstairs, and pay the delivery guy, and lug up all the bags. Both my guests jump up and help me as I enter my apartment.

"Hey, this should be on me," states Philip. "I won a thousand bucks with a certain lottery ticket. It's wonderful knowing you, Kailey." My mouth opens wide, and I could kick myself. It makes me wonder—if I kept it for myself, would it have been worth anything when I scratched it?

After much eating, talking, and a transformation and clothes change for Philip—I guess to even the ground—the boys seem to warm up to each other, almost to the point of forgetting about me. They even come up with a plan for Conner to help Ladimer with his foster situation. I'll kind of miss Philip, though.

The men eventually say their goodbyes and arrange for
Conner to come over another day.

Ladimer leaves first, and asks me to walk him out. "Be
careful, please," he whispers. "I know you like him, but how well
do you really know him?" He looks me in the eyes, and just as I
think he's going to kiss me, he heads to his apartment, where he
will quickly change into Philip before Karen arrives home.

Upon returning to my own place, I see Conner putting his
shoes on. "Thanks for dinner and the company, Kailey. Thanks for
my gift, too. I know just where I'm going to put it. He stands close
to me and stares intently into my eyes. "Be careful of Ladimer. You
have not heard all the stories I have. My mother and father told me
lots of Renhala tales, and Ladimer played a few parts in them. He's
a powerful and dangerous man."

I agree to watch my back, and before he leaves, he leans into
me, stealing my breath as his lips press to mine. I hope he tastes
the strawberry lip gloss I reapplied after dinner. His hand is at the
lowest part of my back, and I suddenly feel a hunger for it to roam,
but he's a gentleman and removes it hastily. I sigh deeply when he
leaves as I stand at the top of the apartment stairs.

As I watch from the hallway window, Conner beeps his horn
as his car pulls out. I hear Ladimer's blinds close as I stand, staring
at nothing. Both warnings replay through my head, and I decide,
after much thought, that I cannot live my life fearing everyone
close to me. My, what help a nice, tall glass of wine could do for
me right now, if I were normal.

Chapter 28

Missing
❧

Time flies when you're busy, and the next few days are just that, but it makes me happy that I can earn a paycheck doing things that help others. In just a week, Helping Hands has helped six individuals complete a difficult task, achieve some lifelong dream, or just plain relax. Life is good, until I receive a strange phone call from Gunthreon.

All I get from the one-sided conversation is that something is wrong with "the connection" and Neda must be found soon. I agree to come see him, since he sounds so distraught. Evan allows me to sneak out a few hours early.

Fidello picks me up straight from work and drives me quickly to Gunthreon's place, Spirit Cave, where I am greeted by Russell. I hug him and ask how the wedding plans are going, but he dismisses my questions and says that he's on his way out to pick up Amber's dry cleaning. "Tell her to pick up her own dry cleaning," I say. He just smiles quirkily and waves goodbye as he drives away.

I find Gunthreon in the room with the disappearing door. He's seated, staring at his urn, which is propped up on a chest. "Gunth, are you okay?" I say. I walk over to stand directly in front of him, and he finally notices he's not alone.

"Do you see it?" he questions.

"Yes, I see the urn."

"No, do you *see* it?"

"Umm, you need to be a little more descriptive right now."

"It's cracking, Kailey," he comments. "The urn is breaking down."

There is indeed a small hairline crack on the urn's lip. "Well, it's old, I'm sure," I say. "If it gets worse superglue works wonders.

There's also this antique place I pass on the way to work that could maybe—"

"*You don't understand!*" As he turns away, I take a few steps back and fidget with the silver ring in my pocket. "Who did you awaken, Kailey? Who answered you?" he says to himself. Thank God he isn't actually expecting an answer from me, because he's scaring the hell out of me. He turns back and the fire in his eyes is so bright that I back up even further, not knowing whether to run away or cower in a corner. He apologizes and, in his persuasive voice, asks me to sit. He eyes the ring in my hands as I continue to play nervously with it.

"Your father's?"

"Yes," I reply as I place it back in my pocket.

"Keep it safe, for it's your only connection to what was once good." He hesitates, then adds, "You must know this urn also has a special connection. It signifies a living link between those who reside on this plane and Neda. You can say that this urn is actually alive," says Gunthreon. "Nobody knows what it is made of, but it's something organic and connected to the living force of Neda. The fact that it is breaking down means we must find Neda, and immediately. Something is terribly wrong. And *we continue to waste time!*"

I switch into business mode. "Okay. I know that you and Ladimer have been attempting to dig up information. Pull this information together to find Neda as a first step. How do we start? Do we need to brainstorm?"

"I don't know how to say this... I have no idea." But *I* have a feeling traveling is involved. *Good-bye Helping Hands.*

We spend about an hour talking about what to pack for our trip to Renhala and who to bring. My need to explain how I've never been camping in my life is overshadowed by Gunthreon's fire and his sudden energy to move fast. "Can I at least bring the s'mores?" I say. It falls on deaf ears.

On my way home, I call my mom to ask if she can dog sit Kioto for a while. She does not agree, because she knows something's going down. Her voice is snotty as she says, "You're going to need my help aren't you?"

"Yes, I need you to help me by watching Kioto." Gunthreon doesn't want my mom along for fear something may happen to her and she may slow us down in some way. Go figure—Quicksilver slowing us down. I guess Gunthreon knows best, or otherwise, he just used that persuasion power to get me to agree that she shouldn't come. "Gunthreon was very specific about each of our tasks," I add, standing my ground.

"Whatever. Fine. I have the spare set of keys you gave me. I'll pick her up tomorrow," she says. "Hey, I got an invitation to Amber's wedding?"

"Yeah, weird, huh? She and Russell have only been dating two weeks, but I'm hoping he may be exactly what she needs."

"I've always liked him. Let's hope so." She hangs up the phone.

I arrive at my place thanks to Flash Gordon behind the wheel of the limo. As I head upstairs, I hear Bu and Ladimer in the hallway in a heated debate. Just as I reach the second floor, I see the hippie couple who live below me shutting their door. All I hear is, "Whoa, man, those mushrooms are killer."

"You guys need to calm down and get out of the hallway," I say to Bu and Ladimer, quietly yet firmly. "My neighbor just saw you! What were you fighting about?"

Ladimer twitters, "He won't leave your door no matter how many times I tell him I live across the hall. He's only jeopardizing you by being here."

Bu adds, "Bu only knows what Bu would do." I think to myself and realize he just admitted he only trusts himself.

"Thanks Bu," I say as I hug him.

They enter my apartment, and I force them both to sit down and stop arguing. Kioto cuddles up next to Bu.

Ladimer glances toward Kioto. "Why big smelly here? I'm the one who walks you." Ladimer looks blatantly jealous. It seems to be a common trait of his nowadays.

But "big smelly" isn't the best thing to call Bu right in front of him, so I change the subject. "Bu, Gunthreon told me how you can fix things. That's pretty cool big guy."

His head turns down in a modest sort of way. "Yeah, Bu just like to see how things work here." Modesty turns to sadness. It hits me that Bu would probably rather live here, but cannot because of what he is.

"Funny, Bu—both you and Ladimer kind of do the same thing. You both know how things work!" Bu looks up, and there's a sudden gleam of pride in his eyes. Ladimer rolls his own. A sudden knocking noise from my refrigerator diverts Bu's attention while I pull Ladimer to the side. "You can change him!"

"What?"

"Make him human."

Like a tornado, Ladimer's energy starts twirling, violently, for no apparent reason. "*No!* I will not!" His intensity frightens me and I take a step back as he takes a deep breath to calm himself down. "Altering living creatures to that degree is wrong. Believe me, I've had experience." He turns from me and heads toward Bu, whose concentration is intense as he reconnects some wires in my refrigerator and blabs something about a thermistor. He then cleans off one of his wrenches.

I turn on the television, and there's nothing on except the good ol' news. The lead story is on a missing physicist, Dr. Martine, who disappeared from his lab in Maryland, and the only clue they found in the lab was a dead chupacabra-looking animal. I click off the TV and move to pack a bag for our trip.

Ladimer turns the news back on. "Don't you want to be up to date on current events?" he says. "Who knows what happened to this guy? He's been working on some pretty interesting things—one's some kind of machine that's able to replicate what might have happened during the so-called 'Big Bang.' You know, more and more occurrences like this are happening around the world. I just heard a week ago there's also a famous biologist missing."

"You sound like a reporter."

"I just like not to be left in the dark."

I stand hands-on-hips in front of him. "Don't you know a lot of this is bull?"

"Yeah, well, a lot is *not*."

He's evidently one of those late night news junkies. I don't want to argue. "We are going on a trip tomorrow, so go start packing."

"Gunthreon already called. I'm packed. I also threw a few things in a bag for big dopey." I give him a look, daring him to say one more insulting remark about Bu.

Bu doesn't hear, and asks if he can take a few of my snacks on the trip. "Go ahead, Bu," I say. "Take whatever you'd like." This gets him very excited. At least someone is satisfied with the simple things in life.

"Well, I'm going to finish watering some plants at home," yaps Ladimer. "And oh, your *boyfriend* is coming over to help me with you-know-who before I leave my apartment next-door for good."

"He's not my boyfriend."

Chapter 29

Desperate

CR

The next day, Gunthreon tells me about the hours spent with Conner and their efforts in speaking with Philip's foster mom. Also, several odd-hour calls to different offices within the Department of Children and Family Services—as well as government employees' homes—were made, resulting in Philip becoming officially off the adoption radar. Conner also agreed to join our quest at the request of Gunthreon, who thought his abilities would come in handy.

Apparently, Conner has had numerous conversations with Russell and Gunthreon about the odd occurrences happening and his own theories. It's decided Russell is to stay in Abscondia, continuing on with his own quest—Amber.

Everyone is equipped with their backpacks, bundles and bags, but nobody truly exudes readiness for this journey, for Gunthreon had given us quite the pep talk about the severity of the matter and the fact we could all die. I feel many nervous jitters, and not just from myself. The uneasiness is thickening the air around everyone, making it difficult for me to gather my own thoughts and strength.

Kioto sits by Bu's feet, watching everyone closely, her eyes picking up every nervous movement. She knows something is up. I fill her water and food bowl and kiss her on the head. Her eyes plead and I whisper to her, "Please stay." She seemingly understands and lies down quietly.

I take a last peek in my bag at what I've packed. I grab a few more toiletries and my iPod, thinking it's small enough to hide from any technology police.

Before I turn to join my motley crew, I take a glance at my dresser and see my father's silver ring lying there, willing me to touch it. I reach over and pick it up and turn it over and over in my hand, attempting to gather the needed courage to go on with this madness of travelling between planes, trying to find some god I never knew existed, to save lives—actual lives. I take a deep breath and think to myself that if I really want to prove something to myself—that I'm strong enough to face anything—I best get this party going.

"I'm ready," I say as I enter the family room. Then wanting to give my own pep talk, I say, "Remember everyone, we have karma on our side, even if she feels like puking, too." Bu looks frightened and falls slightly deeper into my couch, so I secretly wink at him and shake my head. He turns away from everyone and smiles to himself.

Conner sits on the couch, and I sit next to him, putting my hand on his leg. "Find a sitter for Cherry?" He nods and his shoulders slump slightly. I feel that he's as scared as I am pretending not to be. He whispers something in my ear, indeed confirming that he's scared as hell, but willing to go on our quest. Ladimer sees the exchange between us and quickly diverts his eyes when I turn toward him.

Then Ladimer stands up before us, as though he's going to give a speech. "So, I wanted to all let you know that I've rented an apartment in this complex as of yesterday—one building over. Kailey," he says toward me, "perhaps you can come over later and... " The look in his eyes makes me shudder as I instantly sweat. "... help me decorate. Here's my phone number." He hands me a piece of paper. Conner and Ladimer exchange a look that isn't entirely friendly.

Conner then says, "You know, in thinking about it, I don't really think the matter of your disappearance from the adoption list was entirely taken care of. I'm sure there'd be lots of media hype on a lost seven-year-old, eh? Might be hard to hide, then." He stands up and Ladimer straightens up, willing a fight between them. I blush from the argument, not knowing what to do as the ego battle ensues. The fear we harbor is going to eat us from the inside out. Bu stands with his hands on his ears, just like a certain monkey I fear.

"Children!" This is from Gunthreon, who seems to have come to his own senses. "Stop this insidious behavior. I'd think you were in grade school, fighting over the new girl in town. Everyone grab your belongings. We are leaving. Kailey, you need practice, so try taking us to Renhala, now." Caught off guard, I just stand there, staring at Gunthreon. "Now, please. Just grasp each person's energy. You can do this."

I think of the only two places I know, and focus on Meadow's Edge, our destination.

We arrive, and when I open my eyes, I jump up and down. "I did it, I did it!" I cry. But Conner shuffles his feet uncomfortably, and Gunthreon swears under his breath. "What now?" I can't seem to do anything right. I twirl around and realize what I've done. No Ladimer. "Shit!"

"You have to go back and get him," states Gunthreon. "He doesn't know where we are."

I instantly go back and find him standing at the window, staring out at nothing. Quietly, he whispers, "Just like Georgie Parker."

"Huh?" He's got me on this one. "What does that mean? Who's that?"

"Nothing. Just take me to everyone, please." He doesn't accept a hug, instead just pushing me away. "We have our quest, remember?" I feel his pain in my own chest and want to make it go away, but I know I can't. It feels as though my mere presence next to him upsets him right now, and his energy is actually repelling my own—a horrible feeling for me.

"Ladimer. Please don't make me feel like the bad guy in all this. Don't humiliate me any further."

"Humiliate you? You don't know the half of it! Just take us now, or you can forget my help."

I struggle to grasp his energy, which is still fighting against my own, but suddenly, we're back with our friends. Conner looks to Ladimer, and Ladimer turns away. As we begin walking across the rocklands, following Gunthreon to Lupa's house, nobody speaks, and poor Bu just trails behind everyone. I stop and walk next to him. "Conner and Ladimer angry," he says, sadly. "Bu wants to cry." He tears up, too. What is it with men and all their issues?

"They're being very immature right now," I explain. "I'd have to say you are the most grown-up one here now, seriously." His hand grabs mine gently, and he kisses it.

The gentleness of his touch soon migrates to pain as we suddenly smell the smoke, hear the screams, and watch as a screaming dragon falls from the sky. The last thing I remember is **Neda save us all** bursting through my head like lightning.

◌

My vision is foggy, but I sit up on my own. Chaos screams around me, and I don't know what to do. My head hurts *again*, and I see the piece of rock that must have hit me lying next to my leg. Meadow's Edge is under attack and the battles have spread to the rocklands. Gunthreon stands beside Lupa, who seems to be using her gardening tools as weapons to fight off some huge creature resembling a giant earwig. Conner uses his sword to slice into a giant squirmy larva that keeps spitting brown liquid at him, and Bu pummels a greble about his size.

That's when I see Ladimer tending to Greer. I run to them and peer into Greer's eyes, sensing a retreat from consciousness.

"Kailey, this is bad. I can't heal him fast enough. My energy is draining," whispers Ladimer. "His injuries are too substantial." Ladimer is pale from giving his all.

"Keep trying Ladimer, please!" Greer's eyes roll back into his head like marbles.

"My energy... I can't do this without your help. Replenishment," he yelps, as he fades fast. The drain he speaks of feels like a malfunctioning vacuum trying to suction, but with a disconnected hose. With a push of his breath, he says, "Kiss me, Kailey."

My eyebrows raise and I don't move. "What?" I ask, dumbfounded.

"Please!" I hear *Kailey* in my head, and the combined pleas push me over the edge as Ladimer passes out. I know I will somehow regret what I'm about to do, but they both need the help, and fast. Conner's attention is elsewhere, so I go for it.

As Ladimer slumps over Greer, I grab his mouth and kiss him with a newfound passion. With all the anger he makes me feel, I still care for him. I take the anger and pry his mouth open with my own, and in a last ditch effort, I gather my own energy and desire and push it into him, transferring it. A profound warmth seems to spread from my own body and travel into his as the hunger I have for him swells inside me like a tornado. I grab onto his waist.

He awakens, and his energy multiplies with my own. I can feel it flow over me and Greer both. One hand is still on Greer, but the other finds my back. He grabs at me and lets me know he's not going to let go until he's through. I allow it. His energy is like fiery water; it's hot, but flows like liquid, and flows slowly over every sensitive spot on my body. I don't want it to end, but am afraid of the power coursing between us. With every second, my body feels renewed and replenished, like when I stepped into the life pool. My respect for Ladimer intensifies with each spasmodic episode, for he is a giver of life and the pleasures life brings. The touch of his hand is magic.

He still holds me and Greer. His face is one of sheer joy, and I hope he feels what I feel. He opens his mouth and I hear, "Just like Luke Levine." This time, the name tickles my memory, but I still don't know what he's talking about. I feel the power parting slowly, and my heart no longer pounds in my throat. Finally, he lets go of me, and I slide down to the ground. I have no energy left whatsoever.

"Kailey, that wasn't only me, you know." Ladimer seems drunk with energy as he crawls down. "That was your power, too. I felt it."

Well, it's about time, you two.

I smile, for I know Greer is okay, but a glance in Conner's direction tells me someone else is not. His attention is directed toward us for a brief moment, and then he quickly turns to the larva, which is gaining ground on him. With disgust plastered across his face, he jabs the creature in the gut with his sword and stands, covered in disgusting goo, staring at me. He then turns back to the fighting as my energy returns and I realize the chaos around us has not lessened.

Greer stands up to his full height, stretches, and bows to Ladimer, then to me, then flies straight up toward another black speck in the sky. My monk's spade is warm and I grab it, embracing its warmth and swinging it through the air, becoming acquainted with it once again. I run toward Bu, who is still fighting the greble, and run my blade through the greble's heart with ease, suddenly feeling a certain undescribable pang (the best way I can put it) in my energy and near my own heart.

"Thanks, Kailey. Bu tired," he says. He sits on the ground almost immediately, then lies on his back.

"This is not the time to sleep, Bu. Get up. Bu, get up." The blood starts to pour out from underneath him. I scream for Ladimer.

"Kailey, you help Bu like you help Ladimer," he pleads quietly.

His pain-filled smirk makes me smile sympathetically.

"Bu, you have to protect me," I say. "Hang in there, buddy." Ladimer comes, and I help him turn Bu over. I can't believe what I see. Bu has an actual screwdriver stuck in his back.

"Ladimer, get it out, and make sure you clean, please," Bu says. With this, he passes out. I kiss him gently on the forehead.

Ladimer heals him easily, and without *my* help. *Sorry, Bu.*

The carnage around me attacks my senses once more. "What's going on?" I ask. "Do you have any idea, Ladimer?" But for once, he is speechless. Gunthreon and Lupa join us, and I see that Lupa is bleeding from a few cuts, but is generally okay. Gunthreon is unscathed, but keeps putting his arm around Lupa, trying to comfort her, or perhaps himself.

"Lupa, what's happening?" I say. She has to know.

"One moment, I'm preparing a stew, and the next, I'm fighting off a giant bug trying to crawl in through my open window. I didn't know until I stepped out that everyone seemed to be fighting. It happened so quickly, even Greer was caught off guard."

Suddenly, Ladimer shouts, "Mortimer!" and takes off running toward town. I try chasing him, but he is too fast. Standing amongst the fighting, I am once again lost. But just as I stop, I feel the sensation of being swept up in the air and almost having the breath knocked out of me. I don't know how to react, or who to scream to for help, and even if I did, I don't think anything would help me at this height.

Chapter 30

Truthful
☙

A great green talon has me in its grasp, and we are flying, and fast, straight up in the air. I recognize the talon as Greer's.

Sorry to startle you, karmelean.

"That's all right, I guess. Where are you taking me?"

My urgent matter has been taken care of, so I want to show you something. Also, I don't trust you'll keep yourself alive in the battle down there. I can see that, overall, the enemies below are retreating.

"I lose the vote of confidence."

I have lived long, Kailey, and have learned a great many things. One of them is to read a person's energy. When you helped me today, I felt your essence, and I know you are one to trust, unlike many others. I also know that you underestimate your powers. You are very powerful, but I feel you need more practice on channeling, perhaps? After all, you're Quicksilver's daughter. She wasn't always Quicksilver you know. She was once just like you: naïve.

Greer's ride is smooth, and I love his embrace. He's extremely gentle, and I can relax in his grasp. He's also very warm, and that wonderful smell of cinnamon emanates from him. As we fly over Meadow's Edge, I can see the all too-familiar rocklands I previously traveled across. I see that the rocks are indeed in a pattern, because they form a giant version of the rune of Meadow's Edge. It is beautiful.

Greer starts his descent, and we land at the life pool.

Does this seem familiar to you?

"Yeah, it's the life pool that I entered not that long ago. It's absolutely wonderful," I coo. "Why are we here?"

I'm glad you used the pool. It is a female Life Pool and can do many a wonder for those who enter. Kailey, believe it or not, you were born in that pool.

I smile for the simple knowledge of one more fact on my birth.

Here in Meadow's Edge, everyone is born in either a female or male life pool. Babies born here alternate. This way, there is a balance, always. The pregnant female is told by a shaman what sex her baby will be, and then she comes to the pool when her contractions start, and all friends and family stand around and witness the birth. I was lucky enough to witness yours. Your mother was absolutely beautiful, standing in the center of the pool, shining like a night star, and she was absolutely ecstatic seeing your face for the first time. You are lucky to have her as your mother. She loves you beyond words. He pauses briefly. *You know, she came to me very recently to visit.*

"She did? What did you talk about?"

I'm going to be honest, because I think we both know that she is not doing so well. Her pain is intensifying. We spoke about the good old days and of our many journeys through this life, and of her love for you. But she's very tired, Kailey.

I think of my mom and feel the tears start to trickle down my face. "I know," I say as I look down at my hands.

The day you were born, your father was here too. My face rises instantly. *He loved your mother very much, but had already begun having troubles. When you were born, the pool lit up with such bright light we all had to close our eyes or turn away. It was as though Neda itself blessed your birth. We could all feel its energy and were awestruck. In my many years of life, I have never witnessed that kind of reaction from a life pool. Your mother then brought you to your father, and*

213

he laid one gentle kiss upon your head. I could sense the energies in you and felt both the good and bad as they exist in newborns, passed on from previous lives' experiences. You see, babies are not truly born devoid of bad energy—only born into ignorance. As they grow, they nurture their energies, either feeding the good or the bad.

"Oh. Nice to know I have evil pumping through my veins," I respond.

I want you to know a piece of your history. Let's say I'm satisfying karma. He winks at me. *Remember, I can feel your energy, and it is good and powerful. Your soul was meant to do something great in this world. I know this. Your family housed a constant struggle between good and bad as you grew, and your father left because he saw what he was doing to his family. Your mother then nursed your good energy as much she could, sheltering you from many of life's complexities. I know now, though, that she knew what she was doing. You are karma full strength, and are here to show us the path. I need you to tell me you understand.*

I just sit, not saying a word, trying to take in everything Greer is saying to me. "I don't know what the hell I'm doing, Greer." Greer studies me intensely with his giant eyes, and when I shake my head no, he nods.

You do, Kailey. Reach deep inside. Make your mother proud, girl.

The tears flow yet again, and I make a promise to both myself and Greer to do the best I possibly can. I try thinking of any evil things I may have done when I was younger—I call them "*Flatliner*" moments—but I have to agree with Greer. I was generally a good kid. Except...

A single act floats before me in my head: the day I broke a little boy's heart. "Georgie Parker!" My thoughts begin to race as I see Ladimer, broken-hearted, standing before me saying "Just like

Georgie Parker." My thoughts buzz in my head at deadly RPMs. How could Ladimer know something like that?

Greer looks at me like I just spoke Greek. ***Now* you *have me confused. What is your little mind thinking right now?***

"We need to find Ladimer. He went to check on Mortimer, but I couldn't keep up. Come on, come on." I snap my fingers.

The great creature before me suddenly laughs. ***If you were anyone else, I would have just eaten you for that. Hold on, little one.*** He puts out a claw, and I grab on as he swoops me up. If life was easy, he'd drop me when we were a few thousand feet above the ground, but then who would save the world? A few maniacal laughs escape my mouth, and Greer peeks at me out of the corner of his eye.

I will never fully understand you humans. And to think I am placing my life in the hands of an extremely strange one. Neda save us all. He laughs, and I whole-heartedly laugh with him.

Mortimer's shop appears below us like a speck of dirt. Greer descends quickly and lands perfectly. I hop off his claw and race to the front door while Greer watches the skies. He seems to be expecting something and he growls a deep, low growl. Sooner than I can say "turnip," he flies straight up. I hope I never happen upon whatever he's been fighting.

The store seems quiet, and I am reluctant to enter. The bell chimes overhead, and I wince, for fear someone may jump out at me. There is silence, and I am afraid, for my monk's spade jumps to life. I take it off my back—I've gotten much better at that at least—and walk toward the back shop area where Mortimer does his magic. Just as I open the door, I see the most gruesome creature staring at me. Paralysis kicks in, and I cannot move an inch. I once thought grebles were the scariest thing ever, but this takes the cake.

The creature is somewhat human, thin, and stands about seven feet tall, but the horribleness is that it is somehow inside-out. *How can it survive with all its internal organs hanging out?* The heart is beating, and I can see the blood flowing to its kidneys, liver and many other nameless items—I was never good in biology. It has two eyes, which still stare at me, and have not blinked once. It has a mouth, for I can see about, oh, a hundred vampire-sharp fangs in it, and it has a black tongue, like some rabid chow.

I grasp the monk's spade a bit tighter, for the paralysis lets up slightly, and that's when it moves. Before I can take a breath, it is standing an inch from my face, again staring. It breaths on me and smells like pork. I vow never to eat bacon again, if I live. It seems to be examining my face, maybe deciding which facial feature to eat first.

It then says one word to me: "Run."

I try and move, but find I'm still stuck.

"Run."

I cannot even open my mouth to give this creature some choice words I've thought up. I send out my feeler, quickly—my attempt at an offensive move. *Nothing.* My eyes opens wide. "It has no energy! How—"

"Run!" This time it screams at me.

My legs have feeling once again, and I do just what it says, just as a meeple jumps toward me from behind a soldering table. The inside-out man lunges at it and digs its teeth into the meeple. The bunny screams a hideous scream, and the blood splashes over my back as its head is ripped off.

Fear creeps up my throat like vomit, and I take off as fast as my feet can carry me. I'm almost to the back door when I stumble over Mortimer and Ladimer, both tied up and gagged. Ladimer stares at inside-out man, and Mortimer has either passed out or died. The creature is just standing there now, not doing anything.

That's when I see the huge ax sticking out of the back of its head.

"How is it still alive?" I turn to my friends and realize they cannot answer gagged. I use my monk's spade to cut through the thick rope they are bound with. Ladimer quickly grabs Mortimer, undoes his belt, and starts to remove his pants.

"What the hell are you doing right now?" I don't know if I want to know. But I soon see why Ladimer was so eager to remove Mortimer's pants: his legs are inside out. He is surely still alive, for I see the telltale blood flow. Ladimer does his magic and Mortimer's legs return to normal.

"Oh my god!" I exclaim. "What the hell is that thing, and why did it kill the meeple?"

The creature pulls the ax from its head, returns it to a hook on Mortimer's wall, and then bends over toward the meeple. It takes something from the meeple's carcass, then leaves.

Ladimer speaks to me. "It's a deathman. Wherever there is death, you will find a deathman. They don't choose sides. They only feed on those who are dying or newly dead, and the only way to avoid them is to be buried beneath the ground before they get you. Deathmen eat souls, and then they dispose of the souls wherever they take them, but nobody really knows where. I must say, though, I've never seen a deathman attack like that." Ladimer looks at the meeple's body.

Mortimer stands up, brushing himself off. "Thank you, Kailey. You saved us," he says. "When I entered my shop I saw Ladimer hanging." I gasp. "The deathman was approaching him, so I grabbed my ax, cut Ladimer down, and then swung in desperation at it. Honestly, I didn't want it coming for me, even if it was my time to go. I'm such a coward." He spews disgust—with himself.

"Mortimer, I would have done the same exact thing, so don't beat yourself up over it." A thought suddenly occurs to me. "Grim Reapers! They actually exist. That's what the cape hides. Gross."

"That damn meeple was too quick for us." Ladimer's words are chock-full of anger. "Damn thing jumped on my mind so quick. When I got here, I was so worried about Mortimer I let my defenses down. It actually made me grab that rope down from a shelf so I could hang myself with it. Mortimer was not even in his shop. Good thing I was here first. That meeple might have gotten Mortimer's lutheose secrets out of him, giving the bad guys a very powerful weapon against us, I think."

"Can we get out of here quick?" I don't want to be here anymore.

Mortimer's face is suddenly one of sheer terror as Ladimer turns to him and says, "You know you need to leave this place for good."

"You know I cannot. This is my life, Ladimer."

"There is evidently a solid reason they keep showing up here, Mortimer," grunts Ladimer. "They will continue until they get what they're after. Every day, they are becoming smarter. They will figure out how to use your gift against us. Lutheose is *your* baby, Mortimer. Don't let them discover the secret."

"Funny, because I don't even know *the secret!*" says Mortimer, with a bit of sarcasm. "I just create it. It just happens. I've never told anyone this," he pauses, "but I essentially black out while I make it. I black out! I don't even know what goes into it. I'm the only one that can do it, though, so everyone gives me the credit and praise. So even if they got me, I don't think they'll ever know, because I don't even know." He stares at his feet and looks very much discouraged. "*I'm* the secret ingredient."

I walk to him, whispering in his ear, "We're in the same boat. I have no clue how these damn powers work and what to do with them. I need direction, too. We need a foreman or something." He laughs again, but this time it lightens my heart.

Ladimer doesn't laugh. "Your brains know how you do it. There's an expanse of brain that's working undercover, and someone is going to learn how to tap that. It's only a matter of time. Let's go."

Chapter 31

Exposed
CR

The fighting seems to have died down, and there are only a few scrappy battles remaining. We find our friends at Lupa's house, all eating homemade pineapple upside-down cake, but they don't seem to be truly enjoying it. Conner gives me a glance and continues eating. There's some blood on his face from a cut, and I step forward to tend to him, but he brushes me off.

"Leave it. I'll be fine."

"Are you sure about that?" I ask, reaching my feeler to examine him, but somehow he blocks my advances as he suddenly stands up and strikes up a conversation with Bu, who seems startled that Conner is talking to him while he's busy eating.

Gunthreon seems oblivious to my many problems. "I think that Meadow's Edge is safe for the time being," he says. "Greer seems to have some things under control for now. This attack had to be Velopa's doing. It seems they all fanned out from Mortimer's shop. I fear for him." Gunthreon looks tired. "I tried persuading information from a captive of mine, but he didn't know Velopa's whereabouts. It could be that only a select few know. But we must continue searching for Neda. I think if Neda was destroyed, we'd all be dead at this point, or prisoners of war. The balance still exists, but it's teetering."

I furrow my brow. "I'm sorry. I don't understand." Without realizing I even do it, I take out my father's ring and run it between my fingers.

Gunthreon nods. "Kailey," he says, then hesitating, "we believe we may be on the edge of another 'Surge.'"

"Oh my god!" I exclaim, truly frightened as I think of Gunthreon's tale of the original 'Surge' –the very one that gave birth to war and strife in Abscondia.

Gunthreon says, "But I myself am confused about the way things are proceeding, like there's a goal, but no organized plan of action. Things are messy and random, unlike anything I've seen before."

"My exact thoughts," adds Ladimer. "Uncertainty creates chaos. It seems as though armies are being sent out with a known mission, but no map."

Gunthreon seems to be concentrating. Finally, after what seems like much gathering of courage, he says, "I've heard from a reliable source that Devoten has been talking of something he calls 'the releasing.'"

I think to myself that the *reliable source* may otherwise be known as Dena May, or Mom.

He continues with, "I have no clue as to what this 'releasing' is. And also, he...has an unidentified informant feeding him some very valuable information *about us*." He looks to each face before him. "Devoten somehow knows we are working to get to the bottom of what is going on, and that we plan on stopping it."

"Whoa!" Conner shouts. "I'm well aware that we are searching for information, but I think of us as 'intelligence' vs. 'the front line.' I suggest we settle on doing the research, then passing it on to those more equipped for fighting a possible war."

I have begun fidgeting even more with my ring and drop it on the ground. It rolls from me, and as I watch, nobody moves to pick it up for me, instead they watch it continue on its seemingly endless roll. I think of Ladimer not touching my pendant.

I walk to pick it up as each look at one another.

Ladimer breaks the silence and says, "And this is what war does, doesn't it Gunthreon? Makes mutiny in your own battalion quite believable. How long have you been sitting on this information? Secrets kept between old friends?" He is offended, and makes sure we hear it in his voice. "Just who might this informant be? Perhaps someone who might be the biggest surprise of all," he looks at Gunthreon, "or maybe someone of whose history we know nothing?" He says this loudly in Conner's direction.

Conner turns, taking the comment as the blow it was meant to be. "Yes, Gunthreon, who among us would have such a past?" Then Conner says something in soulspeak, and we all turn to Ladimer, knowing Conner has spoken something to the effect that he's innocent.

Ladimer, frustrated, turns to each of us, examining our expressions, then walks out Lupa's door. I run after him, grabbing at his arm. He tries to pull away, but I'm ready to put up a fight. I continue holding his arm.

"Georgie Parker, eh?" I say. "Tell me, how would you know about that, Ladimer?"

"How would I know of a heartbroken little boy who was the only one not invited to your ninth birthday party? Take a guess, Kailey. You're really not as dumb as you appear." He tries to walk away again, but I refuse to let him go, even if he's trying to hurt me.

"Luke Levine?"

He sighs. "Kissed for the first time by the cutest little redheaded vixen." I hear his words, but cannot believe what I am finally realizing—a unique coincidence. A scar below each of their left eyes. Georgie's scar freaked out my best friend, hence no invitation to my party, and Luke's was mysterious and intoxicating, hence my affection.

"Why?" I say, shakily. Scared, I let go of his arm, now knowing that Ladimer, blessed with his special abilities, has been present in my life for longer than I know. Flashbacks of Philip's strange touches and odd behaviors play in my mind. I'm afraid of

Ladimer's deception—how deep, and in what direction it may be running—yet I feel nothing harmful from his energy. But, he is indeed powerful and I consider the possibility of his powers managing a change in his energies.

"What? Think I've been scheming all these years to get you into Velopa's hands?" he says. "Well, perhaps I had a good reason for following you around your whole damn life. Maybe I was actually foresworn to protect you—karmelean, daughter of Quicksilver. You see, once upon a time, a young woman gave birth to a very special girl. This mother feared for her daughter and asked one of her very best friends to follow her through life, protecting her, for the girl's father had fallen from grace. So, this best friend wasted a portion of his life following a girl he grew to love in so many ways. I gave up fighting in my own realm to live here, in this stupid, good-for-nothing realm. The complexities of living as different people, of different ages, is in no way a blessing, Kailey. It's been a curse." He pauses to look at me with his wet eyes. "And the one day I was needed most, I wasn't there, and the beautiful girl I swore to watch over was hurt, badly. So, yeah, maybe I am not to be trusted, for I cannot even carry out what I have sworn to do." He then looks away.

I am filled with such mixed emotions it feels as though something is eating its way out through my gut. He seems to feel that it's his fault I suffered the assault by the monster, that unforgettably painful day in my apartment. "Ladimer, I... " I don't know what to say.

"No need. I must leave now, for I am not trusted here. I will not allow myself to feel more pain from you and my so-called friends. You could never even *begin* to understand the angst I've experienced throughout your lifetime. Goodbye, Kailey."

With this, he turns and walks toward the rocklands. I sit on the nearest patch of grass. Then I see movement out of the corner of my eye. It's Conner.

"I'm assuming you overheard that, right?" I ask.

"Yes, I did. Let him go," says Conner. "Does he speak the truth?"

"He's not you, but yes, I believe he does."

"You know straight from my soul that I am faithful to this mission, Kailey, and I will not let anything bad happen to you while I am on it. I care about you, and will *not* deceive you," he says. I start to say something, but he shakes his head. "Do not patronize me and tell me you care about me too. I want more than that. I saw that kiss with Ladimer, and *ours* should not be resultant of some life-threatening situation." His hands move slowly to my face and then slowly, once he sees no rejection from me, his lips meet mine. There's a small shock of static electricity as he touches me. "What, no strawberry lip gloss?" He's spews determination, yet there's an underlying sense of uncertainty—an undercurrent of something shaky.

Despite my confused feelings, and need for something concrete in my life—something I can lean against without fear of falling—to Conner's surprise, and mine, I pull him in with more force and kiss him back, tasting my salty tears as they run between us. My need for some sort of solid foundation has me suddenly reaching for his nervous energy and gently coaxing the uncertainty away, wanting him to be the support I desire. He opens his eyes, definitely feeling my workings, and I feel the muscles relax in his kiss. He whispers in my ear that everything will be all right as I realize that I may have just taken advantage of Conner, and that he honestly must believe that everything will be all right—exactly what I need.

∞

At night, I sit near the window closest to the fireplace, watching and hoping for Ladimer to return. He never does.

Before bed, Lupa makes us all some deliciously smooth and creamy hot cocoa that goes down easily—not too sweet, not too thick. I myself am falling in love with this woman, for her love and ability to cook make her something special in my eyes.

Soon, Gunthreon starts shooing us to our rooms, as he wants us all to have a decent night's sleep. I ask to sit a bit longer, because the fire calms my nerves. After several assurances that Gunthreon never knew of Ladimer's promise to my mom, Gunthreon and Lupa agree. They say their goodnights.

Conner lingers a bit. He sits next to me and kisses me on my head while he covers my feet with my blanket.

"You need sleep, Kailey," he declares. "He will return in due time. I can honestly admit we need him on this journey."

"You need sleep, too. Today was a rough day for everyone," I say. "Goodnight." He stays seated, just staring at me. I see the fatigue in his face, but that doesn't make him any less handsome. His whirlpool blue eyes steal my thoughts, and I want him to whisk me away on a current to some secret island, where there is no fighting and I can sit beneath a willow tree and drink wine and eat gummy bears and be merry all day. He smiles warmly at me, and I smile back.

"You sure are something special," he whispers. "I hope you realize that."

It's what every girl wants to hear, but for some reason it's something I can't truly believe of myself. "Yeah, well, I wish I could believe that. But I know me best, and I feel I cannot live up to what everyone thinks I am."

"Ladimer's stories aren't the only ones I've heard from my parents, you know," says Conner. "I've heard stories of great ones to come, and within you my dear, I feel something great and powerful." I think of Greer's words near the life pool. "Don't be afraid to let it out, Kailey. Be the woman to spark a thousand more stories," he says.

These words, and his firm belief in me, ignite something deep within me, and the emotion I sudden feel has my hands on his chest holding him down, and again we feel the same static shock, but it fires my emotions further. "Wow, that's a start," he says. He's surprised, but a twist of his weight flips our positions, and he's suddenly on top. I feel a flame of power inside which awakens a bit of anxiety, and increases my breathing, but he whispers in my ear and it all melts away, replaced by a hunger so strong I cannot hold back. "Relax, Kailey. You know you can always use the whistle." Again, that wonderful sexiness of his soulspeak warms me up. He smiles, and I laugh a throaty laugh, full of want. I pull his lips toward mine, and he holds back, still looking in my eyes. "Are you sure?"

"Relax, Conner." Cool moonlight highlights his face, and his magnetism is mesmerizing. His hands are gentle, but his want for me is not. The eyes staring back at me are puddles: mirrors for reflection, but of shallow depth, for his need of me is concrete and unporous, preventing the escape of a single hint of contemplation. His hair has fallen in my face, and it smells like summer sex—beach, cocoa butter, and sweat. I breathe in, and it makes all my worries disappear, like clouds dissipating as the sun bursts with heat.

My pulse rises as my head clears, bringing forth my simple need and want for him. He breathes in my ear, whispering sweet truths to my soul, then lowers his face to mine, and his kiss is enrapturing, giving birth to a passion so intense, that when he grabs a handful of my hair, it sends a spark of energy between us, extending to the furniture, along the floor, and to the walls.

His hand finds my breast and caresses with such care that I squeeze his hand, harder, wanting more from his grasp. I quickly work my shirt up and off. He grabs a nipple with his fingers and squeezes, sending me pleasure that bows my back as he kisses my neck. I find him under the blanket, and he's ready for me, which only makes my own need so intense that I start pulling his shorts down with my legs and feet. My pajama pants make their way to my knees, and he finds me and the wet heat that seems to increase with every second. My power increases and I feel energy pulsing through my veins, quickening my heartbeat even more, while opening my mind to the same pleasure I felt while kissing Ladimer. *Ladimer.*

Before I can control it, at the same exact moment Conner enters me, I scream at the top of my lungs, expelling an energy to the walls, surrounding us, and once the room is fully engulfed in the energy we create, a huge explosion of light and sound threatens to wake everyone within three miles. Every hair on my body stands straight up, and I see nothing but light. An ethereal song is being sung and I am suddenly standing naked before a huge castle. I'm afraid, but feel drawn to this magnificent castle, which reeks of age and of stories untold. I touch the entry doors, and they whisper to me secret tales of happiness, tainted with moments of pain and sorrow. The doors are heavy, surely guarding treasures within, but I push with determination and they open, moaning from the intrusion.

The great room I enter threatens me with a sense of looming danger, but I walk on, stubborn with my need to find the source of a pulsating energy calling to me. I admire the beauty surrounding me; the tapestries mounted on the walls are lush and the cool, marble floor is covered with the largest, softest, most detailed rug I've ever seen. Vibrant, fresh flowers adorn antique vases in every nook and cranny I spot.

I walk slowly through the great room, but I am drawn to a spiral staircase that leads upstairs. Upon closer examination, it seems to be carved from one single piece of wood. That this is possible amazes me. My hand brushes the wood as I travel up, and a scene of druids and fairies dancing around a massive, ancient tree plays like a movie in my head.

Soon I stand before a wooden door adorned with carved creatures of magic. Unicorns and dragons battle amongst troves of deathmen. It's eerie and beautiful at the same time. I know what I seek is behind the door. It slowly opens before me.

He turns to me, his face full of surprise, but also despair. "Kailey, how did you—why are you—" His face is quizzical as I stand before him naked. I hold my arms out to him, but before he reaches me, I'm back in Lupa's front room with Conner balled up in the corner in his boxers, holding his knees to his chest, Gunthreon, Bu, and Lupa beside him.

As I appear before them, Gunthreon runs to me and covers me with a blanket.

For a moment, they all simply stare at me, waiting for me to speak. Finally, Bu breaks the silence, "What did you do? Bu was sleeping, the world exploded and then you were at a castle."

I'm as confused as they are. "You saw me at a castle?"

"You walked in the front door of the castle, and then I was back in bed."

Gunthreon holds my hand. "Where did you go, Kailey?"

"I don't know."

"Well, what did you see?" He seems eager for something worthwhile.

"I saw Ladimer."

Gunthreon smiles the biggest smile I've ever seen him wear.

Lupa also smiles. Bu sees them smiling, so he smiles, not knowing why. Conner is *not* smiling.

"You soulsearched!" Gunthreon is practically drooling, and his eyes are wide, like a hopped-up druggie.

"And travelled within," whispers Lupa to herself.

"Okay... "

"Let me explain," says Gunthreon. "We travelers can usually only travel to areas where we have been before, unless brought by someone else—this I've told you. But you—you can do something different. You can feel for someone's energy and then travel to that energy—anywhere in Renhala! This gift has very rarely been seen, at least in my lifetime. You had to have been thinking of Ladimer, right?" As he says this, he realizes he put his foot in his mouth. "Oh."

"Well, Bu was evidently there, too," I say, trying to save the situation.

"You felt you needed Bu's protection," Gunthreon adds, surely adding more fuel to Conner's fire.

Conner stands up and walks toward the bedrooms. "You must excuse me," he comments. "I'm exhausted, and this conversation is going in a direction that might prove detrimental to any good thoughts I have left of this night. Goodnight, good lady." His accent no longer sounds sexy, but dangerous. He bows toward Lupa and disappears into his room, totally ignoring me.

I am so embarrassed, and I turn to Lupa for help. "You know, I really do care for him," I confide. "He makes me feel strong and alive, but... " I cannot make eye contact with her.

"But Ladimer haunts your thoughts." I feel Lupa's stare as she talks to me. She leads me into the kitchen and shoos Gunthreon away. A beautiful teapot is set on the stove, and she begins to prepare some tea for the two of us. "Honey, believe it or not, I know where you're coming from." She looks into some distant past that seems to be playing on the rough surface of her kitchen wall, and her face softens, revealing the young Lupa she once was. "Many women have suffered this same fate. Decisions, decisions. Like my mom before me, I will give you this advice: Follow your heart. It will not lead you astray."

"Lupa, I appreciate the advice, but I know you know it's crap." She looks at me and starts to laugh, her crow's feet deepening near her eyes.

"Or you could go with the nicer butt!" She doubles over, and we're both laughing as Gunthreon walks by ever so slowly to grab a cookie. We both glance at his butt and crack up even more. He looks as though he's been publicly groped.

Lupa hands me a spoon, a jar of wildflower honey, and some additional advice: "I think you need sleep. We all need sleep. Finish your tea and hit the hay, girl. You've all got a long journey ahead of you still. Today was nothing." She pinches my cheek. "Please, no more explosions in my house. I don't think my tea cups can take it."

"Oh, believe me, that will *not* be happening again"—at least tonight. My body reacts to the thought of Conner against me, whispering to me. I sip my berry-tainted tea, realizing I am thoroughly confused.

"I'll make sure that power-hungry Gunthreon doesn't try to sneak to your room to make you talk about what happened," says Lupa. "I'll keep him busy." She's suddenly got a devilish glow about her, and I love this woman even more.

"Thanks for everything, Lupa. Gunthreon's a lucky man." She turns and heads for her own room. I wash the dishes, and eventually end up climbing into the bed she made for me. The linens smell of lilacs, and I burrow my face in the pillow, deep enough for near suffocation.

Chapter 32

Cold

☙

I open my eyes to dirty stone walls, and the stench of decay makes me grimace. It's cold in this dungeon of a place, the dampness of the air sticking to my skin. I am alone, and I feel like something is very wrong. There are chains attached to the walls, and bones, non-human and human alike, scattered here and there. My ears home in on speech, and I run to the nearest wall and peek around the corner.

There, I find another room like the one I am in, but much larger. I see a greble—make that the greble who wants to eat my brain, Tartarin—and someone else I cannot see. In the middle of the room is a huge metal box that seems to be perspiring. The sweat from the machine trickles along the floor, threatening my feet with dirt and grime. The container is at least fifteen feet high and fifteen feet wide, littered with dials and levers of all sorts. It appears that one side of the box opens on giant hinges.

"You better be doing your job right, you stupid human," barks Tartarin, as jolly as ever.

"I know what I'm doing. He's happy with my progress, so let it be, you ugly pile of horse manure."

Tartarin moves quickly, and before I even blink, he pulls this person into view. I don't recognize him. He wears a lab coat with a pocket protector and looks human enough to me, even though I can see someone did a number on the left side of his face. Tartarin pushes him away, practically throwing him to the ground.

Just then a door opens and another person enters. I recognize the cloak.

"Please get up, Dr. Speck. Tartarin, you touch him again and I will make you eat your own hands for breakfast," says Devoten. I

231

hold my breath, hoping that his dark energy—sudo-abominor—will not hunt my energy down, for I feel it wake up, and almost sniff like a bloodhound.

"Who knows if he's really doing his job?" says Tartarin, looking mighty pissed-off.

Despite his cloak hood over his face, I know Devoten is staring at Dr. Speck. "Oh, he knows what he must do, don't you, Doctor?" A small trickle of the dark energy that's Devoten's sneaks toward me. I can feel it approaching, slowly.

"Yes, sir, I do. Your happiness is important, sir. We really do need the metal, though, sir." He actually smiles at Devoten, and it's a loving smile, which makes me want to pull out Devoten's own eyes for making this man experience the unfortunate emotion of infatuation. "Is she strong enough yet?" asks Dr. Speck.

Devoten turns in my direction as I hear him say, "Let's all hope she is. Otherwise, we might have a date with some deathmen." A small yelp escapes Dr. Speck as he turns an odd, greenish hue, and the dark energy crawls up my leg, grasping it like a thorned weed.

☙

I wake up in bed in Lupa's house, shuddering at the remnants of my experience. I attempt to climb out of bed, then land on my butt as my water-drenched slippers come in contact with the stone floor.

As I lie still, the sun gleams in my face, cheerily informing me that, despite the fact that I'm totally exhausted, it's morning. I feign stupidity as I close the curtains and climb back into bed, shuddering as I think of Devoten and what technology he may have brought to Renhala. Two more hours of sleep won't hurt.

☙

"Let her sleep a little longer," whispers Lupa as she walks past the bedroom door.

"Kailey." This is whispered by Bu. I try to fake a snore, but have a feeling it doesn't matter what I do. "Kailey." His voice is slightly louder.

"I'm sleeping, Bu."

"Oh. Sorry." He turns to walk away. "Hey, wait. You silly, Kailey." He trounces in my bedroom and sits on the bed, practically tipping me out of it. "Lupa made breakfast. You have to come eat. They keep telling me to save some for you, but, but—"

"Just save me a cup of tea and a biscuit. You can have the rest, Bu." The speed with which he jumps off my bed and into the hallway makes my head spin. The talking in the kitchen gets louder as Bu exclaims he can eat most of my portion.

"Tell her to get her lazy ass up and save her own biscuit." Conner sounds like he must have gotten some real good shut-eye. Who is he to talk about *my* biscuit anyway?

I drag my legs off the bed and sit up, not wanting to stand. My body feels like I ran a marathon and a half. I feel my head and my crazy hair, which is especially knotted this morning. A simple pat doesn't really do the job, but I don't have to impress anyone this morning, not even the handsome gentleman with the killer blue eyes who hates me now.

The kitchen smells yummy, and I plop my butt on one of Lupa's chairs. Bu gives me the smallest biscuit I've ever seen and a cold cup of tea. He smiles at me with crumbs all over his face, and I do my best to return the smile.

"Hon, I can whip you up something else, too, if you want." Lupa is as fresh as ever; she's almost glowing. Gunthreon looks just as fresh, so I am happy at least someone had a pleasant night.

Gunthreon sits with a map spread out before him. "We're planning our route, and we'll want to leave as soon as we can," he says. "Make sure to pack your things up soon."

I frown. "How come we need to pack up our bags?" I ask, upset. "Can't we just transport ourselves where we need to go—you know, travel between places we need to search?"

"Well, generally, we are not supposed to be able to 'travel' within Renhala—only from your realm to Renhala and vice versa. Travelling within Renhala is usually done the old-fashioned way—with feet," says Gunthreon. "But after what you did last night, maybe we would be better off. Try bringing us somewhere, just me and you, within Renhala."

He stands before me with a smile plastered across his face, expecting me to do what I did (twice) last night. I close my eyes and do my best, but we end up in my apartment three times.

"I'm sorry Gunth, can't do it," I say once we're back at Lupa's place.

"That's fine. We'll work on it," he chatters, with a sense of displeasure. "Just go get your stuff ready, because we want to leave sooner rather than later."

"Can I go clean myself up?"

He grunts first, then gives me a yes that is not the most pleasant as he walks toward Conner, who examines the map. "From what I've heard," says Gunthreon, "we need to head east, to Socola—the mooncats' land."

Conner frowns. "Are you sure? That may be a little tough for those of us less experienced." He nods in my direction.

"What, aren't I powerful enough, eh?" I say. "You all keep telling me I am. Starting to doubt, aren't you?" I say with a small amount of hostility towards them. "Whatever. What the hell is a mooncat, anyway? It sounds like a dessert." I'm quite brave this morning after my debaucherous night.

Bu stares at me. "You don't know about them? They scare Bu, and they are *not* desserts."

"Bu, no offense, but I think everything scares you." Tears instantly well up in his eyes. "Sorry, Bu. I'm just tired this morning. I know you're not a scaredy-cat. You have been very brave."

I hear Conner clearing his throat. "Mooncats, for your information, are perhaps the most seductive creatures in Renhala. They are beautiful and enticing, but you must *never* be alone with them, not even one. Make sure you always have one of us with you. Understand?" Conner tries to make his point without looking directly at me.

"Sure, whatever you say soulspeaker—and who made you an expert? I think I can handle a few cats, though."

Conner laughs under his breath, cockily, and Gunthreon gives me a stern look, making me take a step back. "You'd better listen to what he's saying, Kailey. Do not underestimate them. Besides, the land of the mooncats is lit only by moonlight, hence their name. Enjoy the sun while you can."

I swallow hard. I think about meeples. If bunnies can be that dangerous... "I hear you."

"Good. Then go get cleaned up, and pack. We leave in twenty minutes."

As I head back to the bathroom, I grab Lupa. "What about Ladimer?" I query. "Will he know where we're going?"

"Don't worry about him. He'll find us if he needs to, or wants to. He has his ways."

"Where was that castle that I traveled to? It was the most hauntingly beautiful place."

She walks to her room and comes back with a beautiful, bound book. As she thumbs through the pages, I see the most vivid maps imaginable, and the scenes actually move slightly—a ripple of water here, a palm-like tree swaying there. Her finger lands on one page that seems to be mostly water. "There, somewhere. Ladimer's family home. His family is the only one that has ever lived on his island. It is not on any map, but is known to be in that sea."

"*Kailey, are you ready?*" I hear Gunthreon yell. "*You have fifteen minutes left!*"

"*Okay!*" I jump up and run into the shower room, pumping the ice cold water in Lupa's rudimentary shower.

"Ahhh!" I shout as I step foot in the water.

Chapter 33

Blue
ℭℛ

There was much arguing in Lupa's room before we left, but there was evidently no convincing her not to join our quest. I don't know if she's resistant to Gunthreon's ability, or if he doesn't use it on her, but I think he could have easily gotten her to stay home if he really wanted her to.

The townspeople are out and about, repairing Meadow's Edge. The baker tosses spoiled goods from her shop, and I see the local doctor pouring lime on a greble whose head is missing. We stop in front of Mortimer's shop, and I see him busy inside. Gunthreon leads us in, and I see Mortimer try to hide as we enter.

Gunthreon says his hello and asks Mortimer a question I do not hear, but gibberish is the only thing that escapes Mortimer's mouth. Gunthreon gives the floor to Conner, in hopes that soulspeak produces a different result. Conner introduces himself and says something I don't fully hear also. The tactic is to see first if Conner can get any information about creating lutheose out of Mortimer, because if Conner can, so can Devoten. After Conner talks with Mortimer, Mortimer's gaze turns foggy, and he again starts talking gibberish. Conner seems confused and looks to Gunthreon, who just shrugs.

"I don't know what he's saying," says Conner, returning to us, "and I always know what one is saying." Mortimer stops talking alien and just smiles. He then shakes his head and furrows his brow.

"I'm not going to have any luck getting his formula or processes, so I would think that would be the same for anyone," states Conner. Then he speaks once more to Mortimer, and again, the same gibberish spews from his mouth.

The second part of the plan is to see if Mortimer can create his lutheose elsewhere, but Gunthreon says, "I'm afraid if we pull him from his shop he may be of no use to anyone—even us if we need his metal. Let's let him be."

"Stay with your shop, Mortimer, and I will speak with Greer before we leave," advises Gunthreon. "We'll make sure you are well-guarded."

Mortimer smiles his own special smile this time. I see that he needs dental work, but it's still a lovely smile. I mention to him that he could create some lovely instruments for the local dentist. He evidently never thought of this, because it's like a light bulb goes off above his head. "Barter, Mortimer." I feel karma working to save his mouth.

"Bye, Mortimer." Gunthreon bows to him.

"Bye." He turns quickly to his sketchbook, and I see him deep in thought as I close the door.

"Be safe, good Mortimer," I say to myself.

The last stop in Meadow's Edge is Greer's lair. Gunthreon and Greer chat privately while we all wait outside, staring out at the land beneath us. I breathe in as much lilac-scented air as I can and feel a bit of sadness come over me as I realize I have to leave my homeland. My anxiety heightens at the thought of separation.

Karmelean, remember all that I told you, says Greer in my head. ***Stay strong. We need you.*** I think back to Greer and picture a tiny ant carrying a nut ten times the size of itself. His laugh is deep and hearty in my head.

"To the mooncats we go!" Gunthreon is cheerful, and seems to have enjoyed the chat with Greer. He later confirms that Greer mentioned he, too, had heard rumors about the east we're to explore. Good to know we're at least heading in the right direction.

"Onward ho," I grunt, the lack of enthusiasm blatant in my voice. The parting from Meadow's Edge, Conner's new attitude towards me, Ladimer's disappearance, and my time away from both Kioto and my mom have me wishing that I was someone else, someone like Amber—safe at home, in a new, but solid, relationship with someone who loves her, unconditionally. How quickly the tides change.

☙

The distance is great between Meadow's Edge and Socola, so it gives me plenty of time to think about things. I wonder how my mom and Kioto are doing, and what they are doing this very moment. I miss both of them, and wonder if they're thinking of me, too. My mom's blood pressure is probably skyrocketing, because she hasn't heard from me *and* she's pissed she wasn't invited. Maybe tonight, if nobody is paying me any attention, I can just pop on over and see them. It would be a fast visit, just to make sure everything is quiet in my realm.

We approach a land that, from a distance appears to be covered in purple. "Are we entering the Land of the Grapecats?" I amuse myself sometimes.

Conner gives me a "don't be stupid" look.

"How quickly we change our game," I say. He's got me angry now.

"Well, it's hard when you're invited onto the winning team, only to learn you're the sacrifice fly."

"Stop with all the stupid talk, both of you," Lupa sputters. "Shall we stop now for some supplies? We may not get the chance again." Gunthreon rolls his eyes. "I take that as a big fat yes," she says, a bit perturbed.

Purple, purple, and more purple is all I see as we come closer—purple houses, purple streets, and purple trees. I also see movement, and as I squint, I see people—very plump people, in fact, like Tweedledee and Tweedledum offspring. "How did we get to Wonderland?" I ask.

"Would you stop already with your dumb comments!" Conner is asking for a fight. I quickly reach to his energy to subdue his anger, but his eyes open wide and he points at me. "Don't even think about it! I know what you're attempting to do. Stay away from me—me and my...energy!"

"Maybe if you stop being so jealous!" My anger awakens as I sense his, and it has awoken my monk's spade, because I can feel its warmth on my back.

"Whoa!" Lupa doesn't seem amused. "You two had better settle your differences, because this is no fun for the rest of us. Understand?" She gets a simultaneous "yes" from Conner and me.

Conner turns to me and says, "We'll talk later."

"We will talk when I feel like it." I cross my arms in defiance.

"Kailey!" Lupa turns red in the face.

"Sorry, Lupa. Fine, we can talk tonight." I turn to Conner's stupid face. "I have time later in my schedule. Maybe I can squeeze you in."

The main strip is bustling. How these people don't fall over or bump into everything in their path is amazing. With all the roundness of the people, I'm ready to see some pinball action. Gunthreon stops us in front of a building—purple, of course—that seems to be some sort of apothecary-style shop called Wafter's Mercentile.

"Goody!" Lupa, having apparently forgotten our bickering already, is jumping up and down, squealing.

Gunthreon turns the purple doorknob and we enter. The man behind the counter hasn't turned yet, but knows we're there. "How can I help you good people today?" he says. Thank goodness the inside of the shop is not purple. As he turns to face us, his eyes widen at the sight of Bu and he reaches behind his counter. Gunthreon persuades him to relax and Conner soulspeaks, letting shop man know Bu is no threat.

"I was wondering if you had some things I need." Lupa picks up a piece of parchment on the counter and starts looking for something to write with. I pull out a rollerball pen and hand it to her. Shop man shrieks as Lupa holds the pen in front of her. Everyone freezes and anticipates his next move.

Shop man stares at Lupa and then slowly walks toward her, looking as though he's actually a bit intrigued. He stops in front of her and looks at the pen, then runs quickly by her and closes his shop curtains. "Travelers?" he says to Gunthreon. Gunthreon nods. Shop man turns to Lupa. "Can I hold that dear woman?" She shrugs and passes it to him. He brings it to his nose and sniffs. "Hmm," he mutters as he sniffs again. "What would I call this smell?"

"Plastic," I reply and he drops the pen on the floor, not wanting to touch it again.

"Nasty stuff! Please continue with your shopping, before I have any unexpected visits from the Unapproved Foreign Objects Enforcements," says shop man.

Lupa whispers, "UFOE—Technology police," to me and picks the pen up and writes down her order, finishing quickly so that I may put the hideous object away.

I wander the store and peruse the aisles, admiring the jars on the shelves. There must be a thousand of them at least. Each jar is the same size and shape; only the label differs. I pick one up and open it, and there seems to be nothing in it—but it does smell. It smells like peanut butter. I find another that reminds me of newly painted walls, and one other jar that smells exactly like a wet dog. "What the hell is in these jars?" I say.

"Don't keep them open too long!" Shop man seems perturbed with me.

"Smells." This comes from Bu, who seems to have found a jar that smells like pot roast.

"That's why they're all fat! It makes you want to eat!" I say this too loud, and shop man's face tells me he may try and strangle me before we leave. I make sure to keep my distance while wandering.

"How can you buy scents, let alone store them?" I find this concept very interesting.

Gunthreon leans into me and whispers, "Some sort of olfactory trick." Lupa is like a kid in a candy shop, running from canister to canister.

I'm not a convert yet. "Yeah, well, what do you do with them?" I say. The shop man squints at me. "Sorry, this is all new to me. I have a feeling you can enlighten me."

Shop man's chest puffs up, and he holds his head up high behind his podium, ready to give his inaugural address. "Well, good lady, don't you realize how important your sense of smell is?" he says.

"Well, sure I do."

He gives me the squinty eyes again. "Haven't you ever smelled something that brought you back to your youth, or makes you suddenly feel relaxed, or even sad? Scents spark emotion!"

"Oh." I think for a bit. "Yes! New asphalt!" Everyone turns to me like I farted publicly or something, and I'm sure even *that* jar is here somewhere. "The smell reminds me of elementary school, after they repaved the recess grounds." *Duh.*

Shop man turns the attention back to himself. "I've seen alliances formed and treaties broken over scents." He leans in to whisper something to us. "Cleopatra, of Abscondia, was one of the founding Wafter's regulars, but shhh, it's a secret passed down many generations." He puffs up again. His eyes close and he breathes in deeply. "They say jasmine followed her everywhere."

He opens his eyes again. "Feel free to keep shopping, I have some business to attend to in the back." Abruptly, he leaves.

I browse the canisters and try to think about my favorite scent. Cotton candy is the first thing that comes to mind, and I wonder if cotton candy exists here in Renhala, so I walk through the isle with the "C" canisters, which are labeled alphabetically. "'Cabin,' 'Cabernet'... 'Circus'... 'Corn,' and—aha! 'Cotton Candy'! I point to the jar when shop man comes back. "Gunthreon, can I get this, please?" He nods.

I am astonished at how shop man maneuvers around the shelves and jars without toppling everything over. Just then, Bu finds something to his liking, and he runs over, but not as nimbly as shop man. Bypassing his usual gracefulness, he knocks jars off the shelf, making shop man angry.

"Sorry!" cries Bu.

"It's all right, Bu," I say. "It was an accident. What's gotten you so excited?"

"Kailey, this one smells like Kioto!"

"Why, that's just up your alley, isn't it?" He comes over and opens his jar. I sniff, and I recognize the wet dog smell. "Guess Kioto needs a bath, eh?"

"Oh, Bu think she smells wonderful!" This, from someone I forgot smells like rotten eggs. I've gotten so used to him. I guess I understand where he's coming from.

Shop man picks up the canisters Bu knocked over and grabs one to fill my order. He then disappears behind the counter to get a small, airtight jar. "You know these only work once, right?"

"No, but I do now. I just open it up, right? Then what happens?"

"You open it up, and make sure you are not in a tight area, for my smells are the strongest in town." He smiles. "It will last for about fifteen minutes, and it is pure delight! Make sure you tell your friends about me, and since you are new to all this, I'll give you a triple dose—free of charge!"

We all buy something, even Conner, then leave the shop. Conner conveniently doesn't let me see his purchase, though. Gunthreon lets me see in his bag. "'Basil,' 'Cedar,' 'Garlic,' and...'Bug Repellent'?"

"Can't help it. It reminds me of Lupa's hugs in the garden—eucalyptus, and citronella oil."

"Hmm. To each his own I guess," I comment. Lupa shows me her jars. She picked up "Sparrow," "Black Dirt," "Peppermint," and "Rose." "Sparrow?" I say.

"To scare away those topola bugs the day they migrate in throngs to my garden. Once they settle on my plants—I got 'em!"

"Okay, then." I then suddenly see Gunthreon's eyes diverted toward two men dressed in black uniforms stopping patrons on the street. He indiscreetly gets us moving away from the area without explaining, and only keeping the conversation going as we move a bit faster. "Bu, what did you get at Wafter's?" he says, his eyes quickly darting behind us.

"Kioto, 'Fresh Cookies,' 'Sausage' and 'Metal,'" says Bu.

"There was a metal one? What does metal smell like, and why would you buy that?"

"It smelled like Bu's pliers." He looks down at his feet.

"Oh, silly me. Of course! What a great find, Bu!" He smiles and goes back to rummaging through his bag. "Oh, Gunthreon, I forgot to ask why everything here is purple."

"The founding father of this town insisted purple had a smell," he explains, "and he was determined to prove it. Don't you smell it?" Both Conner and I take the deepest breaths we can. Gunthreon turns to Lupa, and they both laugh.

I roll my eyes and frown. "Ha ha, joke's on us. You're cruel."

Bu sniffs the air. "It smells like blue to Bu," he says. We all laugh together.

Chapter 34

Cute
ɑℛ

From the land of purple, we travel what seems to me like five miles or so, and my feet grow blisters by the second. It's also been the most boring time, because 1) Bu doesn't hold conversation well, 2) the two lovebirds have been holding hands and chatting the whole time, and 3) Conner has been ignoring me, and I in turn, am ignoring him until tonight, supposedly.

We encounter several towns on our journey—some ravaged, just like Meadow's Edge, and some totally abandoned.

Now, Gunthreon leads us into a forest, and to a small open area surrounded by thistle. The clouds above us rumble and brief shots of green lightning flash across the skies. "We are going to stop here for the night," Gunthreon says. He throws down his bags and scopes out the area quickly. "Conner, how are you at scouting? Russell tells me you're quite the camper." I then notice nobody brought a tent.

"First place in the Summer Quadrant Games, two years in a row." He puffs up and resembles shop man. I withhold the comment.

"Great!" yaps Gunthreon.

"I'll do it," Conner says, then looking at me, "I've got nothing better to do anyway." He leaves his bag with us and walks off toward the setting sun.

I look around again, searching for a tent. "Gunthreon, um, where's the tents?"

"No need for tents here." The sky lights up green and a loud boom has me jumping in place. I stand, staring at Gunthreon as he lays down his sleeping bag—directly on the ground.

"Bu and Kailey, tomorrow we reach Socola," says Gunthreon. "I know I shouldn't have to repeat myself, but I feel the need. You must remember to at least stay in pairs. Many a person has been lost to the mooncats. They are a very slick race. Bu, you remember last time we were in Socola?"

He shivers slightly. "We lost Haren."

"Who was Haren?" I ask. "How'd you *lose* him?"

Gunthreon sighs. "He was a friend of ours who was travelling with us. The transformation was beyond anyone's control," he says, giving me yet another ambiguous answer. "Let's just stay on our path to finding Neda. The mooncats are quite resourceful when they choose to cooperate—which is never—but we are going to try our damndest."

Bu starts rummaging through his bag of smells. "Can Bu open one, Gunthreon?" he asks.

"Sure, Bu. Make sure you savor it!"

Bu takes out his "Fresh Cookies" jar. He pulls out his blanket, curls up on the ground next to me, opens the jar, and lays it right next to his nose. "Mmmm," he murmurs.

I lean over and sniff, and my mouth starts to salivate. "I think I'll wait to use mine," I say. "I've had my share today."

Conner trudges back from deeper in the forest. "All's well," he comments. "I found a few forest friends, but nothing dangerous."

"'Forest friends' like raccoon-and-possum-level'? Or bear-and-wolves-level?" I ask, my eyes open wide. "Or Jason-level?" Having never been camping, all the camping movies I've ever seen reel through my head, creating a fear that increases with every scary forest sound. Ghastly green lightning then flashes its brightest throughout the sky, illuminating the forest around us. My eyebrows raise and I point to the sky while looking at Gunthreon.

"It never rains here, in this part of Renhala at least," he says. I look again to the sky.

Renhala

"I'm just going to leave it at forest friends," Conner responds. "Gunthreon sent me, and he knows what I mean."

"Thanks," I hiss. "If something tries to eat me tonight, I'll make sure and remind them there are more succulent pieces of meat at this campsite." Bu shrieks under his blanket. I make sure I talk loud enough for him to hear: "And we all know greble doesn't taste as good as human!"

Lupa sets up a nice, cozy, fire and pulls a set of pots out of nowhere. "I'll fix us a nighttime snack," she says. "We've got a few minutes, so why don't you two have your little chat?" She looks around like she's lost something. "Where did that honey go? I just put it down." She looks at Bu accusingly.

Damn this woman. "Fine! Conner, let's go." We wander off far enough so nobody can hear us argue, but still close enough to see the firelight.

"Conner," I say, then pause, thinking to myself it takes too much negative energy to be upset with him. "I'm really sorry about what happened. I was enjoying myself—really enjoying myself—but this whole energy trick of mine confuses me. It was so rude of me, but I couldn't control it. I'm attracted to you, really." I blush in the dark.

"Yeah, but not exclusively. Remember, I saw the kiss you shared with Ladimer, and he's got something for you—you know, the history of following you and all. And I don't want to compete with someone who honestly scares the hell out of me."

"But Ladimer told me to kiss him! And it saved Greer, didn't it?"

"And you just always do what people say? No. I don't think so. You're not as weak as you think you are."

I take in a deep breath. "Conner, you're exactly what I need, but—"

"'Need'? I much rather hear 'want.'"

I stand, not giving a reply, and then decide to just let it out: "I'm not used to attention from men! There!" His eyebrows shoot up. "My whole life I've been hidden behind Amber—the one watching her back while all the men ogled." My speech becomes shaky as I try to hold back from crying. "I want to be with someone. The fact that the two most intriguing men I've ever met happen to be travelers to another realm throws a little wrench in my plans." I start crying as I continue talking. "I just don't know what to do, especially with this talk of an informant. Doesn't this make you feel a bit suspicious of everyone around you?"

"Kailey, I've never felt for someone like I do you, especially after only knowing you for so brief a time—granted, maybe you're using your abilities to make me feel this way, but—" I attempt to talk but he places his hand on my mouth, causing me to jump from the static shock.

"What's up with that?" I ask.

"No idea, but's it a little annoying, ain't it?" he responds. I nod and he continues talking, brushing off the fact we keep shocking each other. "Please know I find you... enthralling." He says the last word a bit quiet.

"Me? Enthralling?" Wiping my tears with my sleeve, I laugh, and his energy quivers. "Well, I can accept that," I squeak, smiling at him, and then puff up my own chest, and pull myself together. "And I also find you—" A rustling sound in the bushes interrupts my sentence and I jump, moving closer to him.

He smiles. "Find me what?" he asks.

I think to myself that "a solid prospect with a hot body" are not the appropriate words, so I say, "Cute."

"*Cute?* That's all?" he twitters, annoyed.

There's a sudden growling noise from the forest and he says, "Just make sure you stay near the fire tonight." With this he starts walking toward camp. I scurry behind him.

I smell baking smells. "Who opened up their jar?"

Bu sits next to Lupa like a dog waiting for scraps. "Lupa cooked!" he says.

She hands out to each of us a small foil packet. I open up mine, and discover it's some sort of fruit cobbler. "Lupa, I love you. Will you marry me?" Bu is staring at me with a disturbed look on his big face. He must not get it. "Bu, it's a joke."

"Oh. Kailey, you funny!"

"Yeah, you seem to tell me that all the time." The fruit cobbler is to die for—nothing less than expected—and with full bellies, exhaustion takes over. An urge then comes over me. "Where do I go when I have to, uh, you know."

"Just go into the forest, find a place, and squat. It's really quite simple." Easy for Gunthreon to say.

"Is there, like, camping etiquette? I mean, do I try and go where someone won't step? But what if I sit in poison ivy and something like that?"

Lupa throws me some toilet paper.

"Abscondian?" I ask as I examine the quilted hearts and squares.

Lupa replies, "I do prefer some luxuries once in a while. I don't think my butt will fall off using it."

Bu giggles, most likely at the thought of someone's butt falling off.

"Fine. But if you hear me scream, someone better come save me." I wander off, find a secluded place, and as I watch a squirmy, oozing bug crawl by my face, I decide I can perhaps wait a bit longer. I pull my pants up and figure this the perfect time to travel and check on my mom, when suddenly I feel a new energy approach.

"Hello?" I say, scanning the area. The energy feels... simply inquisitive. Just when I'm about to grasp the exact location of it, a small yellow animal with a very long tail crawls out from behind a rock. It looks up at me with large eyes and "snuffs"—at least that's the best way I can describe it—then turns around and scampers away.

I then travel. I end up in my living room, with no lights on. "Hello? Mom?" I check out the place, but nobody's there. She must have already taken Kioto to her house. I try and call her house, but I get no answer. It's around the time I usually walk Kioto, so I just leave things at that. I travel back to the bush I squatted near.

"Why don't you just soulsearch? I know you can," says a female voice, somewhere near me.

I twirl around where I stand. "Lupa?" My heart pounds as I hear giggling. "Who's there?"

"Booooo! A forest friend. Booooo!" Whoever it is is mocking me. I reach for my monk's spade and swing it around in front of me. "Ooh …" And with that, I see a tiny little female thing standing in front of me. "I've never seen one of those. What is that?" she says, seemingly mesmerized by my weapon. She's about five inches tall, dressed in what appears to be squirrel hide with matching boots. She has twigs all knotted up in her hair, and her neck is adorned with a necklace made of holly.

"Why did you tell me to soulsearch, and how did you know I can?" I'm tempted to bend down to her like you would with a small child, but I really don't know what this thing is capable of doing. She might rip my throat out.

"If I tell you, will you let me touch it?" She eyes my monk's spade feverishly.

"Yes, but only for a second," I state. "First, you *must* tell me the truth."

"But I don't have *that* power. Your boyfriend does," she says. "You wouldn't know if I was lying to you or not. Wait! You might. Energy reading."

"He is *not* my boyfriend."

"Sure."

"Fine. I'm just going back to camp." I turn to walk back.

"To go see that handsome man? He's quite pleasant on the eyes." I start walking. "No, please don't. I want to see your weapon and touch it, if I may."

I turn around and walk back to her.

"Come down so I don't have to shout," she pleads. "I won't hurt you."

I crouch, then sit Indian-style. She comes over and sits the same way next to me, very, very closely.

"I'm Jenna, woodsprite of the tribe Uriben." She extends her tiny hand, and I shake it with two fingers.

"You gonna tell me how you know so much about me?" I say.

"Well, besides the fact I just saw you appear out of nowhere, that's what we woodsprites do. You don't know this?"

No. I'm kind of new to Renhala." I twiddle my thumbs.

"You're from 'there'?"

"Yes, from Abscondia."

"It really does exist!" she shouts, wide-eyed. "Is it all dangerous and scary like the tales? Oh! Are there really soul-drainers who steal your life force by sucking it from your ears?"

I laugh, hard. I eventually calm down. "You mean you've never met someone who travels from Abscondia?"

She shakes her head. "I don't make friends too easily," she admits, kicking around dirt.

"You know, I don't have many friends either, so don't feel bad! And as to your question, no, there are no 'soul-drainers' in Abscondia. Well, if you don't count the government...or those crazy bible thumpers...or ear muffs," I joke.

"Well, Neda gave us the power to see auras—yours is beautiful by the way—and know what powers one possesses," says Jenna. "It comes in handy sometimes. If you're messing with a traveler and stealing her campsite food, you know whether you might get caught and what the consequences might be. That honey was delicious, by the way."

"Oooh, if I let Lupa know, she might strangle you."

"No, she won't."

"Of course. You would know, right?" I say.

"Your female friend's like me, kind of...a friend to plant life."

"So that's her secret!" I exclaim. "She's got special powers, and that's how she grows those man-size squashes. Aha!"

"Yep. She respects them, as I do." Jenna hugs the nearest weed. I squash a bug trying to crawl up my leg, and she shrieks. "You should hug a tree once in a while, you know!" she says.

This makes me laugh, and I imagine myself in tie-dyed clothes with flowers in my hair and a peace symbol painted on my cheek.

"They give you the oxygen you breathe, and food and shelter," she says. "They watch us all, constantly."

"Okay, but that creeps me out. They don't have eyes, so how can they watch me?"

"They do in their own way." She waves to a nearby tree. The wind blows, and the tree sways. "See?"

I just laugh. "Whatever you say."

Jenna scoots a bit closer to me so that she's practically in my lap, near my weapon. "Can I touch your weapon now?" she says.

"Sure, I don't see why not." I take my monk's spade off my back and slowly lower it to her, then hold it back. "Wait, tell me one more thing: What does my aura look like? Is it really pretty?" I say, wanting to hear it from her again. I feel a chest puff coming my way.

A second before she can touch it, Gunthreon rushes out of the bushes. "*Do not* let her touch that!" he yells. Jenna stands up and snarls as Gunthreon runs toward her. "You evil little thing! Go away!" Gunthreon shouts and then shoos her.

"You gonna *persuade* me to go? I don't want to!" Gunthreon towers over Jenna. She doesn't budge. "You don't scare me," she says. "Now, if you were her, you'd for sure scare me." She points to me.

"Why me?" I ask.

Jenna laughs a cute little tiny laugh. "You don't have any clue, do you? That's right. You're new. Let me just say that karmeleans that are able to soulsearch aren't born very often—try like ever."

Gunthreon turns to me. "'Forest friends' like this little one are like wolverines. Give them the chance by listening to their sweet talk, and they tear your weapon from you. Then they sell them on the black market. Isn't this right?"

Jenna sticks her lizard-like tongue out at Gunthreon. "I've gotta make a living somehow."

I walk over to Jenna. "You were really going to take it, weren't you? How could you carry this anyway?" I once again think of ants.

"Actually, I wasn't sure if I was gonna take it yet. I don't even know what that thing is. I was kind of scared to." She seems genuinely embarrassed. "I probably would have tried, though. I haven't eaten a good meal in a while."

I say to her, "You did have that honey."

"You call that a meal? What do you eat in Abscondia?" she whines. "You should come with me sometime where I can show you a good meal, for a price of course. Wildabug and dewjuice and, yum, mealworms!" She looks like a starving dog with a giant ham bone held out in front of its nose, told to stay.

"Yuck!" I blurt, disgusted.

Gunthreon puts his arm out to me. "Kailey, come back to camp with me. Leave her here."

"Let her make her own decisions!" Jenna says, sticking up for me.

He replies, "So you can take off with her blade?"

Jenna seems to try to keep up her tough exterior, but she looks discouraged now. She turns her head down toward her bare feet. "I'm not going to take it. I just like her. She's got good energy. I'd much rather have her as an ally than an enemy."

"Kailey is not an item I can bargain with, and I need to keep her safe. Good day to you."

I walk with Gunthreon back to camp, but not without a glance toward the tree that Jenna waved to. Creepy.

"Weren't you kind of rough on her?" I say.

"Like most creatures here in Renhala, you cannot underestimate even the tiniest of beings."

The others seem to have found their own place to crash, and are bundled up all snuggly to protect themselves against the night chill. Bu snores, his jar of cookie smell totally exhausted, and Conner, in his sleeping bag, reads from a rather thick book. Lupa drinks something steamy from a tin cup and smiles at us as we return.

"Glad you're safe, hon," she says with warm eyes. "We were kind of worried about you. *All* of us." She nods in Conner's direction, but he's clueless, well into whatever thought-provoking words he's reading.

"A little woodsprite named Jenna almost nabbed my weapon."

Lupa laughs. "Yeah, they're almost as vicious as pixies."

"Pixies?"

"Get some shuteye, because we're all getting up at the crack of dawn. We're gonna need plenty of energy and brainpower for those mooncats."

Lupa informs me that Conner set me up a sleeping bag. She points to it next to Bu—evidently Bu moved it there after Conner set it up closer to himself. Conner was quite the gentleman, too, because I see he gave me the much warmer one with a Sherpa liner.

I climb into it, and as I inhale, I can smell his cologne. I suddenly sit up and shout, "Tomorrow is Monday! I have to call into work. I'll be right back."

I stand up and right before I travel home to leave a message for Evan, Gunthreon shouts, "Stop! Don't go."

"Hey, I'm still working. At a job. Where I have responsibilities. Don't tell me I can't leave a message for my boss."

"There is to be no travelling to Abscondia during this mission, Kailey."

"Why?" I keep to myself that I've already broken that rule.

"Because every time someone travels, both Velopa and Neda know this person has travelled," he states.

"And why is that bad? That's our whole reason for searching! To find them, right? I could just travel back and forth like twenty times and maybe Neda will come and slap me on the hand."

Gunthreon shakes his head. "You don't understand. That may draw attention to you, in particular. We must be guileful about this. Every time you travel, it gives one small clue as to your exact location. You want Velopa sneaking up on you while you're indisposed?" His eyebrows are raised high.

"No, probably not," I mumble. I see Conner indiscreetly watching my reaction.

Conner stands up and says, "I'll do it for you. I travel often, so neither Neda nor Velopa will pay me any heed. Give me your work number and I'll leave a message for you. Is that okay, Gunthreon?" Gunthreon nods after some thought.

"Thank you," I say softly to Conner. I tell him the number and he travels home. As I lie in my sleeping bag, staring up at the flashes of lightning, I close my eyes and reach to my campmate's energies, examining each, closely, looking for even a hint of deception, hidden somewhere. I find nothing.

Chapter 35

Uncomfortable
☙

The night is cruel to me. Every single noise wakes me. I nearly put in my iPod earplugs, but the thought of not hearing something important changes my mind.

When the sun rises, I realize the pounding I hear is not from the forest, or from Lupa clanging her pots together, but from my head. Seeing everyone else wake up looking well-rested makes me want to kick them. The imaginary birds and animals I conjure up following Lupa around, Snow White-style especially don't help.

"How did any of you get sleep last night?" I squint as my eyes cannot take the burning sunlight. In fact, even turning toward Lupa's glowing face makes me wince.

"I got enough that I feel ready for our journey today," says Gunthreon. I'm not even going to look at Gunthreon when he's talking, because even he sounds wide-eyed and bushy-tailed.

Conner is already packed and smiling.

"What are you so cheery about this morning?" I glare.

He turns to me. "Did the woodsprite you encountered last night wear a holly necklace?"

"Why yes, she did," I respond. He smiles widely. "And she is quite smitten by you." I laugh when he drops his smile.

"What?" he chirps.

"Oh, she just thought you were adorable."

He blushes, and it makes me sneer. He recovers quickly, though. "I was just happy I actually saw her," he says. "Woodsprites are quite sneaky, and very clever. I thought my tracking skills were improving. Now I know she might have wanted me to see her though—or she just grew lax in her ability to hide because of my blinding good looks."

256

"Whatever. Maybe you could go find her, and you two could have some 'dewjuice' together and talk about your dreaminess." I am so going to be crabby all day.

"My, my, so this is how you are first thing in the morning, huh?" spouts Conner. "I'm more of a morning person. And don't knock dewjuice." He smiles again. "Just finish packing. We can't lose any daylight."

"Lose daylight? It's like five o'clock in the freaking morning. How much could we possibly lose?" I try turning toward the sun, but it's so not worth it. "Oh, and aren't we also going somewhere where it's dark all the time anyway?"

"Conner's right, Kailey," says Lupa. "We have to move fast. We have to make sure we stop at a few places on the outskirts of Socola first, and we definitely want to get there in the daylight."

"How come I always seem to be the one totally left out of the preparation plans?"

"I think you work best when you don't know what to expect, Kailey," replies Gunthreon. He waits for a response, but I actually don't have anything to say.

We double-check to make sure we've packed everything, and I say a secret goodbye to my first campsite. *Note to self: If this is what camping is like, I don't think I like it.*

I make sure I leave a small piece of my breakfast sandwich behind for a certain forest friend while nobody is watching. I can't help it—I've always secretly fed strays. As a child, I'd save all my leftovers and feed them to the pigeons—everything from potato salad to chicken. They always left the onions, though. Life's all about karma anyway, right? Maybe someday, I'll be saved by a giant pigeon. You never know.

We travel through some wetlands, which stink like a concoction of cooked broccoli, dirty diapers, and pigpen. It makes all of us cranky, and gives us all horrendous headaches. Lupa ends up cracking open her peppermint jar to let us all use it for a few minutes each. Surprisingly, this helps tremendously, for our heads seem to clear.

An hour after we leave the wetlands, I still stink of broccoli. *What I would do for a life pool right now.*

After we travel the majority of the day, Gunthreon finally stops and turns to all of us. "We are approaching the outskirts," he says. "There's a few things we need to do while outside Socola, and talking with some locals is one of them. There are a few more necessary supplies we should pick up, and then we can stop and catch a bite to eat, and maybe get some information while we're at it. I'm hoping to get to Socola right around nightfall, because it will seem more natural for us."

"What kind of information are we searching for exactly?" I want to make sure I do my best and don't do anything stupid.

"We're searching out the mooncats' alpha cat. Rumors are spreading of direct connections to the Higher Ones here."

I laugh out loud, but nobody else does. "They have an *alpha* cat?"

"Yes," replies Gunthreon, "and if you were smart you would mind your manners if you happen to meet him."

I do my best salute toward Gunthreon.

A glance at Bu tells me he's troubled. "What's wrong, Bu?"

"Bu just scared. Bu don't like them." He holds his locket and gently caresses it. I show him my own ring which I am secretly fondling in my pocket. He smiles and takes a deep breath.

"Bu, remember who you're with: your friends who love you. And we are all here to take care of you. Okay?"

"Bu worried about Kailey."

"Why me?" I say. "Don't you worry about me. I have my handy-dandy spade on my back, and am ready to use it if need be. How about we just watch each other's back? Then we'll be fine." I take his hand in mine and squeeze it.

Conner comes over and clasps Bu's other hand. We all enter town holding hands, and must look like the weirdest bunch around. I don't care, though.

We continue walking through the town. Gunthreon enters a butcher shop while we all wait outside. When he finally emerges, he's carrying a particularly large package wrapped in white butcher paper. It's handed over to Lupa, who opens her pack and places it inside with her other goods. I must remember to ask her if her pack is secretly a never-ending abyss.

We all follow, and Conner points out a peculiar storefront with a picture of a giant mouse eating a particularly large piece of cheese, the words "The Big Cheese" carved into the cheddar.

"Shall we stop for a few nibbles?" Conner turns to Gunthreon who nods.

My stomach screams at the mention of food. "They better not just sell cheese here," I yap. "I could use a nice, big, fat, juicy burger. Okay, maybe with cheese."

Gunthreon peeks inside through the foggy window. "We could all use some nourishment right now," he says. "And a tall glass of something bubbly."

Lupa follows him inside, her head turning quickly to and fro. Most likely, she's scanning the crowd, seeing if there's any potential danger inside this dark and dingy establishment. I puff up my muscles and walk in with a gangster's stride.

The "crowd," I see, consists of two people. There's one harmless elderly man and a haggard woman who could possibly be a call girl—make that woman, and seasoned at that, because she's definitely got age on her side. Lupa quickly spots what she's actually searching for. She practically flies toward the exit for the outhouse. Gunthreon grabs us a table and some chairs. He even finds a chair big enough for Bu to sit in comfortably.

The menu is written on slate on the wall in the sloppiest handwriting I've ever seen. The only thing I can somewhat read is some sort of steak and potatoes, and that sounds scrumptious to me, so I decide to go with it. If it's close enough to cow I'll eat it.

The waitress comes to our table after what seems like an eternity, and she's not the most cordial. "What'dya all want?" she says, squinting and not even carrying a nice little pad to write on. I feel as though she's not talking about food. She stares at us—at whom directly, I don't know, because both of her glass eyes swivel in her head every which way at once.

Gunthreon says, "We'll have some of your rosabread and olives to begin. Thank you, kind lady."

"Uh-huh." She eventually stops staring and walks away into the kitchen.

"Gunthreon, I have a question for you," I say. "We're on a search for these Higher Ones, and I don't even know what they look like. Are they things, or people, or what?"

"I've seen them as floating, glowing balls of energy, but I have also heard people say that they take different forms. Neda has been a dragon, a tree, a dwarf, and even a greble, from what I've heard. Velopa has been mentioned as many a thing also. It all depends on the individual who finds them. The only thing I know for a fact is that you can feel their strong energy, even if you're not an experienced reader, if you are within a certain distance of them. Again, whether the experience is good or bad depends on the individual."

The waitress comes back and practically throws our food onto the table in front of Bu. His eyes swell, and I can see he wants to devour it all as much as I do. It smells delicious. We order our meals, and she leaves again.

Turns out rosabread is much like a sweet bread, but lighter and flaky, and the saltiness of the olives is the perfect complement. The spread that accompanies it is somewhat peppery, and also extremely tasty.

My stomach begs to eat the whole serving of bread, despite the other beings sitting here with me. Conner enjoys his portion as much as I did mine, and I sit and stare as he licks each finger, slowly, savoring every drop of olive juice. He catches me staring, and I cannot help but blush as I turn my head elsewhere.

"Wow, this is so good," I mumble quickly. "I would think there'd be more people here, with such delicious food."

"It's probably the fact that the food here is not worth the danger," says Gunthreon.

"Huh? There's no danger—"

Just then, the elderly man attacks Bu from behind with a mace-like object. Bu's quickness saves him, and he suffers only a brush to the shoulder as Lupa draws a rather sharp garden spade against the man's throat, forcing him down on the floor. I glance at Conner, and he, too, is amazed by Lupa's speed. I shove the last piece of bread in my mouth.

"You attempt that again and you are dead," yells Lupa. "You should be ashamed of yourself." She lets up on her grip.

In an old tired voice he grunts, "Why are you here?" The man sits up on the floor. "You know I had to."

"Well, he was with us! Couldn't you see he's civilized?"

"Yes, but you know I had to, as keeper."

I don't know what the hell is going on, but I try to pretend like I do, giving this man my toughest badass poker face.

Lupa moves away, and Gunthreon stands over the man. "If you were wise, you would give us information."

"What do you want?" he responds with a snarl.

"What is the current situation in Socola?" asks Gunthreon. "We are a party in need of any information you may have on Neda. That is all."

The gears churn in the old man's head for what seems an eternity, until he apparently decides it is information he can provide. "As far as Neda, we, on the outskirts, have our own

261

scouts searching. The mooncats have recently received some word of a higher power, I believe. We here are also in search of Velopa."

"Thank you, keeper. We have no quarrel with you," says Gunthreon. "We'd like the rest of our food, and we will leave you peacefully."

The waitress appears with a helper, and they both carry huge trays of food to our table. She lays them down far more gently than she did the bread, and the food before me makes me want to shed a tear. My steak, whatever it may be, is dripping blood-red, salty juice into the spiced potatoes, which still simmer on my plate. Everyone at the table holds their breath at the spectacular spread.

Bu also ordered a steak, his raw, but he ordered some sort of giant vegetable patty, too, which I *must* try. He lets me take a slice—since I keep staring at it—and I place it on an extra plate next to mine, since there's no room on my own. I gorge on the steak, lost in my own little culinary amusement park. A greble army could march in right now, and I wouldn't even know move a muscle—except to bring my fork to my mouth.

After my steak, I decide to try the vegetable patty and see that the portion Bu gave me is much smaller than I thought. He's already finished his own portion.

As we eat, with a full mouth, I say, "So why is that guy called 'keeper'? Keeper of what?" I only dribble a little.

Gunthreon replies, "Keeper for the mooncats. They have several spies around, keeping a watch on the outskirts. The mooncats are not very trusting of outsiders like ourselves. They pay the keepers in many ways—sometimes gold, jewels, or even sex."

"Oh." I peer out the window, and I can guess where Socola starts because, about a half mile from us, the skies suddenly seem to turn an ominous black. I turn back to eat my last bite of the vegetable patty and discover it's gone. I frown at Bu, but he's engulfed in his own merriment from the food he frantically shovels into his mouth. *Oooh, I wonder if they have dessert*, I think.

262

Just as I'm about to ask, Gunthreon says, "We must go now. Finish up your last bites, please." Bu's hands move the fastest I have ever seen, and he swallows everything in front of him in one mouthful.

Gunthreon pays the waitress and nods at the keeper, who actually nods back. We head onward.

Chapter 36

Seductive
◌◌

The walk to Socola is one of absolute silence. My travel companions, I'm beginning to feel, are extremely nervous, the fear thickening each of their energy fields. I even catch Bu crying a few times. My energy reaches to his and I softly touch it, stroking it, and willing some happiness from him. He glances at me briefly as he continues walking, and takes a deep breath. As we approach Socola, I break the silence.

"Gunthreon, how can Socola have no sun?" I question. "How can it be that the sky turns dark right where their lands begin?"

"Well, in the beginning," says Gunthreon, "Velopa and Neda worked together by defining the lands harmoniously, yet making each one unique, and all the while having fun with it. This was when the good lands, like Meadow's Edge, were formed. But once the arguing began, things changed, and we got places like Gernwood, where Bu lives. Each land we travel to can have its own fauna or animals, or, like Socola, have its own moon. Renhala is like a giant puzzle—all the pieces are different, but they fit together to form one giant, awe-inspiring picture." He smiles. "It's such a magical place, and this is why we have to protect it. And by protecting Renhala, we protect Abscondia. We must have Velopa withdraw its troops from Abscondia."

The sky is black and the coolness of night lingers in the air as nameless bugs buzz and chirp. The only difference between a real nightfall in my realm and this is that there are no stars. There is a moon, though, and it is *huge*—a ginormous, breathtaking moon. I feel like, if I keep walking, I'll be able to walk right up to it and put my hand on it. There's no man in the moon, but definitely craters, holding secrets of their own. The moon shines upon the endless expanse of forest beneath it. I hope to see light somewhere, possibly lights from a town or even a campfire, but there is nothing—just blackness. A big, black, flying bug lands on my chest and clicks loudly at me while trying to pierce through my thick sweatshirt with a long straw-like beak.

Lupa quickly swats it off with a stick. "Damn bloodsuckers!" My eyes open widely at her. She explains, "Broofwings. Just don't let them touch your skin, please. They're like giant, nasty fleas to the mooncats—and are especially dangerous to us humans."

"Why?" I ask.

"Just do as I say!" she replies, and catches up to Gunthreon.

Bu walks right next to me, and every time I move, he moves with me.

"Bu, sorry, but I need some space. You're gonna trample me."

"Sorry, Kailey. Bu scared."

"Yeah, big fella, I know. We're here with you so don't—," I hear something rustle in fallen leaves, and I jump, "—be scared," I say, gathering myself. I soon find myself walking closer to Conner.

He looks at me. "Kailey, sorry, but I need some space."

I stick my tongue out at him in the dark. "So, who are we supposed to meet? How do we know where to find them?" I want this over and done.

"They know we're here. We have to wait for them to come to us," says Gunthreon. He seems sure of himself, which is slightly comforting. Lupa walks right next to him, holding his arm a bit tight.

Before we have a chance to take another step, I hear more rustling. Gunthreon turns toward the rustling sounds.

"We come in peace. We are here to speak to your alpha cat," he states. "Can you tell me who currently holds this position? It would be greatly appreciated if we can address him correctly."

Gunthreon faces forward, but I know he sees nothing. I turn away from the moon so that I can see better. It's like when you glance at the sun, and it leaves that splotch in your eyesight, and you can't see anything because your eyes are so dilated.

Blocking the moon helps slightly, and I see something coming toward us ever so slowly. Bu does his owl-head thing to look in the direction of the creature and it growls, slightly.

"Hello," says Gunthreon. "We bring no danger with us. Do not fear our greble if you mean no foul play. I am Gunthreon, and this is Lupa." He tries raising the arm to which Lupa hangs on with a death grip. "Conner, Bu, and Kailey. I ask your name."

The creature comes closer, and as it does, I can see that it's about the size of an oversized puma or jaguar. As it slinks toward us, it begins to talk, its voice rich and full of seduction. I find myself so enraptured, I don't even hear the words being spoken. The sound is thick and soft, and I feel like I could reach out and stroke the velvet-like words. Once it comes into full view, its slick, gray fur is even more alluring than its voice. I imagine the creature brushing against me with the full length of its body, adding its scent to my own, and it makes me want to nuzzle my face against its neck and breathe in its savageness. When I reach to its energy I recognize it as cautious, yet intrigued, and a bit of regality flows along the edges, almost making one feel small in its presence. This creature is absolutely magnificent.

"Kailey, don't." This is Gunthreon, and he sounds a bit further away from me than I remember him being.

"I am Nayla," speaks the cat. "It seems as though your Kailey has never met one of our kind." The sound of my own name rolling off her tongue wakes me from my trance, and I realize that I am standing within five feet of this awesome creature. If I would close the gap between us, I could touch and embrace it.

"Kailey." It's Gunthreon again, and he slowly pulls me away. He turns back to Nayla. "You know this is meant as no disrespect to you, but as an acknowledgment of your great power." He walks backwards slowly, pulling me with him.

Nayla's voice creeps up into my ears again: "Understood." She sits on her hind legs, just watching us. Bu looks away, pretending he doesn't even see the giant cat in front of us.

"She's absolutely stunning," I say. Nayla purrs loudly.

"Yes, Kailey, she is. Just stay back here with Lupa." Gunthreon hands me over to Lupa.

Nayla's voice is soothing and warm: "It is mating season, you know. It would be smart to keep a watch on such a lovely girl." I want to run to her and kiss her forehead and scratch behind her ears.

After getting a glance from Gunthreon, Conner speaks to Nayla. He tells Nayla we mean no harm, and he asks of her alpha male.

"Yes, of course. It is Michel," says Nayla.

"May we speak with him directly?" Gunthreon talks with a bit of sternness in his voice.

"If you let me smell her." This catches me off guard. She was definitely staring at me when she said that.

"If you promise not to harm her."

"Well, you come in peace, so I have no reason to, right?" Gunthreon frowns, but must agree with her.

Lupa holds onto my arm firmly and doesn't let go. If anything, she tightens her grip as Nayla moves forward. I also sense that Bu has moved forward, despite his fear of her. Nayla moves in very stealthily and brings her face up to mine. I close my eyes and feel a tingling sensation all over my body, making my hairs stand on end. She sniffs me all over and lingers in certain places, making the energy in me wake from its lumbering sleep. My monk's spade is warm, and she steps away from it.

"Keep her at bay, or I might need to defend myself, and that could get ugly, no matter how pretty she is. I feel her power," replies Nayla.

Lupa speaks in my ear. "Kailey, relax, please."

"Why does everyone keep telling me that? Geez. I'm fine, really I am," I say.

Nayla stops directly over my backpack and takes several deep breaths. She seems satisfied, and purrs again. "She smells divine. Michel would love her."

"You know we must take that as a threat, Nayla," states Gunthreon. "We would like to speak to him if he is available. We have let you do as you like, now return the favor."

"No need for hostility, Gunthreon. You know what we are. I shall carry your request. You may travel ahead and take shelter until you hear from us again. Goodnight, lovely one." This, again, is meant for my ears. My arm hurts from Lupa's grip.

Nayla turns and begins walking away, but then she stops and turns her head back to us. "Better keep that small one in your pack, because she may seem a little too appetizing to some of my friends." With this, she sprints away into the darkness.

As she leaves I spring back to my usual self—unfazed by giant cats. I immediately take my pack off my back and open it to find a certain woodsprite huddled up in a ball, shaking with fright. "Please, oh please, don't let them eat me!"

"Jenna! What are you doing?!" I shout. "That was *so* stupid."

Gunthreon, infuriated, marches over, and I wince as he reaches for my bag. "How dare you!" he blurts. "I have a mind to leave you on a silver platter skewered with some vegetables!" He pulls her out by her stringy hair.

"Owww! Put me down!" She tries to scratch him, but cannot reach his hand or arm.

"You shall not jeopardize our mission here. Go home!"

I try to reach out for her, because at this point, I'm afraid Gunthreon may dropkick her. I get a hold of her and take her in my hands.

"Let me talk to her. Alone," I request, my mother hen instinct kicking in.

"Fine, but hurry it up," grumbles Gunthreon. "We must move forward."

I carry Jenna away from the group. "Jenna, why are you here?"

Jenna has tears in her eyes. "Why does he hate me so much? He doesn't even know me."

"I don't really know. You haven't answered my question."

"You seemed like you could be my friend. I don't really have many friends. I also thought that maybe I could talk to him." She points to Conner. "Sorry I ate your vegetable patty."

I laugh. "That was you, huh? I was gonna blame Bu."

"You can't leave me here. Please," she pleads. "I will surely be mooncat dinner. If you want, you can leave me at the next town you visit. I'll be as quiet as a fluffmouse, I swear!"

"If you can behave, I'll carry you, but I can't hide it from Gunthreon, though, so you need to convince him you can be trusted." She nods. We walk back toward everyone.

"Well?" I can tell by his stance that Gunthreon wants to be rid of Jenna.

"Come on, Gunth, you know damn well that I can't leave her here," I say. "She's agreed to leave us at the next town we visit. Is that good enough for you?"

"Fine," he clucks. "I am not a monster, you know. Do you forget I could have just persuaded her to jump in Nayla's mouth?" Gunthreon stares at Jenna. "Next town and you're gone, agreed?" Her head nod seems to satisfy him.

Conner walks over to her and holds out his hand out. "I'm Conner," he says. "It's a pleasure to meet you."

She blushes the deepest red and grabs his finger with her hands, shaking it. "*My* pleasure."

"I can carry you a bit if you like. Give Kailey a rest." I didn't even know she was in my pack, all two pounds of her. I know it's just an excuse so he can have Jenna all googly-eyed over him.

"Whatever," I say, handing Jenna over to him. She snuggles in his hands.

When only his eyes can see, I stick my finger down my throat. He just grins and mouths, "Jealous?"

We continue deeper into Socola, looking for a comfortable place for shelter. Eventually, we find an opening to a rather dark and scary cave, which resembles the mouth of a moaning deathman. "This is it." Gunthreon stands in the mouth, willing us all inside.

"No," Conner says, shaking his head. "We could get ambushed, and there would be no way out."

"He's right, Gunthreon," adds Lupa.

"Bu stay guard." We all turn to Bu, surprise splashed across our faces. "Bu want to stay outside to watch. Please, Gunthreon."

"He *does* have the speed and strength to be a good bodyguard, I think," I say.

"Do we have a majority?" asks Gunthreon. Lupa, Conner, and Jenna all nod. "So it shall be. Who will make the fire? It will surely get cold tonight."

Bu hugs me. He lowers his voice to a whisper: "Bu won't let them hurt you, Kailey."

"Thanks, Bu. I think we'll be all right, especially with you on watch." He leaves the cave and attempts to hide behind the nearest bush, but he is clearly too big, for I see his arms and top of his head sticking out.

"Time for a snack, I think," Lupa says, digging into her bag. "Food always calms my nerves."

"Lupa, where are you packing all this food?" I ask.

Jenna jumps down from Conner's hands. "Did you already forget her gift?"

It suddenly hits me what she means. "Oh yeah, that's right! Show me something amazing, Lupa."

Lupa walks over to me, holding the smallest tomato, still on a piece of vine. She displays all sides of it like a magician and covers it with her hand, and in seconds, the tomato is the size of a small pumpkin.

Jenna claps. "Well done, Lupa! Can I help you at all?" I see her glance out of the corner of her eye toward Gunthreon. He pretends to not hear her.

"Why, yes, you can. Come on over here, and I'll show you how to make some root flowers." Jenna springs up and follows Lupa.

It takes some time before Jenna runs over to show me her blooming root flower, clearly proud of her accomplishment. But as she runs to me, her eyes widen at the sight of something at the entrance of the cave, right behind me.

Chapter 37

Welcomed
❧

I'm afraid to turn around, but for fear of something attacking me from behind, I whirl around anyway, grabbing my spade. My eyes adjust to the figure standing in the doorway, and I only see the silhouette. I wonder where Bu is, and why he slacked off at his job already.

We all stand on guard with our weapons in our hands, ready for a fight if need be. The figure moves forward into our firelight, and it's a small female—a thin, meek, scrawny woman, shorter than me. She moves a bit closer, and I see she's a plain, unattractive brunette with thick librarian reading glasses on her face and a giant mole the size of Texas on her chin. She wears dirty, torn, baggy, clothes, in odd, mismatching colors. In reaching her energy, I feel the strangest sensations, all coming in flashes. First confidence, then boredom, then surprise, then anger. It makes me dizzy and unable to focus. She eyes me, carefully.

"How can we help you, dear lady?" Gunthreon moves forward toward her, looking out behind her to where Bu should be.

The woman speaks in a fragile voice, "I was just wondering if you could help a fellow traveler who needs company, and possibly some food?"

Lupa looks her over and pulls some bread out of her bag. "You may have this, honey. If you'd like to sit near the fire with us, you are more than welcome."

Jenna sneaks over to Conner, and I hear her whisper, "She's powerful."

Conner grabs his blade and holds the stranger back before she can even approach the fire. "What is your name, and what are your intentions?" He says it in soulspeak, asking her soul to reply.

272

"Leave her alone!" Lupa shouts, nearly screaming. "She just wants to eat, for Neda's sake." Gunthreon says nothing, but watches closely. I move to stand near Conner and Jenna.

The woman freezes in place and smiles at Conner. "I mean no harm," she informs us. "I am known as Fannie, and I am hoping to find an elusive creature."

Jenna whispers, for my ears only this time: "She's a giver." I furrow my brow because she lost me. "You know, of life and death."

I step toward the stranger. "We are also on a mission for an elusive creature," I state. "We have room for one more, as one of our party abandoned us. We're probably better off without him, though, because he liked to whine." Fannie's face contorts, and she steps toward me. Everyone moves in unison, but before anyone can stop me, I run at Fannie, grab her, and give her the hardest kiss on her cheek I possibly can.

For a moment, Fannie is as stunned as everyone else, but then she giggles. The giggle turns manly, and within seconds, Fannie's head becomes Ladimer's. Bu then enters the cave and starts laughing, because the sight of Ladimer's head on a little itty-bitty body is quite comedic. Finally, Ladimer fully transforms.

Ladimer nods at Conner, and Conner returns the nod. "You've got to work on your soulspeak questions," says Ladimer. "Be more specific."

"Yes, I see that now." I can tell he is fighting between the relief of having another strong soldier back in our travelling party and his strong feelings of competition against Ladimer. He simply walks away and out of the cave.

"How did you know?" Ladimer asks.

I point to Jenna. "Nice try, though."

"Oh, I see," Ladimer responds.

Jenna stares wide-mouthed at him. "You know *him*?"

Ladimer smiles at me. "Soulsearching now, eh?" I blush, because the last time I saw him, he saw *all* my goods. He sees my embarrassment and grins widely. "You'd better learn how to control it, karmelean."

"I'm sorry I gave you away, Ladimer, sir," whimpers Jenna. "I was only trying to protect my friends."

Ladimer tilts his head to the side. "Wow, Kailey, you've befriended a woodsprite? They don't really have friends, you know."

Jenna's face blushes, but she still walks up to Ladimer and holds out her hand. Ladimer is resistant. "I am Jenna, and I'm glad to meet you. I've heard great stories about you. Don't worry, I'm not going to do anything stupid here." Again I see her eyes move to Gunthreon.

"Gunthreon running you through the ringer?" asks Ladimer. "Well, any foe of Gunthreon's is a friend of mine."

"Nice," replies Gunthreon.

Ladimer starts laughing and adds, "I don't mean to spoil the party, but I did see some mooncats moving this way on my way in." Our laughter stops all too quickly. "To be honest, the mooncats don't really care for me, so I had to make this transformation. I thought this one would be the least threatening." He once again transforms into Fannie.

I notice one thing. "You got rid of your scar."

"No need to keep ugly reminders, right?"

"Thanks, Ladimer." Gunthreon shuffles all of us together near the fire. "Just remember, we're here for information on Neda—nothing else. No moonlit strolls or parties!" He sees my odd expression after his comment. "Kailey, remember when I said that you must always be with someone?" I nod. "The mooncats have power that can cost you your humanity." He pauses. "They can make you one of them."

I shudder, then actually give that option a thought. "They can make me an actual cat? Tail and all?" I think what it might be like to be a cat, and the lounging about all day makes me consider it, but only briefly. I don't think I'd like mouse too much. Too lean.

"That is how we lost Haren, who was one of Bu's best friends. Bu saw it happen. They got Haren when he was enjoying the scenery by himself one beautiful summer evening. The mooncats are a tricky race, and can get you to do things without thinking twice. This is the last time I will tell you to be careful."

As Gunthreon finishes his sentence, Bu catches our attention with a whistle.

"They're here," Gunthreon sings, in *Poltergeist* fashion. Bu and Conner stay outside, waiting for us to join them. I want to pee in my pants as Gunthreon pulls me aside and whispers, "If what they say is true about this Michel, you may want to pretend you're already 'involved' with someone. It may help."

As we step into view, I am suddenly in awe of the brood before me. About six giant cats prowl around the cave's entrance, and they seem to be of all different varieties. I recognize Nayla and wave hello, and she purrs back loudly. One cat in particular just sits, watching everything going on around him. He stares me down as I proceed to leave the cave and step out fully before him. I assume this is Michel, and I bow before him. If he's like a king to them, I feel he deserves this courtesy.

Gunthreon walks between us, shielding me from Michel, and I decide to stand next to Conner. "Blessings, great king," says Gunthreon. "We are a traveling band searching for any information you may have on the Higher Ones' whereabouts. We mean you no harm." Nayla sniffs the air in Fannie's direction. Though I hope Ladimer's cover doesn't get blown, I have to wonder why the mooncats dislike him so much. It's probably one of the "many stories" I keep hearing about.

Michel sits still before us, only his eyes moving—large, gorgeous tiger eyes. His physique is much like a tiger's, but he's a bit bulkier, with huge muscles rippling under his skin, like the big burly guys at the gym who make love to themselves in the mirror.

For a giant cat, he is handsome and alluring. "I welcome you to Socola, if you indeed mean us no harm," he says. "I am wondering what you have brought as a gift for the king. This is our custom, you know." He stares at me again and suddenly, his arrogance is like a slap to the face. I take a few baby steps closer toward Conner and grab his arm. He does not object and slightly flexes his muscles.

Jenna disappears behind Bu's leg and he picks her up and holds her gently.

As Gunthreon takes a bit long with his reply, I wonder if he did, in fact, know of this custom. All the other cats still walk about slowly, except for Nayla, who sits, slightly in front of Michel, like a bodyguard. Her tail gently swishes back and forth. She gets up and rubs herself against Michel, and he purrs underneath his breath. As she does, I see her sneak a whisper in his ear. He laughs.

"Nayla is very much hoping your gift is the red one, and to be honest, I think I am, too."

Conner speaks this time, in soulspeak, as he lets everyone know that "the red one" is taken. I realize he must really think so, if he's able to say it. He adds that, unless someone is willing to fight, it will stay that way. I worry that that sounds too much like an offer.

"Of course we have brought you a gift," says Gunthreon quickly. "But as king, you should know that *our* kind do not give away friends as gifts."

"Yes, of course. One can only hope that maybe one day you will change your ways. What have you brought me?" Michel sniffs the air.

Lupa places her pack on the ground, reaches in deeply, and removes the butcher's package. She then walks to Michel, lays it before him, and opens it up. "I hope you are pleased with our gift." Lupa bends down her head.

"A pig? That is it?" Michel examines the pig. He must then see something he likes, for he licks his lips.

"Not just any pig," replies Lupa. "A pregnant female, farm-raised, who fed off the highest-quality feed."

Gunthreon better have done well, I think.

Michel once again licks his chops. "I see the branding. You've brought us a rather nice gift: a Bushingshire export. I accept your gift," he says. "They rarely sell their pregnant pigs, for there is a shortage of females, I hear. Thank you." All the cats seem to move a bit closer to Michel, hoping for a taste. He growls underneath his breath, but allows Nayla to sniff the pig. She smells its belly and proceeds slowly to cut it open with her claw, licking the blood as it trickles down and over the crisp, white butcher paper. Once the piglets are exposed, she walks away, leaving the way open for Michel.

I glance at Bu and see a trickle of light slide down his face. He hides it quickly, and I hope nobody else sees this sign of weakness. He's supposed to be our bodyguard, and tough, badass bodyguards do not cry about piglets.

Jenna strokes Bu, trying to comfort him. When a giant tabby moves a bit too close to him, Jenna bares her teeth. Gunthreon was right about her resembling a wolverine; her teeth could probably shred through the toughest leather without her breaking a sweat.

One of the other cats, a long-haired beauty, kind of reminds me of Amber. She seems high-maintenance, and has the greenest eyes I have ever seen. She keeps licking herself and stroking her fur with her paw, ignoring what's transpiring around her. This reminds me that I'd still like to have a conversation with Gunthreon about the lovebirds, and whether or not Amber might know of Renhala.

277

My mind stops wandering once Michel decides to start eating the pig sprawled out before him. I have to look away, and Conner just hugs me, letting me bury my face into his shoulder. I still have to peek, though.

It's like a train wreck. Michel pulls out each piggy, then actually crunches them, like he's eating a handful of chips. Dark, rich, red blood circles his mouth, and he makes no attempt to wipe it off. He takes the last piglet and throws it to Nayla, who savors it while she eats. Michel then eats the fatty parts of the mother, sucking on the enlarged nipples and staring up at me while doing so. This disturbs me greatly and also Lupa, for her energy reeks of disgust and loathing. It's strongly repulsive. Once he is full, Michel walks away and lets the rest of the cats feed. They rush in and attack the food, fighting for the best leftovers.

"I am willing to share information with you," states Michel, "but there is one favor I request."

Gunthreon turns angry quickly. "We have given you a great gift, which you have recognized, so what more could you expect of us?"

"I want you to share food and conversation with us at a gathering tomorrow night," he says. "You shall be our guests of honor. We will not take no for an answer." At this last remark, all the cats enclose us in a circle. They are motionless, and awaiting movement from us. *This sounds like a party to me.*

My monk's spade is warm, and I feel the heat from Conner's own blade rising. Gunthreon locks eyes with Michel, and I feel his power of persuasion creeping over us. "Dear king, would it not be better for you to give us what we ask? We will leave your land with no quarrel."

Michel laughs. "Oh, your powers will not work on me. Have you forgotten what I am? Are *cats* not known for being surly and insusceptible to persuasion?"

Gunthreon smiles at Michel and bows. "You are indeed powerful. We must agree to join you at your 'gathering.'"

But I'm surprised, because I know that, for some reason Gunthreon did not do his best. His weak energy was quickly expelled. *What is he planning?* He and the newest member of our party, Fannie, make eye contact.

"I will send you escorts tomorrow night," says Michel. "Feel free to roam our land, for you will be under our protection. However, you must let us mark you."

I gasp. "You want to pee on us?"

This produces laughter from all the cats. Fannie laughs, too, and I frown at her. Conner gets points for *not* laughing.

"Pardon our naïve one, sir," cackles Fannie. "I am Fannie, by the way. Kailey, he means for the cats to rub up against you, distributing their pack scent upon your body. That is all."

"Oh." I now feel stupid, but what's new? I can't help staring at Fannie's giant mole. Fannie rubs it and turns away from me.

The cats slowly approach us. Michel remains seated. Nayla rubs against Gunthreon and Lupa, while the other cats rub against Fannie, Conner, and Bu, who holds his breath and closes his eyes, standing motionless as one of the cats rubs slowly against him.

Nayla walks to Jenna and teases her, swatting at her like a cat playing with a mouse. Jenna bares her little dagger teeth at Nayla. "Calm down, woodsprite. I'm just playing," laughs Nayla. She then licks her on the head, but I have to laugh as her tongue gets stuck in Jenna's matted hair. Jenna and Nayla fight to free her tongue, and I feel Nayla's anger. "Ooh, I should have just eaten you and gotten it over with!" she exclaims. Her tongue is eventually freed.

Rising now, Michel approaches me, and I feel his strength as he comes closer. The arrogance and superiority blare like subwoofers from him, making me cringe. But my own power rises to match his, and we both feel a sort of electricity as he rubs against me ever so gently. His tail slowly caresses my face and lips, then moves between my legs, but I quickly jump away, and Conner steps forward. Michel laughs deep in his throat as I tremble. "I feel your power, little one," he says. "Your group is marked. We will see you tomorrow night—at the moon's highest point."

Suddenly, they all run away into the dark, only Nayla lagging behind, taking up the rear. She is soon gone.

I speak to Gunthreon, restating something he told us—something that I know everyone is thinking: "You said no parties."

He frowns. "This one is unavoidable, I fear."

As I point to the cave entrance, I ask, "Well, shall I unpack my bag for our night's stay in our cuddly cave?"

I jump from face to face, and it's Fannie who answers: "I guess this *is* the best place, as long as someone keeps watch. I'm willing to watch tonight, and I'm sure Bu would be happy to relinquish that duty?" Bu nods.

"Gunthreon," I say, approaching him privately, "I have to ask you why you didn't really try to persuade Michel."

"Ladimer had it right. We have to appear as though we are not a threat," he says. "It will give us a bit more flexibility."

"Flexibility for what?"

"For us to do what we must, when we must."

"Thanks for the Greek."

"Anytime."

Fannie says her goodnights and disappears out the mouth of the cave. Jenna walks over to me. "You know, with some practice, I bet you could be as strong as him someday," she says. "There is so much one can do with energy, Kailey. If you can feel it, you can grasp it, if you can grasp it, you can eventually manipulate it—to great proportions."

"I will never be that caliber." I then ponder what she just said.

"That's what you say." She then walks to Conner and snuggles next to him. He covers her up with the corner of his

280

blanket. It's rather endearing, and makes me think again of what he said earlier about me being taken. It kind of makes me feel warm and fuzzy.

"What Kailey thinking about?" I jump and realize I must have been staring. Bu jumps when I jump, because he didn't expect me to.

"Oh, nothing. Bu, can I sleep next to you tonight?" He smiles, and I take it as a yes. He rolls out his blankets, and I roll out my bag next to him. I curl up in the fetal position, and am out within five minutes.

Chapter 38

Unsuspecting

❧

I wake up to the smell of cinnamon toast, and it smells delicious. *How I love thee, Lupa.* My mom used to make me some cinnamon toast every winter morning before school. I'd get out of bed and find, in the kitchen, a big bowl of oatmeal with a plate on top of the bowl to keep it warm, and on the plate would be buttered cinnamon toast. And next to it, I'd always find a big, frosty glass of milk. It's things like this you don't cherish as a kid, but as you get older, and life kicks you around, you realize there's comfort in simple pleasures—like cinnamon toast.

I turn over toward the smell, and suddenly I realize I'm not lying next to Bu, but am instead in Amber's spare bedroom. I quickly roll off the bed and lay beside it, away from the door. I try peeking around the bed and out the door. I can't see anything, but I hear talking. A peek outside the window informs me it's still dark outside.

"Will you just eat it! I finally cook you something, and you just stare at it." Amber sounds frustrated.

"I will. Sorry, I'm not feeling good this morning." Russell sounds horrible.

"Whatever. Did you get your suit cleaned?"

"Yes." He starts on the toast, and it sounds like she must have made it quite crunchy. Typical.

"I can't wait," says Amber. "They're just going to flip. I can't wait to see her face." She sounds ecstatic. "Did you happen to buy me those olives, and vanilla bean yogurt? I can't believe I already have the crazy cravings. Ugh."

She's pregnant? I am so startled by this I gasp.

"What was that?" This from Amber. "That sounded like something was in the bedroom," she whispers. "Go see!"

Russell is already at the bedroom door before I can travel, and we make eye contact. His eyes widen. "There's nothing here. I'm going back to bed," he says. He sneaks over to me. "Are you with my grandfather?"

"I was. I'm sorry I'm here," I respond. "Amber's pregnant?" He nods. "How—" is all that I get out before he covers my mouth.

He whispers. "You're a big girl. I think you know 'how.'"

I hear Amber approaching as Russell says, "Just tell him—," and I travel, for fear Amber might see me.

It must still be the wee hours of the morning, for I see everyone sleeping and can hear Jenna snoring. Her snore is almost as loud as Bu's. It appears nobody has noticed I left. I lay my head back down, insert my iPod earphones into my ears, and count sheep, trying to fall back asleep.

But I can't help but think how Amber and Russell got so busy so fast—marriage, and a baby, already. Thinking about Amber's past relationships, I pray for Russell that it's actually *his* baby, and if it *is*, that he sticks around to be a good husband, and father. Amber cannot be abandoned with a child—it would break her. I pray that the faith I have in Russell and his ability to deal with a hormone-crazed female like Amber will pay off.

As I contemplate telling Gunthreon about what I witnessed, Bu turns over and puts his arm around me, and I feel like I'm in a giant cocoon, unable to move. His stink has grown on me, and now it will probably *be* on me.

Sleep soon takes over.

౪

I am awakened by a hissing noise right near my head, and jump up at the sight of Jenna baring her teeth at me. Her eyes are opened as wide as can be, and she hisses at my iPod. "Evil magic! Kailey, get up! It has snakes in your ears!" She reaches out to me and rips out the earphones, then bites them with her teeth, tearing—no, shredding—the cords. She then manages to chew on the iPod itself, breaking pieces off.

"No! Jenna—" My voice chokes up with displeasure. "You better sell a few weapons to replace what you just broke!" Gunthreon moans slightly, but checks himself fast. Jenna frowns. I pick up the iPod and it won't turn on. "What the hell?! Damn, Damn, Damn!" I shout. Seeing my displeasure, Jenna starts crying, realizing she made a mistake.

I look at her and her energy feels as though *it's* crying—it's so full of sadness that I crouch down near her, realizing I'm overreacting. "Sorry. I know you were only protecting me. It's all right. You see, I bought this. It plays music, and those 'snakes' were only cords to bring the music to my ears. Don't be upset. I can replace it someday." I throw the iPod down in the corner of the cave and salute it. "Rest in peace, dear Marley, Morrison, and Bono."

Conner walks over to me. "I know someone who could get you a *really good* deal on a new one," he says. "Remind me when we get home, and I'll give you his number." Gunthreon overhears the conversation and looks disturbed as Conner talks about his inside connection. Gunthreon looks the other way as his energy swirls with a sort of uneasiness.

"That would be great, thanks," I reply, downhearted, as Conner squeezes my shoulder. He's being nice to me this morning.

Jenna walks toward Conner and I hear, "You know a magician who makes those things?" They continue their conversation as I shed tears internally, not expressing what I truly feel right now.

Everyone starts packing up their stuff, and I do the same—slowly, thinking of my lost music, and humming "Cat's in the

Cradle," to myself. *Cats*. Mooncat thoughts soon shadow my
sorrow over my lost music. Bu's expression of sheer panic surely
reflects his own thoughts as he fiddles with his fanny pack. I pull
out my own ring and stare at it, tracing the braiding with my eyes,
finding no seam. I then look up to Gunthreon, who is still
bothered by something.

I shove the ring back in my pocket and ask him to come
with me outside the cave. It has to be morning, but it's still totally
dark outside. This will take some getting used to.

"What's on your mind, Gunth?"

He stares at me.

"You can't hide it from me."

He sighs. "Remember when I told you that I was not always
a friend in a high place?"

"Yes?" I say, suddenly overwhelmed with eagerness to learn
a deep, dark secret. His energy wavers and I feel embarrassment
leaking through.

Gunthreon looks out in the distance, apparently gathering
courage. "I used to be not such an honest man."

"Yeah, well, we all have moments of weakness."

"I...used to run with some woodsprites." He says it so
quickly I can feel his breath pushing the words out.

My jaw opens slightly, and my head tilts to the side. "And
what does that mean?"

"I used to buy weapons from the woodsprites and sell them
to the highest bidders. I was so young, and I misused my
persuasion, not understanding that karma would eventually find
me. I was awful." His face is darkened by the shame he has been
holding onto too tightly, most likely for decades.

I dig into his energy, and he scratches his chest, where I've
touched, not realizing it's me. I reach in deep, trying to find
something to help his remorse.

"Everyone does stupid things when they're young," I say. "As long as you make a turnaround at some point and lead a better life, which you've done, higher powers will recognize this—whatever or whomever they may be." I then find what I seek, inside his energy field.

Gunthreon stares into the darkness as I add, shyly, "I feel something wonderful in your energy. I've dug—maybe I shouldn't so deeply—into yours, and I've found a most endearing quality." He continues scratching his chest, then looks to me, realizing what I've just done, then looks at me with an odd expression. "I've found you possess an *honest* willing of self-sacrifice. You are risking your life to save others, others you do not even know. What's more unselfish than that? You're a good man."

He breathes deeply, not saying anything. I then feel him build up an extra energy layer around himself, something I've never experienced before. I step back slightly, and continue watching his face.

"Impressive, Kailey," he says, pulling himself together, and standing a bit more straight. "Thank you for the reading. I *needed* that." He then turns and whispers to himself, "You are definitely ready for this."

"What?" I ask, not understanding.

"Nothing. Let's go back in."

"You do have to do one thing for me."

He turns to me with a quizzical face. "What?"

"Give a certain someone else the benefit of the doubt. Give her a chance. You turned your life around. She can, too."

"Oh, yes, of course. I'll try," he responds. "It's just that I see her, and everything comes back to me." I nod. He leads me back toward our friends, and back toward the smell of something cooking. "Let's head out, everyone," he requests of the group. "Jenna, can I talk with you?" He doesn't look at her directly when he asks, and I see her eyes widen with fear.

"Why?" She's not going easily.

"Please, Jenna," he pleads. I feel Gunthreon's energy change as he makes a conscious effort to keep his temper in check. I nod to Jenna. Then, I make sure I'm close enough to eavesdrop.

"I need you to every now and then run ahead of us to check out the area," Gunthreon says. "Could you do me that favor? You wouldn't be in much danger, because we'd be near enough, and I know that you are stealthy enough not to be seen. I'd really appreciate it." He looks directly into her eyes.

"No persuasion—a genuine request," grunts Jenna. "All right. I will do that for you." Gunthreon extends his hand to her. She studies his face, but eventually holds her tiny hands out to him.

Jenna is still holding Gunthreon's hand when she says, "Only thing we need is a call in case something is up. Do you know the cry of the speckled witherling?"

Gunthreon makes a guttural sound from deep in his throat with a high-pitched shrill at the end. Lupa jumps, and both Gunthreon and Jenna laugh. From Jenna's face, it must be the perfect rendition of a speckled witherling. *Glad to see there are no longer any enemies in our party*, I think. *Let's see how long it lasts.*

Fannie, packed, sits, waiting for Lupa to finish making some delicious smelling pancakes on a tiny, camp-sized griddle. I have to ask about the griddle. It's the last straw. "Lupa, where on earth are you storing all these things?" I say, picking up a saucepan lying next to her. She hands me a plate of pancakes and I start devouring them.

"I acquired the coolest everything pack when I was shopping in Nanorea a few years back," confesses Lupa, as she hands me her plain, tan linen bag, embroidered with a blue spiral. I look inside and there is nothing. "It was quite pricey though, and I even had to cut a deal for *that* price! The mayor was in a contest for garden-grown roses, and I helped him out just a little bit. I know it's probably cheating, but the pack is the best!"

I turn the bag upside down and shake it. "Lupa, you've lost it. There's nothing here."

She reaches over, sticks her hand in and pulls out a metal colander.

"What?!?"

She laughs. "So I've lost it?"

"How?"

"When you put something in the bag," she explains, "you make sure you get a good mental picture of it and think of it as you place it in. Then, when you need it again, you think of it, stick your hand in, and voila! It's in your hand."

"Can I try?" I ask.

She hands the bag back to me and I look around. I grab a fork, and then think of it as I stick my hand in the bag, placing the fork inside and closing the bag. I then look in it and it's empty once more.

"Okay, now retrieve it."

I think of the fork and place my hand in the bag. A sudden coldness envelopes my hand and I feel around, only feeling linen, until suddenly, I grasp metal. I pull the object out and it's the same fork. "So I bet you have to be the one to get it. I couldn't reach in and take anything because I don't know what's in there. It's the perfect safeguard against thieves!"

Lupa smiles. "You got it."

"I want one!"

"Works in your realm, too" she says, a big smile across her face "You could borrow mine someday if you like. It's kind of scary to think how this thing really works. I mean, where does everything go?"

"Thanks, that would be cool," I laugh. "But what if you forget about something you put in there?"

"Well, most likely, you would remember it at some point. The only way to lose something would be to never think of it again."

We all finish eating and pack up. I pick up my bag and sling it over my shoulder. That's when I smell the odor wafting from my own body. "Good god! Will we ever be able to shower?"

"You'll have to wait at least until tomorrow," says Gunthreon. "We're marked, remember? You can't wash that off if you plan on exploring Socola today."

"You better all stink as bad as I do," I mumble. "I don't want to be the only one making our hosts' eyes water tonight."

Lupa reaches in her bag and throws me a bottle of white powder. I smell it, and it smells faintly of lilacs. I think of my mom and immediately feel a pang in my heart.

"Move on out!" Gunthreon leads the way, as Jenna scouts ahead. Gunthreon smiles to himself.

I walk behind Bu, and whenever he's not paying attention, I sprinkle some of Lupa's powder on him. He's totally oblivious and doesn't even wonder why he keeps sneezing. I take some and rub it under my shirt, hoping to ease my pain and suffering from my own stench. I see Gunthreon smile to himself.

"So what are we going to do with ourselves until tonight, considering we can't see anything?" I inquire.

"Well, whatever we do, we need to slather up with some protection from the broofwings, first. I am *not* ending up in an infirmary," Lupa says. She reaches into her everything pack and pulls out a container of some smelly, yellow lotion, and slathers her body.

Conner pulls out his own tube.

"Let me use some of that." I hold out my hand. He raises his eyebrows at me, and I feel there's going to be some form of IOU, or else he just wants me to beg, which I will not be doing. "Please," I say quickly.

"Just don't get it in your eyes or mouth."

"Yessir."

As we continue walking, Fannie covers the rear, staying quiet. I hold back a bit until she catches up to me. "So Fannie, want to play dress-up later? I can put some makeup on you and give you pointers."

"Funny, Kailey. No help needed."

"That's what you think."

"We're being followed," she suddenly states. I turn. "Don't look! The only thing I can say is that it's not by mooncats—something smaller, and not Jenna. Just keep your guard up, and don't let them know we know."

"Okay," I drone.

But it's hard to pretend I don't hear them behind me, so I find myself repeatedly talking nonsense about nothing in particular. I also talk a bit louder for some reason. I also stretch out my energy feeler and get nothing back. "So, the weather is so strange here. Hey! That rock looks like Elvis."

Fannie turns to me as we continue walking and whispers, "Just act normal, Kailey."

"You should have never have told me we were being followed. How can I act normal?"

Suddenly, Fannie disappears behind the huge Elvis rock. For a moment, I hear nothing, wondering if something awful became of Fannie.

"Ow!" she suddenly shouts. "Why did you bite me?"

"Ladimer—Fannie—you okay?"

She returns, nursing her hand, which I see is bleeding slightly, but she heals it quickly. "Just a damn ceetchan! I don't know what it's doing here—probably hunting for food and wandered off. It's pregnant. Maybe it's sick and wants me to make the nausea stop. I get that a lot." Fannie pulls me forward to keep us with our group.

I stop mid-stride. "Pregnant?"

Fannie stops with me. "Yeah, so what?"

"Hold on a minute." I run back to where the ceetchan was and do not find her. I hurry back. "Just thinking something. Sorry, let's go."

We continue walking, and after a half mile, I hear something behind us again. I turn around quickly with my monk's spade in hand.

Behind me and Fannie is the fattest, cutest pregnant ceetchan, a patch of white hair over her eye. I walk to her, and she lets me pet her head. "No way." I immediately wipe my hand over my pants. She feels like a dog that hasn't been bathed in years.

"Don't pet it!" spits Fannie. "You don't know what diseases that thing is carrying. It'll bite you, and I will not heal you."

"I know her."

"What do you mean, you know her?"

"Just that. I've met this ceetchan before," I explain. "Actually, partially in Abscondia."

Fannie's eyes squint for a brief two seconds. "There are hundreds of thousands of those things around. Maybe you saw one similar to this one."

"You don't think it's strange she let me pet her? And why is she *here*?"

Fannie furrows her brow at the creature, and it growls at her.

"You're just mad because she doesn't like you," I say. I pull a piece of beef jerky out of my pack and let her eat it. I take a piece also, then spit it out, as I somehow got bug lotion on my tongue. My tongue begins feeling numb as I try wiping it on my sleeve. "Blah!"

"And you're going to waste your food on it, too! Neda save you, Kailey," yammers Fannie. "We need to keep walking, because everyone else is far ahead of us, and we don't want to be alone here right now."

I hold up the ceetchan's head and look into her eyes. "You need a name. I'm gonna call you Cheeto! Why are you here, sweetie? Have you been following me this whole time?" Cheeto just stares up at me, clearly wanting more jerky, so of course I slip her another piece.

"You've really lost it. Come on!" Fannie runs forward, and then I realize it's just me and Cheeto. I start running, too, and Cheeto does her best following me, waddling as fast as she can. I guess I can assume I've attracted another party member. Gunthreon is going to just be so happy, I'm sure. I decide to divert his attention.

As I catch up to him, he sees the ceetchan. "Gunthreon, I have to tell you that I traveled last—"

"I see you found another forest friend, eh?" He stares at the ceetchan. "A pregnant friend. You know she may hold you back if you get attached to her."

"Don't worry, Gunthreon. About my traveling—"

"I was wondering where you went last night," says Gunthreon. I saw you were gone and was quite happy when you reappeared. Where did you go this time?" He peeks up at me, inquisitively.

"Amber's place. Russell was there, too." Gunthreon's eyebrows rise slightly. "And?"

"Ummm... "

"She's pregnant," he blurts.

"You knew?" I ask. "Why didn't you tell me? How did you find out? Aren't you supposed to wait three months before telling people that? Why am I always the last to know!"

Gunthreon smiles a quirky smile at me. "He *is* my grandson, you know. I really wouldn't know about the three-month thing you speak of."

"I hate to say this, but are you thinking what I'm thinking?" I query.

"That Lupa is especially beautiful this morning?" he says with a giant smile, looking in her direction.

"Yeah, she's awesome," I respond, quickly, "But no!" I feel a bit embarrassed, but need to express my doubt to Gunthreon about Amber's fidelity. "You know, it's only been a few weeks that they've known each other, and Amber's not...always 'exclusive.'"

Gunthreon actually smiles. "Let's just say, that, Russell, being what he is, is extremely...capable. Extremely. And I'm sure he's captivated her." My eyebrows scrunch, questioningly. "*He's potent!*" Gunthreon says, his embarrassment evident by the redness in his cheeks. "Let's leave it at that, Kailey. I no longer desire to speak on the matter."

Definitely radiating discomfort, Gunthreon "humphs" and I decide to change the subject for both our sakes.

"Oh! Then what was it he wanted me to tell you?" I say, puzzled. "It seemed urgent, but Amber interrupted us."

"Keep your eyes open. We are near an encampment and you don't want to miss anything," states Gunthreon, brushing off Russell.

"What does that mean?"

"You'll see. Preparations."

We come upon the top of a hill with, despite the darkness, a wonderful view of the valley below. There are plenty of fires lit, and several mooncats roasting numerous foods over them. We can see hundreds of mooncats scattering hither and thither.

"What's going on? This can't be just for *us?*" My blood pressure rises and I can hear Bu's heart beating even though I'm standing six feet away from him.

"They only have a few hours to get ready for the party," says Gunthreon. "They sure know how to do it up." He squints, apparently trying to see more of what's going on below. All I can see is that there's an elephant involved. "We might as well start trekking down there."

"What?!" I exclaim, an alarm going off in my head. "Maybe they don't want us to see them preparing. Let's just be surprised tonight." I imagine us walking into an ambush of wide-open feline jaws, slashing cat claws and thousand-pound, stomping elephant feet. My imagination dances without rhythm, and it's an ugly dance.

"Yeah, that sounds like a good idea Kailey," agrees Fannie. Clearly, she doesn't want to walk right into their hands—claws—either.

"No," responds Gunthreon, having none of it. "We are going down there, whether you like it or not. Would you rather have a glimpse of what they are preparing for us or be entirely shocked when it's spread out before us tonight?" From the look on Conner's face, he agrees with me and Fannie, but he isn't going to speak up against Gunthreon, who happens to be standing hands-on-hips.

Jenna appears beside us, returning from her scouting mission, and suddenly, bares her teeth again, this time at Cheeto, who shows her own teeth. "What is that thing doing here?" she yaps.

"She's under my watch, so leave her alone," I howl. "Hey! You were also under that watch once, too, weren't you?"

"But it's a *ceetchan*!" Jenna stares at Cheeto, her hands on her hips—mirrored image of Gunthreon. "You making it your pet now?"

"I guess you can say that. Her name is Cheeto."

I see the disgust in Jenna's eyes. "You *named* the ragged mutt?"

Cheeto's big eyes turn up at Fannie as she wags her tail.

"She likes you now. Look." I caress her head and remove my hand, and pat her head briefly, twice.

Fannie grunts. "Well, I don't have to like *her*. She probably only likes me now because she senses what I am." Under her breath, she adds, "Everyone wants something." She walks off.

Our little woodsprite friend says "whatever" with her body language—hands dropped, and a wave of her hand towards me and Cheeto, and turns her attention back to the current situation. "I'm scared, but I agree with Gunthreon," she says. "I took a quick look down below, but really, we all need to go to assess the situation. Hopefully, we can figure out what to expect from tonight's festivities."

My, my, Gunthreon's made himself a brave little detective.

Gunthreon decides to not wait for our approval and starts the descent with Lupa. "They know we're here, so be on your best behavior," he warns us. "Don't appear as shocked as you may feel at the sight of their festivities."

As we start our journey, I turn back and see that Bu is still at the top of the hill. I walk up and stand beside him. I lay my hand gently on his and look up into his face. He then turns to me and simply says, "For Haren."

Then, I am then the one being led downhill. The firmness of his grip on my hand is that of a boy facing his darkest challenge with adult-like dignity, but also a shitload of fear. Cheeto follows us as closely as she can. As we approach the bottom of the hill, I find myself walking very slowly, but Bu keeps his own pace and lets me fall behind. I can smell the lilac powder as he walks to the others. Gunthreon, Fannie, Lupa, Conner, and Jenna have already reached the encampment, and are greeted, or, I should say, sniffed, by several mooncats.

Just before I continue, a random thought of my mother races through my head and the anxiety I feel from not being able to check on her safety floods my current anxiety from the situation below. I close my eyes and take a breath, holding it, and imagine her standing before me, smiling—simply for comfort. Then, I imagine the feel of her energy—that kind of humming that goes on in your head when you're around someone else—which also possesses its own kind of texture, at least to me. I send out my feeler, letting my energy call out to her, and wait for her energy to respond.

I feel my movement, and my eyes slowly open as I quickly brace myself, discovering that I just traveled. I find that I'm standing on a rather tall rock, and not on a level plateau, but on the peak. My foot slips, and I grab onto the rock with both hands, regaining my balance and keeping myself from falling to my death. I do my best to see into the distance all around me, but I do not see my mom, let alone any living creature. A puddle of green goo at the foot of the rock lets me know exactly where I am: Gernwood. Why I repeatedly show up here, I do not know—especially if this was a semi-involuntary act of soulsearching.

Sudden activity to my left forces me to crouch down, and I try hugging the rock, making myself less visible.

"He says to check out the yards and holler if there's any trace." I peer down below and see a somewhat short and thin greble—by greble standards—using a long staff to balance himself as he stands. Next to him is a dirty, gray-haired meeple, who from the looks of it, has seen many a year.

The meeple glances wearily over the scenery. "In my opinion, he's losing it. That plan of his scares me to death." The meeple grunts loudly, and the greble nods his head, assuring the meeple he indeed feels the same. They both turn around, walking back in the direction from which they came. "Damn Devoten. Whatever haunts him must be something nasty, making us walk all the way out here because he 'feels' something. Yeah, let him *feel* my foot up his butt!" They both laugh and continue on, not seeing the redhead perched up above them like a cardinal in a tree.

I make a judgment call and decide not to search the area. My lame attempt at soulsearching—even if subconsciously—a failure. I prepare to travel back quickly, but before I leave, I can't help but notice a figure in the distance—a figure I quickly recognize as a deathman. It stands as still as can be, just staring directly at me. It grins, and I take this as my cue to return from whence I came.

As I travel, it dawns on me that I just did once again what Gunthreon said no one ever does: traveled within Renhala.

Chapter 39

Pitiful
ɡ♋

The elephant I suddenly find myself perched upon moves slightly as I appear on its back. Its trunk comes near me, and it sniffs me, tickles my ear, then blows snot at me.

"Gross!" I yell, gripping firmly with both hands. "Why on top of an elephant?"

Its elderly, gray-furred owner laughs as he watches me gripping the elephant for dear life. He's rattily dressed in dirty old clothes, but his fur is combed back neatly as he lovingly pets his elephant. He laughs merrily to the point of tears. "I'm not gonna ask where you just came from," he giggles. "I only want to say, thanks so much for the laugh. Haven't had one in months."

"Kailey, get down from there this instant!" Lupa has her hands on her hips, resembling Gunthreon for a brief moment. "You're going to fall and kill yourself. How did you get up there?"

Conner turns his attention to me and starts laughing when he sees the goop all over my face. Jenna joins in the laughter.

The elephant owner and Bu help me down. The tissue Lupa hands me barely makes a dent in the snot.

"Glad you're back," Gunthreon states, his face clearly revealing the sarcasm spoke. I cringe. Gunthreon pets the elephant's trunk. "Kailey, were you searching for your mother?"

"I didn't mean—" I say as he puts his hand up.

"You haven't seen her in a while. Any luck?" I shake my head. "I'd probably be defying me too, if I could. But Kailey, it's important that you stop. As of right now." My nod satisfies him. "Let's keep walking."

Lupa stops in front of a bunch of mooncats preparing a substantial amount of brown stew over a large fire. She sniffs the air. "Excuse me," she says to a rather tiny little thing, something resembling a Siamese cat. "Are you using mountain fern?"

The cat smiles. "You have a discerning nose. Well done. I'd offer you some, but the rules are no tasting until later."

"Totally understandable. Thank you for sharing your herbal secret." Lupa bows to the Siamese. The cat stirs the stew in the kettle, and I gasp when I see a pair of green eyes disappear into the depths of the broth. The eyes had a familiar glare to them.

Lupa turns to us. "Do you have any idea how rare that is? I feel like royalty! I wonder how they came about such a huge quantity of mountain fern."

"Or how they can eat their own kind."

Lupa gasps as the words exit my mouth. "Why would you say that?"

I tell her that I saw a pair of eyes that we met the other night. "I'll leave it at that," I state.

"It's dark and your eyes are playing tricks on you," responds Conner. "Mooncats are not known cannibals."

"Thanks, Mr. Walking Encyclopedia."

"He's right," declares Gunthreon. "They eat flesh, but never their own."

Conner pulls a "me," sticking his tongue out in my direction. As I make a stupid face back at him, crossing my eyes and all, I trip over Cheeto, who has been walking as close as possible. My body gains momentum, and I then trip over a rope holding up one of the tents. My hand lands on a grill covered in roasting rats.

"Ow! Damn! Ladimer!" My hand screams at me, and I can see the blisters forming already. The pain is excruciating.

The realization then sets in as to what I just said.

Fannie is beside me before I even have the chance to be dumbfounded. "You better shut up," she howls, "or else you're going to get me killed!" She pulls me by my hair as the mooncat manning the grill watches us with squinted eyes. The cat, a cheetah

299

and definitely male, flips his rats methodically, keeping his other hand on a chef's knife a little longer than I'd like.

"I have some salve for that, if you'd like," says the cat, pulling a small metal container out of a bag.

"Yes, that would be so kind of you," replies Fannie. "Your food smells scrumptious!" Fannie holds out my hand as the cat man puts the salve onto the burn. I hope he doesn't notice that Fannie is squeezing all the blood out of my hand, or that my nail is trying to burrow itself into her finger to get her to let up a bit.

"Just keep this dry, and you shouldn't have a scar." Cheetah man winks at me. He's kind of cute. I blush.

"Thank you. I'm Kailey." I shake his paw with my good hand. He responds a bit awkwardly, but I don't know the cat equivalent of shaking hands. As long as it doesn't involve smelling his rear, I can handle it. He then licks my hand and I blush, again, and giggle.

"And I'm Fannie." Fannie does not shake the cheetah's paw.

"Conner." Conner does a guy-nod.

"I am Leon," purrs the cat. "Sorry I couldn't catch you in time, but you fell so quickly! Your little friend here believes you will keep her safe, eh?" He stares down at Cheeto.

Fannie says, "Stupid animal has grown attached to our clumsy... "

"And flirty," adds Conner.

"... Kailey," Fannie finishes, ignoring Conner.

Leon checks all of us over, head to toe. "Do not underestimate an animal's intuition, *Fannie*. That could prove to be stupid in itself down the road." He pauses. "You folks enjoy the pre-show and we will see you tonight. I gotta get back to the cooking."

"Thanks again." I hold up my blistering hand.

"Any time." He winks as Conner and Fannie start walking away. I blush again, then run to catch up with them.

300

Cheeto catches up to me and rubs against my leg, then looks up at me with her big eyes. I lean down, scratch behind her ears, and tell her how cute she is. She smells my hand where I burned it and starts to lick the wound. It hurts, but I let her anyway. I always believed the claim that a dog's mouth is cleaner than a human's, so maybe it's the same for a wild raccoon with fangs.

When I catch up to my friends, Jenna is jabbering away in Gunthreon's ear. It puts me in a brighter mood, because he actually let her talk rather than demean her or talk over her.

"They are always ready for a party," says Gunthreon, "but I do have to say, this one seems especially extravagant. Imported food, rare animals, handmade silks, and tapestries—it must be costing them a fortune." As we continue forward, Gunthreon stares at a showcat whose headdress, from the look of it, could very well be made of real emeralds and sapphires.

I turn to what I think is Bu's direction and soon find that he's nowhere in sight. "Guys, where's—"

My words abruptly stop as I stare at a horrible scene before us. Lupa buries her face in Gunthreon, Conner gasps, and Fannie and Jenna are wordless. Even Cheeto growls and bares her teeth.

I turn away, no longer able to look. Conner puts his arms around me. "How—how can they do that?" I cry, into his shoulder.

"I don't know," Conner replies, solemnly. As he holds me I sense his emotions—a faint sense of hopelessness mixed with pity, and I don't like it. *Pity*.

"Shouldn't we do something? Shouldn't *someone*?" I sob, pulling away from him and scanning the huge crowd surrounding the abomination while everyone simply stares, murmuring to each other, and thanking their gods that it's not them.

"We are a bit outnumbered, and we're in their territory, Kailey," states Gunthreon. "They have their own ways of doing things here. We cannot do a godforsaken thing."

Lupa sobs loudly, but tries to hold it back for Gunthreon's sake. He hugs her and whispers in her ear. She wipes her tears from her face and turns to me.

Memories instantly flood back. *Defenseless and soon hopeless. It's what he's hoping for—I can sense it. My pleas only serve as satisfaction— satisfaction for the fact I broke. I held on for so long, after so much blood shed, but there's* always *a breaking point. Humiliation can break one just as easily as immeasurable physical pain.* I wonder if *she* broke.

My monk's spade burns my back, and I grab a hold of it and take it off, only set on finding the one responsible for her pain. No defensive moves this time, but a willingness to hunt—to track the very soul who took pleasure in the humiliation. I suddenly swell with confidence as I swear to avenge.

As I march forward, I hear Gunthreon calling to me—his persuasion calling, calling me back—but I'm full of an unstoppable energy, even to him.

Fannie steps in front of me, and says, "Calm down. She's simply a mooncat who could of easily turned on you at any moment, Kailey. You hold no allegiance to them, so why defend her? Maybe she deserved—" she stops as she looks into my eyes, now realizing my motivation. Fannie steps aside.

"Who is responsible for this?" I ask, as I scan the crowd, searching for anyone who might reply. No answer. "*Who?*" I grab my spade with both hands and try to control the anger that flows through me and into my weapon. Then, I walk to the beautiful creature that has been dismembered and hung from a tree in a hammock. I cut the hammock down, and Fannie helps me lay her on the ground gently.

"Oh, Nayla," I whimper. The loss of beauty makes me cry, and my tears glow as they streak my face. Her body is motionless as I touch the tender area where her legs were once attached, now sloppily sewn up with butcher's twine.

To make it worse, the legs are on giant skewers, dripping her blood into the fire pit below them. The cuts are fresh, and I turn to Fannie who has put her hand on Nayla's brow, and Fannie's eyes rise slightly. This is my clue there is a chance. Fannie rips a piece of her shirt and uses it as a tourniquet around one of Nayla's legs where the stitches have ripped open.

"This was done while she was still alive!" I exlaim as I bury my hands in Nayla's slick fur and feel a slight electric current, and below that, her own energy, barely pulsing. I keep my hands on her and somehow, intuitively know that the current I sense is from her assaulter. I raise myself off the ground and send out my feeler toward the crowd; nothing coming back to me.

Everyone is motionless, and silent, waiting for a response from us. It makes me so angry that I push the feeler out even further, and that's when I feel it: a tiny response from an energy distancing itself in a hurry. As I embrace my find, as well as my knowledge of the power inside me, a small tear drips from eye, and I am no longer broken.

I turn to Fannie. "Take care of her."

"Kailey, I can't without them knowing. I'm sorry. I can lessen her pain, though." She looks down at Nayla with compassion.

I inhale and grab Fannie's chin, gently, turning her head toward me. "Help her for those you couldn't save in the past."

I take off running before Gunthreon or anyone can stop me. I run toward the familiar pulse, responding to my own energy. I never even see the rocks I sprint over or hear the hissing of the cats around me. My mission controls me, and I am bound to find the respondent. The feeling grows stronger, and I sense the presence of the one who owns the energy I seek. I approach a tree with a huge hole in the side—perfect for hiding.

"Come out. I know you're there," I spit. My grip on my monk's spade is as tight as I can make it, and I am prepared to use it. "I will give you a fair fight." The sudden laughing I hear from the hole in the tree makes me shiver to my bones, but I hold tightly to my anger. "Come out so I can see your yellow belly before I kill you."

The laughing grows louder. A voice filled with immense power responds. "Who do you think you are? You are nothing but a child with a sharp toy. You do not even know how to use that spade, so why bother? Devoten is foolish for keeping you alive. You should have been the one in that damn cat's place."

I am instantly overwhelmed with the feeling that I indeed do not know how to use my spade and that I am not worthy to hold it. I drop my weapon to the ground, but hold my ground firmly. "No matter who she was, no living creature deserves something like that," I say, with a bit less confidence.

The meeple steps out of the darkness of the tree hole and laughs at me. It sits on its haunches, pretending to sharpen its talon against the bark of a tree, breaking off huge chunks as it does so. It is then that I see a quick movement above us.

"Oh, is this just too close to home, Kailey?" the meeple teases, smiling. "Are you seeking out revenge for your own misfortune, perhaps?" I swallow as I hold my tears back. I will not allow this miserable creature a chance to humiliate me. It's clear it knows what happened to me, and I question how, but I'm choosing to fight, and fight with all I've got. I see movement once again from high above, and cannot wrap my mind around what I think I saw.

"What? Praying that quickly? Come on, I gotta see you sweat first," the meeple rambles, slowly taking a step forward. I see the movement again above us and interpret in my brain what's going on. *That damn woodsprite was right!*

Just as the meeple takes another step, ready to strike me while my spade is down, tree branches swoop down, pick up the meeple, twist its neck, and drop it to the ground as I stare in awe. I

304

stand, motionless, not wanting to move an inch as the branches go back to simply swaying in the wind.

There is no further threat, but there is a rustling of leaves that seems to be getting closer. I crouch to the ground, turning my head toward the sound, straining my ear to make sure I know exactly where it's coming from. It is then that it appears, all disgusting and creepy: a deathman.

It walks straight to the meeple, not paying me any attention as it picks up the carcass and stares at it, while kneeling. It lays the meeple back down and holds its hands a few inches above the creature, moving them back and forth, methodically, over the body. Slowly, a beautiful, round, iridescent specter escapes and hovers above the body. The deathman stares at the ball for a moment, then grabs it, puts it in its mouth, and swallows. It climbs to its feet, and before walking away, seems to wave at the tree in a neighborly sort of way.

The deathman leaves, and I still stand motionless in front of the tree.

I look up, waiting for more movement. "Umm... Thank you?"

I turn around to start my walk back to the encampment, and hear a whisper that resembles the wind: "You're welcome." My walk quickly turns into a run.

Chapter 40

Proud
ଓଃ

As I head back to camp, thinking to myself that karma just scored, I remember Gunthreon's words of the Higher Ones intervention with karma: I'm simply the beacon. In thinking that Neda surely must be involved, I intend to tell Gunthreon, when I suddenly realize camp's much quieter than I remember it, so I approach with care. I hear Gunthreon's voice above all noises, using his persuasion to calm the crowd. Fannie holds Nayla, and I whisper, "Is she gone?"

"No, she's still hanging on somehow, but I do not know for how long." She pets her head gently.

"Any idea why this was done?" I ask.

"Both Gunthreon and Conner are working on it, but aren't getting any concrete answers," she replies, continuing to stroke Nayla's head.

"It was a meeple," I state as Fannie's head suddenly turns to look at me, "and it knew my name."

"Why would one be here, of all places?" she asks. I shrug. "Mooncats and meeples never mix well. Where did it run off too?"

"It's not running any longer. It's dead," I respond. Fannie stares at me, looking a bit too shocked.

"Not by my hands," I say, disappointingly.

"Maybe not by your hands, but you *definitely* had something to do with it." Fannie answers.

In looking over the crowd, I see someone heading toward us and realize it's Bu. "Quick, take her into the forest and help her," I plead. Fannie glares at me. "Please!"

"You're gonna be the death of me!" Fannie gets up and drags Nayla into the forest on a blanket while the mooncats stand and stare.

Suddenly, a proud and exhilarated mass of energy approaches. I know instantly who it is behind me. "Kailey! Bu's got something for you! Kailey will be happy!" Approaching, Bu holds out his hand, revealing my iPod. Cheeto is waddling after him.

Oh, Bu. Jenna broke it, so I left it."

"Kailey." He shows me the iPod again. I see that the cords are wrapped and the iPod is on, so I put the earbuds in my ears and, sure enough, it works.

"Bu, you are so awesome." I say. "How did you do it?"

"Bu also made these for Jenna." He shows me a mini set of earphones, made with tiny pieces of some kind of spongy organic material.

"I don't think she'll even go near this thing, but it was very nice of you to think of her."

"Bu doesn't want Jenna to be afraid of these things. They are not bad," he says. He then realizes that something is going on around him. "What's happening?" In a heartbeat, I see proud Bu disappear and nervous Bu reappear. He picks up Cheeto and starts caressing her head.

"At least you aren't afraid you'll get something from her," I say, as I smile warmheartedly at Cheeto.

"Grebles don't catch ceetchan diseases," Bu comments.

"Oh, great."

As I explain everything to Bu, Gunthreon returns, looking exhausted. He overhears that a meeple was the culprit. "That tested my limits," he says. "At least everyone is going back to their business. We've got nothing—except a few comments on a 'new reign,' which means Michel. Why would a meeple be here? I wonder if Michel is aware of the situation. We must talk to him as soon as possible." Gunthreon stares at me as though he wants to say something.

"I tried, too, and got nada," admits Conner as he approaches. He sits on a rock nearby and looks like he's thinking too hard. He looks and *feels* worn out. I smile at him, warmly, and then notice a slight change in his energy—a sense of appreciation.

A sudden crunching noise—sounding like sticks and leaves—from the forest alerts us that we must move. We all move as fast as we can without catching anyone's attention. I lead, and we find Fannie and Nayla quickly.

Nayla's regenerated eyes are wide open, and she has her two front paws again. Ladimer, not Fannie, stands over her. They both stare west at a figure approaching slowly. No energy emanates from this creature, so instinctively I yell, "Deathman!"

Gunthreon yells, feverishly, "We must find out what happened! Get her underground! Lupa, did you pack that shovel?" Gunthreon shakes Lupa. "Lupa, get with me!" She then snaps out of it and hands him a shovel from her everything pack.

Bu stares at Nayla, tears trickling out of his eyes, lighting up his face. Shovel in hand, Gunthreon turns to Bu. "Bu, she'll be okay, but you have to help. Start digging!" Gunthreon has already started a hole, and Bu quickly joins in with his big hands. I take my monk's spade and use the shovel-sided end.

"Didn't think you'd actually be using your blade for its original purpose, did you?" says Gunthreon with a smirk, grime on his face. I remember that this is what Gunthreon said the monks used the shovel spade for: to bury people. "We have to get her buried before it gets here."

The deathman moves ever so slowly, evidently seeing what we're doing but not caring.

"Just make sure you give me a large enough hole to breathe through," requests Nayla, suddenly conscious and aware of the approaching deathman.

"Oh, beautiful Nayla, be brave," I say. She softly purrs.

When our hole is big enough, Conner and Ladimer lift Nayla and put her in it. The deathman stops, but continues to stare. "Cover her with dirt, now!" shouts Gunthreon. He's so busy throwing commands, and everyone else so busy throwing dirt, that only I notice that the deathman is staring at me.

I want to say, "What?" but my better judgment tells me not to. The deathman continues staring as one of its fingers points up at me. Nobody else seems to notice.

"She's covered," mumbles Conner, breathing heavily. The deathman turns to where Nayla is, looks down toward the newly covered hole, shrugs, and heads back in the direction from which it came. Ladimer, with closed eyes, has his hands in the ground, trying to heal Nayla while she's buried.

"I can't tell if it's gone." I shiver and glance down at Cheeto, who grooms herself as if nothing else is going on around her. Jenna hides behind a rock.

Gunthreon starts to brush the dirt off Nayla. "It's gone. Come on."

Soon, Nayla is out, coughing up some dirt that got up her nose and in her mouth. Thanks to Ladimer, she is fully healed. "I thought so," she says to Ladimer.

He attempts to pull off her tourniquet, but Nayla keeps it on. "I'm going to keep it...as a reminder."

He nods, knowing exactly what she feels.

"I put nothing past a mooncat's nose," states Ladimer. "Are you going to try and kill me now or later?" He asks it rather simply.

"I can't. You may have a death warrant on your head, but you saved my hide. We are definitely even."

Gunthreon moves in quickly, while she's still in the talking mood. "Nayla, you have to tell—," but he doesn't have time to finish, because a band of cats suddenly springs upon our party and circles us. Michel brings up the rear.

"My dear Nayla, what is going on?" asks Michel. She puts her head down. "Many mouths have brought to my ears news of a tragedy. I seek the tragedy and find nothing but a dirty cat." He turns to Ladimer with a devilish grin, his mouth still open. "And a dirty fool!" Several cats move toward Ladimer, and we all grab our weapons—Conner first—ready to defend Ladimer, as well as ourselves. Gunthreon begins to open his mouth to talk.

Ladimer throws up his hands in our direction. "Do not defend me. I must go with them. Rules are rules, after all. There will be no more bloodshed on my behalf."

"But Ladimer," groans Gunthreon, his face creased with worry.

"Let it be, my friend," Ladimer responds. Gunthreon takes a step back.

I turn to Gunthreon and whisper, "What's going on?"

"Just listen to Ladimer."

"We will take Ladimer *and* Nayla," barks Michel, authoritatively. "These tragedies, however, will not stop our party, so please be prompt tonight, and my deepest apologies for these little unfortunate events."

Two rather burly cats reach out to take Ladimer's hands. In the briefest of moments, Ladimer's palm brushes against one of the cat's paws. The cat convulses, then falls to the ground, motionless. Ladimer puts up his now free hands and says, "Oops. So sorry. Accident."

"Fabian! Nolan!" Michel yells. Two more cats emerge, these carrying gloves and spears. Ladimer allows them to approach as he puts his hands behind his back. They bind his hands and cover them with the gloves. The cats lead him away, and Nayla follows without a word. She turns her head back, and I see a small shake of her head. Michel nudges her along with his muzzle. They all leave as we stand, dumbfounded.

I hate being in the dark, in more ways than one. "I'll ask again," I say. "What is going on?"

Gunthreon, speaking forlornly, replies, "Well, long ago when Ladimer was new at his powers, he kind of made a stupid mistake."

"And that would be?"

"He created the first mooncat."

My jaw drops as I stand, looking in the direction in which Ladimer left, remembering our conversation about making Bu human.

"I'll explain, but after we clean up. Let's go," says Gunthreon.

Chapter 41

High
ᘓᔕ

It's near midnight and we are all as well-groomed as possible, thanks to a warm freshwater creek where we rinse off the cats' scents, and Lupa's endless supply of grooming products from her endless bag.

I think about Ladimer as I finish scrubbing up.

"Why would the mooncats be mad at Ladimer for creating them?" I query. "I'd think they would revel in the fact they get to meet him. But, wait, how old is Ladimer really?"

"You wouldn't believe it if I told you." He stops combing his hair and sits on the nearest rock. "The reason they are so mad, I believe, is that Ladimer did it on a whim, for the sheer pleasure of a pixie who had a fascination with cats and wanted to see the extent of Ladimer's powers. So she coerced him although his subconscious told him how bad an idea it was. Ladimer had drunk too much mead that evening, and the devil on his shoulder won," says Gunthreon, very solemnly. "He melded a lonely human traveler and one of the pixie's cats into one being: the first mooncat. It was laughed at wherever it traveled, for it couldn't figure out the simplest things, like holding a cup. Ladimer tried to help, but the creature was elusive, and eventually disappeared." He pauses. "Wouldn't you be a little angry if you were considered a joke?"

"That's quite the grudge to hold for so long," I respond. "They seem a proud race, so why would they pass that from generation to generation? And what's the deal with pixies? You all talk as though they are dangerous."

"Just remember pride can fog the conscience. And speaking of consciences, pixies have none, only an unyielding power over all things male." Gunthreon looks to Lupa, who just shakes her head from side to side, showing her disgust in the matter.

I still don't understand what's so special about them. "So you're sure the mooncats will not kill Ladimer before we get there?"

Gunthreon starts polishing some loafers that Lupa pulls out of her pack. She walks off to help Jenna get ready. "They would want to make something like killing him a spectacle—maybe even a national holiday," he says to me. "First matters first. We still have to find out why that meeple was here, and retrieve any information the mooncats have on Neda. The mooncats have always been a neutral party, but love sharing information—for a cost of course." I stare as he suddenly disregards Ladimer's situation. "Ladimer is my friend, but there are other matters at hand," he says. "Save one, or one *million*, Kailey?" He briefly drops down his guard and I feel his energy, and realize his words are forced. He's hurting just as badly as when Bu disappeared. Suddenly, his energy wall builds itself up. "Kailey, I'm glad you are using your powers, but please remember it's also an intrusion. And it seems as though, in time, my powers may be null against you." He pauses, looking as though he's lost something very dear to him, forever. "Anyway, Ladimer can take care of himself. He's quite resourceful when he needs to be." But then he just stares at me, not looking very convincing. "I have to finish getting ready, and have much to think about." Gunthreon marches off and I see his hands rise to his face when he thinks nobody is watching.

I walk over to Conner. "You've been awful quiet. What's going on in that pretty little head of yours?"

"I can't believe we're in this mess. Tell me karmelean, what have I done to be put in this situation? I know I agreed to help, but I can't help think of how my life at home was easier—simpler, at least."

"I've been asking myself that same damn question, for months," I profess. "And honestly, I think that no matter what the level of strife, we'll be asking ourselves that same question. Life will never be perfect, and there will always be something giving us heartache, but I know, deep within my heart, that everything happens for a reason. We were all sent here, specifically, for a purpose. There's got to be a light at the end of the tunnel."

"Yeah, that's what they say about death." Conner gets up and walks away from me, helping Lupa comb Jenna's nappy head.

I look to Gunthreon and while concentrating on him, feel he's an unhappy, unsettling mess of energy. Something is bothering him deeply.

Bu, another mess, approaches. I try building up my own wall of energy to block any intermingling, but I instantly feel downhearted. "Bu did not know Ladimer was responsible," he states.

"You can't know of every story Bu. Ladimer was young. You can't hold that against him, okay? Even if it was because of a pixie, floozy, whatever, hmph. But that's still something heavy to hold on your conscience. Maybe that's why he went so easily." Bu nods and pets Cheeto, who snuggles next to him. I see her peeking at me every now and then, but when I look directly at her, she closes her eyes, feigning sleep just like a certain dog I miss with all my heart. As I eye Cheeto, it seems like she's going to pop at any moment and have the twelve babies she must be carrying.

Lupa looks marvelous, but I would, too, if I had an everything pack. "Lupa, did you leave anything at *home*?" I tease, as she laughs.

"Gather round, please." Gunthreon gestures for us to come close. His face is one of serious thought as we approach and I can practically feel his guilt like a dagger in my back. "This is getting too dangerous for everyone," he says, confirming what I feel. "I brought you all into this, and I'm realizing how selfish I've become and how this mission is jeopardizing all of you: my love, my son, my once best friend—everyone. I think it's taking over my better judgment. And perhaps the fear of an informant makes this easier for me." Lupa has surprise written all over her face as Gunthreon speaks. "It is not fair that you all risk your sanity, and life, for my cause—if you are indeed committed to this mission. I also fear that giving up any valuable information we find to the very creatures we are battling against is probable, if an informant is kept in my party." Gunthreon eyes us all, slowly. "You are free to do as you choose, henceforth." He bows at us and keeps his head down.

The sudden change in Gunthreon has us all examining each other's faces and body language, not really knowing what to say. The possibility of leaving seems especially appealing, but the thought of handing Velopa my realm without my best effort overshadows any actual action toward me leaving Gunthreon. Nobody speaks. I know everyone is contemplating going back to their respective homes, especially after the loss of Ladimer, as well as the stress of an informant among those we have grown close to.

I've made my decision. "Well, lucky for you, you're stuck with me," I say. "I agreed to do this, and I keep my word. I was given my powers for a reason, and I know I am meant to do something meaningful with them. You can't get rid of me *that* easy. If you try to lose me, I'll find you and your energy—wherever you are," I say, looking Gunthreon straight in the eyes, with no hesitation.

Jenna stands up straight and replies, "Well, don't forget, I see all of your colors. And I see a beautiful rainbow before me. I am drawn to follow." She smiles. "Plus, I don't know how to get home from here." I throw a towel at her and she ducks.

"I couldn't find anything better to do this weekend," Conner laughs. "Real estate listings are down at the moment."

Lupa simply says, "You persuaded me." Gunthreon's face twists to say he didn't, but then he sees she's slyly smiling at him. He returns the grin.

Bu takes his cue: "Bu follow wherever you go. Bu love you, forever. Bu would never betray." Gunthreon's face reflects his melting heart.

Cheeto pants at us and wags her tail. I think we can count her in, too.

Gunthreon holds out his hand to Lupa. "Looks like I'm stuck with all of you. Just remember I gave you all the out." He pauses as we all sit motionless. "Fine, let's do this." Lupa takes his hand and squeezes it, and caresses it against her cheek. "Let's discuss our strategy."

The next twenty minutes are spent deciding what to do, and this time, I am graciously accepted into the discussions. I pray to higher powers that the plan works.

Afterwards, I feel I need some pumping-up, so I turn on my iPod, stick in my earphones, and crank up some Black Eyed Peas. Jenna's eyes widen as she watches.

"Jenna, isn't it cool Bu fixed my iPod?"

"*Bu* fixed it?" she stutters. "I didn't know grebles had any magical skills. I must have been mistaken in thinking they were all brawn." I can tell she's angry at Bu for fixing it, and so can Bu. This embarrasses him, so I show Jenna her very own set of earbuds. "No way!" she shouts. "Over my dead body!"

So I turn the volume as high as it will go and start dancing around, wiggling my butt and shimmying to the best of my ability. Conner tries not to watch, but being the male he is, he cannot help admire the jiggling going on. I catch Jenna watching him watch me. Then Lupa and Gunthreon turn to watch.

"Fine." She grabs the earbuds from me and I pull mine out. We plug hers in, and as she puts the tiny foam pieces in her ears, she immediately winces in pain. I turn down the volume for her

316

sensitive ears and restart "Let's Get It Started." As the music begins, she stands motionless, but eventually her body starts swaying, and then her arms, and soon enough, she's wiggling her own butt for Conner, as everyone else laughs away their fears. When the song ends, I can tell I hooked Jenna in.

"Another one!" she hoots.

"Over your dead body? How quickly we change sides, Jenna," says Gunthreon. I give him a face that says, "Stop it, or else." He clams up quickly.

"Kailey, how about one more as we trek to our destination. Please?" asks Jenna, begging with both hands together. How can I resist a convert? Scrolling through my songs, I decide that Beethoven's Fifth is not the best choice, so "Rockin' Robin" it is. It turns out that Jenna actually has quite a bit of rhythm. She plays this one over and over.

"We're here," says Gunthreon as he stops. I hear the beginnings of activity up ahead. As we cut through the dense shrubbery and approach the source of the sounds, I am awestruck at the sight that suddenly looms before us. A huge village hangs high up in the trees, comprised of hundreds of tree houses and actual buildings—several-story buildings—made of wood, stone, and mud.

"How?" is the only word that escapes my mouth.

"They are very clever beings," Conner responds, sounding as astonished as I feel. His eyes are focused on what seems to be a pool of water in a large wooden basin, in which several mooncats bathe, again, up in the trees. "Amazing."

Leon, my cheetah friend, waits at the entrance gate, smiling as we "ooh" and "ah." "Welcome, friends," he chants. "I am your personal escort this evening. Kailey, how's the hand doing?"

"It's doing fine, thanks for asking." I blush, again.

I feel Conner lessen the distance between us as he gently grabs my good hand and squeezes it. Leon ignores the gesture.

"Shall I take you to our main ballroom, then?" asks Leon. I mouth the words "Main ballroom?" to Conner. With a bow, Leon pushes open the front gates for us.

As open fires blaze in stone pits, the scent of charred meat and fat drippings have us all filling our lungs with deep, full breaths. The bright, twinkling fire-lit sconces brighten every corner, continuing up for what seems miles into the sky, and as the flames sway with the wind, I imagine living here, in a world high above all others—a world hidden from humility.

The mooncats are busy with their families, hushing their curious children, and last-minute prepping. With plenty of food to fill the body, and elaborate set-ups of luxury within the trees, one would think the cats would exude happiness, but as I walk and take in the many emotions around me, I sense a heightened feeling of strain—a worrisome feeling. My thoughts turn to Ladimer as I envision him caged, like an animal.

Leon takes us to a staircase that seems to be cut into the base of a giant redwood tree, spiraling toward the heavens. "Stairs or pulley?" he says.

"How about we conserve some energy and take the pulley?" Gunthreon replies.

Leon points to Cheeto. "I recommend not letting her into our confines. Can she wait outside?"

Cheeto once again wags her tail and smiles at me. I bend down to her. "Honey, you be good and wait out here for us. You have to stay." But as we begin to walk forward, she tries to follow. "Stay!" I point at her, and she stands motionless, looking sad, with her downturned ears. "Leon, does she have to?"

Simultaneously, Jenna and Conner roll their eyes at my resistance.

"Yes. I am sorry. We do not allow such creatures inside camp. They carry too many diseases."

"Again with the diseases!" I wipe my hands on my pants. "Lupa, you got any kind of antibacterial goop in that bag?"

"Nope, sorry. I actually forgot that one," admits Lupa.

"Spice jars are much more important, of course."

"Oh, don't go there."

I turn to Conner. "Conner, you talked to Kioto once. Can you tell Cheeto to stay?" He nods, then speaks to Cheeto. Amazingly, she sits.

As everyone moves forward toward the pulley, I hold Leon back. "Leon, how is Ladimer?"

"Let's just say that, for the time being, he is fine. We will make his last few hours 'comfortable' for him," says Leon. "He knew better than to cross Socola's border. He played his own fate for the worse, but I must say he is cooperating rather well for a man on a death walk."

"That's nice to hear," I grunt. Of course, my hope is that we will *all* get out of here alive.

Cheeto sits and waits patiently, her head on the ground. I wave at her, and she closes her eyes as though taking a nap, and rolls over on her back with her legs sticking straight up in the air.

"Let's go, my lady." Leon leads us toward the party.

Chapter 42

Sufferable
↷

Once we're up the pulley, the walk to the main ballroom is lengthy, considering we're only walking through tree canopies. But the place is bustling, and there are plenty of cats who stop us on our way, giving us yummy treats and presents. I watch Gunthreon as he continues checking on me over his shoulder. As I lag behind the group a bit, a rather old soul emerges out of one of the smaller, older, sturdier huts and stops right in front of me, nearly knocking me down. I then recognize him as the older, gray-haired elephant trainer. He grabs my hand and places into it a trinket, then turns and slips back into his hut.

When I open my hand, it contains a pendulum, much like the one I lost in my first battle with the meeple. Upon close examination, I see the pendulum is a beautifully carved woman with a stunning, flowing head of hair, a furry creature at her side. It seems to be made of a colorless crystal or stone of some sort, almost perfectly clear and flawless. As I hold it, wonderful thoughts of my childhood come flooding back to me—things I forgot about through the years: thoughts of my mom and of laughing so hard we couldn't breathe, like the time my mom served Amber a plate of rubber chocolate candy and how after picking one, she continued to gnaw on an especially delicious looking piece until my mom and I were hysterical with laughter. Then, this vision morphs into a time when I'm much younger, and my mom is smiling at someone standing, looking over me as I pretend to sleep. I am peeking through slit eyes as I see a figure, hugging my mother tightly.

I wipe a tear which falls down my cheek and suddenly, I think I feel movement in my hand, waking me from my thoughts. I look at the pendulum again, but it's lifeless; only the eyes seemingly follow my moves.

I turn back to knock on the door of the hut, but see the old cat snuff out the lamplight inside. I tuck the pendulum into my pocket alongside my father's ring. They seem to chime when they touch.

"Kailey, we must keep up," clucks Gunthreon as he startles me, touching my shoulder. Gunthreon's nervous energy wipes away my blissful thoughts. We continue onward as I touch my tokens inside my pocket.

Leon holds back next to me as Lupa and Conner walk ahead of us, admiring the trees and whispering to each other. Lupa giggles and grabs his arm and they continue arm-in-arm, walking and soaking in the scenery.

I tighten up a bit as Leon sneaks a peek at me. "They are friendly, aren't they?" he whispers. "And you don't like it, I can sense it."

"I can't lie to you. Yes, *she's* a bit too friendly." We watch as Lupa lets her hair down and it rolls over Conner's arm.

"She may have seen many a moon, but she is captivating in her own way," Leon hums. As Conner turns around toward us, Leon grabs my hand. I see Conner's jaw clench and Leon then squeezes my hand. Gunthreon moves forward to Lupa and Conner separates himself, turning to Jenna and picking her up as we walk on. I let go of Leon's paw.

The very large and elaborate ballroom is unmistakable as we ascend even further into the sky, on another pulley. Beautiful, serene music reaches our ears as we reach the last step to the entrance.

Just before Leon puts his hands on the extremely large and heavy door, a scream rises to our ears, making the once wonderful music suddenly haunting. I recognize the voice and scream, "Ladimer!" The agony imprisoned in that one scream is enough to drive one crazy.

Leon hesitates before opening the door. "Your friend is all right," he says. "He's just being questioned by our leading inquisitor. Ladimer will be joining us for dinner, so you may say your last words to him before dessert." Leon's tone is emotionless, which matches his energy field. I wonder what kind of life these mooncats are living. I look up at their moon, and it shines as brightly as ever, daring onlookers to stare too long.

I move next to Bu and grab his hand, because we both need the comfort. "We're just going in to enjoy a little party and do what we need, and then we'll leave," I say to Bu. "You will never have to come here again."

"They're hurting Ladimer. What are they doing to him?"

"Ladimer is a giver. He can heal himself. Stop worrying about him, Bu. Let's just try and keep together and remember to watch each other's back, okay?" His shaking lessens and I feel his nervous energy retreating. "I love you, Bu."

"Love you, too."

Leon opens the door, and the lobby practically knocks me on my butt. It's filled with flowers of every species imaginable, and the scent floating on the air tickles my nose. Lupa, enthralled, stops to smell each and every one as she walks through. "Wow. I didn't even know they could grow these," she mumbles. "They have to be imported." While Leon is busy talking to Gunthreon, Lupa pulls a small, white flower off the stem, and the petals shiver, then flap like butterfly wings. She wraps it in a wet towel she miraculously pulls out of her everything pack.

"Why don't you just pull out your backyard and plant it while we're walking?" I tease.

"You're just jealous. You have no idea how much that seed I just pulled off is worth. If I can grow these at home, I'll buy you a summer home in Meadow's Edge. We could be neighbors." She makes me smile, and my mind wanders to Meadow's Edge, but unfortunately, that leads to my mom, yet again, and guilt creeps over me for not being home, watching over her. Lupa, seeing my sadness, grabs my arm and squeezes gently.

The next doors we approach are intricately carved, and standing next to them is an older, silver-haired cat, who seems to be carving something into the door. Thoroughly involved in his work, he does not pay us one iota of attention.

Studying the pictures on the door from left to right, they seem to be a historical and artful rendition of the mooncats' journey in time. My heart skips a beat, however, as I reach the work in progress. It's clearly a picture of Ladimer kneeling head-down before Michel, who holds a rather large sword over Ladimer's head, ready to strike with all his might. I gasp.

Conner works his way over to me. "Be strong for him and stick to the plan."

"Leon is staring at us," I whisper. Conner looks up and soulspeaks in his direction.

Leon nods. "I understand," he says. "He was one of your traveling companions—one of your pack. You'll see him soon."

Lupa then sneaks a peek at me as she comments, "Conner, you know that soulspeak of yours is absolutely spellbinding. You can whisper in my ear anytime."

Stick to the plan, Kailey. "How 'bout you keep your comments to yourself, Lupa."

"How about you learn to share, my friend," she taunts. I lurch forward as Conner holds me back.

"Come on, girls, you mustn't fight." Gunthreon puts his hand on Lupa's shoulder. "Let Ladimer's last few hours be ones of peace." Lupa and I exchange our best pre-girlfight faces.

The artist steps aside. "Welcome to our ballroom," says Leon, opening the door.

The room beyond is the largest I have ever seen—big enough to hold at least a hundred elephants, if need be. There are circus acts everywhere, and mountains of food, with diligent servers working each table.

One section of the room is decorated in black, and my eyes are drawn to the walls. An endless array of whips and chains and nameless items hang in neat rows, just within arm's length of a rather large masked cat, who appears to be deciding which whip he wants to take down next.

On a chair next to him, I see a human male sitting with his back to us—not Ladimer. Other cats stand around the man, clearly enjoying the show. When I turn to Gunthreon, he motions zipping his mouth shut.

Jenna's eyes focus on the several large, over-the-top-muscled cats standing at each entrance. The word "juggernaut" pops into my head. "Why the guards?" Jenna's question is directed at Leon.

"We wouldn't want any unexpected visitors ruining our fun, now, would we?" responds Leon. This leaves an unpleasant feeling in my stomach.

As Leon leads us around, I see a head table at the front of the room, with Michel seated in the middle and Nayla at his side. Her head is down, and I see a fresh wound near her ear.

I sneak next to Gunthreon. "Did you see Nayla?" I ask. He nods. "Something is very wrong here."

"Glad we're in agreement."

Leon leads us to the table closest to the head table. There are seats for each of us, and even a large, Bu-sized chair. Next to Jenna's place seating, they have placed small pillows on the table for her to sit upon.

As we planned, Gunthreon tells Leon that Lupa and I should be separated so that he may keep his sanity. Leon grins and whispers, "Of course. Please, make yourself comfortable, and your servers will be with you shortly. I hope you enjoyed the walk through our village. If you need me, I'll be seated at the table over there, near the door." Leon bows, then goes to join his table, but not without first sneaking me a wink.

The numerous cats captivate us with their diversity and ability to eat large quantities of meat in single bites. For the moment, they all seem to be involved in their food, only sneaking brief peeks at us.

Michel, however, is a different story. He is motionless, and his eyes are *glued* to us. Nayla briefly sneaks a glance in my direction. I risk a sly smile to her, hoping she recognizes it as a response to her need for help. She immediately looks down toward the table.

Then, Michel stands up and reaches for a bell next to his plate. He rings it loudly and silence immediately fills the room. "Thank you, everyone, for joining in this celebration," he says. "We have very special guests today, as you may see." He holds out his paw in our direction, and the cats look quickly, then return their eyes to Michel. The tension in the room doesn't match the expressions in the room and I sneak a glance at Gunthreon. I reach a feeler toward one cat in particular. As I dig into its energy layers, searching for something, it suddenly hisses at the cat nearest it. A guard tromps heavily to the table and both cats sink back into their seats. I quickly withdraw.

Michel continues with his speech. "Please enjoy as much food as your bellies will take, and as much conversing as your mouths, and *others' ears,* can take." A handful of the cats laugh, while others clench their jaws in silence.

"Lastly, as you may all know by now—I know how word travels fast—we have an extra-special guest, one with much history connected to our race. Each and every one of us has grown up with whispers of his name in our ears, and have been told numerous bedtime stories that brought us countless nightmares, *but* we must all thank him for the one gift he has given us: birth. He is truly a miraculous creature, and he deserves at least that."

Michel motions to another juggernaut, who moves from his position at the door. The door opens, and two cats lead Ladimer into the room, holding his bound arms. He is naked, save for a newly acquired, and still bloody, snow leopard's hide. My eyes widen and I immediately reach to him with my feeler, but Gunthreon shakes his head at me. I withdraw it, almost immediately.

Ladimer does not seem to be hurt, and I feel relieved, until he lifts his head and reveals his once-beautiful face. There are deep, dark wells of purple skin under his eyes, and his mouth droops as though plagued by Bell's palsy. His eyes tear, and it looks as though he has aged twenty years. My eyes well up, and I try my hardest to keep the tears inside. But when Ladimer looks at me, the pain inside my chest screams so loud I turn to Bu, who seems to have winced at the same time. My guilt for essentially sacrificing Ladimer forces me to gather my emotions and churn them into something usable. Determination. Determination to hold up long enough to continue with our plan.

"Please seat him at our head table, near me," requests Michel. Ladimer is pushed down into his chair with a mighty shove and slap to the face. Conner makes a slight move to stand, but Gunthreon stops his further movement with a head shake. Michel smiles at Ladimer. "Everyone, I am pleased to bring before you, your creator, our father, Ladimer the Giver." He begins clapping, and it seems nobody knows what else to do but clap along with him. The clapping dies slowly, and Michel sits, whispering in Ladimer's ear God only knows what, most likely bent on crushing Ladimer's hopes. Ladimer's eyes rise to Gunthreon, who stares back at him, giving him the slightest of nods. Ladimer then begins speaking to Michel, engaging him in some form of conversation, keeping his head down in mock submission. Michel eats it up.

Our servers work our table quickly, bringing us numerous plates of food, but none of us seems able to even think about eating. After a dollop of what looks like mashed potatoes is thrown on his plate, Gunthreon turns to me and says, "Kailey, Conner and I are going to have a few 'conversations' with some guests, so you and everyone else just sit and go with the flow." As a server walks by, he stands up and puts his arm around the cat. All I hear is, "I would highly recommend that you..." as they walk to the next table. Michel seems too caught up in his favorite guest even to notice what anyone else is doing.

Jenna and Bu only sit, not touching the food on their plates. Jenna turns to Bu. "Let's eat," she says. "We don't know when our next meal may be. This could even be our last." Bu lifts his fork and starts nibbling on what seems to be brisket, more or less picking at the food, as a similar feeling of guilt as my own flows over him. He feels helpless.

"We are going to get through this," I whisper. "Just stick to the plan." I then catch Lupa's eyes, which watch Gunthreon's every move. He nods toward her, and she at Conner. Conner walks toward Lupa and sits next to her, whispering something in her ear. She laughs loudly and then hugs Conner and kisses him lightly on the lips. She actually makes a bit of a scene, unbuttoning the top buttons of her shirt for air, as I turn red in the cheeks. She's apparently an expert flirt. The cats around us begin to stare at them.

I stand quickly from my chair and march toward Conner and Lupa.

"Hands off," I snarl at Lupa.

"Oh, calm down, Kailey. You are so jealous all the time!" says Lupa, still smiling, with her arm around Conner.

I tug her arm off of Conner and all the cats pull in a breath, simultaneously.

Standing, and speaking in her most annoyed voice she barks, "You are such a bitch, Kailey!"

"You bring out the best in me, don't you? Stop flaunting yourself in front of Conner!" Bu looks up from his brisket. Without warning, Lupa splashes her drink in my face. This shocks me, because I totally didn't expect it, but I go with the flow, grabbing at her and pulling out the hair extension she put in for the occasion. A nearby cat's mouth drops at the sight, spilling out food.

"Stop it, stop it!" Michel yells, clearly annoyed. "You're ruining the party!" Leon walks over to Michel and whispers something in his ear. "Kailey, why don't you come up here and sit at the head table?" says Michel. "It's clear you two need to be separated even further."

I hesitate. "I'm sorry," I apologize. "I am so sorry for the disturbance. It's just our Lupa here seems to not be able to keep her hands to herself." Lupa lunges at me, but Bu grabs her and holds her back. "See?"

"Up here now!" Michel has a juggernaut add an empty seat at his table, right in-between Michel and Ladimer—thank karma. Gunthreon believed Michel would want me near, to admire my feistiness closely. "Sorry, everyone," he says. "We seem to have the 'catfight' under control." Michel laughs, generating nervous laughter throughout the crowd.

"Yes sir," I say. I grab my bag and walk up front. On the way, I steal a glance at Gunthreon, and he seems satisfied. I needed to get the closest I could to Ladimer, and we couldn't have gotten any better an option than this.

I brush Ladimer's shoulder as we pass. He feels my energy near him and tries to lean in for more. As soon as I am seated, I reach under the table and grab his leg. He shudders and I already feel my energy flowing to him. I see his excitement revealed in manly fashion, and he adjusts his hide.

"Everyone, continue on please." Michel then turns to me, touching my shoulder, softly, and whispering to me, "I'll allow you to converse with your friend. He hasn't much time left. But after, your attention must be mine." Michel then sees Gunthreon walking around. Curious, he gets up and walks in his direction.

I whisper to Ladimer, "What did they do to you?"

"They called in a shaman." Ladimer's voice is raspy. "He tried to drain me of my power. Pretty ironic, eh? The torturer tortured by the tortured. Another little setback created by karma. See why I can't ever make a mistake like that again?"

"I see that. I'm sorry."

"Don't be sorry, Kailey. Everything happens for a reason."

"Did they really drain you of your power?" I ask. "Is that even possible? What can I do?" My powers sense nothing from him—no vibration, no movement, no layers of emotion whatsoever. I only feel as though he's running on empty.

Ladimer gathers enough strength to smile mischievously at me, making my blood pump a little faster.

"Within reason, of course," I murmur, giving him a stern look, attempting to disregard the increase in heart rate.

"I'm too weak to do anything, so a little kickstart might start me up. Too bad Michel can't tell if he needs to watch *us* or Gunthreon," he says, watching Michel. "Skin-to-skin contact is best for me." I look to his face and the lack of energy sickens me.

I close my eyes and imagine our kiss above Greer, but my nerves won't settle, because I'm too afraid as Michel eyes our table after seating Gunthreon. My eyes settle on Conner, who sits patiently, moving around food on his plate with his fork. He looks up to me, knowing what my goal is—clearly not liking it—but willing to do what is necessary to save lives.

"Only do what you're comfortable with, Kailey," responds Ladimer.

Conner turns his gaze away from me and I then bend over near Ladimer and put my hand over my mouth, like I am whispering to him, but in fact I gently kiss his ear. I smell his sweat. He takes in a quick breath and I feel a spark of power from within him. I kiss him again and exhale in his ear, slowly. He shudders and suddenly his energy flows, warm and fluid. As I feel it reaching to me, my eyes widen at the sudden heat of his desire—hot and unquenched. I want to give in and allow his energy to engulf me.

He looks up and the need in his eyes is relentless.

He wants me badly, and I long for the touch of his magic, but know what I must do. "Keep your face down," I demand of him, seemingly breaking the frenzy rising in him.

"Okay," he grunts, suddenly looking down. "That was good. Very good." His energy feels restored and even overflowing.

I leave him and sneak over to Nayla. "Nayla, are you hurt bad?"

"No, just a little cut," she responds. "Kailey, you need to get out of here and soon. Michel is—,"

"Michel is what?" Michel leans over the table, bringing his face close to ours. "Nayla, you wouldn't be spilling any secrets, now, would you?" Nayla sinks lower in her chair, and Michel's energy spews conceit, making my anger flare. He's cocky, and holds no fear of what his actions may spark.

I give Michel a glare that could kill. "She was only telling me you plan on cutting off Ladimer's head with a sword!" I spit. Ladimer looks up, then quickly puts his head back down. I feel certain that Michel won't think of the door carving.

"Nayla. You *did* give our secret up! No dessert for you," says Michel. "Well, since the surprise is ruined, I suppose we must simply continue. Guards!" Two juggernauts come at Michel's command. "Fetch me my lovely one, please."

Michel hands one of the guards a key as he moves closer to the crowd, and the guard heads toward a lovely armoire that seems to be made of solid gold. The key fits perfectly into the lock, and as it is turned, the armoire plays a beautiful tinkling song, like a giant music box. The doors slowly open, and a long drawer extends outward. The guard reaches in and removes a shining, tri-colored metal sword, far more beautiful than the piece of furniture that sheltered it. The crowd murmurs, and the guard's eyes become clouded as he holds the sword—the most magnificent sword in the world. It shines brilliantly, and I feel a need to get closer to examine the workmanship.

"Guard!" Michel, impatient, snaps the guard—and me—out of our twilight. "You wouldn't want to suffer the same fate as our guest, now, would you?" Awakening from the fog covering him, the guard shakes his head and marches toward Michel, sword far away from his body. Michel takes the sword quickly in his paw and grins a grin worthy of the Cheshire Cat.

He motions for the guards to take Ladimer and bring him forward. They grab Ladimer, who, again, puts up no resistance. My heart pounds, and I pray this does not end badly. Michel stands proudly before the crowd, demanding all eyes.

Nayla leans in my direction, whispering, "If you are going to make a move, let's pray you do it soon." Her eyes meet mine.

Michel puffs up his chest. "It is finally here: the time we have all been waiting for." But when I see a particularly scrawny cat roll his eyes at Michel's words, it's clear that not all of the mooncats are in league with Michel. I scan the crowd and see several cats fidgeting in their seat and shaking their heads. Some are even crying. Evidently, they follow him strictly because he's their alpha male. Hopefully, that will make Gunthreon's job easier. "We have before us Ladimer, head bowed in submission, ready to give his life to us—his children." Michel grinds his teeth as he speaks; whether it is from his impatience to get the matter over with, or excessive elation, I cannot tell. "By taking your life, we shall no longer be laughing stock."

He stands over Ladimer, sword at his side. Then, suddenly, he turns to Gunthreon, who sits besides Lupa. "Oh, how rude of me. Gunthreon, we never even discussed your request. You must excuse my actions. I have become too involved in my conquest." He laughs. "You and your party came here not only to hand over this idiot, but to seek knowledge of our missing Neda, is this right?"

Gunthreon nods. "Yes, Michel."

Michel laughs as would a lunatic. I feel I am not alone in my fear of what this cat may do. "I must say, honestly, that I have heard nothing, and that I actually do not give a damn!" Gunthreon's shoulders slump slightly, but he recovers quickly, aware that action awaits.

Michel walks slowly toward Gunthreon's table. "Do you not notice all the luxuries around you?" he grumbles. "Do you think that Neda would give us anything of this value? That *Neda* would give a damn about our race? That *Neda* would care *what happens to you*?!" Michel screams this at Gunthreon, looming over him. Gunthreon sits motionless.

"I thought so. Well, for your information—that *is* what you came for—we have decided that the other side is much more fun. And I've invited a few more *friends* to share the occasion with! They've been waiting so patiently since you arrived." The Cheshire Cat appears again. As Michel raises both his arms, I feel the mass of energy approaching the doors. Quickly, I yell for Gunthreon.

In an instant, several meeples and grebles burst through all doors, weapons in hand, running toward my friends. Bu is the quickest to respond, and as a meeple runs toward Jenna—who stands firmly, her knife unsheathed before her—he lifts it in the air and throws it against the nearest wall, knocking it unconscious. As the other cats run around like chickens with their heads cut off, I see Gunthreon's mouth moving, and I hear his words in my head clear as day. He calls for all cats to fight back.

As I watch Bu, I see a gross, slimy creature sneaking up behind him. Before I can yell to him, I see a black cat jump on top of the creature as Bu turns around.

"Haren?" Bu says, standing, shocked.

The cat who he thinks is Haren stops and stares at Bu. A moment is shared between them as they lock eyes. Bu, saddened, frowns, and Haren then takes off, chasing a smaller meeple, but not before taking one last look at Bu.

Various cats draw serving utensils and knives, and try their best to attack the intruders. Some even pick up the priceless vases from their tables and whip them overhead. A greble holds Conner in a headlock, attempting to choke the life out of him, but instantly, Conner's own blade is out, stabbing at its arm.

My monk's spade glows brightly in my hands, and I search the crowd for Michel. I find him back at his table, standing over Ladimer.

"Any last words Ladimer?" asks Michel, determined to finish him off despite all the other activity going on around him.

Ladimer looks up, grins at Michel, and sings, "Transformers: More than meets the eye." Michel, confused and, angry, swings his sword where Ladimer's neck would be if he were still a grown male, but Philip appears in his place, ducking as the sword swings by. As Michel recovers from the swing, Philip gets up and runs underneath the table, dragging the huge snow leopard skin. Michel runs after him, poking his sword underneath the table as Nayla approaches Michel's back, revenge glowing in her eyes. I'm so engaged by the scene that I forget to watch my own back.

"Put down that weapon, you disgustingly pathetic creature," hisses a meeple from behind. I lower my spade. "Your friends are losing the battle. Why don't you be a good pet and *sit?*" My legs obey, and I sit, observing the fighting around me and my friends. Some are bleeding. Some are screaming. Soon, the sounds of battle disappear, and I realize it would be far easier just to give in now and let this meeple finish me before we screw things up any further. Tears trickle down my face, my hope fighting a losing battle. This must be my destiny, humiliation.

Seconds before the meeple reaches me, I feel an intense energy approaching fast. "Hey, dinner's served!" Leon, running at us, throws steaming, saucy, hot vegetables at the meeple's face, then grabs my hand and pulls me up. "Come with me now!" he demands. I throw my bag on my back and let myself be dragged out the doors. Leon picks me up as we slide down several wooden tunneled slides, emerging at ground level. I continue with him as we exit the village gates and run into the chilly forest.

Chapter 43

Accidental
ɷ

After I fall several times, he stops. It's not so easy keeping up with a four-legged beast. "We can hide here," he mutters, pulling me behind a fallen tree. I worry for my friends as we hunker down amongst some wild mushrooms and soft greenish-blue moss. I can feel Leon's hot, moist breath on the back of my neck, and his soft purring soothes my nerves. He puts his arms around me so I will not move or make any noise. The warmth emanating from his fur is inviting, so I nuzzle in as best I can. "Let's not move for a bit," he says. I just nod, my mind beginning to cloud.

Slowly, my fear of what is going on in the village ballroom and what fate my friends are facing dissipates. Sitting and waiting for orders from Leon feels far more intriguing than anything else I can think of.

The sound of nearby movement threatens us. I hold onto Leon tight and wait, holding my breath. "Don't move, Kailey," he snaps as two deathmen appear, stepping out from behind a giant red-barked tree. They pay us no attention, instead on a mission I can guess will lead them to the ballroom. *Deathmen. Ballroom. My friends.* My mind triggers a need for action and I try to get up and follow, but Leon pulls me down, tightening his grip on my body. "Kailey, if they are gone, they are gone. There is nothing you can do."

"But my friends—!"

His grip does not lessen. "I can take care of you now, but you need to relax." He strokes my hair gently.

"Take care of me?" I respond as my muscles loosen up, and my mind clears of worry. His grip is solid and I can't move a muscle.

"Relax..." That single word holds a mysterious magic which resonates, forcing me to submit. Leon purrs softly, and it's so comforting that my worries don't seem so important anymore. "Relax..." The sound of his voice caresses me as I melt deeper into his fur. His mouth comes close to my ear, and he speaks words that invoke thoughts of ancient rituals and spark animal instincts as I answer Leon's purring with my own. I want to nuzzle longer with Leon, shedding all inhibitions and rubbing against each other for comfort as cats do.

My skin recedes as the hair on my arms grows longer, but I do not feel remorse. Rather, I encourage the fur, daring the transformation to quicken. I long to stretch my legs and run beside Leon in full stride.

My hearing picks up cats approaching, as well as humans. There are harsh words exchanged. It seems the battle has moved outside to the forest. Angry from the intrusion, I am annoyed and worried at the same time. A most awful and incessant barking joins the clamor, and I will it to stop. My instincts urge me to run, but there is something so familiar about the sound that I stay, curiosity rooting me where I stand.

"She's here! I know it!" This is yet another familiar noise—a noise that brings to my senses thoughts of food.

"Conner, behind you!" Screams and shrieks and noises of many varieties draw closer. Leon falls on all fours, growling, prepared to take on whatever emerges from the brush. Any second now, we should become part of the battle. The source of the barking emerges, and I hiss at it. The four-legged creature stops directly in front of me, tilting its head to one side. A human emerges, followed by several others. They stop and stare at me.

"Kailey!" This noise is from the familiar one. She approaches me, and I hiss at her, baring my new fangs. As Leon jumps toward her, she produces a long, shiny sword, moving so quickly he falls into a tree stump and knocks himself unconscious. More cats join the scene, bringing great confusion to my brain. In the throngs of action, I stand motionless as an ugly, three-legged giant crashes into me, spilling the contents of my bag all along the forest floor. I hear a loud, metal clinking sound, and soon all the cats and myself are drawn to a smell—a wonderfully intoxicating smell emerging from the jar that has fallen and burst open. As the cats begin to roll and pounce around, forgetting the battle, a male human grabs me and drags me away as I attempt to claw him.

"Now's our chance! I must say, our karmelean is quite the valuable asset, isn't she? Catnip! Why would she buy catnip scent?" These words come from a little human with gray fur on his head and squinty eyes who watches me attempt to scratch my captor. I make contact at least once, forcing a yelp out of my captor's mouth. The female I first encountered cries and shows me some shape with her fingers, and again a sense of familiarity creeps into my mind, but I still want to bite her fingers.

She speaks amongst the humans: "Can you help her, Ladimer? Oh, please, say you can." She pets the annoying barking creature as I continue to hiss at it. "Sit, Kioto. Stay. Good girl. It took me so long to find you all. I was almost caught in Gernwood, but some dirty old meeple and a lazy greble let me get away." A vision of my human-self teetering on the tip of a rock appears in my head, but soon dissolves as the dog keeps sniffing in my direction. My claws extend as its nose gets closer, daring me to scratch it off.

The male called Ladimer holds me with both hands, and his energy crawls along my skin, forcing me still. The fabric he wears smells of another male, one that brings thoughts of mating. Then, my fur starts to disappear as quickly as it came, and my fine-tuned hearing goes with it. I no longer hear cats crying in the village, but only my mom crying in front of me.

"Mom! Kioto!" I sputter. I run to them and I hug my mom as tight as my arms will let me. Kioto licks my face violently, and I have to hold her off before she smothers me. "What the hell just happened?"

Lupa smiles at me and responds, "Long story. All I can say is that it might be beneficial to start growing some catnip in my garden."

Conner approaches me, handing me his scent jar. "Why are you giving me this now? What is it?"

He laughs to himself. "I thought I'd save this for when you ran out of your own, but it seems you never had one to begin with."

I open the jar and breathe in. "Yum, cotton candy," I hum. I must have picked up "Catnip" by accident. Conner kisses me gently on my forehead.

Gunthreon, who holds Michel's sword, turns and glances behind him. He hands the sword to Lupa, who places it in her everything pack. I then notice a ceetchan waddling toward us, and Jenna behind her, shooing her to move faster.

"Damn creature!" shouts Jenna, as she squints her eyes at me.

Chapter 44

Exhausted
☙

The race off Socola land is much anticipated and as fast as we could have hoped for. Each and every one of us, including Cheeto, looks as though we've seen much better days. Our clothes are disheveled and littered with cat hair, while our own hair on our heads is littered with stray bits of food. Strange thing is, I don't feel as horrible as I appear to be. Dead-tired, yes, but forlorn, no. We are alive at this point and I am thanking my lucky stars.

I razz Lupa about her amazing ability when it comes to flirting. "You know, you did that all too well," I tease, pointing my finger at her.

"How do you think I won over this fool?" she answers, bumping her hip against Gunthreon's.

Gunthreon ignores it—after gaining back his own momentum—and explains that the mutiny rumors of the East were of Nayla. She had already started forming a coup to dethrone Michel in an attempt to restore their non-allegiance to either higher power. My arrival in Socola proved the perfect opportunity for Nayla to take action—karma willing—and that was why the meeple attacked her, to stop her and her army from rebelling against the current Velopa-sided reign. Nayla's hate for Michel and his reign must have grown so immense in her time forming the coup—with no available outlet—that when finally given a chance at revenge, Nayla went all out, for Gunthreon cringes as he describes her wrath once I left with Leon. Conner speaks in soulspeak, also confirming the scene was indeed graphic.

After Gunthreon finishes, he informs us he needs to speak to one other inhabitant of Socola before we leave. As we continue on in silence. I walk besides my mom. I begin to notice how many times she stumbles. "Mom, how are you feeling?" I send out my feeler to her before she answers, and suddenly feel ill.

Gunthreon finds the cave he was searching for and enters with Lupa, leaving the rest of us outside.

"I'm fine, honey—just tired from all the traveling." She doesn't make eye contact with me, and I know what that means, before even feeling her energy—she's lying.

"You know, Mom, I'm not twelve anymore, in case you haven't noticed. You can be honest with me. We've both been through a lot and deserve at least that. And you feel..."

Before I finish my sentence, Ladimer works his way over and puts his arm around my mom—the shirt he's wearing a bit too large for his frame. "Dena May, Kailey knows."

My mom stops mid-stride. "Knows what, Ladimer?" Danger lurks in her tone, and it has me cowering for Ladimer.

I hear the gears working in Ladimer's head while he's thinking. "Simply that I was always there, watching over her."

"Were you really?" Anger reverberates through her words, and Ladimer drops his arm. Conner turns toward my mom, looking fearful.

"Stop!" I shout. My mom's eyebrows raise and I feel surprise from her. We're all tired and I see this going nowhere good. "I'm just happy to be alive at this point, as I am sure all of you are, too. But if there's going to be all this nastiness, I give up."

My mom takes a deep breath and nods her head. "I'm sorry, hon," she says to Ladimer softly. "I am just so damn..." Before her sentence is complete, she collapses to the ground like a pile of bricks.

"Mom!" I pick her head up off the ground. She's alive, but limp.

Ladimer moves in and placing his hands on her—one on her chest and the other on her head—he says, "It's okay, just simple exhaustion. Let's get her home. She needs to rest." But I don't thoroughly believe him as I sense his energy. A withering sensation reaches me, then instantly retreats behind an energy wall. He's hiding something.

"Let's take her to my place," I request. "I can take care of her."

Gunthreon emerges from the cave and kneels by my mom, taking her hand as Lupa wipes her sweaty hair to one side. "Let's all go back," he says, looking at me, and I feel an underlying current of frustration.

Conner picks up my mom and holds her with ease.

Suddenly, I hear crying and look toward Jenna. "Jenna, what's wrong?" She doesn't answer me.

Gunthreon stands up. "We made an agreement," he states. I remember the agreement made for her to leave our group after Socola and feel a pain in my chest. Gunthreon's face shows no emotion as he turns and faces the opposite direction.

Jenna looks up at me and I bend down toward her. Her tears are tiny balls of light, dripping to the ground. I look to Gunthreon, and see him turn his gaze quickly from us. "I know what I have to do. I just want you all to know that I care about you, and I hope to see you again," she cries. She walks over to me and wraps her tiny little holly necklace around my wrist, then kisses my cheek. She smiles at Bu, and blows both him and Conner a kiss. She pats Cheeto on the head once, then wipes her hand on her leg. "Thank you for giving me the chance, Gunthreon," she says. She then bows toward him and starts to walk away, shoulders slumped.

Gunthreon lets her get a few yards away before he turns around toward her. "Well, I think I may have a new mission for you, actually," he says. She turns around slowly, then freezes like a statue, staring intently at his face.

"Yeah?"

"I think that maybe you'll have to come back with us while I explain the plan. Think that's doable? We have to go soon, though." He nods toward my mother.

Jenna runs back as fast as her legs will carry her and, when he bends down to her, hugs his face. She simultaneously reaches over and snatches back her necklace from my wrist. I twist my face at her.

It's decided that I am to bring everyone back at once. "Are we all ready?" I ask. I turn to look at my beloved friends—family, now, perhaps—a second before transporting them and it's then that I notice they are all wearing sunglasses—even Bu, wearing those giant plastic carnival glasses. "What?! Hey!"

Chapter 45

Grumpy
∞

*S*hit! It's morning and the sun blinds me as I open my eyes. After being in Socola, you forget how unforgiving the morning sun can be. Ladimer has to lead me around my apartment until all the blinds are shut.

Jenna sits on my couch, exhausted, while she listens to my iPod. I see her eyes wandering around my apartment, taking in anything electronic, or plastic. She exudes a bit of fear, but sits nicely, not budging. Bu sits on the floor, petting Kioto, whose hawk-like eyes are glued to Cheeto, who sniffs around. One growl from Kioto as Cheeto approaches her food bowl sends Cheeto in the opposite direction rather quickly. Ladimer, Conner, Gunthreon, and Lupa, all looking ragged from lack of sleep, have already spread out a map on my dinner table, discussing something rather quietly. I choose to ignore that conversation and instead check on my mom, who Ladimer sent to my bed.

I find her curled up in the fetal position, her hand in a ball near her mouth. This is a sleeping position that I have unfortunately inherited, and I use it when I am especially worried. So this has me worried about how much pain my mom really might be feeling. My senses reach to her as I close my eyes, but like Gunthreon, I bump into an energy wall.

"Kailey, you need to stop worrying. It's giving you frown lines," she says, lying on the bed.

"Some say lines give you character." I examine my face in the mirror.

"Yeah, I'd say a wrinkled-up pear has lots of character." I pick up the nearest pillow and whip it at her. She, of course, catches it mid-air, then lies back down, closing her eyes.

"Mom, save your energy. We have a wedding to go to soon. Oh, and guess what! I know a secret," I say in a sing-song sort of way. She's fake snoring, but I see her eyebrows rise slightly, making it obvious she wants to know.

"Guess who's pregnant!"

"Kailey!" This gets her sitting up faster than I can say "not me."

"Settle down! Amber."

My mom doesn't smile. "What?" She sits on the edge of the bed, her mind wandering.

"Mom, what are you thinking?" I ask, knowing my answer.

"Wasn't that rather fast?" she says. "Is Russell the father?"

"Thank God someone thinks as logically as me!" I reply.

"Well, I wouldn't say *that*," my mom says. I frown. "It's just that Amber always seems to make mistakes. I know she's your best friend and all, but she makes bad choices."

"Gunthreon says it's Russell's," I respond, then a bit quieter, "Seems his 'swimmers' are pretty strong."

My mom looks perplexed.

"You know...sperm?" I say, embarassed.

My mother laughs loudly. "Yes, Kailey, I know what 'swimmers' are—semen, spunk, baby gravy."

"Ew. Stop! Baby gravy, really?"

She stops laughing and her facial expression is one of seriousness. "Last time I saw Russell he didn't seem like a new father-to-be, that's all."

"Amber is just difficult," I say. "She's probably tiring him out with all the running out at two a.m. for ice cream and pickles."

"She has cravings?" my mom says.

Ladimer peeks in and smiles at us. "I brought refreshments," he says, holding a tray full of cookies and milk, which he sets down in front of my mom. There's a also a single pink rose. She picks it up and holds it to her nose.

"They were always my favorite," she murmurs.

Ladimer comes over, lays his chin on my shoulder, and gives my mom puppy-dog eyes. "Still mad?"

"Yes, *pissed!*" Before I know it, she has Ladimer in a headlock.

"Damn, Dena May!" shouts Ladimer. "Let go. You know I hate it when you move so fast." She lets go.

With a downturned face, my mom says, "I knew she'd find out someday. I should ask if *you* are pissed at *me.*" She faces my direction.

"Honestly, I *was* at first. Then Greer showed me a few things, and I think I understand."

My mom laughs heartily. "Greer! Did he threaten to eat you?"

I laugh. "Yes, he has threatened to eat me," I say, "with pickled rootflowers?" My mom laughs. "He doesn't scare me." To myself, I say, "But that Tartarin on the other hand... "

"Tartarin? How do you know of Tartarin?" I hadn't realized I was speaking aloud. "Has he tried to hurt you?" snaps my mom, her face turning the color of cherries as she sits up straight in bed. "Where have you seen him? Was he alone?" She seems hysterically interested in Tartarin.

"I've had a few run-ins with him, that's all. Calm down." My mom turns to Ladimer, who looks out the window, suddenly interested in the weather. "Mom, Ladimer cannot follow me everywhere! I can take care of myself."

"Maybe you *think* you can, but Kailey, you don't know the half of it." She stops abruptly, her head turning downwards toward her socks.

"Do you have something else to tell me?" I sit down next to her.

"It's just that you're so new to Renhala, and Kailey, it can eat you alive," she replies. "I wish you could just stay here and be safe and quit it with all of Gunthreon's wild goose chases."

On cue, Gunthreon enters the bedroom, and says, "Honk." Then he sits next to my mom, holding her hand. "Kailey chose this, just as you did once. It's all karma. You know she's special. Dena May, both our worlds are in trouble. The urn is breaking down." Her head lifts with lightning speed, and I see fear in her face, as well as feel it from her energy field as her wall crumbles.

"Our trip to Socola didn't bring us any closer to Neda or Velopa," says Gunthreon, "thus I feel we have achieved no goal, only twiddled our thumbs. We've started the journey, and I need her with me to finish it. I just know it. She was born for this."

My mother's fear dissipates and determination takes its place. "You better watch her! She's all I got."

"We are doing everything we can to save our realms, but keep our karmelean safe, too."

"Just remember she's not something to be 'owned.' She has a right to say no—make her own choices," states my mom as she looks at me.

"Kailey has exhibited the ability to block my 'suggestions,'" says Gunthreon. A sudden jolt in my mom's energy tells me she's quite surprised. "It is evident she *will* make her own choices," he says.

Just as Gunthreon finishes his sentence, the phone rings. I don't answer it, but it stops mid-second ring. Conner then walks in with the phone.

"It's Amber," he says.

"You're answering my phone now?" A small smile escapes the corner of my mouth.

"I saw Russell's number on the caller ID, so I picked it up, that's all." He throws me the phone. As he walks away, he snarls, "Jenna, will you turn that damn song off already!"

I put the phone to my ear. "Hello?"

"You know it's me, Kailey." Amber sounds ornery already.

Everyone in the room stares at me silently. Holding my hand over the phone receiver, I say, "Isn't it a little crowded in here?" They all fidget, then agree to leave the room, except my mom. "Amber, what's up?"

"Just wanted to make sure everyone was still coming for the wedding. Conner's over, I see," she says, with a smile on her face— I can hear it.

Cheeto wanders in my room and jumps up on the bed, tracking muddy paws on my nice, clean, comforter. "Cheeto!" I yelp. She just smiles at me, panting heavily.

"What are you babbling, Kailey?"

"Sorry, just dropped some food on the floor. Pointing it out to Kioto."

"Isn't it kind of early to be eating Cheetos? Never mind, who cares. With all that junk you eat, you'll be fat soon enough."

"What is with your attitude?"

For a moment, she's all quiet on the other end. "You know, I didn't have to invite you *or* your boyfriend to the wedding, *or* even your mom and her date!" she yells. "You ungrateful bitch."

I drop the phone, then pick it up quickly. Her pregnancy is getting the best of her. "I know you're all hormone-y and crap," I say, "but give it up—"

"What the hell does that mean? Have you been talking to Russell?" Her voice is rising, and I can feel her reaching through the phone to choke me.

My eyes scan my room, trying to come up with some good excuse to hang up. I spot my birth-control pills on my dresser. "It's just that we're on the same cycle, remember?"

"Oh. I forgot." Suddenly, she starts crying on the other end.

"Amber, are you all right?"

"I'm fine. Just anxious, I guess."

"Maybe we can hang out together sometime this weekend? We haven't done that in a while," I say. "How about a movie?" I know drinking is out of the question for her.

She pauses. "Uh, well, I have things to do with Russell, so I don't think I can. Maybe next time. I'll see you when you decide to show up for work." She abruptly hangs up. I feel as though I'm losing my best friend. I know it's inevitable, especially with starting a family, but it still saddens me. I sigh.

Sitting on my bed, I pet Cheeto on her head. Kioto enters the room with a bone in her mouth and drops it right in front of Cheeto. I pet her, too, as she sits on my feet. Cheeto starts to chomp on the gift, and at this point, I don't even care about the mess on my bed. "Why don't you have your babies right there while you're at it?" She ignores me, and I just laugh to myself, thinking how warped my life has become, and how exhausted I am.

Chapter 46

Transfixed
ଔ

After everyone crashes in my apartment for a brief nap, which turns into plenty of hours, I wake up to find Jenna—her energy field much more relaxed—and Gunthreon deeply involved in a conversation of cell phones and laptops. Conner and Lupa study the map as Bu fidgets with my refrigerator, once again. He's so involved, he doesn't even budge when I pull out the Devil's Food cookies I hid in my cabinet. "Where's Ladimer?" I ask.

Suddenly, shouting emerges from the hallway outside my apartment door. Jenna and I simultaneously jump up to peek outside. It's Ladimer and his foster mom going at it.

"I should call the cops right now! Who the hell are you?" she shouts. I see her holding a towel up around her breasts.

"Sorry, Miss. I thought Kailey lived here. Wrong door!" Ladimer has a dumbfounded expression on his face I would love to capture on film right now.

Her eyes narrow as she stares intently at his face. "Do I know you?" she asks, tilting her head like a dog hearing a dog whistle.

"Uh, no, no. Oh, look, there's Kailey now," he responds, blushing—such a rare occurrence. "Hey there. I, uh, accidentally entered your neighbor's apartment by mistake." He pushes past me to get into the room. I look at my neighbor's door as I stand halfway in my doorway. Karen now peeks through the hairline crack she's allowed with her front door.

"He's always doing stupid things like that," I say. "So sorry. You know what? I'll bake you a cake!" With this, I quickly close my door, and glare at Ladimer.

"What the hell?" I say.

"I kinda forgot I don't live there anymore—momentary loss of placement. I was going to check on the plants and grab an orchid clipping for your mom, that's all." I realize how nomadic his life is, and how hard it must be to switch from one life to another so quickly.

My mom laughs as Ladimer walks by her to check on Bu's progress. "Hon, I'm going to go home," she says to me. "I can't sleep in your bed. Mine is much more comfy." I see her grab her back, exactly over her right kidney. "I'll talk to you during the week." She hugs Kioto farewell, then leans into me for one too.

As she lets go, I whisper in her ear. "Thanks for coming to my rescue. I owe you."

She takes my hands in her own and looks into my face. "I hadn't heard from any of you—even Gunthreon—so I just had to make sure you were safe. You don't owe me. *No more* IOU's between us, *please*, Kailey. You no longer need to be my guardian angel. Understand?" I nod, knowing she indirectly speaks of my constant intervention in her medical conditions. "I'm tired," she says, simply, but to the point. She attempts to walk away, but I hold tightly as the tears in my eyes trickle out. "Kailey, it's time," she murmurs, breaking from my grasp. I reach her energy, grabbing at it as she shakes her head, asking me to release her. I do, sadly. She says her goodbyes to everyone and asks Ladimer to walk her to her car.

"Sure." He holds out his arm to her and she actually takes it. She then signs me our special gesture. I do the same to her. They leave my apartment.

Conner appears beside me. "You okay?" he asks, genuinely concerned. I shake my head and he wraps his arms around me as I cry into his shirt. "The love between you and your mom is special—strong. Just know that it's something indestructible, no matter what karma throws at you. Unlike beating hearts, true love exists for eternity."

I cannot help but glance out my window as Ladimer and my mom stand by Fidello's limo, Conner's arms still around me. My mom does all the talking as Ladimer just stands and nods, repeatedly. He glances up at my window as he continues to nod, and nod, and nod. He's surely getting an earful. A small laugh escapes my mouth as I wipe my tears away and release myself from the comfort of Conner's chest.

"Thanks."

He wipes a stray tear from my cheek. "Anytime."

The discussion at my dining room table would seem to be the last thing I want to involve myself in, but I know I must. I almost trip over Jenna as she darts past me to play with the computer on my desk.

"Hmmm." She tries lifting the CPU.

"Hey! Be careful with that!" I yell.

"Sorry, Kailey. I'm just starting my preparations," she says. Busily, she zooms around my apartment, examining everything, everywhere. She lands in my bedroom.

I see her pulling out my dresser drawers. "Hey! Get out of there!" I sure don't want her to pull out something I might be a little embarrassed to admit I own. I race over and slam it shut. "Dresser drawers off-limits!" One glance at her face and I see she doesn't really hear me. She's in the zone. "What preparations?" I query.

She looks to Gunthreon, who nods at her. "My new job, that's all," she replies.

"And this involves items in my dresser drawers?" Gunthreon ignores my glare, and I see Conner, who, from his face, is clearly contemplating what must be so secret in my drawers. Jenna then sits in front of my television and turns it on, then off, then on, and off again.

"Uses electricity," Gunthreon states without turning from the map. "Out." Then she spots my stainless-steel toaster and runs over to push all the buttons. "Out," says Gunthreon. "If it has a cord to the wall, forget it."

I stand motionless, staring at Jenna with my hands on my hips. Then it hits me. "You're going to sell this stuff in Renhala, aren't you?"

The biggest grin imaginable stretches across Jenna's face. "Lovely idea, eh?"

"If so many Renhalans are afraid of this stuff, why bother?"

She stands before me with my iPod. "I'm a convert, aren't I?" she says. "If Gunthreon *and Bu*—" she then whispers to me, "—who's afraid of everything—" she then stops whispering, "aren't afraid, I choose to not be afraid, also."

"Really? Hmph." I see the enthusiasm in her face. "Jenna—" *She* puts her hands on her hips this time, "I actually think you could pull it off." She jumps up, elated, clapping and dancing around. "You, I think, are quite capable of outwitting the UFOE." Then she stops jumping and freezes, as though she has just realized something horrible.

"Oh yeah," she says. Her head shakes like she's trying to force some bad idea out through her ears. "I *can* do this—you're right, Kailey. I *will* do this." Her journey through my apartment continues, and she spots my handheld *Yahtzee* game. She picks it up and examines it closely, noting all buttons. It starts blaring its delightfully entertaining music, and she drops it, evidently not expecting it to make so much noise.

"Can you answer me one thing," I ask. "How do you plan on acquiring these items? You're surely not selling my things."

With her eyes not leaving the game, she replies, "There are a few details I still need to figure out, of course, but all the answers will come in due time. Fascinating."

Conner is in the kitchen, preparing cups of tea.

At the dining table, I spot an open seat next to Lupa, so I sit and finally take a look at the rather large map. As I sit Indian-style, the contents of my pocket spill out onto the floor—both my ring and pendulum. I pick them up and lay them out in front of me, turning over the rather curvaceous womanly-shaped pendulum I received in Socola, and tracing the figure with my finger.

My ears don't hear Gunthreon until he's practically on top of me.

"Kailey!"

"Huh? What? Why you shouting at me?" I say.

"Maybe because you have not answered one question since you sat down." Gunthreon, Lupa, and Conner all stare at me with quizzical faces.

I seriously heard nothing. "Sorry," I apologize. "I thought maybe you were talking to somebody else."

"Where did you get that?" he asks. His eyes are bigger than plums as he stares at my trinkets. "Holy mother of Neda." The only thing that has moved is his mouth. He makes no motion even to touch anything.

"You're talking about the pendulum, aren't you? Isn't it awesome?" I say. I stretch my arm to pick it up, and he grabs my hand with such force that I retract it for fear he'll break it. Ladimer comes back in and makes his way over to see what all the hoopla is about.

If Gunthreon's eyes were plums, Ladimer's are now grapefruits. Their eyes alone scare the shit out of me. "*What!* Someone tell me what it is!"

Lupa and Conner shrug. "Must be an elders' thing," responds Lupa as Conner puts cups, hot and steamy, in front of us. Gunthreon and Ladimer seem to hear nothing around them, but only continue to stare at my pendulum. When I put my hand over it, they shake out of their trances.

"I'll ask again, what is it?" Gunthreon tries moving my hand away from the pendulum, but I refuse to budge. "Answer me first."

"What you are covering with your hand is perhaps one of the most valuable missing pieces of Renhalan history," states Ladimer. "To make this easy for you to understand, I'd say it's like finding the Ark of the Covenant." My jaw drops, and I fall off of my chair with no grace whatsoever.

I recover quickly. "How did the pendulum wind up with *me*?" I ask. "What am I supposed to do with this? You take it." I try handing it to Ladimer, but he jumps back. Gunthreon shakes his head. You'd think I had the plague. Conner moves quickly beside me, sticking out his hand. I place the pendulum in it, relieved that someone else is willing to touch it.

"Some old mooncat just walked up to me and put it in my hand," I say. "How did *he* get it?"

Gunthreon walks over to Lupa and asks for her everything pack. He opens it slowly and pulls out Michel's sword. "Maybe the same way we ended up with this: a won battle." The sword he holds is no less beautiful then when I saw it previously, and I want it. Gunthreon sees my face, then holds it behind his back, bringing me back to reality.

"Why do I want that so bad?" I ask, realizing the intense feelings I felt when the sword was exposed.

"The power these items hold calls to your soul, rather like how Conner talks to the soul," answers Gunthreon. "It *wants* you to want it. You have to try your best and resist. After enough exposure to these items, you'll do it involuntarily, except if it catches you off guard, like it just did me and Ladimer. I've seen many a person killed over pieces like this."

Ladimer finally puts out his hand to hold the pendulum. Conner hesitates. "Please," says Ladimer. Conner places it in his hand, reluctantly. "Items like this predate Gunthreon here," Ladimer says. Gunthreon just grunts. "They are from the harmonious time of Neda and Velopa. The Higher Ones worked jointly once, knowing that their relationship held Renhala together. Items like these antiquities were made as gifts for one another, recognizing the other's importance, and they were deeply treasured by the Higher Ones. When times went sour, the 'Lost Treasures of the Surge,' as we call them, were either destroyed or hidden away. Upon rare occasion, they are rediscovered. The strong will of the mooncats proved valuable on passing these priceless artifacts. How we ended up with three is beyond belief."

"Three?" I say.

"The urn is also one."

At the word "priceless," I see Jenna's eyes wander over and fix upon my pendulum. "Don't even think about it, Jenna!" I tease. I grab my ring off the table, deciding I best put it away before losing it.

"Kailey, that hurts my feelings." But Jenna just giggles, and I smile at her. Despite her history, I feel a trust between us that I hope is genuine.

I walk into my bedroom and kiss my ring before placing it in my grandmother's beaded clutch that I keep in my closet. On my way back to the map, I stop by Bu,—all slimy with grease—who is standing in front of my refrigerator. "Bu fixed your icebox. It should be true to its thermometer now," he says.

I watch him carefully place his beloved tools in his fanny pack. "Bu, you are truly amazing," I say. "I think I may still have a couple T-bones I forgot about in the fridge."

"Yes, you did. Bu saw them." He wipes a drip of salty blood from his mouth.

"I *did*, eh? Well consider that payment for your services. It was nice doing business with you." We shake hands, then I continue on to my dining room table.

Ladimer carefully examines the pendulum, turning it over and over in his hands.

"Do the Lost Treasures of the Surge have names, like they do in fantasy books?" I watch Ladimer as he sniffs the stone carving.

Gunthreon holds the sword before him and places it on the table. "Kailey, meet Evlengard," he says. "You may pick it up if you like. Just remember what I said. And we are both here—", he glances at Ladimer, "—if the need to intercept arises."

"Oooh. Are you sure? I really probably shouldn't." But I am already at the sword, feeling the grip. It's much lighter than I imagined. Both Gunthreon and Ladimer are stiff as boards, watching me with deep intensity. "Don't worry, you two. I'm fine," Thoughts of battle roll around inside my head, and visions of triumph and waving flags appear before me. Before I know it, I'm slicing the air around me inside my limited-space apartment. Ladimer is suddenly at my back, grabbing my arms. Conner steps forward, quickly, grabbing Ladimer's arm. Kioto growls at both of them as she comes to my side.

"I wouldn't do that," Ladimer advises, looking at Conner's hand. "I'm simply protecting *our* Kailey from herself." Kioto continues to growl, her haunches ready to jump at anyone who attempts to do me harm.

Conner says, "I think you do more endangering than protecting," as he releases his hand and soulspeaks to Kioto. Gunthreon takes the sword from my hand. But once my hands are free, I slap Gunthreon in the face. Both Conner and Ladimer's jaws drop. Kioto's growling stops and her ears rise.

The speed with which Lupa moves would rival my mom, but Gunthreon tells her to sit. He wipes his face where I slapped him. "Foolish me," he says, "I should have seen something like that coming, considering the situation. Evidently, you cannot handle this yet." Evlengard ends up back in the everything pack. "Let's take a try at the pendulum. It's most likely safer." He picks up the pendulum and holds it above his opposite hand. "This is known as the Hand of Wohmin." The pendulum starts swirling around in an even circle, picking up speed. His eyes are closed, and he smiles.

"What did you ask it?" I ask. His eyelids flutter before they open, and I see a sort of haze over his eyes, almost like cataract film. "Ewww." He briefly shakes his head, and his eyes clear.

"Wow." Gunthreon still smiles. "I didn't ask it anything. It just showed me something—something rather pleasant. Hmm."

"What?"

"None of your business, that's what."

It's clear I won't be finding that out. "Alrighty, then," I say. "Can I have another try?"

Gunthreon thinks about my question, then must feel that it's safe enough, because he puts it in the palm of my hand. "It was given to you after all, not me. It is now yours, Kailey, and it seems harmless enough."

Once I grasp the pendulum, I feel a movement in my hand, something resembling a snake slithering. I drop the pendulum immediately. "It does move!"

"Yes, that's what pendulums do."

"No, this was different."

Gunthreon smirks. "It's a different pendulum, now, isn't it?"

I grab the chain, and, again, there is instant movement. It feels as though the pendulum is reaching toward the map, pulling me to stand directly over it.

Ladimer comes to stand next to me. "Ha," he blurts.

My hand moves slowly over the map in the direction the pendulum pulls. It finds a location in what Gunthreon and Ladimer state is only vast prairie, which appears to be surrounded by lakes. The only land access to this area seems to be an area to the west, called Glamor Glen.

The pendulum focuses on the prairieland and keeps circling, until it circles so fast I drop it. "Why is it pointing here?" I ask.

Ladimer grunts loudly. "Don't know," he says. "And if Gunthreon plans on going there, I'm out."

My confusion must cover my whole face, because Lupa whispers "Pixies" in my ear as she points to Glamor Glen. "Oh." I understand Ladimer's hesitance. "You know, the only way to get past a fear is to face it head-on."

Ladimer rolls his eyes at me.

Gunthreon says, "We must go where we must, Ladimer."

"There's nothing there! It's practically lifeless. I know this from experience," Ladimer hesitates, "for I've sent many a traitor there, to fend for their pathetic lives." Lupa frowns as Ladimer's face suddenly looks aged. "And there's definitely no need to travel through Glamor Glen."

"Of course he refuses continuing where our mission takes us," says Conner, angrily. "Not because of putting others at risk, but because of his own selfish pride. Or *maybe* it's an informant's move." Ladimer moves quickly and grabs Conner by the front of his shirt.

Suddenly, my cell phone starts ringing. I see that it's Amber, but being such an inopportune time, I can't answer the phone, so I mute the ring and place it on my table. It then vibrates, *loudly.*

Conner only stares back into Ladimer's face, willing him to make a move. After an eternity, Ladimer slowly lets go of his shirt, wiping away the creases, as he says to Conner, "Spoken by another, who, also, has never met a pixie."

"I've heard tales," retorts Conner, defiantly.

Ladimer laughs, and says, "Tales, tales, tales. Until you become one of those stories, you have no room to speak! So step back off your high horse, youngling." He hesitates. "And soulspeak would just be the perfect tool for someone needing to relay information, wouldn't it? They would know without a doubt that you weren't deceiving them, the deceivers." Ladimer's eyes penetrate Conner.

Gunthreon jumps in and snaps, "Calm down, both of you! You will stop insulting each other, now. Focus on something else besides belittling each other. Do you need to be put in separate corners?" Gunthreon stands between them, examining each of their faces. They both walk away in opposite directions.

Bu and Jenna sit on the floor—Bu petting Cheeto, and Jenna petting Kioto. They both stroke with nervous hands, simultaneously.

Since the first mention of pixies I've imagined cute little images of Tinkerbell and her friends fluttering around my head. Ladimer and Conner, in my opinion, clearly want to fight over *anything*—for when near each other their energies flare. I break the tension for everyone by saying, "Are they like the size of Jenna here, or smaller?" I say, leaning toward Gunthreon with my question because I'll only get some smartass comment from Ladimer.

"They are anything they want to be," says Gunthreon. "Whatever will get them what they want, when they want it, is what they will be."

"So they're shapeshifters?"

"I suppose, except they are always women—female to the bone."

"Any way we can hold off traveling for another day?" I ask. "I understand the importance of finding Neda and Velopa, but we all must keep a grasp on our sanity. We need a break—even just a short one."

Gunthreon scouts the room and sees the hunkered shoulders and weary eyes. "Your place is a bit small for all of us," he responds. "I must ask you all to come to Spirit Cave. Consider it a mini-vacation. You can even bring Cheeto, Kailey."

I grin ear-to-ear. "You're on! I've got to pack again. Lupa, need anything?" She just shakes her everything pack at me. I then look to Gunthreon. "You live at the bar? There must be more to the building than I've seen?"

Lupa smiles at Gunthreon as she replies to me. "Oh, you have no idea."

"Better hurry up, then, because Fidello has returned and is waiting downstairs." Gunthreon picks up his pack, ready to leave.

"*How* do you do that?"

Ladimer peeks out the window. "Let me run and grab some stuff, too. I'll be back in a flash."

"Kailey, the invitation extends to your mother, too, if she wants to come—and Kioto," says Gunthreon. Kioto turns to him as she hears her name and wags her tail. Gunthreon gets up and gives her a biscuit from her treat container.

"I'll call my mom later, because I know she's gotta be resting now. Thanks, G."

Bu and Jenna stand side-by-side, resembling lost puppy dogs—mastiff on steroids and a litter runt Chihuahua. Gunthreon laughs. "You'll be going too."

Bu starts dancing about. "Yeah! Bu can't wait to see SharkBoy!"

"I don't even want to ask about that one," I say.

Lupa laughs in Gunthreon's direction. "One of his *many* strays," she says. They both laugh together and then it hits me.

"Hey!" They laugh even harder, for a bit too long.

Chapter 47

Shocking
❧

Getting Bu out of my apartment without anyone noticing turns out not to be as easy as I thought. Bu really wants to travel via limo, so we throw an extra-large comforter over him. Ladimer's foster mom opens her door right as Bu walks out of my apartment, but she quickly slams it shut. As I run with Bu, hippie neighbor, carrying his Wild Oats groceries, walks from his car with his mouth agape, tripping over the one step to the front door. Thank the Higher Ones he only shakes his head and continues inside. I shove Bu into the limo, then Gunthreon and Lupa slip in.

Conner comes running with Kioto and Cheeto. Kioto pants heavily, knowing with her animal senses that she's going on a trip in a way unnatural for animals—a motorized vehicle. Cheeto, wearing a pillow case with holes cut out for her legs and eyes, spots Kioto's anxiety and sits outside the limo, becoming dead weight as I attempt to lift her into the car.

Ladimer comes bounding back from his apartment with a small backpack and allows me to struggle with Cheeto as he watches. "Bit off more than you can chew with that one, eh?" he teases.

I finally shove her inside, then stick my tongue out at Ladimer.

Once we're all inside the limo, Jenna crawls out from underneath Bu's comforter so she can peek out the tinted windows. As we pull away, however, she hunkers down and grips onto my pants leg for dear life. Her greenish hue as we drive away makes me break that grip, however; I'd rather her not puke on me.

"Jenna, look out the window at the horizon," I advise her. "If you only sit on the floor, you will definitely throw up. Here, just in case." I hand her a plastic grocery bag as I smile to myself, finally justifying five years of carrying one in my purse "just in case."

"How can this thing move? There's no aura! It's not alive." Jenna grumbles. She's on the brink of barfing, but manages to sneak the words out.

Gunthreon holds back a laugh. "It's called a car, and more specifically, a limousine. It runs on slightly-altered natural resources. My driver's name is Fidello." Fidello, almost on cue, lowers the divider, and I see his eyes in the rearview mirror.

"Nice to meet you," he says. "Got enough room, big guy?" This is clearly directed at Bu.

In a shy voice, Bu answers, "Yes, thank you, sir." Fidello nods and rolls the window back up.

Bu leans over to me and very quietly, whispers, "He's a namakon."

"A who?"

"Fidello is a namakon," says Gunthreon. "N-A-M-A-K-O-N." I sound it out as I see the letters appear in my head. "Namakons have a unique gift, which Fidello was willing to share with me. I saved his life and, for this, he has bonded to me as a, well, servant type."

"That doesn't sound like a pleasant life," I say.

Gunthreon holds up his hand and shakes it, brushing me off. "It's what he's born to do. A namakon's talent allows him to bond, mind to mind, with one other creature. All thoughts are exchanged between the two, making them wonderful adversaries."

"Or prying menaces." Lupa folds her arms, clearly uncomfortable with Fidello's ability.

"Honey, we have been through this three thousand times— at least," sputters Gunthreon. "You know damn well that Fidello has come to my aid many a time, and many a time returned the favor of saving my life. I am still here because of that fellow."

Lupa knows she has struck a sore spot, so she warmly smiles and holds Gunthreon's hand. "I'm just cranky and tired," says Lupa. "A good night's sleep will cure everything." She pinches his thigh, and Gunthreon pushes her hand away, as if it tickled.

"We are *all* going to enjoy a good night's sleep," I say. The motion of the moving car knocks me out in a minute flat, as I slump over on Conner's shoulder.

ƆȢ

When I wake up, it's to the sensation of being carried. I fear that I've traveled and landed in some compromising position, but when I quickly open my eyes, I find Bu cradling me like a child. I stick my thumb in my mouth and "wah" like a baby. "Kailey, you silly!" Bu laughs, and it's a more mature laugh than I remember. Bu places me down on my feet gently past the back door of Spirit Cave, runs inside, and then disappears through the kitchen door.

Lupa heads in after him. "Gunthreon, your fridge stocked?" she queries as she opens the ceiling-height refrigerator door. "Pizza it is!" She frowns and closes the door.

"I thought we were going to be gone longer," responds Gunthreon. "And I was not expecting company."

I offer to call in the pizza, and Gunthreon says, "Be my guest."

I play waitress and take everyone's order on a notepad, and make sure that I remember Bu's request for extra anchovies. He'll be getting his own special pizza, for sure. But before I dial the number, I notice another missed call from Amber. Right as I'm about to return her call, I see Jenna just sitting on the ground, playing with her necklace, oblivious to what is going on around her. The sadness emanating from her immediately saddens me.

I sit down next to her on the floor. "What's up?"

"It's just that I miss Renhala already, mostly the forests," she whimpers. "It's too noisy here. There's this constant buzzing in the air, and I can't hear the trees. Don't you hear it?"

I hear the hustle and bustle of Chinatown through the closed windows around me, but nothing that resembles buzzing.

Downheartedly, she says, "It's just different, that's all."

Fiddling with my phone, I feel her pain in some strange way. "I have an idea," I say. "Would you like to call in the food order?"

She brightens up and grabs the phone from me. "What do I do?" I show her the numbers to press, and place the notebook in front of her, adding Gunthreon's phone number. She dials, starts to breathe quicker with each ring, and practically drops the phone in her lap when they answer and speak to her. I pull in close to her to hear the conversation. "Uhhh," she slurs. I tap on the notebook. "Oh yeah. I would like to order... " she says, looking confused, so I mouth the word "pizzas" to her. "...pizzas?"

"What?" says the barely-sixteen boy who answered the phone.

Jenna furrows her brow, then speaks again, a bit louder. "Pizzas. I want to order some."

The boy on the line fumbles the phone and I hear, "Dude, I don't know what this person's saying—speaking alien, again, or Polish. Maybe Chinese. Steve, you take it. "

We hear Steve on the other end, "Hello?"

Jenna tries again, but a bit perturbed. "Pizzas! Can I get 'em?"

"Yes, of course. What would you like," Steve asks.

She then rattles off the order, adding her own request of fried gundworms (which they don't seem to have today) and says, "Bye." She passes the phone to me, and I show her how to press the "end" button. Her eyes wide, she's junkie Jenna again, which, by me, is much better than sad Jenna.

Gunthreon gives me the tour of his apartment, and it is absolutely stunning, as though he hired the world's top interior designers. Every item is unique in its own way, holding some special secret.

"Wow. Can I hire you?" I ask. "Give me the friends and family deal." He just smiles at me.

I spy Conner standing in the corner, staring in a mirror. He is motionless, and it's kind of creepy. Ladimer walks over to him and pulls him away by the back of the neck. Conner shakes his head, and "What the hell?" escapes his mouth. I stare from afar at the mirror, wondering what he could possibly have seen.

"There is many an item here that will pull you from your reality, but nothing dangerous," Gunthreon states, unpacking his bags. "Go ahead, Kailey."

I turn to Conner, who is puzzled, but intrigued. "Go ahead. Nothing bad," he says.

So I stand before the mirror, staring at myself. Nothing happens. But just as I'm about to turn away, everything behind me disappears, and instead of me in the mirror, I see my mom. She is beautiful, standing before me in my clothes, and as I move, she moves, mimicking each smile, each frown, each raspberry. "How?" I don't dare turn from the figure just yet. But within seconds, the figure is no longer my mom, but a male figure with red hair like my own. My mouth drops and I suddenly see Gunthreon standing next to me.

"That's enough. The pizza is here."

"Was that—?"

"Yes."

"How can that mirror do that?"

Gunthreon laughs. "Magic, of course."

The image won't escape my mind as I keep thinking about the male face in the mirror staring back at me, and how closely his mouth and nose resembled my own. I am tempted to go back and look in the mirror, but Gunthreon reads my mind.

"It will only show your true lineage once," he says. "If you look again, it will only be your beautiful face staring back."

But I can't help trying again. As I walk by to grab a slice of pizza, I stop before the mirror and stare, but alas, I see nothing but myself, just like Gunthreon said. "Conner," I say as I pass him. "did you see your parents, too?"

"Yeah. Kind of freaky, huh?"

I shrug. "Where did you get that mirror, Gunthreon?"

He frowns and says, sadly, "One of my many conquests way back when." His head tilts toward Jenna, and I realize what he's trying to get across to me.

"So where did Bu run off to?" I ask, quickly changing the subject. "He's got to be as hungry as I am, or more so. I'm surprised he hasn't smelled it already."

Lupa, with her mouth full of gooey cheese and vegetables, mumbles with her finger pointed, "You'll find Bu down that hall, through the door on the right. It will have an aquarium scene carved into it, and beautiful work, I must say." She keeps chewing, drooling a bit out of the left side of her mouth, but she catches it skillfully with her napkin.

"SharkBoy?"

A nod is all I get as she gulps her fruit punch.

"Do you mind if I come, too?" Conner's plate is already empty, and he stands with his hands in his pockets, looking cute and innocent.

I can't help but allow him to follow. "Sure." Jenna doesn't even know what's going on around her—her pizza is untouched—because she's still playing with my phone. My cell phone bill will definitely be checked with more gusto come next month, because I wouldn't be surprised to find a cross-country call to 123-456-7890. "Jenna, call this number and ask my mom if she wants to come over and hang with us." I write down her number and slide the paper in front of her.

I pile on my plate two more pieces of pizza then go grab a few anchovy pieces for Bu. I decide to put his in a plastic Ziploc I found on the counter because I don't want any of his anchovies touching any bit of my pizza. Conner grabs one more piece for the road as I shove the baggie in my pocket.

As we walk, Conner clears his throat. "You know, the stupid bickering we've been doing is going nowhere. Let's start from scratch." The apology—or at least that's how I'm taking his words—releases tension in my shoulders that I didn't even realize I was carrying until now.

My pizza balances nicely on my hand as I extend my other to shake. "Nice to meet you. I'm Kailey," I state. Conner shakes firmly, and I feel that familiar static electricity dart through my hand. "Stop with that, though."

"Honestly, I'm not doing that. It must be you."

"Uh, no. I don't do that. Maybe if you'd pick your feet up more when you walk." Our walk slows down as our voices get louder.

"I've never done that with anyone," sputters Conner. "You're the one with the hidden powers after all, remember? Maybe you're like 'Super Shock,' the superhero, or something. No, better yet—'Karmelean: your personal defibrillator.' Yeah!" He laughs at his own joke, but stops quickly as his pizza slides down the front of his shirt.

"No need to reheat later, Sparky McGee!" I prance well ahead of him and find the door Lupa mentioned. The workmanship is indeed superb, giving each sea creature a life of its own, suspended in wood.

"Wow." Some of the pizza sauce still lingers on his shirt. "This is a hundred-dollar shirt, you know," he whines. He speaks without taking his eyes off the door.

"Looks like you got robbed," I say.

Just as he is about to return the fire, a low-pitch rumbling noise leaks from beyond the door. We look to each other and both grab the doorknob. The shock from that simple touch sends an electrical current up the door, which reaches out to each fish and anemone carved into it. For a brief three seconds, the creatures are alive, swimming to and fro across the door.

But as quickly as their lives began, they freeze and are once again carved into the door where they last swam.

"Beats the Shedd Aquarium any day!" says Conner. He turns the knob and opens the door ever so slowly, revealing the room beyond, foot by magnificent foot.

To imagine standing on the bottom of the ocean floor with all your clothes on, breathing air as schools of fish swim between your legs does not even come close to the experience even of standing in the doorway of this room. Bu floats in the center of the room, his back to us. He talks, but I cannot understand his words or see who or what he may be talking to. As I gather the courage to step inside the room, Bu's head turns 180 degrees and he smiles. No matter how much I love and trust Bu, that simple movement still creeps me out.

"That is horror-film material," mumbles Conner, shaking.

"Glad we can agree on something." As we enter the room, the door disappears behind us and the room gets very moist, as though we have entered a rainforest. The moisture grows heavier and heavier, until we are totally saturated to our underwear. Overwhelming dizziness takes over my body and I wobble, feeling as though my head might explode. I look to Conner and see gills on his neck. "No way!" I yelp. My words are drowned as I reach to my neck and feel my own set of gills.

Chapter 48

Wet
ॐ

I panic and start pawing frantically at the water in front of me. Quickly, Bu holds my hands down to my sides as he and his friend, indeed a SharkBoy, start talking again, but without the use of their mouths.

Kailey, you relax. The familiar tickling of someone else in my head makes me forget the weirdness of the water not flowing up my nose.

You were right. She is pretty...appetizing. SharkBoy swims directly in front of us, more shark than boy, and winks at me with his boy eyelids. Only his face is one of human youth—large blue eyes, small stub for a nose, and thin, beautiful, delicate lips. The rest of his body is full-blown shark, fins and all. I shiver as SharkBoy's lower line of teeth appears over his top lip in his attempt at smiling at me. He swims quickly around Conner, scoping him out. *Your heartbeat is speeding up. That's tempting.* His smile is at full capacity now, and it's as scary as hell, looming in front of us. I cannot help but stare at the abomination floating before my eyes. I freeze, not even being able to sense his energy. Conner moves closer to me, his hand moving towards his hidden weapon.

SharkBoy, you stop messing with Bu's friends. Bu slaps SharkBoy on his back like an old fishing buddy.

SharkBoy stumbles forward in the water, then winks at me once more. In my head, I hear a laugh. *Sorry. I hardly get any visitors these days. I'm beginning to forget I'm still a predator. Nice to meet you guys. Bu already trusts you like family. He's not making any mistakes, is he?* He indiscreetly flashes his knife-sharp teeth as he quickly gulps up a few rainbow-colored fish swimming by.

My mouth opens to reply, and I take in saltwater. The whole switch of communication methods throws me a bit. *Bu is very important to me*, I think. *Rest assured, your dear friend is in good hands.* I swat away a handful of shrimp-like creatures who keep yelping in my ear. *Are we in Renhala or Abscondia? If we're in Abscondia, how is this room possible? I can't even see the walls.* The strange, dizzy feeling remains, but is less pronounced as I float in the water.

SharkBoy answers: **This may be hard to understand, but you're in both. This is a small piece of Renhala residing in your realm. Your friend Gunthreon is a very powerful man, and is capable of many a thing, such as this.** My feeler senses a bit of fear at the mention of Gunthreon. **My waters were once threatened by some very nasty poachers, and Gunthreon did what he could for me, for a price of course. I owed him my kingdom for what he did.** He laughs to himself. **Well I guess I kind of gave it to him, didn't I? After all, we are all in his second-floor apartment. Me and my kingdom.** He holds out a fin to the many creatures floating distantly around him.

How long have you been here? Conner thinks.

Bu stops playing tag with a fish that reminds me of my neighbor's Scottish terrier. He answers, **He's here long time.**

SharkBoy nods. **I'd have to say since long before you were all born, but I continue to be called SharkBoy.** He nods toward Bu. **I may look young to you, but I've lost many a tooth.**

I think back to elementary school science, and the day we studied sharks. *I'd say you still have many more years to live*, I think. Hundreds, probably. *I have to ask—do you feel the recent imbalance, too, living between realms?*

His head drops, and his expression is one of great sadness. **I was hoping it was just some effect from living as I do, but I** *would have to say something bad is happening. We sea creatures can no longer feel the cradling hands of Neda. Something is definitely wrong. Being the predator I am, I no longer feel as prey-driven as I should. I settle for eating this.* With his fin, he pulls out a bunch of seaweed from a coral bed next to him and munches on it. *Aside from Neda distancing itself, I must admit Velopa's pull has weakened, or even disappeared.*

This puzzles me, as well as Conner, from the expression on his face. *I thought Velopa's army was becoming stronger? Wouldn't you feel Velopa more than ever?* I think.

You would think so. SharkBoy swims next to Bu and rubs up against him like a beloved pet. Bu giggles like a child and pets SharkBoy's dorsal fin. *We are relying on Gunthreon, and your group, to find some answers. After meeting you, Kailey, I can sense something extraordinary in you—something capable of finding us answers.*

Suddenly, SharkBoy raises his stub-for-a-nose and almost seems to be sniffing the water. He swims over to me, and I realize it's the side with my pocket stuffed with anchovy pizza.

If Bu wants to share, I believe you might enjoy this, I think. I pull the pizza out of the baggie and let it float in the water before me. SharkBoy's eyes widen, and he turns to Bu. Bu simply nods. Instead of devouring the pizza in one huge gulp, SharkBoy somehow breaks tiny pieces of the pizza off and lets them sit in his mouth a bit.

I absolutely love these tiny fish. They're my favorite! So salty. See, you've won over me and my loyalty already. He winks at me yet again. *Someone else approaches.* The door opens and closes almost simultaneously as Ladimer steps inside. SharkBoy bows, as much as a shark can. *Hello, and welcome to my home. Am I safe in assuming you are Ladimer, the Giver?*

You are absolutely correct, and thank you for not eating me upon entry, King Xotylenan. Ladimer then proceeds to speak to SharkBoy in what sounds like whalespeak, or something close to it. Whatever it is, it's very loud. I wonder how many enemies Ladimer must really have, and whether he made SharkBoy, too.

I swim over to Bu and ask if he's ready to go back to air-breathing. He shrugs his large shoulders and says, telepathically, goodbye to SharkBoy, who replies: *Until later, my friend. Come see me again, all of you.* He turns to face Ladimer. *I will get word to you if I hear or see anything.*

Ladimer speaks to SharkBoy, *Thank you, dear king. Shall we go, guys?* He pats Bu on the back and thinks a goodbye to SharkBoy as I cover my ears, which does no good whatsoever.

The exit out of SharkBoy's kingdom happens quickly, and I feel my neck to make sure the gills aren't permanent. I consider how weird the transition was and how dry it actually is in Gunthreon's apartment, almost enough to make my nose bleed.

Chapter 49

Fiery
❧

Ladimer leads us back down the hallway to Gunthreon and Lupa, comfortably sprawled out on a couch. Turns out Gunthreon, quite the movie buff, has his own small movie theater, with squishy reclining chairs, a giant movie screen, and personalized popcorn bowls. Lupa is already in her pajamas, flipping through pay-per-view movies as Gunthreon once more scans a map.

"Just no sappy love stories, please," says Ladimer pleadingly. "I didn't bring my Kleenex."

"Or scary movies," adds Bu.

After searching through Gunthreon's plethora of movies, we all decide on watching *Chocolat*. We fit two chairs together for Bu, and he climbs in and covers up with an Elmo blanket he keeps here at Gunthreon's. I climb into my own comfy chair and snuggle what I think is a down pillow, until it starts to turn warm where I lay my head. I pick my head up and feel it with my hand, and it indeed becomes warm where my hand touches the pillow.

"Phoenix feathers," Gunthreon states with a smile.

"So I'm gonna be, like, sleeping here and my head might catch on fire? No thanks."

"It is only the bird's will that controls the explosion. Your hair is not going to start on fire. It's your choice. Use it or pass it on."

Ladimer, seated to my left, reaches over to me. "I'll take it," he says.

I consider the probability of my hair catching on fire and decide that the novelty of sleeping on warming feathers is worth it. "Sorry, I'm keeping it."

"Good luck," he teases, reclining his chair.

I snuggle in my pillow and turn my body in the opposite direction, toward Conner. He stares at me, and I at him, then he closes his eyes.

I turn again, adjusting my body, trying to get comfortable in the chair, but just cannot seem to.

Gunthreon sees my struggle and then gets up and offers his hand. "I can take you to your room if you like," he says. I take his hand, and make sure to snatch up my pillow, as Ladimer was moving in a little too close.

Gunthreon leads me to a room, at once luxurious and homey-comfortable, something I never thought possible. Bamboo sheets adorn the king-sized bed, brushing against my skin with their coolness as I climb in, but they warm to me quickly. The room smells of fresh flowers, though there are none in sight. One dimly lit nightlight glows on the nightstand, tossing stars along the ceiling, reminiscent of a lamp I remember having as an toddler.

"Goodnight, Kailey. Sweet dreams." He eyes me for a moment. "Remember your meditation techniques."

I'm out before he closes the door.

⚬

"He's starting to resist!"

"Make him finish it. If you do not, prepare to live your life in constant agonizing pain, your only relief from the thought of possible death."

The familiar voice makes my eyes pop open. I find myself standing outside a castle in my pajamas, below some open windows. As I rise up to sneak a glance, I see the all-too-familiar hooded cloak, its owner sitting at a desk, apparently staring at some parchment sprawled across his desk and not the meeple standing before him, which rolls its eyes. It begins to leave the room, but then turns around and simply says, "And the girl is almost at her peak." It turns and leaves the room, slamming the door behind itself.

Devoten then stands and walks toward the window, in my direction. I crouch down as low as possible, then crawl to the next window, which is also open, and slowly rise to look inside. I gasp and cover my mouth before any sound escapes it. There before me is a haggard figure, stirring a giant cauldron of what looks like molten metal over a giant fire. Mortimer stirs with both hands, his eyes white with only the occasional flicker of color that I recognize as consciousness.

"Mortimer," I say in a soft voice. "Mortimer. Mortimer!" The last is a hushed scream, and his eyes flicker as he turns toward me.

"Kailey?"

The door to his room opens and the meeple enters. I sink down low, my eyes peeking in through the corner of the window. "You almost done?" it asks.

"Um, I don't know."

"Dumb creature. How could you not know?"

Mortimer's voice trembles. "I told you already, I don't—" His speech turns to a blood-curdling cry as the meeple sticks his talon into Mortimer's ear.

"You'd better finish, or next time, this will slice your head in two."

Mortimer's scream turns to sobbing as the meeple leaves the room, once again slamming the door behind itself.

I rise a bit and speak to Mortimer as he stands at the cauldron. "Oh, Mortimer. What are you doing?" I ask. "Come on. Come with me. I can transport you to safety." But he just continues stirring. "Mortimer!"

He looks up, then shakes his head. "They'll always find me," he cries. Almost on cue, his eyes turn white again, and he is lost to me. I slump down to the ground, searching for a solution. If Devoten has Mortimer, I fear that Velopa's weapon armory may be complete. If only I could find Neda on my own search. *Soulsearch.* Sudden thoughts of Gernwood and my attempt at finding my mom come to mind as I realize it almost came to fruition.

Just as I'm about to close my eyes and reach for Neda, I'm interrupted by a loud explosion and footsteps running to and fro. I crawl toward the sound and look through one more window, where I see the giant metal contraption I spotted the doctor and Tartarin working on during my nighttime trip four days ago. But it's not the same place. They're moving it. *Why?*

Grebles and meeples run around terrified as Devoten steps slowly into the room, with what looks like a human, uniformed soldier—the letters UFOE embroidered across his chest. They are untouched by the chaos around them. "He's done. Bring him in," says Devoten, his energy suddenly shooting across the room and grabbing me firmly. Sudo-abominor, most likely excited by the pandemonium and fear, is aroused and sensed me almost immediately. "We must also deal with our infestation problem—a particularly nosy little fluffmouse!" With that, he points at me.

As he starts stealthily running toward me, I hunker down, trying to rip off the energy that's squeezing me tightly. I send out my own energy from within, trying to fight against sudo-abominor. As my energy pushes outward, it struggles in vain, so I will myself to have the courage to do something heroic, and quickly. I don't know Neda's energy, but in hoping my karmelean beacon works, I take my own nervously-hyped energy and blast it with all my might outward, waiting for something to recognize a fragment of me and pull me in.

Seconds before Devoten grasps me over the windowsill, I find myself transported.

I appear in the middle of an open, dusty, vacant field, nothing around me except some longer, dried-out grass and wilted plants. The air is devoid of moisture, and the two orange suns seem to battle for dominance, taking turns spitting solar flares toward the other. "Hello?!" I yell, but nobody responds. "Anybody?" I spin around to nothing but the same golden-hued land stretching beyond my sight in all directions.

I sit on the ground and close my eyes a moment before traveling and think of Gunthreon and the cozy bed I left with those stars shining above me. My mind begins relaxing, thinking threads of thoughts. *Stars along the ceiling. Stars that chase away a toddler's fear of gruesome monsters. Monsters that could hurt you and eat you alive. Monsters that bleed black ooze. Monsters that now threaten to destroy the new generation of children. Amber's child.* Tears trickle down my cheeks and drip into the dried grass as I make a decision to carry on in my search—to not run, but to have confidence in my abilities.

To my amazement, small, delicate flowers of all colors begin to sprout where my tears have fallen, filling the barren land with life.

But before I can marvel any longer, I am suddenly beneath Gunthreon's stars again, sprawled across the bed. I sit up, sensing someone else's energy in the room with me. Gunthreon sits motionless in the armchair across from the bed, staring at me.

"Gunthreon, you scared me!" I sputter.

He sits still, dark in the shadows. "Where did you go this time, Kailey?"

I smell a hint of accusation in his voice and it makes me fidget in bed. "He has Mortimer!" I exclaim. "And the UFOE are involved!"

"Who has Mortimer?"

"Devoten!"

"Visited Devoten again, eh, Kailey?" he says. "It seems you know a lot for such *brief* travels." He hesitates and his energy begins rippling, slowly turning to larger waves of hot fire. "Don't dig too deep...without reinforcements. I'd hate to find out this is a trap of some sort—a camouflaged abyss. It would be most unpleasant for those involved, don't you think? One wrong step, and you'll find *yourself* falling. I think it best we don't mention this to the others." His energy sizzles and ebbs.

I sit, totally befuddled. Not knowing where he's going with this, I just agree. He gets up and leaves the room, not making a sound, and as he stands in the doorway, he seems to grow in size, looming above me. Then he's gone.

I spend my time lying there, with my eyes open, too afraid to sleep, thoughts of deception twirling like a tornado in my head. The single word *informant* brings pain to my stomach as I lie, considering possible motives for each and every being around me.

When the sun rises, it comes with fear of what the shadows hide.

Chapter 50

Inquisitive
 CR

The day spent with my fellow travelers is short and not so sweet. The memory of Gunthreon's silhouette in the door frazzles my nerves as I watch him move about Spirit Cave, chatting with everyone, individually. He catches me watching him and smiles. His once charming smile, is now just eerie.

Gunthreon ignores my animals, so in my mind, they're safe territory. Kioto loves my attention at first, but finally gets tired of me, giving me a low growl and walking away when I try painting her nails. Cheeto steps in and takes her place, but there's only so much ceetchan-petting one can take.

When my smartphone rings, I pull it away from Jenna. "Hi, mom. Whatch'ya up to?" I ask.

"Not much," she replies. "Just trying on some old dresses of mine. I shouldn't complain, but they're all too big on me now. Maybe you can have them."

I laugh at her jab. "And did you keep the matching leg-warmers, too?" We both know she hasn't been in a dress since the mid-eighties.

"Smartass."

"I take after my mom."

I hear her closet door close. "Did you have fun at Gunthreon's place?"

"Uh, sort of." My voice lowers a bit. "Mom, how much do you trust Gunthreon?"

She pauses for longer than I'd like. "About ninety-nine percent. Why?"

"So only ninety-nine."

"The only person I trust wholeheartedly is you," she states. "I put my faith in Gunthreon. Why do you ask?"

Just before I can respond, Gunthreon appears next to me. "Kailey, tell your mother we missed her last night," he says. His eyebrows rise slightly.

"Mom, I gotta go. Love you."

Conner approaches alongside Bu, who bounces from foot to foot like a child engaged at play, clearly ignoring the signs that he's got to pee. "Gunthreon, Bu and I are going to my place," Conner says. "I've got some business waiting for me, and my buddy here has agreed to take a look at the sump pump that's been giving me problems." Bu fidgets with his fanny pack as he looks to Gunthreon for an "Okay." He doesn't get an immediate answer.

Instead, Gunthreon says, "Everyone gather round, please." We all look to him. "I have come up with some plans, and I need to know if you are all still behind me." Everyone nods, except for me, but he seems to ignore it anyway. "Here it is: Tomorrow, Kailey, you are to live your life like normal—go to work, go out with your girlfriends, do whatever you like. Only thing is, Jenna and Cheeto will be staying with you. Conner, you go about your daily business also, and when Bu is finished with your sump pump, Fidello will take him back to my place. Lupa and I will be doing some traveling. We will be unreachable." Lupa's quizzical face makes me believe she wasn't really aware of Gunthreon's new plan. "Oh, and Ladimer, just get used to your new adult life in Abscondia. The only thing I ask is that you stay here and do not travel to Renhala."

It's Ladimer's turn to look confused. "Excuse me, Gunthreon, but I think you're outstepping your boundaries on that one."

Gunthreon suddenly gets testy, for his energy heats up around him. "All I ask is that you keep your distance from any hotspots. That's all." He inhales and cools down.

Ladimer shrugs. "I guess I can try."

Gunthreon smiles. "I shall see you all soon." He moves, then pauses. "At the wedding, as a matter of fact." He bows, grabs Lupa by the hand and disappears.

"Oh my god!" I shout. "The wedding! And what the hell?" I stand with my hand on my forehead, dazed.

Ladimer's energy is confused, as well, for it begins swirling around him, in an anxious and nervous sort of way. "Gunthreon's a smart man, and I put my faith in him, despite these latest antics." He seems to be convincing himself more than me.

"Why would he just leave now? He cries how important things are and that we need to take action, yet he abandons us," I say.

Ladimer shrugs. "Let's just go along with the plan for now. Just one thing: Kailey, keep your guard up. If that means against me, too, sobeit. I need you safe."

I nod at him as Jenna comes near, tugging on my pants. I look down at her as she displays the hugest grin I've ever seen on her face.

"Yeah! Let's go to your place, Kailey!" She turns, and Ladimer and I follow her lead as Fidello pulls up to Gunthreon's place.

Ladimer, apparently sensing my uncertainty, says, "Namakon." I recognize his hint that I mustn't say anything in front of someone with a direct link to Gunthreon.

As we all climb into the limo—Bu and Ladimer directly across from me and Conner—Conner says, "Am I still your date for Saturday?"

"Of course," I reply, as Ladimer meets my eyes.

"Good," he says, grabbing my hand, softly, in his warm and comfortable grasp.

CR

My day goes by more smoothly than I could have imagined. Except for the occasional disappearance of minor appliances and a few blood spottings from Cheeto, everything is golden.

Friday morning arrives and the thought of leaving Jenna alone in my apartment conjures thoughts of fire engines and police. "Jenna, what do you think about going to work with me?" I can hear her heart pounding as she thinks it over in her tiny little nappy head. I have to admit her presence will also help me after my time away. I feel so different from the Kailey I was, less than two weeks ago.

She quickly climbs into the larger white, leather replica Prada bag I carry to work. "You know this is not real animal hide," says Jenna. I thought only Amber would know. I just tell Jenna to mind her own business.

We make sure both animals are fed and have emptied their bladders outside in back, Cheeto more discreetly. She's so pregnant now that she can't even get up the stairs, so I end up carrying her back to my apartment. They both get one treat and a stern talking-to about getting along and having no parties while I'm at work. Jenna just stares at me like I'm crazy.

On our way to the bus stop, we pass the neighborhood gangbangers on the corner. Joe is slurping down a convenient store slushie—his mouth stained red—and the others are engaged in a game of dice. I speed up, hoping they miss me, but the comments begin flowing freely.

"Hey, hot momma! Why in such a hurry?"

"Did my cuz, Jose, sell you that replica?"

"No pepper spray today?"

Instead of walking faster, I turn as I walk, yelling, "Go to school and get an education, hoodlums!"

Jenna snickers inside my bag.

"Shut up," I squawk.

Just as I'm out of earshot, I hear Joe say, "Dude, definitely insane. Look. Talking to her bag." They all laugh.

Later, when Jenna sees the bus approaching, she thinks it some square sort of dragon, but after my continual reassurance that it's not going to digest us once we board, she agrees to ride. After sitting down, I adjust my purse so that she can peek out the window without anyone seeing her. Several quiet shrieks later, we hit our stop and I exit the bus, stepping onto the Mag Mile—Michigan Avenue—known for shopping galore.

"How you doing, Jenna?" I whisper into my purse, getting a thumbs-up from a homeless woman rummaging through the nearest garbage bin. I just wave back.

After walking for a block, while waiting for a particularly long light to change, Jenna starts frantically moving around in my purse, snarling. My hands start shaking the bag, hoping that she'll settle down. "Kailey, Kailey! She sees me!" exclaims Jenna. "Hurry! Go! Go."

"I can't! Who the hell are you talking about? There's nobody around us," I say. "Are we being followed?" Fear overwhelms me, and I make sure my pepper spray is in the front pocket of my purse.

"That creature! It keeps staring at me, even when I flash my teeth. It has no aura." She then whispers, "Must be a deathman in disguise."

A look at a nearby storefront's window turns on the light bulb above my head. "You dumbass! That's a mannequin. You must not have any of those in Renhala. She's made of plastic. Totally inanimate."

"Oh. We do not have any, at least where I've been. That's so stupid. Are we almost at your place of occupation? This is tiring me."

As I cross the street, I make sure to put up my dukes toward each mannequin as we pass.

"I get it," grunts Jenna. "Knock it off before I shred your wallet."

"Behave yourself, because we're close," I say. "When we're there, you *have* to stay hidden. If something stupid happens, I could lose my job. You'd see *me* out here digging through garbage cans."

My arrival at work is much quieter than normal. I enter our lobby and smile widely at our frowning receptionist as she says, "Deciding to grace us with your presence?" I ignore her.

My boss gets a simple wave from me as I run to my office, but of course, that doesn't stop him. Before I get to close my door, he sticks his foot in. "Nice to see you," Evan says. "Hope all is well?" He squints at me, as if trying to peer inside my head through my eyes.

"Oh, I'm good, thanks," I respond. "I sure have a lot of work to do. Better get to it." I try and shut the door, but he pries it open again.

"So who's the gentleman that called in for you?" he asks, raising one eyebrow. "Sounds a little old for you, don't you think?" It's meant as a joke, so I just smile at him.

"My uncle," I reply—being the first thing that popped into my head.

"Uh huh. Hey, I wanted to tell you that I had a dream about you last night."

He has captured my interest. "Yeah?"

"All I can remember is that some guy named Vladimir stabbed you right here" —he points to the location on himself— "on your shoulder blade. Strange, eh? I've been known for having a few premonitions. Just wanted to let you know, just in case." I

384

frown and he notices my worry, his energy transforming into regret. "Oh, god. I'm so sorry, maybe I shouldn't have told you." He pauses. "I've also been known for putting my foot in my mouth, perhaps more often."

"Don't worry. I appreciate your warning. I'm okay. Really. Maybe you should lay off the early morning bourbon." He laughs as he leaves, because he hasn't had a drink in ten years, or at least that's what he tells me.

Once he's gone, my calculator seems to strike Jenna's fancy, so I put it and her on the floor under the desk, by my feet. Some music to work to sounds like a good idea, so I switch on my inherited AM/FM radio—which I've been told has been here since Helping Hands opened its doors. I find something with a fun beat and log into my computer, my fingers tapping to the music. Plenty of e-mails sit in my inbox, waiting for my answer.

Time flies, and before long, it's close to lunch time. A familiar smell floats to my nose and I wonder who made the popcorn.

"Jenna, you hungry?" I ask. I look toward where my small friend should be and realize she's not there. At that moment, a shriek from a nearby office sends me out of my chair and racing down the hall. Lisa, of the editorial department, weighing in at around three hundred, kneels wobbily on her chair, looking down toward the pile of papers on her floor. Her popcorn is spilled everywhere.

"Kailey! There is a mouse in my office. A big one! I *hate* mice. Go get Sienna!" she shouts. Sienna is our office manager, who deals with all matters other employees would rather think they are above doing, like picking whether the office kitchen should be supplied with teaspoons or soup spoons.

I hold out my arm to her. "I'm fine with rodents, so let me look," I respond. "Why don't you just jump down and wait outside? It's okay. But run fast!" Her speed is amazing. I close her door.

"Jenna! Out *now*!" I yap. Jenna's crazy hair slowly rises from behind a pile of manuscripts. She has popcorn shoved in her mouth and stuck in her hair. Slowly, she comes out into the open, carrying two more pieces in her arms.

"I was hungry, and this stuff smelled *delicious*! You were starving me, and your feet stink. No harm anyway, she thought I was a fluffmouse."

"They do not stink!"

"Yes they do, just like cricket dung."

I look at my feet, knowing they may smell, slightly. "What the hell does cricket dung smell like?"

"Your feet."

I make Jenna crawl into a nearby UPS box. As I walk out of the office, Amber stands near Lisa.

Lisa shrieks, knowing I have the creature in the box. Jenna wiggles around for fun so I shake the box, once, really hard. "Everything's fine now," I say. "Let me go get rid of this varmint." Amber's insinuating smile bothers me, but I smile back.

After an encounter with a mouse while working at Burrito Burgers, she's well aware of my unnatural and over-the-top fear of small mice. "Can I come see you after I dump this?" I ask.

"You know where to find me," she says, heading back toward her office.

I take the back exit, and once outside, in case anyone's watching, I bend over to let the "mouse" free in the bushes. I carry the box back in with Jenna still inside and dump her once again in my purse. "Stay," I say. Rummaging inside my desk drawer, I find two caramel almond granola bars. When I violently toss one into my bag, I hear an "Ouch!" The wrapper starts rustling, and then there's silence. "A few more hours of work and then we can head home."

"You gotta stop talking to yourself. You may be scared at what answers back," says my boss, suddenly in my doorway. He throws a stack of papers on my desk. "Next client. See ya."

I browse the file, then search the internet for over an hour, trying to find out any information on a Ms. Carmela Johnson, an old, retired English teacher from Louisiana chosen by us for a special award. The search turns up nothing useful. Fortunately, there are just two requests: a fancy lunch and a well thought-out gift of some sort. Simple enough. A call to my contact, Demetri, at the new three-star restaurant, True, guarantees me a table for two when needed, and a guarantee from myself to call him when I'm bored one evening locks the deal completely. Of course, I'll never be *that* bored.

I laugh when Jenna tells me how disgusting I am. "What would your boys think?" she says with righteousness and sarcasm.

"*My boys*? I don't think so." I smile to myself.

When Jenna points to the clock, it knocks me out of my sinister, and very personal, thoughts. I get up to leave. As I head toward Amber's office, I find my boss still sitting in his chair, tapping away at his computer. "Staying late?" I ask.

He nods to me as his fingers fly over the keyboard, his face glued to the screen. "See ya," he says.

As we approach Amber's office, Jenna says, "You owe me a favor for making me hang out at your boring work all day. As always, I was the only excitement in anybody's day."

"Oh, I do?" I say. But it *was* boring...and she was indeed the excitement of the day.

I find Amber sitting in her chair, admiring the rooftop pool across from our building. "Should we crash that sometime?" I ask.

Startled, Amber jumps in her seat, grabbing at her stomach. I look to her hand, and she quickly removes it. "Damn you Kailey!" she yelps. "You forget how to knock? You don't return my calls, but you can barge in like you own the place." Her hands move

387

from folder to folder on her desk, and across the headlining page of today's *Chicago Tribune*. It's an article about a mysterious pack of mutant dogs on the loose.

As I look at the paper, I say, "That's some pretty scary stuff, ain't it?"

"It is. Wonder what the government's doing about it. It's gotta be a hot roundtable topic, you think? Maybe summit-worthy?"

"Wow. Them's some big words for you. I don't think I've ever even heard you say the g-word."

She squints her eyes at me, angrily. "Russell and I do more than just fuck, Kailey." My cheeks redden. "We have decent conversations. He actually respects my opinions, and thinks I have great ideas. Enough with the superiority complex."

"What? No. I didn't mean anything disrespectful. I'm just razzing you." I say, sitting in one of her chairs, changing the topic of discussion. "What can I do for you before the wedding? You know we never even had a bachelorette party! I've been so busy with stupid crap that I haven't even checked in with you. I sincerely apologize. Nice best friend I am." I give her my ashamed face. "Want to go out tonight maybe, just for a little bite to eat and a stripper or two?" I ask, enthusiastically, with a smile plastered on my face.

"Yes, you *have* been missing in action. What've you been doing?" I just stare at her, speechless, and she adds, "Nevermind. That's your business. Honestly, your offer sounds so tempting," she says, "but I don't think I'm up to it." Her face is not enthused, and she looks exhausted. "I've got to save up my energy. It's my big day." I sit and look Amber over, noticing a difference in her—both in her looks, and her attitude. She has seemingly matured and in my absence, has grown into a responsible woman, in so short of an amount of time.

"Well, just promise to put some time away after the wedding for me so we can hang out again. I miss you." I say. "We can catch up, maybe share new secrets?" I hesitate, giving her an in to blab about her pregnancy, but she ignores it. "It seems that our lives have gotten so busy lately. You're my best friend, Amber, I'm not letting you go away once you get married and all."

She laughs playfully and grabs my hand. "You always know how to make me laugh," she says. "Now you go home and get some beauty rest for tomorrow. You surely need it."

"Bitch."

"Tramp."

From there, Jenna and I head out. As we ride the elevator down, she says, "How about we go shopping for an outfit for you? I looked in your closet, and you have nothing worth wearing to this wedding you speak of."

Unfortunately, she's right. "I wish you were invited. You'd be the life of the party!" I say this with true sincerity, and she nods.

We find an awesome boutique, and it doesn't take me long to find a dress that fits rather nicely: a lavender (one of only two colors that looks classy against my red hair), sleeveless, short-length number, with a plunging, yet classy, V-neck.

After she escapes my purse, I find Jenna biting the foot of a rather thin and pale mannequin. But she does find me the perfect jewelry: a long, sterling rod pendant with a beautifully-faceted amethyst gracing the bottom tip, adorning a delicate sterling chain, and matching earrings and bracelet.

We make it home after a long day and agree that a pizza and some TV is the perfect way to end it. Jenna does the honors of ordering, and I turn on WGN's nine o'clock news as I change into my pajamas. I decide to keep it on for Jenna, so she can learn a little more about my realm.

The top story is about the missing physicist and biologist. They show an outdated—from the looks of the polyester brown button-down he's wearing—and unflattering picture of Dr. Martine with a pair of huge, nerdy glasses on his face.

Quickly deciding that that's enough news, I start flipping through the channels, finding something more interesting on PBS—something about butterflies.

Later, as I'm about to call it a night, Jenna gets up and stands in front of me, looking anxious. "I was wondering if I can call on that favor now, before the evening is over," she says. I don't remember exactly agreeing to the favor, but I agree to hear her out, though my heart races a bit, fearful of what she may ask.

"Can we possibly do a little experiment involving this?" She holds up my smartphone.

My eyes widen a bit. "What kind of experiment? Am I going to need Bu to put it back together again?" I snatch back the phone.

"I hope not."

As I start dialing, I tell her, "Just let me call Conner before we do our little 'experiment.' Deal?"

"Okay." I walk away into my bedroom for some privacy.

He answers after the first ring. "I will be wearing a lavender tie. Will it match?" he inquires.

"As a matter of fact, yes."

"You look good in lavender." I can hear his smile as he speaks. "I went out and bought a present from their registry," Conner says. "You don't mind, do you? There was so much left on it. I kinda feel bad. Maybe they'll get a windfall of cash from everyone else. I thought we could both go in on the gift, if you want? I got a card, too." My amazement keeps me silent, except for the loud slap to my forehead. "Hello?" he says, checking to see if I'm still on the line.

"Sorry. I've had no time, so I was just gonna shove money in a card last minute. You, at least, put thought into the gift," I say. "And, I'll most graciously accept their thanks for a gift I've selfishly signed my name to. Ugh, how pathetic. She's my best friend!"

"I've already wrapped it too," he says. My shoulders can't slump any further. "You can sign the card when I pick you up. I'll see you tomorrow. I'm sure you'll look ravishing." He pauses a bit. "And I'll definitely be asking you to pay up for your half."

My cheeks redden a bit. "I'll make sure to clean up nicely for you. See you tomorrow." I'm suddenly very nervous.

Jenna runs in and sits on my bed as I change into pajamas. "Let's check if it works."

"Huh?"

"That," she says, pointing to my smartphone. "I want to see if it works if I try calling you from Renhala," she says with a mischievous grin that scares me.

"I don't think that it will. Anyway, G warned us about travelling."

"But you don't know until we try. And who is Gunthreon to boss everyone around? Who knows what he's really up to?" She watches my facial features. "And I'll be back super quick!"

I feel reluctant to try, but she's right. I can read his energies, but I don't know the details of his brain. He could very well be betraying us all, and we're just going along for the ride, following in his wake.

"If you run off, I swear I will hunt you down and strangle you with your little holly necklace, so don't even think about it," I warn. I point at her, and she tilts her head ever so slightly. "Here." I hand her my phone, then write down my apartment phone number and hand that to her. I don't let go as she puts her hand on it. She smiles at me and disappears in an instant.

Slowly, I count to ten as I sit on my bed, staring at the spot she just disappeared from. "I have faith in you. Don't let me down."

I sit by my apartment phone, waiting. After five minutes pass, I start pacing back and forth, back and forth. Kioto and Cheeto both know something is up, for they both avoid eye contact with me. A second before I'm about to call my cell phone, Cheeto lets out a single yelp of pain. She stands up and slumps back down, yelping again. Kioto starts licking her face, and I know what's about to happen.

"No no no! Not now, Cheeto. Damn! What do you need, girl?" The yelps soon turn to screams, then stop suddenly as she gets up and hides underneath my dining-room table. I try to crawl underneath with her, but she bares her deadly sharp teeth at me. "Sorry, girlfriend," I say. My pacing starts up at freakish speed again as a pool of blood spreads out underneath Cheeto. *Why is there so much blood? It's so dark—almost black.* I feel fear growing inside me, like a tumor, forcing me to retreat in what room is left inside. My thoughts return to the day of my assault. *My warm blood drips from my neck as the creature reaches out a hand, collecting a drop, and bringing it to his mouth. It smiles as*—Cheeto starts panting fast and heavy. I look to her and her pathetic little face. She needs me. I choose to wipe away the memories as I reach to her,—she who needs me—reaching for somewhere to grasp. I find it, and as I take hold, she turns and looks at me. Her breathing slows as I caress gently along her body, helping her complete her task. She allows me to continue as I gently caress her belly area. Her muscles contract, her body responding to the need. A pushing sensation from deep inside her has me adding my own energy—my strength, when suddenly Cheeto starts screaming again, and her eyes bulge. I retract my energy as I stand, helpless as she closes her eyes and trembles.

At the same moment I feel my energy heating up from fear, Kioto starts growling as Jenna appears, running at me full speed.

"Kailey, run!" she yells. "Bring us somewhere safe, and *now!*" Her hand still grips my phone, her voice weak as I bend down to her.

I hear a loud thump outside in my hallway, and we both stop and hold each other, staring at my front door. Kioto stands next to me, her hair on her back standing straight up. She moves to stand between the door and Jenna and I. I notice blood running down Jenna's arm, dripping onto my hand. As Jenna's gaze meets mine, Cheeto screams in agony. I don't know what to do.

"*Now!*" Jenna screams with all her might, directly in my face. Something takes over my body, and then I am somewhere hidden inside myself as my mouth screams a word in an unidentifiable, alien language. Jenna's mouth drops, and we are transported— somewhere.

Chapter 51

Hidden
ॐ

There is absolute silence.
Nothingness.
A change in consciousness.
A feeling of being watched.
The smell of mud, of earth.
The sensation of birth, of life, of love, of complete wholeness.
The sensation of pain, of desperation, of loss, of falling apart into a
million pieces.

A voice as loud as a sonic boom breathes a simple word: "Continue." It seems as though time stops.

Our sense of being arrives back in Abscondia, and we seem almost to step back in time. We stare as Cheeto's second pup pops out. She lovingly licks off each newborn pup. Both sets of little eyes are already open to the world, staring at their mother.

Kioto stands, staring at me, but when I walk to her, she cowers in fear. I walk toward her, reaching out my hand, but she turns her head, only her eyes watching my every move. "What's wrong, girl?" She slinks away into my bedroom.

I turn to make sure Jenna is also witnessing this, and she shakes her head back and forth ever so slowly. She then looks at her hand. "Oops" slips from her tongue.

I look at her hand, and my anger brings me to my senses too quickly. "Damn it, Jenna!" My smartphone is gone. "You are so going to get me a new one. I don't know how, but..." But I'm distracted. I try rolling over the strange place and strange feelings in my head, but they're already fading, slowly becoming a lost experience. Within five minutes, no memory is left of our brief trip to wherever we went, and only a feeling of fright for Cheeto's little babies remains.

"Jenna, what happened?" I ask. "What was chasing you?"

"I was expecting to arrive in my forest, near my hangout, and I did, but what was there was horrible," Jenna wails. "It's like they were waiting for me—and the trees! Poor Lamlut. Oh, poor thing! They burned him! There were grebles everywhere, and with them were these pet things they had on chains. I've never seen anything like them. I felt the fear of Velopa. I don't know what they were doing there, but they saw me, and I came back as fast as I could. I think we're safe here."

"We need to call someone—my mom, no, Ladimer. No more travelling! Where's my phone?"

Jenna looks to her hand, then starts walking around, looking for it. "I don't know. I just had it! You sure you didn't take it?"

"No, I didn't...I guess I'll have to use my apartment phone while you look for my cell."

The phone rings and rings, but there's no answer at Ladimer's place. I try my mom and she, too, is unreachable, except for her ancient answering machine: "You've reached the machine. You know what to do." It's one of the many antiquities she loves.

With no other option, and the inability to shake the feeling that something is just not right, we hang out on the couch, not saying a word. I grab a biscuit for Kioto and try coaxing her from my bedroom, but she won't move from underneath my bed.

"Your aura is different, Kailey," Jenna says, looking at the air around me.

"How?"

"It's just *different*. Can't pinpoint it, exactly."

We make sure Cheeto has enough water and food under my table. I attempt to pet a pup, but Cheeto's not keen on the idea, so we decide to let her have her mommy time with them. "Let's name them tomorrow," I suggest to Jenna.

"Ugly and uglier."

"I'll keep trying to reach someone," I say, as I call my mom and Ladimer again. No luck.

I pick up my new pendulum and cradle it as I continue my attempts to reach someone by phone. My last thought is that maybe I should call Conner, but I'm too exhausted even to move an eyelid. Me and Jenna eventually fall asleep on my couch, hugging one another.

જ

When I open my eyes, the prairieland seems absolutely deserted. My pajamas blow in the dry wind as the swift smell of dried flowers travels up my nose, sending me back, to a time of holding onto my mom's pant leg as she cruised through the local hobby shop's floral department. It makes me smile.

It looks like death has planted itself here, but I know deep inside that this place is full of life—life hidden to the normal eye. *Why am I here?* The ground crunches underneath my feet, and I sit, examining the dirt beneath me. I let it run through my hand, and as it falls to the ground, each small piece grows legs and scurries away.

A panting noise from behind makes me grab my monk's spade as I jump up and twirl around, striking the pose of a deadly ballerina. Three ceetchans sit before me—one momma and two tiny pups. The pups crawl to me and lap at my feet as Cheeto watches. "Can I pet them?" I ask. She shows no resistance, so I bend down and pick them up in my arms, caressing their little heads and kissing them on their eyes.

Cheeto stands and turns in the opposite direction, walking away from me. She stops and looks at me as though I am to follow. I snuggle her pups in my arms and follow as Cheeto leads me to some kind of burrow a few yards away, tucked under a single tree. Her butt disappears as she enters the hole in the ground. "I really

hope you don't expect me to fit in there," I remark. I wait for her
to come out. Finally, her nose peeks out, and she waits for me to
come face to face with her before she descends back down the
hole. Her babies follow her willingly.

I can barely squeeze my shoulders through the hole, but
then, almost like magic, the hole widens, and I fall hard into the
dirt floor below. I look up, and the hole is tiny once more. "Why,
call me Alice," I say, but as I stand looking up, I suddenly rock on
my feet, losing my balance for a brief few seconds as an intense
energy brushes past me. It swims around me, then dissipates.

Cheeto continues to walk down a long corridor of dirt and
tree roots. I follow, eager to find what she has to show me. She
rounds a corner.

"Oh, sweetie, come here and let me see your babies!" speaks
a woman's voice, speaking out from beyond the dirt wall. I freeze
in my tracks. "They are *adorable*. Here, come drink some fresh water
and lie down for a spell. The meek shall inherit the earth." I
tremble as the voice talks, wanting to bow in submission before
her, yet fearing for my life. "I know you're there, honey," says the
voice. "Why don't you come and sit with us, too."

I peek around the corner, and we both see each other. I
proceed slowly and cautiously in her direction. I know instantly
whose presence I stand in.

An old, wrinkled face sits before me, with long, soft, gray
braids wrapped with multi-colored feathers piled neatly behind her.
She's an old black woman who looks like she's led a hell of a hard
life.

The room consists of Neda on a rocking chair, a small
table—smoothly weathered from age with one, alabaster stone
bowl atop it, and two copper-hinged cedar chests.

Neda rocks in her rocking chair made from the tree roots
that descend from the earth above our heads. Her feet do not even
reach the ground, but still she rocks, and it's the roots themselves

rocking her, slowly, as she sits with her hands busily knitting something in her lap.

I do what seemingly comes naturally these days, and reach my feeler to her, approaching with caution, but awe. As I am centimeters within her energy, she breathes in and smiles, then puts her arms out from her sides, as one does when being frisked. "Go ahead dearie. I will allow it this once." She closes her eyes and I dive into her energy. It swoops me in and swirls my consciousness around and around. I taste warmth, sadness, coolness, calmness, frustration, happiness—an emotional cocktail if you will— everything, all at once. It sends my mind reeling and I withdraw my feeler, opening my eyes, and suddenly noticing I stand directly in front of her, within a foot.

She is so familiar to me, but I cannot place where I've seen her. She spews love and comfort, compelling me to sit near her feet. As she drops her knitting needles to the ground near me, I gulp loudly, for they are clearly made from weathered bones. Whether human or not, I do not ask. But her hands are gentle as she caresses my hair, working it behind my ears. The tears flow from my eyes, and I cannot stop them, no matter how hard I try.

"It's all right. Let them flow. You're safe here," she says. "It's hard, I know. You're doing a fine job, girl."

After my tears stop flowing, I look up into her eyes. "Neda?"

"I'm known by many a name. Call me what you will," she responds. "You're not afraid of me, are you?"

I shake my head no, but I'm partially lying. *Can one partially lie?*

"Good. You know, my natural form is far more hideous than your deepest fears. I like this now—makes both me and you comfortable. Good choice, Kailey." My eyebrows scrunch in confusion. "My elemental form is far too boring. Stupid ball of light. Hmph."

"What do I need to do?" It escapes my mouth without any thought on my part.

"My, my, you just jump right in, eh?" She giggles to herself and slides off her rocking chair. I stand and grab her hand as she wobbles over to the nearest table. "It is not my job to tell you what to do," she says. "I will, however, share what I know with you, and how about you take it from there?" From the stone bowl—suddenly full—she hands me a small, round, bulbous thing, and takes one of the same. Quickly, she pops it into her mouth and chews. "Yum. Go ahead, I'm not going to poison you." I smell it, then toss it in my mouth and chew. It's actually very sweet and soft, and reminds me of candied sweet potatoes.

"That *is* yummy."

"First off, we need to make an exchange. I sense something on you. If you give it to me, I will give you information. Deal?" she says, standing in front of me. My hand moves involuntarily and rises up slowly, letting the pendulum hang and twirl.

"Ah, I knew it! May I have it back?" I hand it over willingly and she puts it in her pocket and pats her pocket, apparently happy with herself. "You, as my child, as everything else living, know all," she states. She walks back and slumps in her chair, smiling, looking at me as if that was it—the one answer for everything.

This time, I laugh. "What?"

"It talks to you, but your technology is too damn loud! Use that brain of yours! I mean it—use it. Use that whole area sitting there, being ignored, being brushed off like you're crazy." She points to my head. "How many times must you creatures be shown your own intelligence? Your own *potential?*" A sense of frustration seems to cover her face and I sneak in my feeler, but she swats at it and I actually feel it—like a slap to the face.

"Think of animals, and how they seem to know before humans that an earthquake or tsunami is coming. They flee. *They listen to this!*" She points to that same area of her head. "Tell me how many dead animals you see lying around that have *not* been killed by your technology, like your cars and trucks." Her stare is intense. "They die on their own, hidden from sight, because they know when they are dying. Oh, and don't even get me started on your 'psychics' and how they seem to know everything. They're revealed images by their own minds, and they decipher them. They may come up with something ridiculous or far-fetched, but they're revealed truth by their own brains, and they *pay attention*. And how about food cravings? Once again, your body is telling you what it needs. Stories of sudden strength? The ability to lift cars in times of need? Hon, I could go on and on, but I don't think I need to. It's making me tired. We have a guest anyway."

She points behind me, and I see it coming before I feel anything. A deathman approaches, carrying a ball of light in its hands.

"Bring it here, peaches," she advises the creature. Before she makes it halfway to one of the cedar chests, another deathman appears. "Ugh. Kailey you've got to do something about this. Since my old friend disappeared, I'm getting them *all*! It's making me just too damn tired. And hiding my energy is exhausting."

"Your old friend? Disappeared?"

"Without darkness, how would we know light?" She stares at me. "Well, anyways, I truly don't know what has happened, and I am fearful, for I don't know how long anything will survive with the imbalance. This isn't how it's supposed to be. It's not fair." The balls are handed to her, and she stands holding them with her eyes closed and slowly places both of them in one of the cedar chests. "How will we judge who wins?" The deathmen wave to her and head off from where they came.

I am totally perplexed. My anxiety starts bubbling slowly inside me. "This is some sort of game?" I grunt. "You're jeopardizing lives for a stupid game? If you are who you say you are, why don't you know the answers? How am I supposed to help? You created all this, so why the hell don't you do something about it?!" I immediately cover my mouth with my hand, mortified.

Neda's eyebrows rise slowly, and as she stares at me, her face contorts to one of the most gruesome things I have ever experienced. Combine every single horror film I have seen and every single nightmarish fireside story my ears have ever heard, and it is all unicorns and teddy bears compared to this. I slump to the ground and cover my head. I want to bury myself as far into the ground as possible. The image of her face is burned into my brain, becoming more horrific with every breath I take.

"So sorry, sweetie. Come on, get up, get up. You are karmelean. It'll come. I only pick the best of 'em." She helps me up with surprisingly strong hands. "Just please, take what I've told you, and also know that bloodshed is not the answer. The force is always returned. I know the temptation is strong—hell, I enjoy it once in awhile myself. But it's not the answer." She exhales. "You must go now. I must admit I am becoming tired of this form, and of this whole situation. I am so tired of you all thinking we are both beginning and end, good and evil. It's not that simple, Kailey."

I have no idea what the hell she's talking about, and it shows on my face. Her glorious face beams back at me, and before I am sent home, the last words I hear are, "We two were not the first, Kailey."

Chapter 52

Shining
CR

"Kailey, wake up!" Little hands tug on my arm. "Kailey!" Cold water splashes onto my face and Kioto jumps off my bed.

"Ahhhhh! What the hell?!" I wipe my eyes and look down at my white cotton pajamas, that are now see-through, revealing my green, polka-dot underwear.

Ladimer stands over me. "I'll turn if you want," he says, but he doesn't, instead grinning widely. I feel blood rushing to places I don't want to admit as I look into his eyes. I pick up the nearest pillow and throw it at him.

"Whoa. You're quick, but not that quick." He grabs the pillow and tosses it back at me. Jenna gets hit in the crossfire and falls off my bed. Kioto wags her tail and jumps on Ladimer, evidently much more cheery, and wanting to get in on the fun. He pets her head and allows her to lick his face.

Jenna's head pops up from down on the floor. "I save your life, and that's how I'm treated?"

"Karma," I simply say as I help her up onto my bed. "Saved my life?"

"You weren't responding to me, so I called him. He answered. What did you do? Where did you go?"

"What do you mean?"

"You met one, didn't you?" she drones, her mouth open wide as she stares at me. "Don't you even try and lie. I know these things. How did you do it?"

I sit, not saying one word, instead looking straight ahead.

"She did," Ladimer replies. "You are karma indeed. I'll fix you something to eat, but promise to tell me the story." He leaves, and I soon hear my pots and pans banging and my refrigerator door opening and closing. I appreciate not hearing the microwave open and close.

Jenna waits for a response.

"I have to say I might have," I play. "How do you know?"

"You have an extra white light in your aura that was not there when you fell asleep. That comes from one touched by a Higher One."

"Uh-hmm."

"That's it? Come on!"

"Let me get up and get dressed, first," Jenna stands and I have to shoo her out of my room. I get dressed as I ponder what information to actually share.

I leave my room and then notice Cheeto and her pups are missing. "Where's Cheeto?"

"She was missing this morning. Probably went home."

This makes me sad, until I look at the bloodstain under the table. "How the hell am I going to get that out?"

Ladimer flips my over hard egg onto my English muffin and says, "OxiClean works wonders," as he hands me the plate.

I sit at the table with them, avoiding the blood as I spill my story—all of it. Both sit motionless, staring at the clock on the wall. "Well?" I say. I hope for some kind of answer or maybe even some questions, but nothing happens—just blank stares and shrugs.

"At least we know Neda is somewhere safe. But why is the urn cracking, then?" Ladimer says. "It's just too bad that Neda depends on creatures like us to do something about the imbalance. We need to talk to Gunthreon. Unfortunately, I have no idea where he and Lupa are. I sent out some spies looking for them and got absolutely nothing." He sighs. "Let's just go on with our day and our plans, because right now, it's the only thing we *can* do. I need to pick your mom up, so I need to pretty myself up. I'll see you at the wedding." His hug is tight, and the kiss on my head is soft. "Oh, and don't worry about that mutt. I'm sure she's fine." The door shuts quietly behind him.

Kioto whines and sniffs under the table. I call her to me, and she looks up at me, pleadingly. "You heard Ladimer," I say to her. "She's fine. Everything's fine." But it's my attempt at reassuring Kioto that makes me realize things are so very wrong.

After sitting, staring out the window for an eternity, running my visit with Neda over and over in my head, I decide the only thing I can do is carry on with my normal day and get ready for the wedding. Gunthreon will be there, and then I can unload my information on him.

I walk to my bedroom and admire the dress and amethyst jewelry hanging on my closet door. "I love this jewelry you picked out, Jenna. It matches perfectly!" I turn to her, and she smiles, but not genuinely as she twiddles her thumbs, sitting on the bed while I put together my outfit, perfume, and makeup.

"Kailey, you'd better hurry up. Conner will be here shortly." She marches off to my front room and watches television.

I get dressed and curl my hair, then spritz on some of my special expensive perfume, making sure to get all the hot spots, especially behind the knees—a trick I learned from my mom. A twirl in the mirror reveals no panty lines and, more importantly, no dog—or ceetchan—hair.

The beaded clutch I inherited from my grandmother gets to join me, and as I pull it out and look at it, I admire the treasures I've recently hidden in it, like my father's ring. I take everything out and lay it on my bed, alongside my makeup and all the things I will need in my purse, including gum. I scan the Silver Certificate dollar bill I will never use, smell the miniature doll that smells like roses, and smile at the squashed penny my mom and I put on the railroad tracks. My dad's ring catches my eye, as always, and I pick it up, admiring the beauty of it.

Jenna walks in. "You look really pretty," she remarks. She smiles a real smile this time. "Your date is here." Her eyes lead to all my trinkets. "Fun!" She holds up the doll.

"Jenna, did you have any boyfriends back in Renhala?" I ask. A sneaky, mischievous rise of the corner of her mouth says it all as she sorts through my belongings. "You little wildcat! How many?"

"Well, if you have a few hours later, maybe I'll have to let you in on my secrets," she replies, smiling. "Don't worry, though, I'm not going to steal Conner. He's cute, but not really my type." I grab her arm and pinch her. She slaps me back as the buzzer sounds. My heart pounds wildly with excitement.

"I do look good, right? You weren't lying?" I throw all my necessities from my bed that I need into the clutch.

"You know you do. Go let him in!"

The thought of an actual date with Conner makes me tremble as I buzz him in. I open my door slightly so he can let himself into my apartment as I rush to the bathroom mirror one last time. A final coat of lip gloss is applied, and then I step out before him.

He whistles at me as he stands near the front door, large gift bag in tow. My eyes then focus on the wonder before me—definite GQ material. "Dolce & Gabbana?" I inquire.

"Why, of course."

I walk around him, checking out everything. "Salvatore Ferragamo shoes? Oh, and Armani tie."

"My goodness, you are quite the fashionista. You knew it all."

Jenna laughs as I walk by her. "Is he plastic, too?" she teases.

"What does that mean?" Conner has no idea we were admiring the very mannequin from which he must have taken his whole outfit—but it only makes him more squeezable.

"Let's go, we're going to be late," Conner snaps, abruptly. "Here's the card." He throws it at me, and it lands on the blood-stained carpet. "What's that?!"

"Cheeto had her babies. She left with them," I say, sadly.

"They're wild animals, Kailey. "You know that," he says. "Her maternal instincts probably kicked in, and she brought her pups to what she knows as home." He picks up the card and puts it in my hand while rubbing my shoulder. His hand lifts my chin up. "Don't worry, they're fine."

"Will you two go already?!" Jenna fixes herself something to eat, giving Kioto tidbits here and there.

"No table food for her!"

"Lighten up, Kailey, and go have some fun," spouts Jenna. "Stay out too late!" She shoos us out the door.

As we leave, Ladimer's former foster mom steps out of her apartment, and I don't even need to reach out my feeler to sense a renewed energy—one feeling carefree and ready to tackle the world. She apparently isn't suffering from the loss of Philip. "Wow, what a couple," she says. "Kailey, you look beautiful! Where you two off to?"

"My best friend's wedding."

"Hold on one second!" She runs into the apartment and comes back, holding a beautifully soft-scented, orange and green lily-type flower she must have taken off one of her many Ladimer-grown plants. "A beautiful girl needs a beautiful flower." She sticks it in my hair, the stem resting over my ear. Conner gives me a nod to say that it does indeed make the outfit.

"Thank you very much," I chirp, curtseying.

She closes the door behind her and she walks with us to the parking lot.

"Have a great time!" Karen says, walking to her new, hot, red convertible.

Chapter 53

Momentous
☙

After much driving, and only asking for directions twice, we arrive at the wedding hall, located in a quaint unincorporated town which looks as though it stepped out of the Victorian era. Conner and I look upward as we stretch our legs out after the long drive. He slips my silky pashmina over my shoulders and tells me once more how beautiful I look, then kisses my hand as he grabs it for the walk to the main entrance. The sky is clear, and has begun darkening, allowing the night stars to make their grand entrance. The hall looks top-notch, for Amber would have nothing else. How she arranged such a beautiful event in so little time amazes me, but then again I feel as though I have been underestimating her all along. I feel saddened that I wasn't there for her to help prepare.

Conner comments, "Gorgeous, isn't it?" as we walk through the lobby.

The front foyer is full of flowers, mostly bright red, with an occasional white rose here and there and some trailing ivy. The enormous chandeliers even have some ivy hanging down, giving the hall an "alive" sort of feeling. The lights are dim, creating an atmosphere of softness. Moss-covered vases and bowls hold delicious-smelling potpourri.

"Wow, Russell and Amber must have paid some wedding planner handsomely," I say. "Probably with some help from Gunthreon."

Conner, enthralled, gazes at the long hallway to the main ballroom doors. "This place is huge. Much bigger than it looks from the outside."

"So cool!" We walk hand-in-hand down the hallway, filling our lungs with the scent of roses and something else—something musky and tantalizing.

We finally make it to the main doors, and as we enter, I am astounded at the number of people already seated, suddenly feeling an overwhelming sense of deja vu, which results in a mean case of vertigo. I wobble a bit as a strangely familiar feeling creeps over me, but I shake it off as Conner grabs me firmly around the waist.

"You okay?" asks Conner.

I'm about to reply when I see Amber, dressed beautifully, glowing like an angel, practically floating before the crowd. Russell stands next to her, holding her hand, not looking quite as angelic. His nervous energy shakes and rattles him.

I wave as I enter the room, and she waves back, rushing to me all giggly. "You look stunning, Kailey, as usual." She kisses me and Conner on both cheeks, Amber-style. Russell makes it over and gives me a hug, then shakes Conner's hand.

I turn to Amber. "I look like a sack of garbage compared to you," I say. "Love the dress. Very flattering." Her diamond-studded tiara flickers as she moves, along with the diamonds on her neck, arm, and ears. "I never saw that set before. They look real."

"I'd hope they look real, considering they are. I inherited them. Never had a chance to wear them until now." Amber's fingers run over the diamonds in her necklace. "Russell, there's Sandy. Let's go say hello. You guys make yourselves cozy at your table. Number three." She runs off, dragging Russell.

Gunthreon and Lupa, along with my mom and Ladimer, are nowhere to be seen. "Wonder if G and Lupa are going to show up," I say.

"I hope so. Russell would be crushed if his grandfather didn't make it. Gunthreon will do his best to be here." Conner looks around at the other guests. "Amber sure has a lot of girlfriends, doesn't she?"

"Hmmm. I don't recognize—,"

"Why, yes I do!" yaps Amber, bounding up suddenly. "Lots of college friends. And a bit of family, too. Not mom, though. Whatever." She pauses, and I feel anger brewing inside her. "Well, you didn't think you were my only friend, did you?" Her laugh is sweet and innocent, but her eyes hint otherwise. "Come meet some." She grabs my hand and drags me to another table—typical social butterfly Amber.

"How'd you organize this and get all these people here so quick?" I inquire as we walk.

"I got help. From someone besides you," she answers, smiling at her guests as she walks by, carefully dragging her train. "And Russell is *loaded*." She stops at a table, almost suddenly, and twitters, "Zanthra, Zoe, meet my good friend Kailey."

Zanthra and Zoe are identical twins, and both nod at me once, very dignified-like. Zanthra stands up and shakes my hand with both of hers. "Pleasure meeting you. Amber speaks of you frequently. Love that color!" she says, twirling me around. I like her.

"Nice to meet you, too," I respond. Zoe stays seated, but smiles as Amber says she must talk to them privately for a moment. As I walk away, the doors open to the ballroom, and in step my mom and Ladimer. My smile spreads across my face as I lock eyes with my mom. She looks dashingly beautiful. She curtsies at me, and I cannot help but hold my breath as my eyes gorge on the sight of Ladimer in his perfectly tailored, black-as-night designer suit, accentuating his porcelain-white and flawless skin.

I walk toward them. "Who knew you looked so good in chartreuse and high heels, Mom."

"There are lots of things you don't know about me," she sasses. This pushes Ladimer into a fit of laughter, and my mom elbows him, falling off her heels. "Stop that, Ladimer. I have to say, you're beautiful yourself, Kailey." She holds my face with her hands and kisses me on the cheek. "I am so proud of you and who you have become." She tears up a bit.

"What's that for?"

"Just a realization, that's all. I was just wondering if I'll be here for your big day." We share a moment of understanding as we lock eyes.

My emotions flare, and I don't want to smear my newly applied makeup. "Stop that. Who else is going to pay for it?"

My mom chuckles. "Well, then, it's gonna be White Castle and Boone's Farm for all!" We all laugh as Ladimer notices the lily in my hair.

"I know where you got that," he says, brushing his hand against my ear.

Amber pushes her way in through the crowd and hugs my mom tight as tears fill her eyes, then disappear.

"You all right, honey?" my mom whispers, genuinely concerned. "Don't cry. This is *your* day—your day to shine, my daughter." She kisses Amber on the cheek.

Amber wipes her eyes. "I'm fine. Please, enjoy yourself, and have a seat at Kailey's table. Thank you for coming. It means so much to me." She points to a seated Conner, who waves. My mom and Ladimer walk over to the table, arm in arm.

As Amber walks away, a hand lands on my shoulder, and I turn to see Russell, who looks like he may lose his lunch. "Kailey, have you seen my grandfather?"

"No, but I'm sure he's on his way."

"Was he travelling?"

I stare at him, not wanting to say a word. "Not sure, actually."

"Since he's not here, I have to ask something of you. I know it's unconventional and all, but can you handle this?" He opens his hand, and Amber's three carat diamond wedding band shimmers brilliantly. My mouth drops open and he laughs. "Amber likes nice—and expensive—things," he grunts.

"You were going to have Gunthreon do the honor, huh? And you have nobody else you trust?" He nods. "I would be honored, Russell." I slip the ring into my clutch and he seems relieved.

I make my way back to table three, joining the conversation between my mom and Conner. "Your compliment means so much, considering your gift," my mom says.

I shake my head at her. "All right already. Enough about how scrumptious you look."

I drape my shawl across my chair, then announce, "I've got to use the little girl's room to powder my nose. I'll be back." I work my way through the crowd, and finally find the bathroom, reeking of Tilex and bubble gum sweetness. I seem to be the only one here, but as I stand adding some blush to my cheeks, I sense an energy that should not be here.

I whip around, scanning the bathroom. "Where are you? I know you're here." I walk silently over to the tall floral arrangement in the corner and move it as quick as I can.

"I couldn't help it!"

I rush over to the door and lock it. "What are you doing here?"

Jenna has her legs crossed and her arms behind her, her face downturned. "I was bored," she mumbles, trying to give me sad eyes. "I just jumped in the gift bag."

"Bored? Oh, Jenna, you better hide, and hide well. You won't fit in my purse today!"

"The colors in this place are all swirly and—" I cover her mouth.

"No excuses! Do not be seen!" I unlock the door and return to the ballroom.

The minister arrives, looking as if he may have kicked back a few already: bloodshot eyes, hair askew, obvious slurring, and an unnatural interest in the happy couple. He asks us all to take our seats. "Thank you, everyone, for coming together to take part in this *very* special occasion," he says. From here, he goes on and on, but I hear nothing as Jenna peeks her tiny little head through the doorway. She seems to be pointing at a guest, and I try to give her the angry face without anyone else noticing. Ladimer does, and he looks toward Jenna. His eyes widen. He then looks as angry as I do, but directs it toward me. I just shake my head.

Jenna keeps pointing, so I look at table seven toward a gentlemen slouching in his seat. The lights have dimmed, so I have to squint to see his face. I don't recognize the man in the glasses and tuxedo. In reaching him, I feel an extremely nervous energy which makes me feel like puking. I also sense *hesitation*? When I turn back to Jenna, she's not at the door.

Inconspicuously, I look along the floor. As I "accidentally" drop my napkin near my feet and bend to pick it up, I notice she's already underneath the table.

"Your friend's powers are strong," she whispers, pointing at the wedding table.

"Yeah, Russell is special."

"What an ugly name to call…that's not—,"

But before she can complete her sentence, Ladimer scoops her up and tucks her under his jacket. "I'll be right back. Excuse me." He heads out the door fastidiously.

Amber and Russell make it up to the minister, and Russell calls me over with his hand. "Oh, yeah," I squeak. I stand off to the side and wait for my cue.

As the minister goes on and on, again, my eyes wander. I see the ballroom doors open slightly as two people enter and rush toward our table. As they appear under one of the lights, I recognize them. Gunthreon and Lupa are dressed for the occasion, but I see that Lupa has a cut on her face and Gunthreon's hair is askew. I also see that Lupa is carrying her everything pack, which is not exactly wedding garb. They sit, and Gunthreon immediately starts whispering to Conner, whose face and energy turn to worry.

"And the ring. And the *ring?*" The last is said much louder, and I snap out of the fog. I reach into my purse and hand Russell the ring. He sweats bullets as he stares into Amber's lovely eyes.

"Now place it on her finger," babbles the minister.

Russell slides the ring on Amber's finger.

Amber screams.

"Get it off!" she cries. "Get it off!" She pulls the ring off quickly and throws it to the ground, tears trickling down her face. My jaw drops. Amber's known for being drastic, but this? Everyone else just sits, looking forward. *Poor Russell,* I think. She's evidently getting cold feet.

I look to the ground for the three carat ring, but I find a different ring—my father's. I had instinctively tossed it into my purse. As I rise, I notice the intricately detailed wood framework around the hall door has started falling off, revealing scribblings underneath. I then look to the ring in my hand and realize Amber screamed not because of the non-existent diamond, but because of the *lutheose.*

I look up and around—in what seems slow motion—and that's when I meet the eyes of the gentlemen in the glasses. My head starts spinning as I look at a more recent face of Dr. Martine, the missing physicist.

I brace myself, for something unknown is about to happen and I feel the heat of my monk's spade on my back.

Amber pulls herself up to full height, with some kind of bubble around her, almost like a force field. I suddenly feel a familiar rush of an energy mass heading in our direction from outside the doors.

I look to Amber and she starts shouting at me. "You! It's all your fault!" She points at me, crying. I stand in shock.

Suddenly, the ballroom doors burst open, and throngs of creatures enter—grebles and meeples and other countless horrors. I grab my monk's spade and stand rooted to the spot. Striding toward us, leading them all, is a swirling mass of evil—and deadly—energy: Devoten.

Chapter 54

Jealous
ღ

The guests at table three are held back against their will by various suddenly-armed guests, the only one missing is Ladimer. My mom stares at Amber, oblivious to the hyena-faced creature tightly gripping both her arms.

Amber turns her anger upon me once more, her face twisted and ugly as she cries and shouts at me. "Kailey, always screwing things up for me! Kailey, always number one! Kailey with the long legs. Kailey with the cool mom. What good did I ever get in this life? Nothing—until *he* came along."

Her hand points not toward Russell, but toward Devoten, master of infatuation. I inhale deeply and reach my feeler out to grasp her true feelings beyond the sudden lunacy, but keep hitting the bubble around her, bouncing off like a trampoline.

"He's evil, Amber!" I shout. I can't even begin to grasp what is happening right now, but know I must do something, possibly before karma steps in.

"No! He's shown me true love. He saw the power hidden deep inside me—something nobody *ever* acknowledged!" The bubble around her vibrates. "He helped me grow and transform into this." She holds her arms up toward her iridescent bubble shield.

I examine it. "This is how you wore the necklace I gave you," I blubber, pointing to the bubble. The corners of her mouth turn up in a malicious grin. "The only reason why bad things happened to you was not because *we* doubted you... It was because *you* doubted you. You never gave the real Amber a chance—the Amber I know and love. All those years—all those moments of

415

trouble—who was there for you? Me," I look to my mom and say, "and her!"

Devoten approaches us in his black-hooded cloak, looking as sinister as ever. "We finally get to converse, face to face, Kailey. You are so pretty." His voice is thick and mysterious, but not enough to divert me from gripping my weapon tighter, for what surrounds him is the horrid and foul mass of energy I previously witnessed. It's pure hatred, but in a falsely-subdued shell. It's sudo-abominor, preparing to unleash its rage, given the perfect moment. I know not to reach toward it, because it may swallow me up forever.

Amber's energy is reflective of her feelings, and I hear it ticking like a time bomb. "My love, tell Kailey of our plans," she rambles.

He raises his hand toward her mouth, and her face turns beet red.

"But—"

"Shut up! I am speaking with Kailey. This is not about you right now."

I look at her, and her eyes do not leave Devoten's face. Knowing Amber as long as I have, I know she's contemplating whether she should take the suggestion or break his arm. Her force field shudders a bit. Then she sits down in the chair to her left and says nothing, tears welling up in her eyes.

The noise behind me tells me someone has broken their bonds, then I feel her. It's my mom, rushing toward us.

"Devoten!" she spits as she approaches. "She's such an innocent little thing. What did you do to her?"

"Nice to see you, *Quicksilver*. You really want to know the details? Is this out of simple curiosity," He smiles as his voice changes, becoming heavier as he talks to my mom, moving just a bit closer to her, "or maybe *jealousy*?"

"Don't move any closer to me," she warns, pulling out her long blade, "and remember, your 'power' is useless against me."

"Fine. Always so difficult," he remarks. "The story is as follows: Amber noticed me one day near their work," he looks to me and Amber, "and began openly flirting for the last seat on the bus as we both boarded. Isn't that right?" Amber nods, tears dripping from her eyes. "She never even knew she was using her power as I watched her in action, enclosing both me and herself in one of these bubbles, closing out a beautiful, but threatening high-heeled, tight business-suited female with beautiful deep brown curls who also wanted that last bus seat." My mind wanders to moments with Amber, realizing she never exhibited signs of competition with other females, ever. "So," says Devoten, breaking me from my thoughts, "I realized her talent—one evidently developed over her *formidable* years of dating, because who would actually make a conscious decision to hook up with such emotional baggage—could be an asset to me. She was such an easy target!"

Amber's past admirers and relationships stream through my mind as I realize she was subconsciously holding the degenerates near, probably making them feel an indescribable sense of safety in her bubble—perhaps developing a false notion of bonding between them. If I only spent more time with her since my assault. Perhaps as karmelean, I could have ripped the layers of Amber apart, revealing her powers.

Amber's lower jaw hangs down, almost resting on her feet.

"Oh, and the best part," says Devoten, laughing to himself, "is how that ninny," he points to Russell, "was the perfect decoy! You all thought Amber was busy with him. Ha! His gift proved detrimental to his own well-being—attaching himself permanently to someone openly unfaithful. How pathetically stupid, but then again, he fell prey to her powers just as all the others did. And how would I know that he wouldn't get her pregnant first?"

We all look to Russell, who is supporting himself against the wall.

Soon, I hear Gunthreon—who has also escaped those holding him—approaching, speaking to those he passes. As he passes me, I hear: "Kailey, disregard any suggestions of Devoten's."

Devoten's gaze meets Gunthreon's, and just as I begin to fear a battle between the two of them, Russell suddenly starts making rather odd movements, first covering his eyes, then his mouth, then his ears. He keeps repeating it, and increasing speed, eventually moving so fast I can barely see what he's doing.

"He's breaking down," murmurs Gunthreon, moving to help his grandson. "Russell, sit and meditate. Relax. Take deep breaths." Russell sits on the ground, with his eyes closed as Gunthreon holds him tightly, rocking.

Meanwhile, my mom stands between me and Devoten. "She's beautiful, Dena May," he says to her, with soft emotion. I feel the horror of his energy, still swirling around him, but a bit slower. A loud sigh escapes my mom's mouth. Both she and Devoten stare at me as I feel an odd sensation coming from each of them: small slithering tendrils of energy, one from each. I close my eyes and feel the two tendrils reaching for each other, yearning to touch. I then interrupt by placing my own energy between them since I don't want his touching my mom's. But to my surprise, her energy pushes me away.

"Resembles both her parents you know," rambles Devoten. "And she's strong, I can feel her power." After their two energies touch and twirl around together, I feel my mom's retract, rushing back toward her body.

"Devoten—Kailey." She is formally introducing us. "Kailey—your father."

A single word escapes both my and Amber's lips: "What?" Then Devoten's cloak falls, and I see an older version of the face I spied in Gunthreon's magical mirror. Spotting my ring on the ground, he picks it up, allowing it to sizzle in his hand as it burns his skin. He then slides it onto his finger, his jaw clenching from the pain.

"See! Ruining my whole life!" cries Amber. "No wonder he's always been so interested in you!"

Anger appears across Devoten's face. "I found this one—," he snaps, pointing to Amber, "—while watching *our daughter* grow up. After I conceived my plan to rule Renhala—and eventually the shitty realm you live in—Amber was a convenience." He smirks as Amber's shoulders drop.

"Rule Renhala?" cackles my mom. "And Abscondia?" She laughs heartily as Devoten stares her down.

"Yes. You and Kailey can still be a part of something wonderful. Change your ways Dena May. Just imagine what we'd be capable of, together, as a...family." I hear Amber inhale deeply, and hold it for what seems an eternity. My mom frowns. "Or would you rather just stand back and watch everyone die as my creatures, once fully unleashed in Abscondia, eat them alive? I can protect you, and Kailey."

My mom looks upset as she and Amber continue watching Devoten's face, and his each and every movement. My mom begins shaking her head slowly, back and forth.

Not liking my mom's answer, he adds, "I stood too long in the shadows. It's my turn to shine. My turn to rule. My turn to play God! *Bring it in!*" he yells loudly.

The giant metal box from my secret, unprovoked, travels to Devoten, is wheeled in, along with a life size statue of the lovely woman from my pendant. Dr. Speck, in a lab coat, follows the statue, then Tartarin, who prods him like a cow with some sort of long, metal tube. Tartarin limps from his injury from our little bathroom brawl, when I stuck my spade in his leg. *"Now, bring in the cauldron!"* Devoten screams. A gigantic cauldron, holding an

419

enormous amount of molten metal, is wheeled in and placed beside the box.

Dr. Martine makes his way toward the box, looking very worried. The box begins steaming profusely, and he yells to Devoten that they need Mortimer.

Then Mortimer is dragged in by his feet by two creatures similar to the one that assaulted me—half man, half grotesquely-green and slimy monster. I freeze. Mortimer's head and arms are cut with deep slashes, and he seems to be unconscious. Twin Zoe hands Tartarin her glass of water, and he sloshes it across Mortimer's face. Zoe explodes with laughter as Mortimer wakes screaming and pawing at the air. As Zoe laughs, I scan the crowd—mostly female—spotting each grin Zoe provokes. It is then I feel it—the duality of the females' energies—on extreme measures—with an unmatched quickness in their ability to change. One second they mimic Devoten's swirling dark energy, the next they are something entirely different, from complacent to happy, but not one iota of regret exists in any of their energies. They are all enjoying themselves, and hoping to be recognized for their part in Devoten's plan—to perhaps rule by his side. Each of their faces slowly begins transforming—an Amber nose here, a Dena May smile there, and several heads of flowing red hair. They are transforming into what they see as their chance at Devoten's attention. *They are pixies.*

I then notice a greble walking to the falling framework around the hall door, placing a sticky piece of slate to the wall. On it is a roughly drawn symbol. *They are closing the entry. And Ladimer is outside.* I try working my way slowly to the piece of slate.

Devoten turns to Amber. "I still need you, honey," he coos. "Remember your part." Her face contorts, and then transforms to one of pure fascination as she looks into her lover's eyes—infatuated with him and whatever plan he has discussed with her.

"This is messed up," I prattle, as a meeple comes between me and the doorway. *I have to be dreaming.* As I watch Tartarin antagonize Mortimer, I suddenly realize the full extent of Amber's betrayal. Anger turns my own face into something twisted and perverse as I turn from my mission at the door. "You have been the one feeding them information...and you let that monster into my apartment building!" I yell. "Someone had to show him it before he could travel, and you used the...key I gave you." Amber snickers under her breath, and her eyes will not meet mine. A sudden thought hits me like a line-drive fastball: "Did you let *it* in my apartment, too? That day?" I stare at Amber, and my energy attempts to coax her bubble to open—somewhere. "Did you have a part in my blood shed? A part in the day my throat was ripped open? A part in the day I almost lost my sanity? *Did you?!*" I yell, as her smirk disappears, replaced by something sad.

"Amber, please say you didn't," mutters my mom, hoping.

"I had no idea how far..." Amber replies as her bubble quivers and a small hole, the size of a pinhead, opens. I thrust my energy in and she shakes and trembles as it rushes at her, inflicting pain as it searches for an answer. In her pain, I find my answer hiding deep—the small amount of regret she holds from her actions. I withdraw, not wanting to touch any part of her, any longer. "I'm sorry," she says, under her breath.

Without even looking at Conner, I sense his reaction to Amber and her admission of guilt. As I look to his face, his expression changes into one of empathetic pain—not pity, but a true hurt from deep within, at the Judas kiss given to me by my once beloved and trusted best friend. He shares my pain and I instantly feel connected to him.

Tartarin laughs and announces, "You have me to thank for that, Kailey! I gave those orders to Amber. Why would I waste my own precious time? I thought it would be much more pleasurable if I had your own best friend betray you in the worst way possible."

Devoten turns his body, suddenly hearing Tartarin's boasting. His face reflects a burning hate and I feel his energy heating up like lava. I send my feeler in and feel his surprise as Tartarin rants. "She even handpicked your assaulter!" exclaims Tartarin, happy with his himself. "Good choice I must say. Too bad he's dead. But anyways."

Two grebles grab Gunthreon, covering his mouth with a napkin and tying his arms behind him as Lupa yells at the meeples guarding her, "Let me go, now! You are going to regret this!" They laugh at her, tauntingly. Gunthreon shakes his head at Lupa and she stops, anger clearly swelling inside her belly. Conner speaks to her as she slumps slightly.

From within the metal contraption, a loud noise shakes the giant box, and I feel something strong and dangerous inside, trying to break free. We all feel it, and I feel the fear, growing even in Devoten.

"One look at wohmin and its wrath will destroy you all—" grumbles Devoten, "—and this whole ridiculous realm! Then I will reign! Amber, release Tartarin." Tartarin turns quickly to Devoten, who smiles, looking like a nightmare. Amber releases Tartarin from her protective bubble.

What follows is a blur as everything happens at once.

The piece of slate stuck to the wall falls, and instantly, Ladimer and Jenna burst in and attack the nearest pixies, all of whom have pulled out small, extremely sharp-looking disks, resembling Chinese stars—which fly and stick into various walls.

A greble starts to unlock the metal box.

Devoten, speaking of love and her place next to his side, coaxes Amber to make her force field strong enough to envelop them and their entire army. Anyone in the bubble is shielded against an attack, yet somehow they can strike the outside from inside, but I can find pinholes here and there, where I'm able to peek inside with my feeler.

As Amber holds up her field, she turns to me. "Look what I'm capable of!"

She laughs, maniacally, but I see my beloved best friend behind the laugh, afraid of returning—afraid of the energy needed to fight Devoten's enrapturement. The force field she tries to control drains her as it reaches all those in her party, and suddenly, I see it slowly begin to shrink, her grip lessening on those furthest from her.

"Please, Amber, my love, do what you've done in our training sessions," begs Devoten. "Come on." A single tear, of no particular shine, falls on her cheek. Suddenly, Ladimer stands near Devoten. "*You!*" Devoten screams. "You will die first. Stealing my family. That's what you wanted all along!" As Devoten reaches under his cloak, he turns his back to my mom, who has finally achieved freedom from the creatures holding her. She jumps toward him, but as her blade starts its descent into Devoten's arm, Tartarin appears out of nowhere and reaches toward her, his claws digging into her from behind, knocking her to the floor.

"Mom!" I scream. "Ladimer!"

The rumbling box grows louder and louder as a foul smell releases into the air. I run to my mom, mounting my spade, and that's when I see the hole in her back. Her blood flows everywhere, seeping into the dirty, worn-down ballroom carpet. "No! Oh, Mom, hang on, hang on. Please! I need you!"

"Kailey, no. Let me go. I need to go," she argues, her voice stifled from the flow of blood.

Tartarin stands over us. "Ha! You pathetic piece of shit!" he snarls. "This lovely little thing moves slightly slower than the rest of your body." Before our eyes, he stretches out his hand, and in it is my mom's transplanted kidney. My mom's grip lessens as Ladimer approaches.

Devoten turns toward my mom. His eyes widen. "*Noooooo!!!*" he screams. "She was mine!" His mouth turns into a giant snarl,

and he shouts something that sounds like soulspeak, but slightly
different—something anciently wicked. As the two creatures
holding Gunthreon release him to cover their own ears, he does
the same. Me, and the rest of our party, also cover our ears, Jenna
shoving something in my mom's ears. Most creatures have missed
their opportunity and begin screaming, themselves.

"They weakened you! Can't you see it!" says Tartarin, with
his own ears covered. He's trying to yell over Devoten's horrible
scream. "You were so concerned about them!"

Ladimer, so close now I can hear him through my covered
ears, explains, "Mad love." All our enemies start continue
screaming and pulling apart everything they can get their hands on,
including their own allies. I see Jenna fall as a pixie dives on top of
her.

"Kailey. Kailey." My mom's words are practically drowned
out, but I still hear them.

"Mom. Ladimer!"

"I love you so much. I'm sorry I..." She chokes out blood
over the front of her beautiful dress. Ladimer bends down and lays
his hands on her. "No!" she sputters at Ladimer. "Don't you dare.
You promised me! Don't." She cries and shakes her head as
Ladimer holds his hands above her, his eyes asking me, and only
me, *the* question. One quiet "please" escapes her lips as my eyes
meet hers.

Conner runs over to hold my mom's hand, and begins
soulspeaking to her. He speaks softly, the beautiful words flowing
from his mouth lighting up my mom's eyes as he speaks of her
unselfishness as both a defender of realms, and as a mother. He
speaks of her impenetrable love for those she trusts, and of her
soul's undying beauty. She smiles a thank you at him as he suddenly
jumps up to attack a greble who's gotten too close to us.

My mom's beautiful eyes slowly change before me as her life
drains away, her energy evaporating. I shake my head no at

Ladimer, knowing it's the right answer, but hating it. Ladimer pulls his hands away from her reluctantly as my mom spits out another mouthful of blood. Her eyes, full of pain, meet mine, and she says, "Take it from me, Kailey."

"Take what?"

"Quicksilver."

She pulls me down with the last of her strength and kisses me ever so slightly, speaking a word into my mouth. I grasp her energy, knowing I can easily replenish it, but only embed the feel of it in my brain, knowing this will be the last time I'll experience it. Then, she breathes to me, "Sorry...your brother—" Then she says nothing else. I look to Amber, evidently pregnant with a baby boy. *But how would she know?*

I feel my mom's power inside me completely. The simplest thought sparks my body to move. Devoten stabs at Tartarin, ripping him open from every angle, Lupa and Conner fight off meeples near their table, Gunthreon has Evlengard in his hand, freely swinging, slicing monsters like butter.

I return to my mother and kneel over her body as her spirit lifts. I try grabbing at the mist emanating from her form, but it slips through my fingers, leaving nothing. The mist condenses, forming her figure high above us. I see her smile one last time as her hand signs, "I love you," which I return to her. Then her head of mist turns slowly toward Devoten, who takes a break from Tartarin to watch my mom. Her smile disappears, and she shakes her head at him, her face turning to a frown. Her hand rises and his eyes widen as she gives him a different universal sign: a flash of the middle finger. The mist that is my mom then shoots off quickly through the ceiling, and she's gone in a flash. Devoten's anger swells, and he returns to his previous project: Tartarin.

"Oh god no!" I cry. Sitting over her lifeless body, I feel a huge hole open up in my heart. I hug her body, breathing in the scent of her hair as I choke on my tears. I hug her for all the times

I was embarrassed by her bear hugs. I hug her for the beautiful life she gave me.

My face rises to the chaos around me, and my blood curdles. I take a last look at my mom's body, once full of vibrancy and a rare intensity for life, now forever empty.

Gunthreon fights his way over to me. "She was given a true death," he whispers in my ear. "She was special, Kailey."

Pain and sadness begin to swirl around and around inside me, creating whirlwinds of devastating proportion. I stand in the middle of the hell around me and see my comrades fighting for their lives. Amber's force field protects her army as they instill damage upon those I love.

A loud moaning emerges from the metal box. It shakes and beeps and groans as the metal distorts. I look to Gunthreon, who simply stands, staring. His head turns to me, and I see his mouth move to form one word: "Velopa." I know what he means. Somehow, Velopa is caged inside that box.

As the word escapes Gunthreon's mouth, he looks to Amber and then speaks something to her that I cannot hear above the noises around me. At that same moment, an energy whip escapes the box and strikes him, knocking him several feet off the ground. He lands like a rock. Drs. Speck and Martine stand by the box, pushing buttons and pulling levers, trying to contain the hideousness lurking inside.

Ladimer crawls up next to me, avoiding the meeple looking for him under the tables. "It was Devoten all along," he says. "Velopa had nothing to do with it." The energy whip lashes out once more, just missing a nearby greble.

Before I can read the energy of the creature lurking behind me, Jenna jumps out of nowhere, teeth and knife bared. Her swing, as she comes down, catches the dog-like creature behind me in its eye, but her arm is not quick enough to stab once more as the dog's claws dig into her back. Her blood splashes out across my face, and this triggers something unimaginable inside me.

As Ladimer crawls to help her, I stand and raise my arms above my head, screaming a word of pure destruction. Neda's words open my eyes to the powers lingering deep inside my brain, connected to my indestructible soul. The walls begin shaking and I feel my body opening to release an energy growing exponentially. Ladimer shakes his head no, then grasps it from the pain I am emitting. The power keeps growing inside me as I look to my comrades, and with one last thought of my mom's shining face, I push my feelers out, out to Renhala, out to every nook and cranny I can find, and pull with all my might. *I can do this. Time for reinforcements.*

Almost on cue, there emerges a huge crash from the hallway. He scrambles, knocking down walls as he climbs to his feet. ***My, my, what big powers we have!*** Greer, in the hallway, feels angry. ***Kailey, this has you written all over it!*** I feel him in my head. The crunching is loud as he munches on what critters attack him in the hallway. ***Good thing I have not eaten dinner yet.***

Nayla, with her still-tourniqueted limb, lies in the middle of the floor, her eyes peeking open as she awakes to the carnage around her. "What the?!" she says. She jumps on her feet, and each and every hair on her back stands on end. Her movements are quick as she registers the situation. She looks to me and nods, turning to the creature to her left which has no idea she even arrived before she slits its throat with her razor-sharp claws.

Bu has appeared, sitting in the corner, eating the giant turkey leg he was enjoying before I pulled him in. I see the fear in his eyes as his head turns around and around. He hides as best he can behind a nearby potted tree.

Fidello stomps in, punching at a pixie who has transformed her face into something haggard and hideous. Fangs, along with her lower jaw, fly as she tries to dig into his neck.

I sense two souls still working on the metal machine, but they are getting nowhere, darting from the energy lashing out at them. "It's useless!" Dr. Speck yells at his colleague. Mortimer stands next to them, trying to help with the abomination he created, but his face is full of the remorse that hinders his reflexes. He turns to Bu, who, having crawled out from his hiding space, rushes to the machine, pulling out his tools. Quickly, he twists and cuts wires with such dexterity that Mortimer, pulling from deep within himself, is inspired to step in. His eyes turn white as he lays his hands on the machine. He seems to call to the properties of the metal, hardening it and strengthening its true power. The two of them together silence the energy within the box.

The fighting around us continues, but has slowed. I find Conner spellbound by a pixie standing before him. She is absolutely gorgeous: big, blue eyes, plump and luscious lips, and flowing blond curls. Her breasts are perfect and enticing underneath her tiny white corset. Her arms reach out to him, pulling him into her. The look of lust on her face and the gleam of her knife behind her back snaps me and my jealousy into motion.

The pixie smiles as she reveals her knife to me. Little does she realize my monk's spade is much longer than her arms and Amber's force field is no longer reaching her. The speed in which I move amazes even myself. I pull the spade off my back and swing as her blade reaches out to me. My blade easily slices her in half.

"Bitch, he's *my* boyfriend!" I spit at her corpse. Conner stands, his brain trying to figure out what just happened.

Amber's shoulders slump as her power retreats. Her face rises to Devoten, and he shakes his head at her. "Waste of energy!" he hisses. "You are no longer needed." He points to Amber as she starts crying, holding her belly.

I close my eyes and listen to something deep within— something that's been whispering to me my whole life—the power and strength to deal with the unknown. I feel Neda's energy near—Neda's love. And then I move.

"That's my girl," says Ladimer, standing.

I run to Bu, ripping the necklace and locket off his neck, then move to Greer and remove a scale on his leg to reveal the Meadow's Edge rock I had placed on his alter.

What are you up to, little one?

Nayla watches as I run to her and rip off the tourniquet off her limb, *her* reminder of Michel's betrayal as king. I kneel on the floor, taking the rock and placing it in the tourniquet. Then, tying it, I attach it to Bu's necklace, creating a makeshift pendulum. I walk to my mom's body and place my finger in the blood spilled along the floor. Then I trace on the tourniquet, a heart, shedding one last tear for the beautiful angel I once called "Mom."

I walk toward Devoten and take his hand in mine. He's caught off guard and his energy wavers. I slip off the ring from his finger and slide it onto Bu's necklace, letting it fall to the tourniquet. I hold out the pendulum, allowing it to move and pick up speed as I call to Neda, and to all those who have left this plane of existence. The pendulum begins circling with such speed and power that I brace myself, holding it above my head. The ground starts shaking, and Devoten embraces me, trying to stabilize his own footing. As he looks into my eyes, I throw up an energy barrier, and then and there realize that I must destroy him—the very man my mother once adored, and whose blood is flowing through my veins. "Goodbye, Devoten," I say.

He starts changing before my eyes. His skin hardens, but his eyes remain, glossy. "My little girl," is all that escapes his mouth as I read his energy—his feelings of disgrace as a father, forcing my eyes to well up, but I continue on. The pendulum keeps twirling and as I think it cannot twirl any faster, a stream of lutheose appears, travelling in the air from the giant cauldron to directly above the swinging pendulum—over me and Devoten. After

429

levitating above us for a brief few seconds, the stream then pours over Devoten, loosening his embrace. The moment he releases me I still feel his energy, clinging to me. It starts creeping along my body, searching. A sudden, stabbing pain makes me scream as sudo-abominor attempts to burrow its way inside me. Just as I think I can no longer swing the pendulum *and* keep up my barrier, Devoten starts shrinking, until finally, he disappears, leaving only a silver key where he once stood. I stand in awe, dropping my energy barrier. The pain of the claws immediately subsides.

Lupa runs over, picking up the key and tossing it in her everything pack.

As Devoten's army starts disappearing one by one, Tartarin, bloody but still alive, sneakily crawls to the metal box and releases a lever, which opens the door. The scream that reaches our ears wants to drive us insane. Without even thinking, I run to Velopa, grabbing at the energy, over screams of protest. Conner's scream is the loudest as he claws at me, but I am too fast.

Chapter 55

Deadly
❧

There is absolute silence.
Nothingness.
A change in consciousness.
A feeling of being watched.
The smell of mud, of earth.
The sensation of birth, of life, of love, of complete wholeness.
The sensation of pain, of desperation, of loss, of falling apart into a
million *pieces.*

The floating ball of light hovers before me. It is Velopa, and it is as astounded as I am.

We are both motionless as I hear a whisper: "You cannot follow her."

Both Velopa and I are thrown to the rocklands with a thump—well me more than Velopa, who hovers. Then before my eyes, it quickly transforms into an animate creature—a giant scarab, with beautiful ancient hieroglyphics—resembling those on my spade—painted on its back. It speaks to me: "YOU HAVE NOT LET ME SEEK MY REVENGE! DEVOTEN, WHO RULED MY KINGDOM SO SLOPPILY, MUST BE DESTROYED! ME—CONTAINED! ME—POISONED! ME—VELOPA...the stern... "

The voice quiets as Neda appears across the rocks. The scarab points at me and shouts, looking at Neda, "She deserves death!"

431

It unleashes one last energy whip, and as it hits me in the back, I feel the most painful burning imaginable. The poison spreads quickly, and I fall to the ground, my last glimpse revealing Velopa smiling at Neda, whose eyes squint. They both turn into energy balls and speed toward each other at G-force speed. As the collision is about to occur, I travel back to the wedding hall—a very small piece of Renhala residing in my plane.

"She's dying!"

"Ladimer, fix her!"

"I don't know the poison."

"A deathman! Do something, *now*!"

I lie motionless, not afraid to die. My blood slows its flow as my heart beats to no rhythm. I feel a pain in my back as Ladimer, rolling me over, slices it open with a knife. I want to scream, but I cannot move. Conner's energy is near, and I sense him holding me.

Suddenly, Ladimer laughs. With the laugh comes renewed energy and life. My heart beats to its familiar rhythm once again.

"Hyacinthus animo, a.k.a. lily of life," says Ladimer, gladly, as he holds the flower from my hair—the flower his foster mom gave me—sans one petal.

I come to with such force I sit up immediately, knocking Conner over. The tear on his face is quickly wiped away by the back of his own hand.

Ladimer stands above me, smiling. "My little karmelean is back with us." The deathman at the door shrugs, turns and heads back out the door—the door that knocks it in the butt as it leaves.

Ladimer hands the flower from my hair to Lupa, and I see her throw it in her everything pack. I scan the crowd, which now only consists of my wedding guest-friends, but I don't see Jenna, or my mom's body.

"Jenna? Jenna!" I yap. "And where is my mom?!"

Lupa reaches her hand inside her everything pack once more and pulls out Jenna, who sleeps, curled up in a ball. "She needs some healing rest," replies Lupa. "This was the only place I could put her while Gunthreon fought Tartarin. He did a fine number on that monster, but Tartarin disappeared. Also—honey, we thought it best to move your mother's body—somewhere appropriate, in order to deal with her burial preparations." I simply nod, not wanting to lose my composure.

I swallow hard and my eyes search for my ex-best friend. My blood begins to pump faster as I think of what she did to everyone. "Where's Amber? She run?"

"Yep." Lupa tucks Jenna back in the everything pack.

Conner adds, "Out the door, dress, tiara, and all."

"Where's Russell?" I ask.

"Someplace safe," replies Conner. "I tried speaking to Russell, but he just stared straight ahead, not saying a word, barely breathing. I'm worried about him." I put my hand softly on his shoulder.

"Ladimer, can you help?" I query.

"No. His break is mental. He needs to overcome that himself."

"Markings of protection over the door?" I say, looking to the falling frame.

"Must have been some strong magic," remarks Gunthreon, appearing behind us.

"You were hit by Velopa," I blurt, shocked to see Gunthreon walking to us unaided. "I saw you."

Gunthreon smiles a humble smile. "I sensed the energy coming before it hit me. I persuaded your friend Amber to cover me with her power."

"How's Russell?"

"We shall see how he recovers. What I need to know is, how are you?" He comes over and gives me the tightest Gunthreon hug I have yet received, and he doesn't let up until my tears flow, as well as a single Gunthreon tear. Everyone comes over to us, and we share in one communal hug until there is no more fluid left in my body.

"Sorry I ever doubted you—any of you," says Gunthreon, sorrow in his voice. "I hope you can place your trust in me once again, Kailey. I would like your permission to give your mom a proper burial. It's your choice."

"I trust you to do the best for her," I whisper.

"I will start the preparations," he says. "Forgive me for my abruptness, but I feel it needs to be done as soon as possible. Oh, and please, may I keep the key for a bit? I would like to have someone I trust look at it and tell me what steps to take." I nod as his kiss sweeps against my cheek as he disappears. Lupa sheds a tear as she turns away from me.

As we leave the scene, I feel a sadness that breaks my heart, but I realize the pain for my mom is over. No more band-aids: brief moments of coverage that only masked her real wounds. My thoughts turn to my mom's last words, and Amber, and the thought that the embryo in her womb is my half-brother.

I lose two pieces of family and gain another.

Chapter 56

Remorseful
CR

I choose a flowing white dress with small, lavender flowers embroidered throughout the eyelet fabric. Next to my chest, I wear both my whistle from Conner and Mortimer's gift. My hair is free, and I wear no shoes. Everyone else is also in white, and shoeless. Jenna, fully healed, stands next to me, her hand on my leg, speechless. Bu, to my back, breathes deep, steady breaths. He's trying to be strong for me, but his anguish throbs as loud as Lupa sobs. Conner stands with me, holding my hand.

Meadow's Edge is quiet today, mourning its loss. Even those who never met my mom attend the service, speaking their deepest sympathies, heralding her heroic actions and crying tears out of respect.

I turn to Ladimer who has come up next to me and whisper, "I think tonight, I may need to take a trip to the ol' Wicked Whale."

"It's already been suggested."

Beautiful music plays as lutheose flutes and harps sing their songs of sorrow and resurrection. The overwhelmingly sad emotions of everyone present is too much for me to handle, and I start crying, praying this is all a bad dream, and praying that I don't fall into another depression—a depression that my mother can't save me from this time.

My mom's body, loosely draped in elegant ivory silk, is carried on a carved bed of logs before us. Releasing my grasp from Conner, I walk to her body and stare at her peaceful face. "No more pain, Mom. I love you," I say before gently kissing her cheek. As my lips touch her cheek, and Ladimer walks up to stand beside me, I hear, from nowhere in particular, "Stay strong. They still need

435

you." My mom's voice then blends in with the whistling of the wind.

A tear drips down Ladimer's cheek and he quickly wipes it away. "I loved her, you know," he whispers. I pull him near me and we embrace as our energies slowly meet and a great sadness is shared between us. He then adds, "And I love you, too."

I grip him a bit tighter, then release him as we all march in procession toward the life pool.

We arrive, and Gunthreon steps out and lays his hand on my mom's head. "Your work was heavy, but you moved with graceful agility," he says. "Your life was hard, but your softness carried you. Your soul was repeatedly tested, but you answered and stood strong, always prepared for more. We ask that this shell be taken and, in return, the gift be given."

My mom's body is lifted off the logs and held in the middle of the life pool, where she is released. Her beautiful body floats for a brief few seconds, then dissolves like sugar into the water. The pool glows a brilliant light, and Gunthreon leads me to the water's edge. "Kailey, you must enter."

I walk into the cold water, which starts warming almost immediately upon my entry. I walk down to the familiar bottom, just standing in silence, wanting to stay down here forever, never resurfacing to live my crummy life without my mom.

The noise of moving rocks reaches my ears, and from deep along the bottom of the pool floor comes an otter-like creature, slowly, holding out in front of itself a box. It stops near me, stretching out its nose, seemingly sniffing the water around it. Its eyes are big and brown, like a teddy bear's. As it swims closer to me, I hold out my hands, waiting to accept the gift. But shortly before it reaches me, it snatches the box back, in a snotty way, shaking its paw at me, as if scolding a child. I put my arms down, and it slowly approaches again. I hold my breath as it comes right up to me, near my ear. As I wait in anticipation, a pain surges from my ear, as I see blood floating in the water. I grab my monk's spade and, as the creature tastes my blood, threaten it. It seems to ponder something briefly, then nods, holding the box out to me. I am hesitant to take it, but finally mount my weapon and take the box.

The sly little creature makes its way back from where it came, leaving me alone with the box and my bloody ear, healing as I stand.

The gift in my hands is a wooden box with a metal rune smack-dab in the center on the top. I turn the box over and over, looking for a hinge or a latch or keyhole to open it, but there is none. I shake the box, and nothing. I pry it with my hands, trying to separate top and bottom, but it does not budge. Discouraged, I make my way back up to the crowd. As I emerge, already dry, they say their goodbyes, turn, walking away from me, back to town.

"Gunthreon, it won't open," I sputter.

"Are you sure?"

"You try."

He backs away quickly. "No—nobody else is to touch that," He sees my frown and when nobody else is looking, attempts to open it, but to no avail. He hands it back to me quickly. "When a child is to be born, the mother prepares a box for the child. When she gives birth in the life pool, she drops the box at the same moment the baby is released. It is only to be given back to the child once the mother is returned to the pool. But you must not be meant to have the gift yet. Sorry, Kailey."

I just stare at the box, turning it over and over, thinking that maybe my mom played one last trick on me, making it some sort of puzzle. Jenna's knife is the perfect size, so I take it from her and try prying the box open once more, but alas, no movement—not even a chipping of the wood.

We all decide to head over to Lupa's house to hang out for a bit. As we approach, I sense heightened emotion in Lupa. "Dear Neda!" she yells, running toward her house, darting over short, fruit-bearing bushes and ducking under hanging, blue-flowered vines. We all simultaneously grip our weapons and secure our footing. "My poor garden!" exclaims Lupa. "Look at these nasty sprouts strangling my tomato plants. Oh! My franglefruit!" She runs around frantically, pulling at the ugly weeds as we all drop our weapons to our sides.

"I love her, but she is crazy, G." I smile at Gunthreon, whose loving face admires his woman, especially her butt as she bends over.

"Uh-hmm," he murmurs. I clear my throat, and when he sees me watching him, he blushes.

"I'm going to rest now, if that's okay," I say. He nods and I walk silently into Lupa's house and jump onto the bed, tears for my mom flooding from my eyes. I cry myself to sleep, asking myself if I could have done more for my mom.

☙

A solid four hours of sleep carries no dreams or travels whatsoever, and I wake to a sense of renewal. As I walk out, Conner is at my door, standing with his hand raised, about to knock. "Ready for some fun, or at least some alcohol?" he says. "I know I am." I throw my hair back in a ponytail, and let him lead me out by my hand. Everyone else is up and standing around, waiting for me.

Gunthreon, looking at me, asks, "Dreams?"

"Nope."

"You got some sleep. Good."

Just looking at him and Ladimer makes me think of my mom. As we make our way to The Wicked Whale, I make several stops just to sit and cry.

"We don't have to go if you're not up for it," says Ladimer. "We can all just hang out—or, if you want your privacy—?"

"No, please. I need you all right now, and a few drinks."

As we enter the bar, everyone notices us, and all make their way to me, hugging and kissing me. In a weird way, it's comforting, and I almost feel as though my mom is in the room with us, listening, and feeling the emotions winding between us all.

The band eventually starts up the music, and people begin dancing hand in hand. I make my way out to them and dance my own dance, twirling and swaying, anger and sadness my partners. I hear nothing else besides the music, and I am entranced, moving for myself and not for the pleasure of others. As the music ends my eyes rise and meet Ladimer's, who has had a few drinks already and the bond between us quivers. He raises his glass to me. Conner, beside him, also watches me. I marvel at the beauty of both men and feel grateful for their love.

The music begins once more, more upbeat, but before I begin another dance, I notice someone standing at the door of the bar—and then the door closes. The energy draws me, and I begin walking toward the door.

I exit and find the poor soul sitting outside on a rock.

He cowers as I sit next to him.

"What's wrong?" I ask.

"I cannot find comfort in anything." His breath smells like mead.

I put my arms around his shoulders. "It's not your fault."

"You lie, but I appreciate the effort. Without that metal contraption, none of this would have happened."

"You did not do anything willingly."

His energy is so full of pain, it hurts my head. "And how do you know that?" I have no response. "I need a favor of you," he says, firmly.

"Anything."

He hesitates. "Kill me."

My arm drops as I attempt to stand above Mortimer. "Listen to yourself! There is so much to be thankful for. I need you with me. Don't do this to me—not now."

"They will always find me," he states. "There will always be someone looking to abuse my talents—my curse—and I feel that someday I may just give in to whomever tempts me with the best offer. I will openly admit this. You would never believe the number of times I've been given offers, and have refused them. I need to eliminate the chance of me, one day, accepting."

"You will always have people ready to defend you—your friends willing to watch your back," I proclaim. I reach to the energy flowing around his body in hopes of quieting the pain, but it jabs—almost like a punch—at me, not wanting to cooperate. "Come back inside, and be with us—those friends willing to fight for you." I retract my own energy from him.

I turn to the door of The Wicked Whale and see Ladimer's silhouette in the doorway. I shoo him off, and he returns to the music, but when I turn around, Mortimer has a golden knife to his own throat.

"My god, Mortimer!"

"I am sorry to do this to you again, but it is for everyone's safety. Tell them all I am sorry." His slash is quick, and it penetrates deeply, cutting off the flow of blood to his heart and redirecting it all over the front of his shirt. I move instantly, but simply stand above his body, not believing what is happening in my life. My energy begins twisting and twirling and screaming, and the fact that Mortimer, having taken his own life, is slumped over before me is menial. Another part of me surfaces—a part I instantly abhor—a part that vows to kill Tartarin and destroy the key that was once my father.

Conner comes running out, maybe sensing what has happened. "Oh no. He did it, didn't he?" he asks, staring at

Mortimer lying in the dirt. "Remorse got the best of him. I'll go get Ladimer and Gunthreon." Then he's off at full pace.

As he leaves, it hits me full-impact—a force wild and unstoppable. I begin running, running from whom I am, running at Quicksilver speed, desperate to grasp my hands around a neck and kill with my bare hands. The karmelean in me fights these newfound feelings. Repulsed by the strength of the hate and the violence of the internal struggle creates a horrifically ugly aura around me. I can feel it—a sight Jenna would cringe at.

As I'm about to reach top speed, loving every minute of my chase, I'm hit by something large and thick, about chest high. My eyes turn up in my head, and that's when I see the tree bark and leaves, right before the pitch black.

I never feel the lapping of tiny tongues on my face, or hear my whistle being blown by the wind.

Chapter 57

Afraid
☙

"**S**he's coming to!"

I cough and drag myself to a sitting position. My body is sore, and I feel like I've just finished a boxing match.

"Why is this always happening to me?" I say as I grab my pounding head.

"Well, well. You've finally decided to come around." Ladimer sits on my bed next to me, petting Kioto. She looks at me out of the corner of her eye.

"What happened?"

Bu comes into my bedroom, bringing me a cup of hot tea. "Kailey all right?" he asks. I can sense his genuine concern.

"Yeah, I think I'm fine," I respond.

"Bu give Cheeto and babies treats. That okay?"

"Cheeto?" As I try to get up, Ladimer lays me back down.

"Your mangy little friend found you before Conner got there. That you ended up as far north as you did amazes me. While you were gone we also took care of Mortimer's body. I had to let him go. He couldn't handle the guilt. He's being cremated in a small town outside of Meadow's Edge, where he was born. The man even made his own urn, knowing his time was coming." His mouth stops moving, but I feel he wants to tell me more.

"What?" I spit, a bit more angrily than I'd normally reply.

"He wanted you to have his urn," replies Ladimer. "You are to be the soul possessor of Mortimer's ashes." I frown, but do not cry, for I have shed all my tears. "He left instructions to have his ashes mixed with powdered lutheose, and they are then to be delivered to you."

Jenna, excited, comes running in and stops right before jumping on the bed. She looks to Ladimer, making a disgusted face—sticking her tongue out and all—and then looks back to me and says, "Nice to see you up." I know she wants to hug me, but is resisting the urge. She speaks to me, softly and sympathetically, which makes me feel she's pitying me in some way, making my anger swell. "Good thing Mr. Syla caught you."

"Mr. Syla?"

Her eyes widen, and her excitement returns. "Yes! He is so cool—grabbed you in motion and held you down until we all came and got you. Trees are very sensitive to the change."

"What change? Why did you make that face?" My blood pressure is so high I feel my eyesight begin to shake slightly, and my hands ball into fists. The fact that I feel remnants of Devoten's appalling energy doesn't help, either. I can feel his prior thoughts, feelings. My monk's spade warms up on my back.

They both stare at me, saying nothing.

Jenna's eyes widen. "Kailey, please calm down. It's just that...you need to calm down." She looks toward Ladimer again.

"You should know..." He hesitates a bit too long for my liking. "You have not only acquired Quicksilver."

My heart beats rapidly as the realization sets in. "No," I blurt, clenching my teeth as my breathing becomes shallow. My anger turns on like an opened faucet. "No!" I scream.

Ladimer rushes to me and hugs me, rocking slowly until I feel the anger subside. "We need to keep this between us, Kailey," he whispers. "It's best that others not know. It resides deep, and is unrecognizable unless you are a seasoned reader, like our little Jenna."

"It's ugly!" she squawks. Ladimer shushes her quickly and she shrugs. "Well it is," she says, quietly. Kioto growls very quietly. "See?" Jenna says, giving Kioto a dog biscuit.

"Promise me that you will fight it, Kailey. *Do not* let it consume you. I am going to do whatever I can for you. I *will* find a way to abolish it."

"I'm afraid, Ladimer," I sputter, shaking a bit.

"We both are, honey."

Chapter 58

Brave
℘

"**A**re you coming with me to work today, or what?" I won't admit it, but Jenna's a small comfort, knowing she's there in my purse witnessing everything I see. It also helps that she recognizes when sudo-abominor awakes before I do, somewhat.

It seems that this morning, sudo-abominor took the liberty of picking out my outfit for the day: black pants, low-cut black shirt and a black pashmina. *How uplifting.*

My boss thought it best I took bereavement leave, but I couldn't handle being in my apartment any longer, so during our phone conversation I begged until he let me have my way. I need interaction, and something to concentrate on besides death. And I also remembered it was my day to have lunch with my client at True.

On the way to the bus, I notice my favorite band of gangbangers hanging out, as usual, on the corner. Today their game of choice is roshambo, and evidently the loser gets five-finger slapped as hard as possible—anywhere on their body and a random obscenity thrown at him.

"What the-" I hear Jenna say as she peeks out at them.

Suddenly, after Joe receives an exceedingly vicious blow to the side of the face, he pauses in place, staring at something near him—something that scares the shit out of him. "Jesus! What is that guys?" He's pointing. As all heads turn and view what he's pointing at, their energies—almost as a combined effort—scream.

They start running, as the creature—a particularly scrawny, four-legged spirithound—prepares to start after them, digging its feet in the ground, and screaming as it foams at the mouth.

I immediately step forward, monk's spade already in hand, and chase after the creature as it starts running after them. After a block, and a wrong turn, Joe and his friends find themselves in a death trap dead-end. I come up slowly behind the creature, avoiding making any sound, but as I approach, Jenna sneezes.

As the creature slowly turns from its catch, my monk's spade swings lightly in my hands, connecting with its neck, at the exact moment its body suddenly disappears, only leaving black sludge on my blade. *Black sludge.* I simply wipe it on the ground and nearest brick wall, not feeling one bit of fear rise.

I look to all the boys shuddering in the corner, hugging each other, and say a simple, "You're welcome...bitches." I then smile as Joe stares back at me, a smile of relief appearing across his face. I start to walk away and hear, "I gotta go change my underwear." I laugh a strong and bordering-on-wicked laugh. Jenna stares at me from my bag.

On our way to the office, I decide to take a different route. "Let's take our time today," I suggest. "It's such a beautiful day— so many people are out already. Oh, and I have to find a gift for that client... What was her name?" I think a bit and then remember. "Ms. Carmela Johnson! English teacher."

"Whatever, boss. You're my ride anyway," Jenna says, munching on something in my purse.

We pass tiny boutiques and antique-ish stores as we walk, but as I pretend to ignore the anguish I am feeling, every mother and baby couple, every steaming cup of hot liquid being drank, and every gaudy angel souvenir I see reminds me of her—my mom— and I cannot help but shrink inside myself.

"I love you, Kailey," rambles Jenna from my purse.

"Love you too," I say, taking a breath which seems to help a bit.

On our route, we come upon a small, hole-in-the-wall bookstore, which seems to be getting a shipment of new arrivals. Upon further examination, they're boxes of recent donations.

The storekeeper sees me rifling through a box. "Take your time," he says. "You might find something grand!" He's an old, wrinkly soul, with a love of typeface all over his hands. A particularly worn book catches my attention. A dusting of the cover reveals a copy of *The Wonderful Wizard of Oz*. Someone has evidently written all along the inside of the cover, but I find it intriguing anyway. And that's when it hits me that karma has struck—the perfect gift has unfolded itself before me. I purchase the book for a modest price and feel a soft glow from my aura around me.

"Why so chipper?" Jenna sneaks a peek out my bag.

"I found an awesome gift." I wave the book which the shopkeeper has wrapped up with butcher's twine.

We arrive very late, but our receptionist smiles at me. Hell must have froze over. "I'm so sorry about your mother," she whimpers, teary-eyed. She stands up, and after I think she's actually going to hug me, she hands me a mug of something warm and steamy. "I made this for you."

"Oh...thanks," I respond, bringing my lips to the liquid. I then realize it's coffee—and not tea. I almost choke on it. "Delicious." She pats me on the back. As I walk to my office I pour the coffee into a potted plant.

As I enter my office, Evan comes up behind me. "Hi," he says. I can feel his sympathy without even looking at his face. I turn around slowly and once our eyes meet, my tears flow. He hugs me tightly. "You should have stayed home."

"No. I need this, really. I'll be okay. Just get me working on my case and I'll be fine."

"Yeah...about that," he says, his energy suddenly twisting with nervousness. "It's been transferred to someone else. Here's a new one to work on." He hands me a manila folder.

"What?!" Sudo-abominor awakes and I hear Jenna shriek in my bag. My boss scrunches his face, looking at my bag.

"I thought you needed to have a little alone time. You might...break down at lunch or something. Please understand, Kailey."

"I've worked hard on that case, before everything in my life blew up. No, I'm keeping it!" Evan's eyes widen, perhaps sensing the suddenly malicious anger growing inside me. I inhale, attempting to quiet sudo-abominor. "Well, then, at least tell me who got it."

"Your buddy. Amber."

The look on my face makes him jump back. "She's here?" My internal hate explodes and the heat generated inside me feels like it's singeing my internal organs.

"Yes, she works here, remember? Ms. Johnson should be here any minute to meet with her. Her case is a boring one anyway."

Grabbing the book off my desk, I stomp toward Amber's office, displacing a few trinkets on a few desks. As I reach the front desk, I see the backs of Amber and who I assume to be Ms. Johnson, just about to exit through the front door. My boss follows right behind me. Sudo-abominor swells inside me, spinning around and around, feeling as though it wants to escape. It tugs at me, but instead of pushing me toward Amber, it almost forces me backwards, away from her and Ms. Johnson.

They hear the commotion behind them and Amber turns, slowly. Despite the look of desperation on her face, I still want to slice her head off. The baby in her belly, my half-brother, wouldn't survive, though, and this thought alone calms me.

When Ms. Carmela Johnson turns around to face me, the book slips through my hands and onto the ground. As she eyes me intensely, examining me inside and out, her eyes soften with compassion, and she cackles, "Oh, my dear." She bends over, her braids hanging low, to pick the book up. Sudo-abominor pulls me two steps away from her. She eyes the card—her name, written in calligraphy across the front. "Beautiful!" As she opens the book, she giggles deeply. "And a signed copy! This is the best gift I could ask for. Absolutely amazing." I cannot seem to make any words come out of my mouth as I stare. "Well, I thank you for this gift. Now, you let me and this pretty little thing"—she grabs Amber's hand softly—"go have a good lunch and some very decent, meaningful conversation." She then leans near me as the energy inside me fights both to get away, *and* to hear her whisper, "Karma will get it straight." She turns back to Amber.

Amber's eyes avoid my own as they turn to leave for *my* reservation at True. She most likely had nowhere else to run, except back to her life here.

And that is when Neda turns to me slowly and winks at me. She turns back to Amber, and her hand on Amber's back is grotesquely disfigured. "Come on, now, sweetie. We've got lots to talk about." Sudo-abominor cannot help but hideously laugh to itself as they leave and enter the elevators, but my conscience feels like I've just delivered a soul to hell. I feel guilt like a lump in my throat.

The internal struggle makes me feel nauseous as I stumble back to my office, where I find Jenna on the phone with Gunthreon. I motion for her to get off my desk. "Yes, I'll tell her," she says, placing the phone down quietly, as she stares at me. "Your aura! Oh, geez. Dear Neda," she eyes me, looking all over my entire body, seeing something that is leaving her uneasy. "You're a mess!"

"I know. Jenna, I pray Ladimer can help," I fall into my chair, feeling dizzy. She comes to me, wiping my hair back from my face. She caresses my face, and whispers, "Gunthreon says the urn is healing. And, it seems that creatures are disappearing across Abscondia by the handfuls. It's on every channel."

I smile, feeling a wave of relief wash over me. The dizziness lifts. "Thanks, Jenna." I look downward toward my desk and spot the new case my boss gave me. I open the folder. It's some carpenter wanting to find investors to make a specialty tool for fixing wheelchairs. "Sounds like something for Bu," I say. With this simple statement and the thought alone, Bu appears in my office. He jumps up and throws his cake in the air, and it lands on Jenna.

"Ahhh!" It drips down her face and her clothes.

But I don't care she has cake on her face—just that I brought a massive greble here, to my work, in my moment of confusion. "Dammit," I swear, running to close my door. "I have to learn to control this new trick. Bu, you gotta leave. Sorry." He stares, cake hanging off his open mouth. Then he disappears.

I look to Jenna and all I can do is laugh. She nervously laughs along with me.

Chapter 59

Released

ℭℛ

Since I currently have no cell phone, I must wait to call Gunthreon back until I get home. Jenna fills me in on her *whole* conversation with him and mentions that he would like to give me back the key, for there is no word on how to destroy it, and after seeing a shaman, there is nothing harmful about it.

Next, I call Conner, asking him if he'd like to come over and...maybe bring dinner with him. He agrees as I sigh, happy that I don't have to leave the house to get food.

I feed my four babies multiple treats as they all play together, nicely, on my apartment floor. Even Kioto has taken a liking to the pups, letting them crawl over her and nip at her ears.

All bags and shoes get thrown on the floor as I sit on my couch. The corner of my eye picks up something new sitting on my coffee table. It's Mortimer's urn, sitting quietly next to my mom's box. Beside that is the key. Ladimer must have dropped it off for Gunthreon.

I pick up the box, feeling and smelling the smooth wood. I shake it again, and it feels as though it's empty—no noise and no weight. I place it back on my table.

Conner arrives with takeout Italian. The meatballs and garlic olive oil smell divine, but I cannot seem to concentrate on eating as I stare at the box, almost feeling my mom's presence.

Jenna steals a peek inside a food container and sticks her finger in, catching a quick dab before I throw a towel at her head, knocking her over.

Conner stares at the urn on my table. I know he knows what it is, but he doesn't seem to want to talk about it. His eyes wander to the box beside it. "Still can't open it?"

"Nope."

As we eat at my coffee table, the strangest sensation crawls along my skin. I look up to both Jenna and Conner, who, presumably feel the same thing. Then the phone rings, loudly. I stand up, and as I reach the phone, I look at the caller ID, which reads "Cellular Call." The number flashing on the screen is my smartphone's. I'm suddenly afraid to answer the phone, so I decide to put it on speaker as I grip the phone with ungodly strength. I push the button. "Hello?"

"Hello?"

Oh my god. "Mom?" My heart skips a beat.

"Kailey?"

That is when the phone disconnects, and her box starts glowing, ominously, triggered by the sound of her voice, and as it glows, a small keyhole appears in the wood. I walk to the box and, slowly, place the key in the keyhole. The box opens, and I reach in, withdrawing the treasure inside. It's a highly-detailed, photograph-looking sketch of my mom, my father, and a child of about four years, the spitting image of my mom. My mom is covering her eyes, Devoten his mouth, and the child its ears.

"How could there be a picture of me in—"

"Kailey, it's not you," stutters Conner, his heart beating as loudly as my own.

It is then I notice a monogrammed "S" on the child's pocket, and a blue wooden horse in his lap. I mumble a simple, "Who?" as my thoughts travel back to the day of my mom's death and her final words—*her words of a brother.*

The phone falls from my hand and knocks over Mortimer's ashes, spilling them over Conner's hand, Jenna, and the box and key. I hear a dial tone as I hold the phone, and the last thing I see is

Conner's face contorting in agony as I fall into the darkness that has become so familiar.

Sudo-abominor awakes with a vengeance.

Acknowledgments

☙

The creation of this book, from the very first word I scribbled down on a piece of scrap paper to the very last header inserted for print, was by no means an easy process. It was actually one of the hardest things I've ever had to do in my life; add it to the list that includes college, home-owning, and childbirth. Really.

There were so many missed moments of life due to stressing during the process, this I know (but I'd probably be stressing about something else anyway), and I will openly admit it, but there were also *many* moments of clarity, moments that I realized who was really there to inspire me and kick me in my butt to jumpstart my forward momentum, and what followed were the very moments I found how proud I was to call myself a writer. Those inspirational and/or bullying compadres are the very reason I have a finished product to call my own and are the reason I have anything to be grateful for. Thanks to you all I have a beautiful child that you helped raise in one way or another.

Thanks to Chris Lutchen, Rita Shafer, Jen Hayes, Anthony Mryc, Elizabeth Delpo, Bob Vitas, Adriana Lucas, Melissa Sperk, Harrison Demchick, Tony Burbatt, Robert S. Kolodziejski, and all the beautiful bloggers out there that have provided their support and triggered beautiful and lasting friendships.

Your actions and words (kind and/or criticizing) will always resonate stongest within my thoughts, and bring a smile to my face, so…stick around for future books, PLEASE. I don't want to force any deathmen to leave their current positions.

www.ingramcontent.com/pod-product-compliance
Lightning Source LLC
Chambersburg PA
CBHW070858260626
47162CB00007B/2491